Desmond Bagley was born in 1923 in Kendal, a rural town in England's scenic Lake District.

He left school aged fourteen and worked for a number of years in the aircraft industry before embarking on an adventure – travelling to South Africa by road and supporting himself along the way by working in gold and asbestos mines.

Bagley spent the fifties in South Africa working as a freelance journalist and critic. He met his wife, Joan Margaret, at a party in 1959 and they became a formidable team – she was his manager, research assistant and number-one critic – and they travelled the world together exploring potential stories.

His first novel, *The Golden Keel*, was based on a true story overheard by Bagley in a bar in Johannesburg, about Mussolini's extraordinary riches and the men who went looking for it. It was published in 1963 to great acclaim and was followed by a further fifteen popular adventure novels.

Bagley's career spanned two decades and his influence can be seen in the work of several highly respected thriller writers. When he died in 1983 his final novel, *Juggernaut*, was completed by his wife.

BY THE SAME AUTHOR
ALL PUBLISHED BY HOUSE OF STRATUS

Bahama Crisis
The Enemy
Flyaway
The Freedom Trap
The Golden Keel
High Citadel
Juggernaut
Landslide
Night of Error
Running Blind
The Snow Tiger
The Spoilers
The Vivero Letter
Windfall
Wyatt's Hurricane

THE TIGHTROPE MEN

DESMOND BAGLEY

This edition published in 2000 by House of Stratus, an imprint of Stratus Books Ltd., 21 Beeching Park, Kelly Bray, Cornwall, PL17 8QS, UK..

www.houseofstratus.com

Typeset, printed and bound by House of Stratus.

A catalogue record for this book is available from the British Library and the Library of Congress.

ISBN 1-84232-018-1

Cover design by Marc Burvill-Riley

To Ray Poynton and all his team.
Fons et Origo,
He the one and I the other.

You reasonably expect a man to walk a tightrope for ten minutes; it would be unreasonable to do so without accident for two hundred years.

Bertrand Russell

CHAPTER ONE

Giles Denison lay asleep. He lay on his back with his right arm held crooked across his forehead with the hand lightly clenched into a fist, giving him a curiously defensive appearance as of one who wards off a blow. His breathing was even and shallow but it deepened a little as he came into consciousness in that everyday miracle of the reintegration of the psyche after the little death of sleep.

There was a movement of eyes behind closed lids and he sighed, bringing his arm down and turning over on to his side to snuggle deeper into the bedclothes. After a few moments the eyelids flickered and drew back and he stared uncomprehendingly at the blank wall next to the bed. He sighed again, filling his lungs with air, and then leisurely drew forth his arm and looked at his wristwatch.

It was exactly twelve o'clock.

He frowned and shook the watch, then held it to his ear. A steady tick told him it was working and another glance at the dial showed the sweep second hand jerking smoothly on its circular course.

Suddenly – convulsively – he sat up in bed and stared at the watch. It was not the time – midday or midnight – that now perturbed him, but the realization that it was not his watch. He normally wore a fifteen-year-old Omega, a present from his father on his twenty-first birthday, but this was a sleek Patek Philippe, gleaming gold, with a plain leather strap instead of the flexible metal band he was accustomed to.

A furrow creased his forehead as he stroked the dial of the watch with his forefinger and then, as he raised his eyes to look about the room, he received another shock. He had never been in the room before.

He became aware that his heart thumped in his chest and he raised his hand to feel the coolness of silk against his fingers. He looked down and saw the pyjamas. Habitually he slept peeled to the skin; pyjamas constricted him and he had once said that he never saw the sense in getting dressed to go to bed.

Denison was still half asleep and his first impulse was to lie down and wait for the dream to be over so that he could wake up again in his own bed, but a pressing necessity of nature was suddenly upon him and he had to go to the bathroom. He shook his head irritably and threw aside the bedclothes – not the sheets and blankets to which he was accustomed but one of those new-fangled quilt objects which fashion had recently imported from the Continent.

He swung his legs out of the bed and sat up, looking down at the pyjamas again. *I'm in hospital*, he thought suddenly; *I must have had an accident*. Recollection told him otherwise. He had gone to bed in his own flat in Hampstead in the normal way, after perhaps a couple of drinks too many the previous evening. Those extra couple of drinks had become a habit after Beth died.

His fingers caressed the softness of the silk. Not a hospital, he decided; these were not National Health issue – not with an embroidered monogram on the pocket. He twisted his head to see the letters but the embroidery was complex and the monogram upside down and he could not make it out.

He stood up and looked about the room and knew immediately he was in a hotel. There were expensive-looking suitcases and in no other place but a hotel room could you find special racks on which to put them. He walked three paces and stroked the fine-grained leather which had hardly a scuff mark. The initials on the side of the suitcase were plain and unmonogrammed – H.F.M.

His head throbbed with the beginning of a headache – the legacy of those extra couple of drinks – and his mouth was parched. He glanced around the room and noted the unrumpled companion bed, the jacket hanging tidily on the back of a chair and the scatter of personal possessions on the dressing-table. He was about to cross to the dressing-table when the pressure in his bladder became intolerable and he knew he had to find a bathroom.

He turned and stumbled into the small hall off the bedroom. One side was panelled in wood and he swung a door open to find a wardrobe full of hung clothes. He turned again and found a door on the other side which opened into darkness. He fumbled for a switch, found it, and light sprang up in a white-tiled bathroom.

While he was relieving himself his mind worried about the electric switch wondering what was strange about it, and then he realized that it was reversed – an upward movement to turn on the light instead of the more normal down pressure.

He flushed the toilet and turned to the hand basin seeking water. Two glasses stood on a shelf, wrapped in translucent paper. He took one down, ripped off the paper and, filling it with water from the green-topped tap, he drank thirstily. Up to this moment he had been awake for, perhaps, three minutes.

He put down the glass and rubbed his left eye which was sore. Then he looked into the mirror above the basin and, for the first time in his life, experienced sheer terror.

CHAPTER TWO

When Alice went through the Looking Glass the flowers talked to her and she evinced nothing but a mild surprise; but a psychologist once observed, 'If a flower spoke to a man, that man would know terror.'

So it was with Giles Denison. After seeing the impossible in the bathroom mirror he turned and vomited into the toilet bowl, but his laboured retchings brought up nothing but a thin mucus. Panting with his efforts, he looked into the mirror again – and reason left him.

When he became self-aware he found himself prone on the bed, his hands shaped into claws which dug into the pillow. A single sentence was drumming through his mind with mechanical persistence. '*I am Giles Denison! I* am *Giles Denison! I* AM *Giles Denison! I am* GILES DENISON!'

Presently his heavy breathing quieted and he was able to think beyond that reiterated statement of identity. With his head sideways on the pillow he spoke aloud, gathering reassurance from the familiar sound of his own voice. In a slurred tone which gradually became firmer he said, 'I am Giles Denison. I am thirty-six years old. I went to bed last night in my own home. I was a bit cut, that's true, but not so drunk as to be incapable. I *remember* going to bed – it was just after midnight.'

He frowned, then said, 'I've been hammering the bottle a bit lately, but I'm *not* an alcoholic – so this isn't the DTs. Then what is it?' His left hand moved up to stroke his cheek. 'What the hell is *this*?'

He arose slowly and sat on the edge of the bed, screwing up his nerve to go back into the bathroom as he knew he must. When he stood up he found his whole body trembling and he waited a while until the fit had passed. Then he walked with slow paces into the bathroom to face again the stranger in the mirror.

The face that looked back at him was older – he judged the man to be in his mid-forties. Giles Denison had worn a moustache and a neatly clipped beard – the stranger was clean shaven. Giles Denison had a full head of hair – the stranger's hair receded at the temples. Denison had no distinguishing marks as called for in passport descriptions – the stranger had an old scar on the left side of his face which passed from the temple across the cheekbone to the corner of the mouth; the left eyelid drooped, whether as a result of the scar or not it was impossible to say. There was also a small portwine birthmark on the angle of the right jaw.

If that had been all perhaps Denison would not have been so frightened, but the fact was that the face was *different*. Denison had been proud in a non-committal way of his aquiline good looks. Aquiline was the last word to describe the face of the stranger. The face was pudgy, the nose a round, featureless blob, and there was an incipient but perceptible double chin.

Denison opened his mouth to look at the stranger's teeth and caught the flash of a gold capping on a back molar. He closed both his mouth and his eyes and stood there for a while because the trembling had begun again. When he opened his eyes he kept them averted from the mirror and looked down at his hands which were gripping the edge of the basin. They were different, too; the skin looked older and the nails were shortened to the quick as though the stranger bit them. There was another old cicatrice on the back of the right thumb, and the backs of the forefinger and middle finger were stained with nicotine.

Denison did not smoke.

He turned blindly from the mirror and went back into the bedroom where he sat on the edge of the bed and stared at the blank wall. His mind threatened to retreat to the mere insistence of identity and yammered at him, 'I AM GILES DENISON!' and the trembling began again, but with an effort of will he dragged himself back from the edge of that mental precipice and forced himself to think as coherently as he could.

Presently he stood up and went to the window because the street noises forced themselves on his attention in an odd way. He heard an impossible sound, a sound that brought back memories of his childhood. He drew back the curtain and looked into the street to find its origin.

The tramcar was passing just below with the accompanying clangour of a past era of transport. Beyond it, in a dazzle of bright sunshine, were gardens and a bandstand and an array of bright umbrellas over tables where people sat eating and drinking. Beyond the gardens was another street filled with moving traffic.

Another tramcar passed and Denison caught a glimpse of the destination board. It made no sense to him because it seemed to be in a foreign language. There was something else odd about the tramcar and his eyes narrowed as he saw there were two single-deck coaches coupled together. He looked across the street at the fascia boards of the shops and found the words totally meaningless.

His head was aching worse than ever so he dropped the curtain to avoid the bright wash of sunlight and turned into the dimness of the room. He crossed to the dressing-table and looked down at the scatter of objects – a cigarette case, apparently of gold, a smoothly modelled cigarette lighter, a wallet and a note-case, and a handful of loose change.

Denison sat down, switched on the table lamp, and picked up one of the silver coins. The head depicted in profile was that of a fleshy man with a prow of a nose; there was something of the air of a Roman emperor about him. The wording was simple: OLAV.V.R. Denison turned the coin over to find a prancing horse and the inscription: 1 KRONE. NORGE.

Norway!

Denison began to feel his mind spin again and he bent forward as a sudden stomach cramp hit him. He laid down the coin and held his head in his hands until he felt better. Not a lot better, but marginally so.

When he had recovered enough he took the wallet and went through the pockets quickly, tossing the contents into a heap on the table top. The wallet emptied, he put it aside after noting its fine quality and began to examine the papers. There was an English driving licence in the name of Harold Feltham Meyrick of Lippscott House, near Brackley, Buckinghamshire. Hair prickled at the nape of Denison's neck as he looked at the signature. It was in his own handwriting. It was not his name but it was his penmanship – of that he was certain.

He stretched out his hand and took a pen, one of a matched set of fountain pen and ballpoint. He looked around for something on which to write, saw nothing, and opened the drawer in front of him where he found a folder containing writing paper and envelopes. He paused for a moment when he saw the letter heading – HOTEL CONTINENTAL, STORTINGS GATA, OSLO.

His hand trembled as the pen approached the paper but he scribbled his signature firmly enough – Giles Denison. He looked at the familiar loops and curlicues and felt immeasurably better, then he wrote another signature H. F. Meyrick. He took the driving licence and compared it with what he had just written. It confirmed what he already knew; the signature in the driving licence was in his own handwriting.

So were the signatures in a fat book of Cook's traveller's cheques. He counted the cheques – nineteen of them at £50 each – £950 in all. If he was indeed Meyrick he was pretty well breeched. His headache grew worse.

There were a dozen engraved visiting cards with Meyrick's name and address and a fat sheaf of Norwegian currency in the notecase which he did not bother to count. He dropped it on to the desk and held his throbbing head in his hands. In spite of the fact that he had just woken up he felt tired and light-headed. He knew he was in danger of going into psychological retreat again – it would be so easy to curl up on the bed and reject this crazy, impossible thing that had happened to him, taking refuge in sleep with the hope that it would prove to be a dream and that when he woke he would be back in bed in his own flat in Hampstead, a thousand miles away.

He opened the drawer a fraction, put his fingers inside, and then smashed the drawer closed with the heel of his other hand. He gasped with the pain and when he drew his hand from the drawer there were flaring red marks on the backs of his fingers. The pain caused tears to come to his eyes and, as he nursed his hand, he knew this was too real to be a dream.

So if it was not a dream, what was it? He had gone to bed as one person and woken up, in another country, as another. But wait! That was not quite accurate. He had woken up knowing he was Giles Denison – the persona of Harold Feltham Meyrick was all on the exterior – inside he was still Giles Denison.

He was about to pursue this line of thought when he had another spasm of stomach cramp and suddenly he realized why he felt so weak and tired. He was ravenously hungry. Painfully he stood up and went into the bathroom where he stared down into the toilet bowl. He had been violently sick but his stomach had been so empty that there was hardly anything to be brought up but a thin, acid digestive juice. And yet the previous evening he had had a full meal. Surely there was something wrong there.

He went back into the bedroom and paused irresolutely by the telephone and then, with a sudden access of determination, picked it up. 'Give me room service,' he said. His voice was hoarse and strange to his own ears.

The telephone crackled. 'Room service,' it said in accented English.

'I'd like something to eat,' said Denison. He glanced at his watch – it was nearly two o'clock. 'A light lunch.'

'Open sandwiches?' suggested the telephone.

'Something like that,' said Denison. 'And a pot of coffee.'

'Yes, sir. The room number is …?'

Denison did not know. He looked around hastily and saw what must be the room key on a low coffee-table by the window. It was attached to about five pounds of brass on which a number was stamped. 'Three-sixty,' he said.

'Very good, sir.'

Denison was inspired. 'Can you send up a newspaper?'

'English or Norwegian, sir?'

'One of each.'

'*The Times*?'

'That and an equivalent local paper. And I may be in the bathroom when you come up – just leave everything on the table.'

'Very good, sir.'

Denison put down the telephone with a feeling of relief. He would have to face people some time but he did not feel eager to do so immediately. Certainly he would have to ask a lot of questions, but he wanted time to compose himself. He could not help feeling there would be a lot of trip wires to avoid in the taking over of another personality.

He took the silk Paisley dressing-gown which he found draped over a chair and went into the bathroom, where he was coward enough to hang a towel over the mirror. After fumbling for a moment with unfamiliar plumbing, he drew a bath of hot water, then stripped off the pyjamas. He became aware of the sticking-plaster on his left arm and was about to take it off but he thought better of it, wondering if he really wanted to know what was underneath.

He got into the bath and soaked in the hot water, feeling the heat ease his suddenly aching limbs, and again, he drowsily wondered why he felt so tired after being up only two hours. Presently he heard the door of the suite open and there was a clatter of crockery. The door banged closed and everything was quiet again so he got out of the bath and began to rub himself down.

While sitting on the cork-topped stool he suddenly bent forward and examined his left shin. There was a blue-white scar there, about the size and shape of an orange pip. He remembered when that had happened; it was when he was eight years old and had fallen off his first bicycle.

He raised his head and laughed aloud, feeling much better. He had remembered that as Giles Denison and that little scar was a part of his body that did not belong to Mr Harold Blasted Feltham Bloody Meyrick.

CHAPTER THREE

The Norwegian idea of a light lunch was an enormous tray filled with a variety of edible goodies which Denison surveyed with satisfaction before plunging in. The discovery of the scar had cheered him immensely and had even emboldened him to shave Meyrick's face. Meyrick was old-fashioned enough to use a safety-razor and a silver-mounted badger-hair brush instead of an electric shaver and Denison had had some difficulty in guiding the blade over unfamiliar contours and had cut himself – or Meyrick – twice. And so, when he picked up the newspapers, his face was adorned with two bloody patches of toilet paper.

The London *Times* and the Norwegian *Aftenposten* both had the same date – July 9 – and Denison went very still, a piece of herring on rye bread poised in mid-air. His last memory as Giles Denison had been going to bed just after midnight on July 1 – no, it would be July 2 if it was after midnight.

Somewhere he had lost a week.

He put his hand to his arm and felt the sticking-plaster. Someone had been doing things to him. He did not know who and he did not know why but, by God, he was going to find out and someone was going to pay dearly. While shaving he had examined his face closely. The scar on his left cheek was there all right, the remnant of an old wound, but it did not feel like a scar when he touched it. Still, no matter how hard he rubbed it would not come off, so it was not merely an example of clever theatrical make-up. The same applied to the birthmark on the rightjaw.

There was something else odd about his nose and his cheeks and that double chin. They had a rubbery feel about them. Not ever having had any excess fat on his body he did not know whether this was normal or not. And, again, Meyrick's face had grown a light stubble of hair which he had shaved off, but the bald temples were smooth which meant that whoever had lifted his hairline had not done it by shaving.

The only part of his face Denison recognized were his eyes – those had not changed; they were still the same grey-green eyes he had seen every morning in the mirror. But the expression was different because of the droop of the left eyelid. There was a slight soreness in the outer corner of that eye which aroused his suspicions but he could see nothing but a tiny inflamed spot, which could have been natural.

As he ate voraciously he glanced through *The Times*. The world still seemed to be wobbling on its political axis as unsteadily as ever and nothing had changed, so he tossed the newspaper aside and gave himself up to thought over a steaming cup of black coffee. What could be the motive for spiriting a man from his own bed, transforming him bodily, giving him a new personality and dumping him in a luxury hotel in the capital of Norway?

No answer.

The meal had invigorated him and he felt like moving and not sitting. He did not yet feel up to encountering people so he compromised by going through Meyrick's possessions. He opened the wardrobe and in one of the drawers, underneath a pile of underwear, he found a large travelling wallet. Taking it to the dressing-table he unzipped it and went through the contents.

The first thing to catch his eyes was a British passport. He opened it to find the description of the holder was filled out in his own handwriting as was Meyrick's signature underneath. The face that looked out of the photograph on the opposite page was that of Meyrick, who was described as a civil servant. Whoever had thought up this lark had been thorough about it.

He flipped through the pages and found only one stamped entry and his brow wrinkled as he studied it. *Sverige*? Would that be

Sweden? If so he had arrived at a place called Arlanda in Sweden on a date he could not tell because the stamping was blurred. Turning to the back of the passport he found that the sum of £1,500 had been issued a month earlier. Since the maximum travel allowance for a tourist was £300 it would seem that H. F. Meyrick was operating on a businessman's allowance.

At the bottom of a pocket in the wallet he found an American Express credit card, complete with the ubiquitous fake signature. He looked at it pensively, flicking it with his fingernail. With this he could draw money or traveller's cheques anywhere; he could use it to buy an airline ticket to Australia if he felt the urge to emigrate suddenly. It represented complete and unlicensed freedom unless and until someone put a stopper on it at head office.

He transferred it to the small personal wallet along with the driving licence. It would be better to keep that little bit of plastic available in case of need.

Meyrick had an extensive wardrobe; casual clothing, lounge suits and even a dinner-jacket with accessories. Denison investigated a small box and found it contained personal jewellery – studs, tiepins and a couple of rings – and he realized he probably held a thousand pounds' worth of gold in his hand. The Patek Philippe watch on his wrist would cost £500 if it cost a penny. H. F. Meyrick was a wealthy man, so what kind of a civil servant did that make him?

Denison decided to get dressed. It was a sunny day so he chose casual trousers and a sports coat. The clothing fitted him as though made to measure. He looked at himself in the full-length mirror built into the wardrobe door, studiously ignoring the face on top of the body, and thought crazily that it, too, had probably been made to measure. The world began to spin again, but he remembered the small scar on his shin that belonged to Denison and that helped him to recover.

He put his personal possessions into his pockets and headed for the door, key in hand. As the door swung open a card which had been hung on the outer handle fell to the floor. He picked it up and read: VENNLIGST IKKE FORSTYRR – PLEASE DO NOT DISTURB. He was thoughtful as he hung it on the hook inside the door before locking the room; he would give a lot to know who had hung out that sign.

He went down in the lift with a couple of American blue-rinsed matrons who chattered to each other in a mid-West twang. 'Say, have you been out to Vigeland Park? All those statues – I didn't know where to look.' The lift stopped and the doors slid open with a soft hiss, and the American ladies bustled out intent on sightseeing.

Denison followed them diffidently into the hotel lobby and stood by the lifts for a while, trying to get his bearings, doing his best to appear nonchalantly casual while he took in the scene.

'Mr Meyrick ... Mr Meyrick, sir!'

He turned his head and saw the porter at the desk smiling at him. Licking lips that had suddenly gone dry he walked over. 'Yes?'

'Would you mind signing this, sir? The check for the meal in your room. Just a formality.'

Denison looked at the proffered pen and laid down the room key. He took the pen and scribbled firmly 'H. F. Meyrick' and pushed the slip across the counter. The porter was hanging the key on the rack but he turned and spoke to Denison before he could slip away. 'The night porter put your car away, sir. Here is the key.'

He held out a key with a tag on it and Denison extended his hand to take it. He glanced at the tag and saw the name, Hertz, and a car number. He cleared his throat. 'Thank you.'

'You sound as though you have a cold coming on,' said the porter.

Denison took a chance. 'Why do you think that?'

'Your voice sounds different.'

'Yes, I do feel a bit chesty,' said Denison.

The porter smiled. 'Too much night air, perhaps.'

Denison took another chance. 'What time *did* I get in last night?'

'This morning, sir. The night porter said it was about three o'clock.' The porter offered Denison a man-of-the-world smile. 'I wasn't surprised when you slept in this morning.'

No, thought Denison; *but I was!* He was growing bolder as he gained confidence. 'Can you tell me something? I was having a discussion with a friend about how long I've been here in Oslo and, for the life of me, I can't remember the exact day I booked in here. Could you check it for me?'

'Certainly, sir.' The porter moved away and began to run through cards in a file. Denison looked at the car key. It was thoughtful of Hertz to put the car number on the tag; he might even be able to recognize it when he saw it. It was also thoughtful of the night porter to put the car away – but where the hell had he put it?

The porter returned. 'You checked in on the eighteenth of June, sir. Exactly three weeks ago.'

The butterflies in Denison's stomach collided. 'Thank you,' he said mechanically, and moved away from the desk and across the lobby. An arrow pointed the direction to the bar and he glanced sideways and saw a dark, cool cavern with a few drinkers, solitary or in couples. It looked quiet and he desperately wanted to think, so he went in.

When the barman came up, he said, 'A beer, please.'

'Export, sir?'

Denison nodded absently. *June 18*. He had reckoned he had lost a week so how the devil could he have booked into the Hotel Continental in Oslo three weeks earlier? How the hell could he have been in two places at the same time?

The barman returned, poured the beer into a glass, and went away. Denison tried to figure where he had been on June 18 and found it difficult. Three weeks was a long time. *Where were you at 6.17 on the evening of June 18*? No wonder people found it difficult to establish alibis. He found it extraordinarily difficult to focus his thoughts; they flicked about, skittering here and there wildly out of control. *When did you last see your father*? Nuts!

A vagrant thought popped to the surface of his consciousness. *Edinburgh!* He had been to Edinburgh on the 17th and the 18th he had taken off as a reward for hard work. There had been a leisurely morning and he had played golf in the afternoon; he had gone to the cinema in the evening and had dined late in Soho, getting back to Hampstead fairly late.

He – as Giles Denison – had dined in Soho at about the same time as he – as Harold Feltham Meyrick – had dined in Oslo. Where was the sense of that?

He was aware that he was looking at bubbles rising in amber liquid and that he had not touched his beer. He lifted the glass and drank; it was cold and refreshing.

He had two things going for him – two things that kept him sane. One – Giles Denison's scar on H. F. Meyrick's shin – and two – the change in the timbre of Meyrick's voice as recognized by the hotel porter. And what did that imply? Obviously that there were *two* Meyricks; one who had booked in on June 18, and another – himself – who had just been planted. Never mind why and never mind how. Just accept the fact that it was done.

He drank some more beer and rested his chin in his hand, feeling the unaccustomed flab of his jowl. He had lost a week of his life. Could so much plastic surgery be done in a week? He added that to the list of things to be checked on.

And what to do? He could go to the British Embassy and tell his story. Mentally he ran through the scenario.

'What can we do for you, Mr Meyrick?'

'Well, the fact is I'm not Meyrick – whoever he is. My name is Giles Denison and I've been kidnapped from London, my face changed, and dumped into an Oslo hotel with a hell of a lot of money and an unlimited credit account. Can you help me?'

'Certainly, Mr Meyrick. Miss Smith, will you ring for a doctor?'

'My God!' said Denison aloud. 'I'd end up in the loonybin.'

The barman cocked his head and came over. 'You wish something, sir?'

'Just to pay,' said Denison, finishing his beer.

He paid from the loose change in his pocket and left the bar. In the lobby he spotted a sign saying GARAGE, so he went through a door and down a flight of stairs to emerge into a basement car park. He checked the number on the Hertz key and walked along the first row of cars. It was right at the end – a big black Mercedes. He unlocked the door.

The first thing he saw was the doll on the driver's seat, a most curious object made of crudely carved wood and rope. The body was formed of rope twisted into a spiral and coming out in the form of a tail. The feet were but roughly indicated and the head was a round knob with a peg nose. The eyes and a mouth twisted to one side had been inked on to the wood, and the hair was of rope teased out into separate strands. It was a strange and somehow repulsive little figure.

He picked it up and discovered a piece of paper underneath it. He unfolded the deckle-edged note-paper and read the scrawled handwriting: *Your Drammen Dolly awaits you at Spiraltoppen. Early morning, July 10.*

He frowned. July 10 was next day, but where was Spiraltoppen and who – or what – was a Drammen Dolly? He looked at the ugly little doll. It had been lying on the driver's seat as though it had been deliberately left for him to find. He tossed it in his hand a couple of times and then thrust it into his pocket. It made an unsightly bulge, but what did he care? It was not his jacket. The note he put into his wallet.

The car was almost new, with just over 500 kilometres on the clock. He found a sheaf of papers relating to the car hire; it had been rented five days earlier, a fact which was singularly devoid of informative content. There was nothing else to be found.

He got out of the car, locked it, and left the garage by the car entrance, emerging on to a street behind the hotel. It was a little bewildering for him; the traffic drove on the wrong side of the road, the street and shop signs were indecipherable and his command of Norwegian was minimal, being restricted to one word – *skål* – which, while being useful in a cheery sort of way, was not going to be of much use for the more practical things of life.

What he needed was information and he found it on the corner of the street in the form of a bookshop. He went inside and found an array of maps from which he selected a map of central Oslo, one of Greater Oslo, and a motoring map of Southern Norway. To these he added a guide to the city and paid out of the slab of Norwegian currency in Meyrick's wallet. He made a mental note to count that money as soon as he had privacy.

He left the shop intending to go back to the hotel where he could study the maps and orient himself. He paused on the pavement and rubbernecked at the corner of a building where one would normally expect to find a street name and there it was – *Roald Amundsens Gata*.

'Harry!'

He turned to go in the direction of the hotel but paused as he felt a hand on his arm. 'Harry Meyrick!' There was a note of anger in the voice. She was a green-eyed redhead of about thirty and she was flying alarm flags – her lips were compressed and pink spots glowed in her cheeks. 'I'm not used to being stood up,' she said. 'Where were you this morning?'

Momentarily he was nonplussed but remembered in time what the hotel porter had thought about his voice. 'I wasn't feeling well,' he managed to get out. 'I was in bed.'

'There's a thing called a telephone,' she said angrily. 'Alexander Graham Bell invented it – remember?'

'I was knocked out by sleeping pills,' he protested. With a small portion of his mind he noted that this was probably a true statement. 'Perhaps I overdid it.'

Her expression changed. 'You do sound a bit glued-up,' she admitted. 'Maybe I'll forgive you.' There was a faint American undertone to her English. 'It will cost you a drink, darling.'

'In the hotel?' he suggested.

'It's too nice a day to be inside. We'll go into the *Studenterlunden*.' She waved her arm past a passing articulated tramcar towards the gay umbrellas in the gardens on the other side of the street.

Denison felt trapped as he escorted her across the street, but he also realized that if he was to learn anything about Meyrick then this was too good a chance to pass up. He had once been accosted in the street by a woman who obviously knew him but he did not have the faintest idea of who she was. There is a point of no return in that type of conversation after which one cannot, in decency, admit ignorance. On that occasion Denison had fumbled it, had suffered half an hour of devious conversation, and they had parted amicably without him finding out who she was. He still did not know. Grimly he thought that it was good practice for today's exercise.

As they crossed the street she said, 'I saw Jack Kidder this morning. He was asking about you.'

'How is he?'

She laughed. 'Fine, as always. You know Jack.'

'Of course,' said Denison deadpan. 'Good old Jack.'

They went into the outdoor cafe and found an empty table with difficulty. Under other circumstances Denison would have found it pleasant to have a drink with a pretty woman in surroundings like this, but his mind was beleaguered by his present problems. They sat down and he put his parcel of maps on the table.

One of them slipped out of the packet and his main problem prodded at it with a well-manicured forefinger. 'What are these?'

'Maps,' said Denison succinctly.

'Maps of where?'

'Of the city.'

'Oslo!' She seemed amused. 'Why do you want maps of Oslo? Isn't it your boast that you know Oslo better than London?'

'They're for a friend.'

Denison chalked up a mental note. *Meyrick knows Oslo well; probably a frequent visitor. Steer clear of local conditions or gossip. Might run into more problems like this.*

'Oh!' She appeared to lose interest.

Denison realized he was faced with a peculiar difficulty. He did not know this woman's name and, as people do not commonly refer to themselves by name in conversation, he did not see how he was going to get it, short of somehow prying into her handbag and looking for identification.

'Give me a cigarette, darling,' she said.

He patted his pockets and found he had left the cigarette case and lighter in the room. Not being a smoker it had not occurred to him to put them in his pocket along with the rest of Meyrick's personal gear. 'I'm sorry,' he said. 'I don't have any with me.'

'My!' she said. 'Don't tell me the great Professor Meyrick has stopped smoking. Now I *will* believe in cancer.'

Professor!

He used the pretext of illness again. 'The one I tried this morning tasted like straw. Maybe I will stop smoking.' He held his hand over the table. 'Look at those nicotine stains. Imagine what my lungs must be like.'

She shook her head in mock sorrow. 'It's like pulling down a national monument. To imagine Harry Meyrick without a cigarette is like trying to imagine Paris without the Eiffel Tower.'

A Nordic waitress came to the table; she looked rather like Jeanette MacDonald dressed for an appearance in *White Horse Inn*. Denison raised his eyebrows at his companion. 'What will you have?'

'The usual,' she said indifferently, delving into her handbag.

He took refuge in a paroxysm of coughing, pulling out his handkerchief and only emerging when he heard her giving the order. He waited until the waitress left before putting away the handkerchief. The woman opposite him said 'Harry, that's a really bad cough. I'm not surprised you're thinking of giving up the cancer sticks. Are you feeling all right, darling? Maybe you'd be better off in bed, after all.'

'I'm all right,' he said.

'Are you sure?' she asked solicitously.

'Perfectly sure.'

'Spoken like the old Professor Meyrick,' she said mockingly. 'Always sure of everything.'

'Don't call me Professor,' he said testily. It was a safe enough thing to say regardless of whether Meyrick was really a professor or whether she was pulling his leg in a heavyhanded manner. The British have never been keen on the over-use of professional titles. And it might provoke her into dropping useful information.

All he got was a light and inconsequential, 'When on the Continent do as the Continentals do.'

He went on the attack. 'I don't like it.'

'You're so British, Harry.' He thought he detected a cutting edge to her voice. 'But then, of course, you would be.'

'What do you mean by that?'

'Oh, come off it. There's nobody more British than an outsider who has bored his way in. Where were you born, Harry? Somewhere in Mittel Europa?' She suddenly looked a little ashamed. 'I'm sorry; I shouldn't have said that. I'm being bitchy, but you're behaving a bit oddly, too.'

'The effect of the pills. Barbiturates have never agreed with me. I have a headache.'

She opened her handbag. 'I have aspirin.'

The waitress, Valkyrie-like, bore down on them. Denison looked at the bottles on the tray, and said, 'I doubt if aspirin goes with beer.' That was the last thing he would have thought of as 'the usual'; she did not look the beery type.

She shrugged and closed the bag with a click. 'Please yourself.'

The waitress put down two glasses, two bottles of beer and a packet of cigarettes, said something rapid and incomprehensible, and waited expectantly. Denison took out his wallet and selected a 100-kroner note. Surely two beers and a packet of cigarettes could not cost more than a hundred kroner. My God, he did not even know the value of the currency! This was like walking through a minefield blindfolded.

He was relieved when the waitress made no comment but made change from a leather bag concealed under her apron. He laid the money on the table intending to check it surreptitiously. The redhead said, 'You've no need to buy my cigarettes, Harry.'

He smiled at her. 'Be my guest,' he said, and stretched out his hand to pour her beer.

'You've given it up yourself but you're quite prepared to pay for other people's poison.' She laughed. 'Not a very moral attitude.'

'I'm not a moral philosopher,' he said, hoping it was true.

'No, you're not,' she agreed. 'I've always wondered where you stood in that general direction. What would you call yourself, Harry? Atheist? Agnostic? Humanist?'

At last he was getting something of the quality of Meyrick. Those were questions but they were leading questions, and he was quite prepared to discuss philosophy with her – a nice safe subject. 'Not an atheist,' he said. 'It's always seemed to me that to believe in the non-existence of something is somewhat harder than to believe in its existence. I'd put myself down as an agnostic – one of the 'don't know' majority. And that doesn't conflict with humanism.'

He fingered the notes and coins on the table, counted them mentally, subtracted the price of two beers based on what he had paid for a beer in the hotel, and arrived at the price of a packet of cigarettes. Roughly, that is. He had an idea that the price of a beer in a luxury hotel would be far higher than in an open-air café.

'I went to church last Sunday,' she said pensively. 'To the English church – you know – the one on Møllergata.' He nodded as though he did know. 'I didn't get much out of it. I think next time I'll try the American church.' She frowned. 'Where is the American church, Harry?'

He had to say *something*, so he took a chance. 'Isn't it near the Embassy?'

Her brow cleared. 'Of course. Between Bygdøy Alle and Drammens Veien. It's funny, isn't it? The American church being practically next door to the British Embassy. You'd expect it to be near the American Embassy.'

He gulped. 'Yes, you would,' he said, and forbore to mention that that was what he had meant. Even a quasi-theological conversation was strewn with pitfalls. He had to get out of this before he really dropped a clanger.

And an alarming suspicion had just sprung to mind, fully armed and spiky. Whoever had planted him in that hotel room and provided him with money and the means to provide all the necessities of life – and a lot of the luxuries, too – was unlikely to leave him unobserved. Someone would be keeping tabs on him, otherwise the whole operation was a nonsense. Could it be this redhead who apparently had qualms about her immortal soul? What could be better than to plant someone right next to him for closer observation?

She opened the packet of cigarettes and offered him one. 'You're sure you won't?'

He shook his head. 'Quite sure.'

'It must be marvellous to have will power.'

He wanted peace and not this continuous exploration of a maze where every corner turned could be more dangerous than the last. He started to cough again, and dragged his handkerchief from his pocket. 'I'm sorry,' he said in a muffled voice. 'I think you're right; I'd be better off in bed. Do you mind if I leave you?'

'Of course not.' Her voice was filled with concern. 'Do you want a doctor?'

'That's not necessary,' he said. 'I'll be all right tomorrow – I know how these turns take me.' He stood up and she also rose. 'Don't bother to come with me. The hotel is only across the road.'

He picked up the packet and thrust the maps back into it, and put the handkerchief into his pocket. She looked down at his feet. 'You've dropped something,' she said, and stooped to pick it up. 'Why, it's a Spiralen Doll.'

'A what?' he asked incautiously. It must have been pulled from his pocket when he took out the handkerchief.

She regarded him oddly. 'You pointed these out at the Spiralen when we were there last week. You laughed at them and called them tourist junk. Don't you remember?'

'Of course,' he said. 'It's just this damned headache.'

She laughed. 'I didn't expect to see you carrying one. You didn't buy this when we were there – where did you get it?'

He told the truth. 'I found it in the car I hired.'

'You can't trust anyone to do a good job these days,' she said, smiling. 'Those cars are supposed to be cleaned and checked.' She held it out. 'Do you want it?'

'I may be a bit light-headed,' he said, 'but I think I do.' He took it from her. 'I'll be going now.'

'Have a hot toddy and a good night's sleep,' she advised. 'And ring me as soon as you're better.'

That would be difficult, to say the least, with neither telephone number nor name. 'Why don't you give me a ring tomorrow,' he said. 'I think I'll be well enough to have dinner. I promise not to stand you up again.'

'I'll ring you tomorrow afternoon.'

'Promise,' he insisted, not wanting to lose her.

'Promise.'

He put the rope doll into his pocket and left her with a wave, and went out of the garden, across the road and into the hotel, feeling relieved that he was well out of a difficult situation. *Information*, he thought, as he walked across the hotel lobby; *that's what I need – I'm hamstrung without it.*

He paused at the porter's desk and the porter looked up with a quick smile. 'Your key, sir?' He swung around and unhooked it.

On impulse Denison held out the doll. 'What's that?'

The porter's smile broadened. 'That's a Spiralen Doll, sir.'

'Where does it come from?'

'From the Spiralen, sir – in Drammen. If you're interested, I have a pamphlet.'

'I'm very much interested,' said Denison.

The porter looked through papers on a shelf and came up with a leaflet printed in blue ink. 'You must be an engineer, sir.'

Denison did not know what the hell Meyrick was. 'It's in my general field of interest,' he said guardedly, took the key and the leaflet, and walked towards the lifts. He did not notice the man who had been hovering behind him and who regarded him speculatively until the lift door closed.

Once in his room Denison tossed the maps and the leaflet on to the dressing-table and picked up the telephone. 'I'd like to make a long distance call, please – to England.' He took out his wallet.

'What is the number, sir?'

'There's a little difficulty about that. I don't have a number – only an address.' He opened the wallet with one hand and extracted one of Meyrick's cards.

The telephonist was dubious. 'That may take some time, sir.'

'It doesn't matter – I'll be in my room for the rest of the day.'

'What is the address, sir?'

Denison said clearly, 'Lippscott House, near Brackley, Buckinghamshire, England.' He repeated it three times to make sure it had got across.

'And the name?'

Denison opened his mouth and then closed it, having suddenly acquired a dazed look. He would appear to be a damned fool if he gave the name of Meyrick – no one in his right mind rings up himself, especially after having admitted he did not know his own telephone number. He swallowed, and said shortly, 'The name is not known.'

The telephone sighed in his ear. 'I'll do my best, sir.'

Denison put down the telephone and settled in a chair to find out about the Spiralen. The front of the leaflet was headed: DRAMMEN. There was an illustration of a Spiralen Doll which did not look any the better for being printed in blue. The leaflet was in four languages.

The Spiralen was described as being 'a truly unique attraction, as well as a superb piece of engineering'. Apparently there had been a quarry at the foot of Bragernesåsen, a hill near Drammen, which had become an eyesore until the City Fathers decided to do something about it. Instead of quarrying the face of the hill the operation had been extended into the interior.

A tunnel had been driven into the hill, thirty feet wide, fifteen feet high and a mile long. But not in a straight line. It turned back on itself six complete times in a spiral drilled into the mountain, climbing five hundred feet until it came out on top of Bragernesåsen where the Spiraltoppen Restaurant was open all the year round. The views were said to be excellent.

Denison picked up the doll; its body was formed of six complete turns of rope. He grinned weakly.

Consultation of the maps revealed that Drammen was a small town forty kilometres west of Oslo. That would be a nice morning drive, and he could get back in the afternoon well in time for any call from the redhead. It was not much to go on, but it was all he had.

He spent the rest of the afternoon searching through Meyrick's possessions but found nothing that could be said to be a clue. He ordered dinner to be sent to his room because he suspected that the hotel restaurant might be full of unexploded human mines like the redhead he had met, and there was a limit to what he could get away with.

The telephone call came when he was half-way through dinner. There were clicks and crackles and a distant voice said, 'Dr Meyrick's residence.'

Doctor!

'I'd like to speak to Dr Meyrick.'

'I'm sorry, sir; but Dr Meyrick is not at home.'

'Have you any idea where I can find him?'

'He is out of the country at the moment, sir.'

'Oh! Have you any idea where?'

There was a pause. 'I believe he is travelling in Scandinavia, sir.'

This was not getting anywhere at all. 'Who am I speaking to?'

'This is Andrews – Dr Meyrick's personal servant. Would you like to leave a message, sir?'

'Do you recognize my voice, Andrews?' asked Denison.

A pause. 'It's a bad line.' Another pause. 'I don't believe in guessing games on the telephone, sir.'

'All right,' said Denison. 'When you see Dr Meyrick will you tell him that Giles Denison called, and I'll be getting in touch with him as soon as possible. Got that?'

'Giles Denison. Yes, Mr Denison.'

'When is Dr Meyrick expected home?'

'I really couldn't say, Mr Denison.'

'Thank you, Mr Andrews.'

Denison put down the telephone. He felt depressed.

CHAPTER FOUR

He slept poorly that night. His sleep was plagued with dreams which he did not remember clearly during the few times he was jerked into wakefulness but which he knew were full of monstrous and fearful figures which threatened him. In the early hours of the morning he fell into a heavy sleep with deadened senses and when he woke he felt heavy and listless.

He got up tiredly and twitched aside the window curtain to find that the weather had changed; the sky was a dull grey and the pavements were wet and a fine drizzle filled the air. The outdoor café in the gardens opposite would not be doing much business that day.

He rang down for breakfast and then had a shower, finishing with needle jets of cold water in an attempt to whip some enthusiasm into his suddenly heavy body and, to a degree, he succeeded. When the floor waitress came in with his breakfast he had dressed in trousers and white polonecked sweater and was combing his hair before the bathroom mirror. Incredibly enough, he was whistling in spite of having Meyrick's face before him.

The food helped, too, although it was unfamiliar and a long way from an English breakfast. He rejected the raw, marinated herring and settled for a boiled egg, bread and marmalade and coffee. After breakfast he checked the weather again and then selected a jacket and a short topcoat from the wardrobe. He also found a thin, zippered leather satchel into which he put the maps and the Spiralen leaflet which had a street plan of Drammen on the back. Then he went down to the car. It was exactly nine o'clock.

It was not easy getting out of town. The car was bigger and more powerful than those he had been accustomed to driving and he had to keep to what was to him the wrong side of the road in a strange city in early rush-hour traffic. Three times he missed signs and took wrong turnings. The first time he did this he cruised on and got hopelessly lost and had to retrace his path laboriously. Thereafter when he missed a turn he reversed immediately so as not to lose his way again.

He was quite unaware of the man following him in the Swedish Volvo. Denison's erratic course across the city of Oslo was causing him a lot of trouble, especially when Denison did his quick and unexpected reversals. The man, whose name was Armstrong, swore freely and frequently, and his language became indescribable when the drizzle intensified into a downpour of heavy driving rain.

Denison eventually got out of the centre of the city and on to a six-lane highway, three lanes each way. The windscreen wipers had to work hard to cope with the rain, but it was better when he fiddled with a switch and discovered they had two speeds. Resolutely he stuck to the centre lane, reassured from time to time by the name DRAMMEN which appeared on overhead gantries.

To his left was the sea, the deeply penetrating arm of Oslofjord, but then the road veered away and headed inland. Presently the rain stopped, although no sun appeared, and he even began to enjoy himself, having got command of the unfamiliar car. And suddenly he was in Drammen, where he parked and studied the plan on the back of the leaflet.

In spite of the plan he missed the narrow turning to the right and had to carry on for some way before he found an opportunity to reverse the car, but eventually he drove up to the entrance of the tunnel where he stopped to pay the two kroner charge.

He put the car into gear and moved forward slowly. At first the tunnel was straight, and then it began to climb, turning to the left. There was dim illumination but he switched on his headlights in the dipped position and saw the reflection from the wetness of the rough stone wall. The gradient was regular, as was the radius of the spiral, and by the time he came to a board marked 1 he had got the hang of it. All he had to do was to keep the wheel at a fixed lock to correspond with the radius of the spiral and grind upwards in low gear.

All the same, it was quite an experience – driving upwards through the middle of a mountain. Just after he passed level 3 a car passed him going downwards and momentarily blinded him, but that was all the trouble he had. He took the precaution of steering nearer to the outer curve and closer to the wall.

Soon after passing level 6 he came out of the tunnel into a dazzle of light and on to level ground. To his left there was a large car park, empty of cars, and beyond it was the roof of a large wooden building constructed in chalet style. He parked as close to the building as he could, and got out of the car and locked it.

The chalet was obviously the Spiraltoppen Restaurant, but it was barely in business. He looked through a glass door and saw two women mopping the floor. It was still very early in the morning. He retreated a few steps and saw a giant Spiralen Doll outside the entrance, a leering figure nearly as big as a man.

He looked about him and saw steps leading down towards the edge of a cliff where there was a low stone wall and a coin-in-the-slot telescope. He walked down the path to where he could get a view of the Drammen Valley. The clouds were lifting and the sun broke through and illuminated the river so far below. The air was crystal clear.

Very pretty, he thought sourly; *but what the hell am I doing here? What do I expect to find? Drammen Dolly, where are you?*

Perhaps the answer lay in the restaurant. He looked at the view for a long time, made nothing of it from his personal point of view, and then returned to the restaurant where the floor mopping operation had been completed.

He went inside and sat down, looking around hopefully. It was a curiously *ad hoc* building, all odd angles and discrepancies as though the architect – if there had been an architect – had radically changed his mind during construction. Presently a waitress came and took his order without displaying much interest in him, and later returned with his coffee. She went away without giving him the secret password, so he sat and sipped the coffee gloomily.

After a while he pulled out the leaflet and studied it. He was on the top of Bragernesåsen which was the threshold of the unspoilt country of Drammensmarka, an eldorado for hikers in summer, and skiers in winter, who have the benefit of floodlit trails. There might be something there, he thought; so he paid for his coffee and left.

Another car had arrived and stood on the other side of the car park. A man sat behind the wheel reading a newspaper. He glanced across incuriously as the restaurant door slammed behind Denison and then returned to his reading. Denison pulled the topcoat closer about him against the suddenly cold wind and walked away from the cliff towards the unspoilt country of Drammensmarka.

It was a wooded area with tall conifers and equally tall deciduous trees with whitish trunks which he assumed to be birches, although he could have been wrong, botany not being his subject. There was a trail leading away from the car park which appeared to be well trodden. Soon the trees closed around him and, on looking back, the restaurant was out of sight.

The trail forked and, tossing a mental coin, he took the route to the right. After walking for a further ten minutes he stopped and again wondered what the hell he was doing. Just because he had found a crude doll in a car he was walking through a forest on a mountain in Norway. It was bloody ridiculous.

It had been the redhead's casual theory that the doll had been left in the car by a previous hirer. But what previous hirer? The car was obviously new. The doll had been left in a prominent position and there was the note to go with it with the significant reference to the 'Drammen Dolly'.

Early morning – that's what the note had said. But how early was early? *Come out, come out, wherever you are, my little Drammen Dolly. Wave your magic wand and take me back to Hampstead.*

He turned around and trudged back to the fork in the path and this time took the route to the left. The air was fresh and clean after the rain. Drops of water sparkled prismatically on the leaves as the sun struck them and occasionally, as he passed under a tree, a miniature shower would sprinkle him.

And he saw nothing but trees.

He came to another fork in the trail and stopped, wondering what to do. There was a sound behind him as of a twig breaking and he swung around and stared back along the trail but saw nothing as he peered into the dappled forest, shading his eyes from the sun. He turned away but heard another sound to his right and out of the corner of his eye saw something dark moving very fast among the trees.

Behind him he heard footsteps and whirled around to find himself under savage attack. Almost upon him was a big man, a six-footer with broad shoulders, his right hand uplifted and holding what appeared to be a short club.

Denison was thirty-six, which is no age to indulge in serious fisticuffs. He also led a sedentary life which meant that his wind was not too good, although it was better than it might have been because he did not smoke. Yet his reflexes were fast enough. What really saved him, though, was that in his time he had been a middling-good middleweight boxer who had won most of his amateur fights by sheer driving aggression.

The last two days had been frustrating for a man of his aggressive tendencies. He had been in a mist with nothing visible to fight and this had gnawed at him. Now that he had something to fight – someone to fight – his instincts took over.

Which is why, instead of jumping back under the attack, unexpectedly he went in low, blocked the descending arm with his own left arm and sank his right fist into his attacker's belly just below the sternum. The man's breath came out of him with a gasp and he doubled up on the ground wheezing and making retching noises.

Denison wasted no time, but ran for it back to the car park, aware that his were not the only feet that made those thudding noises on the trail. He did not waste time by looking back but just put his head down and ran. To his left he was aware of a man bounding down the hill dodging trees and doing his best to cut him off – what was worse, he seemed to be succeeding.

Denison put on an extra burst of speed but it was no use – the man leaped on to the trail about fifteen yards ahead. Denison heard his pursuer pounding behind and knew that if he stopped he would be trapped, so he bored on up the trail without slackening pace.

When the man ahead realized that Denison did not intend to stop a look of surprise came over his face and his hand plucked at his waist and he dropped into a crouch. Sun gleamed off the blade of the knife he held in his right hand. Denison ran full tilt at him and made as to break to the man's left – the safe side – but at the last minute he sold him the dummy and broke away on the knife side.

He nearly got through unscathed because the man bought it. But at the last moment he lashed out with the knife and Denison felt a hot pain across his flank. Yet he had got past and plunged along the trail with undiminished speed, hoping to God he would not trip over an exposed tree root. There is nothing like being chased by a man with a knife to put wings on the feet.

There were three of them. The big man he had laid out with a blow to the solar plexus would not be good for anything for at least two minutes and probably longer. That left the knifer and the other man who had chased him. Behind he heard cries but ahead he saw the roof of the restaurant just coming in sight over the rise.

His wind was going fast and he knew he could not keep up this sprint for long. He burst out into the car park and headed for his car, thankful there was now firm footing. A car door slammed and he risked a glance to the left and saw the man who had been reading the newspaper in the parked car beginning to run towards him.

He fumbled hastily for his car key and thanked God when it slipped smoothly into the lock. He dived behind the wheel and slammed the door with one hand while stabbing the key at the ignition lock with the other – this time he missed and had to fumble again. The man outside hammered on the window and then tugged at the door handle. Denison held the door closed with straining muscles and brought over his other hand quickly to snap down the door catch.

He had dropped the car key on the floor and groped for it. His lungs were hurting and he gasped for breath, and the pain in his side suddenly sharpened, but somewhere at the back of his mind cool logic told him that he was reasonably safe, that no one could get into a locked car before he took off – always provided he could find that damned key.

His fingers brushed against it and he grabbed it, brought it up, and rammed it into the ignition lock. Cool logic evaporated fast when he saw the man stand back and produce an automatic pistol. Denison frantically pumped his foot on the clutch, slammed into first gear, and took off in a tyre-burning squeal even before he had a finger on the wheel. The car weaved drunkenly across the car park then straightened out and dived into the Spiralen tunnel like a rabbit down a hole.

Denison's last glimpse of daylight in the rear-view mirror showed him the other car beginning to move with two doors open and his pursuers piling in. That would be the ferret after the rabbit.

It took him about ten seconds, after he hit the curve, to know he was going too fast. The gradient was one in ten and the curve radius only a hundred and fifteen feet, turning away to the right so that he was on the inside. His speed was such that centrifugal force tended to throw the car sideways over the centre line, and if anything was coming up he would surely hit it.

He could be compared to a man on a bobsled going down the Cresta Run – with some important differences. The Cresta Run is designed so that the walls can be climbed; here the walls were of jagged, untrimmed rock and one touch at speed would surely wreck the car. The Cresta Run does not have two-way traffic with a continuous blind corner a mile long, and the competitors are not pursued by men with guns – if they were, more records might be broken.

So Denison reluctantly eased his foot on the accelerator and risked a glance in his mirror. The driver of the car behind was more foolhardy than he and was not worrying about up-traffic. He was barrelling down the centre line and catching up fast. Denison fed more fuel to the engine, twisted the wheel and wondered if he could sustain a sideways drift a mile long.

The walls of the tunnel were a blur and the lights flicked by and he caught sight of an illuminated number 5. Four more circuits to go before the bottom. The car jolted and pitched suddenly and he fought the wheel which had taken on a life of its own. It did it again and he heard a nasty sound from the rear. He was being rammed. There was another sound as sheet metal ripped and the car slewed across the whole width of the tunnel.

He heard – and felt – the crunch as the rear off-side of the car slammed into the opposite wall, but Denison was not particularly worried about the property of the Hertz Company at that moment because he saw the dipped headlights of a vehicle coming up the Spiralen towards him. He juggled madly with wheel, clutch and accelerator and shot off to the other side of the tunnel again, scraping across the front of the tour bus that was coming up. There was a brief vignette of the driver of the bus, his mouth open and his eyes staring, and then he was gone.

The front fender scraped along the nearside tunnel wall in a shower of sparks and Denison wrenched the wheel over and nearly clipped the rear of the bus as it went by. He wobbled crazily from side to side of the tunnel for about a hundred and fifty yards before he had proper control, and it was only by the grace of God that the bus had not been the first in a procession of vehicles.

Level 2 passed in a flash and a flicker of light in Denison's eyes, reflected from the rear-view mirror, told him that the car behind had also avoided the bus and was catching up again. He increased speed again and the tyres protested noisily with a rending squeal; the whole of the Spiralen would be filled with the stench of burning rubber.

Level 1. A brightness ahead warned of the approach of another vehicle and Denison tensed his muscles, but the tunnel straightened and he saw it was the daylight of the exit. He rammed down his foot and the car surged forward and came out of the tunnel like a shell from a gun. The fee-collector threw up his arms and jumped aside as the car shot past him. Denison screwed up his eyes against the sudden bright glare of sunlight and hurtled down the hill towards the main street of Drammen at top speed.

At the bottom of the hill he jammed on his brakes and wrenched the wheel sideways. The car heeled violently as it turned the corner and the tyres screamed again, leaving black rubber on the road. Then he literally stood on the brake pedal, rising in his seat, to avoid ploughing into a file of the good people of Drammen crossing the street at a traffic light. The car's nose sank and the rear came up as it juddered to a halt, just grazing the thigh of a policeman who stood in the middle of the road with his back to Denison.

The policeman turned, his face expressionless. Denison sagged back into his seat and twisted his head to look back along the road. He saw the pursuing car break the other way and head down the road at high speed out of Drammen.

The policeman knocked on the car window and Denison wound it down to be met by a blast of hot Norwegian. He shook his head, and said loudly, 'I have no Norwegian. Do you speak English?'

The policeman halted in mid-spate with his mouth open. He shut it firmly, took a deep breath, and said, 'What you think you do?'

Denison pointed back. 'It was those damn fools. I might have been killed.'

The policeman stood back and did a slow circumnavigation of the car, inspecting it carefully. Then he tapped on the window of the passenger side and Denison opened the door. The policeman got in. 'Drive!' he said.

When Denison pulled up outside the building marked POLISI and switched off the engine the policeman firmly took the car key from him and waved towards the door of the building. 'Inside!'

It was a long wait for Denison. He sat in a bare room under the cool eye of a Norwegian policeman, junior grade, and meditated on his story. If he told the truth then the question would arise: *Who would want to attack an Englishman called Meyrick*? That would naturally lead to: *Who is this Meyrick*? Denison did not think he could survive long under questions like that. It would all come out and the consensus of opinion would be that they had a right nut-case on their hands, and probably homicidal at that. They would have to be told something other than the strict truth.

He waited an hour and then the telephone rang. The young policeman answered briefly, put down the telephone, and said to Denison, 'Come!'

He was taken to an office where a senior policeman sat behind a desk. He picked up a pen and levelled it at a chair. 'Sit!'

Denison sat, wondering if the English conversation of the Norwegian police was limited to one word at a time. The officer poised his pen above a printed form. 'Name?'

'Meyrick,' said Denison. 'Harold Feltham Meyrick.'

'Nationality?'

'British.'

The officer extended his hand, palm upwards. 'Passport.' It was not a question.

Denison took out his passport and put it on the outstretched palm. The officer flicked through the pages, then put it down and stared at Denison with eyes like chips of granite. 'You drove through the streets of Drammen at an estimated speed of 140 kilometres an hour. I don't have to tell you that is in excess of the speed limit. You drove through the Spiralen at an unknown speed – certainly less than 140 kilometres otherwise we would have the distasteful task of scraping you off the walls. What is your explanation?'

Denison now knew what a Norwegian policeman sounded like in an extended speech in the English language, and he did not particularly relish it. The man's tone was scathing. He said, 'There was a car behind me. The driver was playing silly buggers.' The officer raised his eyebrows, and Denison said, 'I think they were teenage hooligans out to throw a scare into someone – you know how they are. They succeeded with me. They rammed me a couple of times and I had to go faster. It all led on from that.'

He stopped and the officer stared at him with hard, grey eyes but said nothing. Denison let the silence lengthen, then said slowly and clearly, 'I would like to get in touch with the British Embassy immediately.'

The officer lowered his eyes and consulted a typewritten form. 'The condition of the rear of your car is consistent with your story. There was another car. It has been found abandoned. The condition of the front of that car is also consistent with your story. The car we found had been stolen last night in Oslo.' He looked up. 'Do you want to make any changes in your statement?'

'No,' said Denison.

'Are you sure?'

'Quite sure.'

The officer stood up, the passport in his hand. 'Wait here.' He walked out.

Denison waited another hour before the officer came back. He said, 'An official from your Embassy is coming to be present while you prepare your written statement.'

'I see,' said Denison. 'What about my passport?'

'That will be handed to the embassy official. Your car we will keep here for spectrographic tests of the paintwork. If there has been transfer of paint from one car to another it will tend to support your statement. In any event, the car cannot be driven in its present condition; both indicator lights are smashed – you would be breaking the law.'

Denison nodded. 'How long before the Embassy man gets here?'

'I cannot say. You may wait here.' The officer went away.

Denison waited for two hours. On complaining of hunger, food and coffee were brought to him on a tray. Otherwise he was left alone except for the doctor who came in to dress an abrasion on the left side of his forehead. He dimly remembered being struck by a tree branch on the chase along the trail, but did not correct the doctor who assumed it had occurred in the Spiralen. What with one thing and another, the left side of Meyrick's face was taking quite a beating; any photographs had better be of the right profile.

He said nothing about the wound in his side. While alone in the office he had checked it quickly. That knife must have been razor sharp; it had sliced through his topcoat, his jacket, the sweater and into his side, fortunately not deeply. The white sweater was red with blood but the wound, which appeared clean, had stopped bleeding although it hurt if he moved suddenly. He left it alone.

At last someone came – a dapper young man with a fresh face who advanced on Denison with an outstretched hand. 'Dr Meyrick – I'm George McCready, I've come to help you get out of this spot of trouble.'

Behind McCready came the police officer, who drew up another chair and they got down to the business of the written statement. The officer wanted it amplified much more than in Denison's bald, verbal statement so he obligingly told all that had happened from the moment he had entered the Spiralen tunnel on top of Bragernesåsen. He had no need to lie about anything. His written statement was taken away and typed up in quadruplicate and he signed all four copies, McCready countersigning as witness.

McCready cocked his eye at the officer. 'I think that's all.'

The officer nodded. 'That's all – for the moment. Dr Meyrick may be required at another time. I trust he will be available.'

'Of course,' said McCready easily. He turned to Denison. 'Let's get you back to the hotel. You must be tired.'

They went out to McCready's car. As McCready drove out of Drammen Denison was preoccupied with a problem. How did McCready know to address him as 'Doctor'? The designation on his passport was just plain 'Mister'. He stirred and said, 'If we're going to the hotel I'd like to have my passport. I don't like to be separated from it.'

'You're not going to the hotel,' said McCready. 'That was for the benefit of the copper. I'm taking you to the Embassy. Carey flew in from London this morning and he wants to see you.' He laughed shortly. '*How* he wants to see you.'

Denison felt the water deepening. 'Carey,' he said in a neutral tone, hoping to stimulate conversation along those lines. McCready had dropped Carey's name casually as though Meyrick was supposed to know him. Who the devil was Carey?

McCready did not bite. 'That explanation of yours wasn't quite candid, was it?' He waited for a reaction but Denison kept his mouth shut. 'There's a witness – a waitress from the Spiraltoppen – who said something about a fight up there. It seems there was a man with a gun. The police are properly suspicious.'

When Denison would not be drawn McCready glanced sideways at him, and laughed. 'Never mind, you did the right thing under the circumstances. Never talk about guns to a copper – it makes them nervous. Mind you, the circumstances should never have arisen. Carey's bloody wild about that.' He sighed. 'I can't say that I blame him.'

It was gibberish to Denison and he judged that the less he said the better. He leaned back, favouring his injured side, and said, 'I'm tired.'

'Yes,' said McCready. 'I suppose you must be.'

CHAPTER FIVE

Denison was kept kicking his heels in an ante-room in the Embassy while McCready went off, presumably to report. After fifteen minutes he came back. 'This way, Dr Meyrick.'

Denison followed him along a corridor until McCready stopped and politely held open a door for him. 'You've already met Mr Carey, of course.'

The man sitting behind the desk could only be described as square. He was a big, chunky man with a square head topped with close-cut grizzled grey hair. He was broadchested and squared off at the shoulders, and his hands were big with blunt fingers. 'Come in, Dr Meyrick.' He nodded at McCready. 'All right, George; be about your business.'

McCready closed the door. 'Sit down, Doctor,' said Carey. It was an invitation, not a command. Denison sat in the chair on the other side of the desk and waited for a long time while Carey inspected him with an inscrutable face.

After a long time Carey sighed. 'Dr Meyrick, you were asked not to stray too far from your hotel and to keep strictly to central Oslo. If you wanted to go farther afield you were asked to let us know so that we could make the necessary arrangements. You see, our manpower isn't infinite.'

His voice rose. 'Maybe you shouldn't have been *asked*; maybe you should have been *told*.' He seemed to hold himself in with an effort, and lowered his voice again. 'So I fly in this morning to hear that you're missing, and then I'm told that you isolated yourself on a mountain top – for what reason only you know.'

He raised his hand to intercept interruption. Denison did not mind; he was not going to say anything, anyway.

'All right,' said Carey. 'I know the story you told the local coppers. It was a good improvisation and maybe they'll buy it and maybe they won't.' He put his hands flat on the desk. 'Now what really happened?'

'I was up there walking through the woods,' said Denison, 'when suddenly a man attacked me.'

'Description?'

'Tall. Broad. Not unlike you in build, but younger. He had black hair. His nose was broken. He had something in his hand – he was going to hit me with it. Some sort of cosh, I suppose.'

'So what did you do?'

'I laid him out,' said Denison.

'*You* laid him out,' said Carey in a flat voice. There was disbelief in his eye.

'I laid him out,' said Denison evenly. He paused. 'I was a useful boxer at one time.'

Carey frowned and drummed his fingers. 'Then what happened?'

'Another man was coming at me from behind, so I ran for it.'

'Wise man – some of the time, anyway. And ...?'

'Another man intercepted me from the front.'

'Describe him.'

'Shortish – about five foot seven – with a rat-face and a long nose. Dressed in jeans and a blue jersey. He had a knife.'

'He had a knife, did he?' said Carey. 'So what did you do about that?'

'Well, the other chap was coming up behind fast – I didn't have much time to think – so I charged the joker with the knife and sold him the dummy at the last moment.'

'You *what*?'

'I sold him the dummy. It's a rugby expression meaning ...'

'I know what it means,' snapped Carey. 'I suppose you were a useful rugby player at one time, too.'

'That's right,' said Denison.

Carey bent his head and put his hand to his brow so that his face was hidden. He seemed to be suppressing some strong emotion. 'What happened next?' he asked in a muffled voice.

'By that time I'd got back to the car park – and there was another man.'

'*Another* man,' said Carey tiredly. 'Description.'

'Not much. I think he wore a grey suit. He had a gun.'

'Escalating on you, weren't they?' said Carey. His voice was savage. 'So what did you do then?'

'I was in the car by the time I saw the gun and I got out of there fast and ...'

'And did a Steve McQueen through the Spiralen, roared through Drammen like an express train and butted a copper in the arse.'

'Yes,' said Denison simply. 'That about wraps it up.'

'I should think it does,' said Carey. He was silent for a while, then he said, 'Regardless of the improbability of all this, I'd still like to know why you went to Drammen in the first place, and why you took the trouble to shake off any followers before leaving Oslo.'

'Shake off followers,' said Denison blankly. 'I didn't know I was being followed.'

'You know now. It was for your own protection. But my man says he's never seen such an expert job of shaking a tail in his life. You were up to all the tricks. You nearly succeeded twice, and you did succeed the third time.'

'I don't know what you're talking about,' said Denison. 'I lost my way a couple of times, that's all.'

Carey took a deep breath and looked at the ceiling. 'You lost your way,' he breathed. His voice became deep and solemn. 'Dr Meyrick: can you tell me why you lost your way when you know this area better than your own county of Buckinghamshire? You showed no signs of losing your way when you went to Drammen last week.'

Denison took the plunge. 'Perhaps it's because I'm not Dr Meyrick.'

Carey whispered, '*What did you say?*'

CHAPTER SIX

Denison told all of it.

When he had finished Carey's expression was a mixture of perturbation and harassment. He heard everything Denison had to say but made no comment; instead, he lifted the telephone, dialled a number, and said, 'George? Ask Ian to come in here for a minute.'

He came from behind the desk and patted Denison on the shoulder. 'I hope you don't mind waiting for a few minutes.' He strode away to intercept the man who had just come in and they held a whispered colloquy before Carey left the room.

He closed the door on the other side and stood for a moment in thought, then he shook his head irritably and went into McCready's office. McCready looked up, saw Carey's expression, and said, 'What's the matter?'

'Our boy has rolled clean off his tiny little rocker,' snapped Carey. 'That's what's the matter. He started off by telling cock-and-bull stories, but then it got worse – much worse.'

'What did he say?'

Carey told him – in gruesome detail.

Ten minutes later he said, 'Discounting a lot of balls about mysterious attackers, *something* happened up there on top of the Spiralen which knocked Meyrick off his perch.' He rubbed his forehead. 'When they wish these eggheads on us you'd think they'd test them for mental stability. What we need now is an alienist.'

McCready suppressed a smile. 'Isn't that rather an old-fashioned term?'

Carey glared at him. 'Old-fashioned and accurate.' He stabbed his finger at the office wall. 'That … that *thing* in there isn't human any more. I tell you, my flesh crawled when I heard what he was saying.'

'There isn't a chance that he's right, is there?' asked McCready diffidently.

'No chance at all. I was facing Meyrick at the original briefing in London for two bloody days until I got to hate the sight of his fat face. It's Meyrick, all right.'

'There is one point that puzzles me,' said McCready. 'When I was with him at the police station in Drammen he didn't speak a word of Norwegian, and yet I understand he knows the language.'

'He speaks it fluently,' said Carey.

'And yet I'm told that his first words were to the effect that he spoke no Norwegian.'

'For God's sake!' said Carey. 'You know the man's history. He was born in Finland and lived there until he was seventeen, when he came to live here in Oslo. When he was twenty-four he moved to England where he's been ever since. That's twenty-two years. He didn't see a rugby ball until he arrived in England, and I've studied his dossier and know for a fact that he never boxed in his life.'

'Then it all fits in with his story that he's not Meyrick.' McCready paused for thought. 'There *was* a witness at Spiraltoppen who said she saw a gun.'

'A hysterical waitress,' sneered Carey. 'Wait a minute – did you tell Meyrick about that?'

'I did mention it.'

'It fits,' said Carey. 'You know, I wouldn't be surprised if the story Meyrick gave to the police wasn't the absolute truth. He was razzled by a few kids out for a joyride in a stolen car and the experience knocked him off his spindle.'

'And the gun?'

'*You* told him about the gun. He seized that and wove it into his fairy tale, and added a few other trimmings such as the knife and the cosh. I think that in the Spiralen he felt so bloody helpless that he's invented this story to retain what he thinks is his superiority. At the briefing I assessed him as an arrogant bastard, utterly convinced of his superiority to us lesser mortals. But he wasn't very superior in the Spiralen, was he?'

'Interesting theory,' said McCready. 'You'd make a good alienist – except for one thing. You lack empathy.'

'I can't stand the man,' said Carey bluntly. 'He's an overweening, overbearing, supercilious son-of-a-bitch who thinks the sun shines out of his arse. Mr Know-it-all in person and too bloody toplofty by half.' He shrugged. 'But I can't pick and choose the people I work with. It's not in my contract.'

'What did you say he called himself?'

'Giles Denison from Hampstead. Hampstead, for Christ's sake!'

'I'll be back in a minute,' said McCready. He left the room.

Carey loosened his tie with a jerk and sat biting his thumbnail. He looked up as McCready came back holding a book. 'What have you got there?'

'London telephone directory.'

'Give me that,' said Carey, and grabbed it. 'Let's see Dennis, Dennis, Dennis … Dennison. There's a George and two plain Gs – neither in Hampstead.' He sat back, looking pleased.

McCready took the book and flipped the pages. After a minute he said, 'Denison, Giles … Hampstead. He spells it with one 'n'.'

'Oh, Christ!' said Carey, looking stricken. He recovered. 'Doesn't mean a thing. He picked the name of someone he knows. His daughter's boy-friend, perhaps.'

'Perhaps,' said McCarthy non-committally.

Carey drummed his fingers on the desk. 'I'll stake my life that this is Meyrick; anything else would be too ridiculous.' His fingers were suddenly stilled. 'Mrs Hansen,' he said. 'She's been closer to him than anybody. Did she have anything to say?'

'She reported last night that she'd met him. He'd broken a date with her in the morning and excused it by pleading illness. Said he'd been in bed all morning.'

'Had he?'

'Yes.'

'Did she notice anything about him – anything odd or unusual?'

'Only that he had a cold and that he'd stopped smoking. He said cigarettes tasted like straw.'

Carey, a pipe-smoker, grunted. 'They taste like straw to me without a cold. But he recognized her.'

'They had a drink and a conversation – about morals and religion, she said.'

'That does it,' said Carey. 'Meyrick is ready to pontificate about anything at the drop of a hat, whether he knows anything about it or not.' He rubbed his chin and said grudgingly, 'Trouble is, he usually talks sense – he has a good brain. No, this is Meyrick, and Meyrick is as flabby as a bladder of lard – that's why we have to coddle him on this operation. Do you really think that Meyrick could stand up against four men with guns and knives and coshes? The man could hardly break the skin on the top of a custard. He's gone out of his tiny, scientific mind and his tale of improbable violence is just to save his precious superiority, as I said before.'

'And what about the operation?'

'As far as Meyrick is concerned the operation is definitely off,' said Carey decisively. 'And, right now, I don't see how it can be done without him. I'll cable London to that effect as soon as I've had another talk with him.' He paused. 'You'd better come along, George. I'm going to need a witness on this one or else London will have *me* certified.'

They left the office and walked along the corridor. Outside the room where Meyrick was held Carey put his hand on McCready's arm. 'Hold yourself in, George. This might be rough.'

They found Meyrick still sitting at the desk in brooding silence, ignoring the man he knew only as Ian who sat opposite. Ian looked up at Carey and shrugged eloquently.

Carey stepped forward. 'Dr Meyrick, I'm sorry to …'

'My name is Denison. I told you that.' His voice was cold.

Carey softened his tone. 'All right, Mr Denison; if you prefer it that way. I really think you ought to see a doctor. I'm arranging for it.'

'And about time,' said Denison. 'This is hurting like hell.'

'What is?'

Denison was pulling his sweater from his trousers. 'This bloody knife wound. Look at it.'

Carey and McCready bent to look at the quarter-inch deep slash along Denison's side. It would, Carey estimated, take sixteen stitches to sew it up.

Their heads came up together and they looked at each other with a wild surmise.

CHAPTER SEVEN

Carey paced restlessly up and down McCready's office. His tie was awry and his hair would have been tousled had it not been so close-cropped because he kept running his hand through it. 'I still don't believe it,' he said. 'It's too bloody incredible.'

He swung on McCready. 'George, supposing you went to bed tonight, here in Oslo, and woke up tomorrow, say, in a New York hotel, wearing someone else's face. What would be your reaction?'

'I think I'd go crazy,' said McCready soberly. He smiled slightly. 'If I woke up with your face I would go crazy.'

Carey ignored the wisecrack. 'But Denison didn't go crazy,' he said meditatively. 'All things considered, he kept his cool remarkably well.'

'If he is Denison,' remarked McCready. 'He could be Meyrick and quite insane.'

Carey exploded into a rage. 'For God's sake! All along you've been arguing that he's Denison; now you turn around and say he could be Meyrick.'

McCready eyed him coolly. 'The role of devil's advocate suits me, don't you think?' He tapped the desk. 'Either way, the operation is shot to hell.'

Carey sat down heavily. 'You're right, of course. But if this is a man called Denison then there are a lot of questions to be answered. But first, what the devil do we do with him?'

'We can't keep him here,' said McCready. 'For the same reason we didn't keep Meyrick here. The Embassy is like a fishbowl.'

Carey cocked his head. 'He's been here for over two hours. That's about normal for a citizen being hauled over the coals for a serious driving offence. You suggest we send him back to the hotel?'

'Under surveillance.' McCready smiled. 'He says he has a date with a redhead for dinner.'

'Mrs Hansen,' said Carey. 'Does he know about her?'

'No.'

'Keep it that way. She's to stick close to him. Give her a briefing and ask her to guard him from interference. He could run into some odd situations. And talk to him like a Dutch uncle. Put the fear of God into him so that he stays in the hotel. I don't want him wandering around loose.'

Carey drew a sheet of paper towards him and scribbled on it. 'The next thing we want are doctors – tame ones who will ask the questions we want asked and no others. A plastic surgeon and – ' he smiled at McCready bleakly – 'and an alienist. The problem must be decided one way or the other.'

'We can't wait until they arrive,' said McCready.

'Agreed,' said Carey. 'We'll work on the assumption that a substitution has been made – that this man is Denison. We know when the substitution was made – in the early hours of yesterday morning. Denison was brought in – how?'

'On a stretcher – he must have been unconscious.'

'Right!' said Carey. 'A hospital patient in transit under the supervision of a trained nurse and probably a doctor. And they'd have taken a room on the same floor as Meyrick. The switch was made and Meyrick taken out yesterday morning – probably in an ambulance at the back entrance of the hotel by arrangement with the management. Hotels don't like stretchers being paraded through the front lobby.'

'I'll get on to it,' said McCready. 'It might be an idea to check on all the people who booked in on the previous day, regardless of the floor they stayed on. I don't think this was a two man job.'

'I don't, either. And you check the comings and goings for the past week – somebody must have been watching Meyrick for a long time.'

'That's a hell of a big job,' objected McCready. 'Do we get the co-operation of the Norwegians?'

Carey pondered. 'At this time – no. We keep it under wraps.'

McCready's face took on a sad look at the thought of all the legwork he was going to have to do. Carey tilted his chair back. 'And then there's the other end to be checked – the London end. Why Giles Denison of Hampstead?' His chair came down with a thump. 'Hasn't it struck you that Denison has been very unforthcoming?'

McCready shrugged. 'I haven't talked to him all that much.'

'Well, look,' said Carey. 'Here we have this man in this bloody odd situation in which he finds himself. After recovering from the first shock, he not only manages to deceive Mrs Hansen as to his real identity but he has the wit to ring Meyrick's home. But why only Meyrick? Why didn't he check back on himself?'

'How do you mean?'

Carey sighed. 'There's a man called Giles Denison missing from Hampstead. Surely he'd be missed by someone? Even if Denison is an unmarried orphan he must have friends – a job. Why didn't he ring back to reassure people that he was all right and still alive and now living it up in Oslo?'

'I hadn't thought of that,' admitted McCready. 'That's a pointer to his being Meyrick, after all. Suffering from delusions but unable to flesh them out properly.'

Carey gave a depressed nod. 'All I've had from him is that he's Giles Denison from Hampstead – nothing more.'

'Why not put it to him now?' suggested McCready.

Carey thought about it and shook his head. 'No, I'll leave that to the psychiatrist. If this is really Meyrick, the wrong sort of questions could push him over the edge entirely.' He pulled the note pad towards him again. 'We'll have someone check on Denison in Hampstead and find out the score.' He ripped off the sheet. 'Let's get cracking. I want those cables sent to London immediately – top priority and coded. I want those quacks here as fast as possible.'

CHAPTER EIGHT

Giles Denison stirred his coffee and smiled across the table at Diana Hansen. His smile was steady, which was remarkable because a thought had suddenly struck him like a bolt of lightning and left him with a churning stomach. Was the delectable Diana Hansen who faced him Meyrick's mistress?

The very thought put him into a dilemma. Should he make a pass or not? Whatever he did – or did not – do, he had a fifty per cent chance of being wrong. The uncertainty of it spoiled his evening which had so far been relaxing and pleasant.

He had been driven back to the hotel in an Embassy car after dire warnings from George McCready of what would happen to him if he did not obey instructions. 'You'll have realized by now that you've dropped right into the middle of something awkward,' said McCready. 'We're doing our best to sort it out but, for the next couple of days, you'd do well to stay in the hotel.' He drove it home by asking pointedly, 'How's your side feeling now?'

'Better,' said Denison. 'But I could have done with a doctor.' He had been strapped up by McCready, who had produced a first-aid box and displayed a competence which suggested he was no stranger to knife wounds.

'You'll get a doctor,' assured McCready. 'Tomorrow.'

'I have a dinner date,' said Denison. 'With that redhead I told you about. What should I do about that? If she goes on like she did yesterday I'm sure to put my foot in it.'

'I don't see why you should,' said McCready judiciously.

'For God's sake! I don't even know her name.'

McCready patted him on the shoulder, and said soothingly, 'You'll be all right.'

Denison was plaintive. 'It's all very well you wanting me to go on being Meyrick but surely you can tell me *something*. Who *is* Meyrick, for instance?'

'It will all be explained tomorrow,' said McCready, hoping that he was right. 'In the meantime, go back to the hotel like a good chap, and don't leave it until I call for you. Just have a quiet dinner with ... with your redhead and then go to bed.'

Denison had a last try. 'Are you in Intelligence or something? A spy?'

But to that McCready made no answer.

So Denison was delivered to the hotel and he had not been in the room more than ten minutes when the telephone rang. He regarded it warily and let it ring several times before he put out his hand as though about to pick up a snake. 'Yes?' he said uncommunicatively.

'Diana here.'

'Who?' he asked cautiously.

'Diana Hansen, who else? We have a dinner date, remember? How are you?'

Again he caught the faint hint of America behind the English voice. 'Better,' he said, thinking it was convenient of her to announce her name.

'That's good,' she said warmly. 'Are you fit enough for dinner?'

'I think so.'

'Mmm,' she murmured doubtfully. 'But I still don't think you should go out; there's quite a cold wind. What about dinner in the hotel restaurant?'

Even more convenient; he had just been about to suggest that himself. In a more confident voice he said, 'That'll be fine.'

'Meet you in the bar at half past seven,' she said.

'All right.'

She rang off and he put down the telephone slowly. He hoped that McCready was right; that he could manage a sustained conversation with this woman in the guise of Meyrick. He sat in the armchair and winced as pain stabbed in his side. He held his breath until the pain eased and then relaxed and looked at his watch. Half past five. He had two hours before meeting the Hansen woman.

What a mess! What a stinking mess! Lost behind another man's face, he had apparently dropped into the middle of an intrigue which involved the British government. That man, Carey, had been damned patronizing about what had happened on top of the Spiralen and had not bothered to hide his disbelief. It had been that, more than anything else, that had driven Denison into disclosing who he was. It had certainly taken the smile off Carey's face.

But who was Carey? To begin with, he was obviously McCready's boss – but that did not get him very far because who was McCready? A tight little group in the British Embassy in Oslo dedicated to what? Trade relations? That did not sound likely.

Carey had made it clear that he had warned Meyrick not to move far from the hotel. Judging by what had happened on the Spiralen the warning was justified. But who the hell was Meyrick that he was so important? The man with the title of Doctor or perhaps Professor, and who was described on his passport as a civil servant.

Denison's head began to ache again. *Christ!* he thought; *I'll be bloody glad to get back to Hampstead, back to my job and the people I ...*

The thought tailed off to a deadly emptiness and he felt his stomach lurch. A despairing wail rose in his mind – *God help me!* he cried silently as he realized his mind was a blank, that he did not know what his job was, that he could not put a name to a single friend or acquaintance, and that all he knew of himself was that he was Giles Denison and that he came from Hampstead.

Bile rose in his throat. He struggled to his feet and staggered to the bathroom where he was violently sick. Again there was that insistent beat in his mind: I AM GILES DENISON. But there was nothing more – no link with a past life.

He left the bathroom and lay on the bed, staring at the ceiling. *You must remember!* he commanded himself. *You must!* But there was nothing – just Giles Denison of Hampstead and a vague mind picture of a house as in a half-forgotten memory.

Think!

The scar on his shin – he remembered that. He saw himself on the small child-size bicycle going down a hill too fast, and the inevitable tumble at the bottom – then the quick tears and the comfort of his mother. I remember that, he told himself in triumph.

What else? Beth – he remembered Beth who had been his wife, but she had died. How many years ago was it? Three years. And then there was the whisky, too much whisky. He remembered the whisky.

Denison lay on the bed and fought to extract memories from a suddenly recalcitrant mind. There was a slick sheen of sweat on his brow and his fists were clenched, the nails digging into his palms.

Something else he had remembered before. He had come back from Edinburgh on June 17, but what had he been doing there? Working, of course; but what was his work?

Try as he might he could not penetrate the blank haze which cloaked his mind.

On June 18 he had played golf in the afternoon. With whom? Of course it was possible for a man to play a round of golf alone, and also to go to the cinema alone and to dine in Soho alone, but it was hardly likely that he would forget everything else. Where had he played golf? Which cinema did he go to? Which restaurant in Soho?

A blazing thought struck him, an illumination of the mind so clear that he knew certainly it was the truth. He cried aloud, 'But I've never played golf in my life!'

There was a whirling spiral of darkness in his mind and, mercifully, he slept.

CHAPTER NINE

Denison walked into the bar at a quarter to eight and saw the woman who called herself Diana Hansen sitting at a table. He walked over and said, 'Sorry I'm late.'

She smiled and said lightly, 'I was beginning to think I was being stood up again.'

He sat down. 'I fell asleep.'

'You look pale. Are you all right?'

'I'm fine.' There was a vague memory at the back of his mind which disturbed him; something had happened just before he had fallen asleep. He was reluctant to probe into it because he caught a hint of terror and madness which frightened him. He shivered.

'Cold?' Her voice was sympathetic.

'Nothing that a stiff drink won't cure.' He beckoned to a passing waiter, and raised his eyebrows at her.

'A dry Martini, please.'

He turned to the hovering waiter. 'A dry Martini and ... do you have a scotch malt?' Normally he bought the cheapest blend he could buy in the cut-price supermarkets but with Meyrick's finances behind him he could afford the best.

'Yes, sir. Glenfiddich?'

'That will do fine. Thank you.'

Diana Hansen said, 'Food may be better than drink. Have you eaten today?'

'Not much.' Just the meal in the police station at Drammen, taken for fuel rather than pleasure.

'You men!' she said with scorn. 'No better than children when left on your own. You'll feel better after dinner.'

He leaned back in his chair. 'Let's see – how long have we known each other, Diana?'

She smiled. 'Counting the days, Harry? Nearly three weeks.'

So he had met her in Oslo – or, rather, Meyrick had. 'I was just trying to find out how long it takes a woman to become maternal. Less than three weeks, I see.'

'Is that the scientific mind at work?'

'One aspect of it.' Could that mean anything? Was Dr Meyrick a scientist – a government boffin?

She looked across the room and a shadow seemed to darken her face momentarily. 'There's Jack Kidder and his wife.'

Denison paused before he turned round. 'Oh! Where?'

'Just coming in.' She put out her hand and covered his. 'Do you want to be bothered by them, darling? He's a bit of a bore, really.'

Denison looked at the tall, fleshy man who was escorting a petite woman. Jack Kidder was the name Diana Hansen had mentioned when he had bumped into her outside the bookshop. If she did not want to mix with the Kidders it was all right with him; he had enough to cope with already. He said, 'You're right, I don't think I could cope with a bore tonight.'

She laughed. 'Thanks for the compliment – hidden though it was. I'll put him off tactfully if he comes across.' She sighed theatrically. 'But if he says that damned slogan of his again I'll scream.'

'What's that?'

'You must have heard it. It's when he pulls off one of his dreadful jokes.' She burlesqued an American accent. ' "You know me – Kidder by name and kidder by nature." '

'Jack was always the life and soul of the party,' said Denison drily.

'I don't know how Lucy puts up with him,' said Diana. 'If you can talk about a hen-pecked husband, can you refer to a cock-pecked wife?'

Denison grinned. 'It sounds rude.' Diana Hansen was making things very easy for him. She had just given him a thumbnail sketch of the Kidders, including names and temperaments. It could not have been done better if done deliberately.

The waiter put the drinks on the table and Denison found he had a scotch on the rocks, a desecration of good malt. He did not feel like making a fuss about it so he raised his glass. '*Skål!*' He sipped the whisky and reflected that this was the first real drink he had had since his transformation into Meyrick.

The familiar taste bit at his tongue and somehow released a wave of memories which washed through him tumultuously, tantalizingly close to the surface of his mind. And with the memories, unrealized though they were, came the fear and the terror which set his heart thumping in his chest. Hastily he set down the glass, knowing he was close to panic.

Diana Hansen looked at his shaking fingers. 'What's the matter, Harry?'

Denison covered up. 'I don't think a drink is a good idea, after all. I've just remembered I'm stuffed full of pills.' He managed a smile. 'If you shook me I'd rattle. I don't think they'd mix with alcohol.'

She put down her glass. 'Then let's have dinner before the Kidders catch up with us.' She stood up and took her handbag from the table. Denison arose and they moved towards the entrance, but then she turned her head and murmured, 'Too late, I'm afraid.'

Kidder was also standing up, his big body blocking the way. 'Hey, Lucy, look who's here. It's Diana and Harry.'

'Hallo, Jack,' said Denison. 'Had a good day?'

'We've been up to Holmenkollen; you know – the big ski-jump you can see from all over the city. It's quite a thing when you get up to it close. Can you imagine, it's only used once a year?'

'I can't imagine,' said Denison blandly.

Lucy Kidder said, 'And we went to the Henie-Onstad Art Centre, too.'

'Yeah, modern art,' said Kidder disparagingly. 'Harry, can you make any sense out of Jackson Pollock?'

'Not much,' said Denison.

Kidder turned on his wife. 'Anyway, why the hell do we have to come to Norway to see an American artist?'

'But he's internationally famous, Jack. Aren't you proud of that?'

'I guess so,' he said gloomily. 'But the locals aren't much better. Take the guy with the name like a breakfast food.' Everyone looked at Kidder with blank faces and he snapped his fingers impatiently. 'You know who I mean – the local Scowegian we saw yesterday.'

Lucy Kidder sighed. 'Edvard Munch,' she said resignedly.

'That's the guy. Too gloomy for me even if you can see the people in his pictures,' said Kidder.

Diana cut in quickly. 'Harry's not been feeling too well lately. I'm taking him in to an early dinner and sending him right to bed.'

'Gee, I'm sorry to hear that,' said Kidder. He sounded sincere.

'There's a lot of this two-day flu about,' said his wife. 'And it can be nasty while it lasts. You look after yourself – hear?'

'I don't think it's too serious,' said Denison.

'But we'd better go in to dinner,' said Diana. 'Harry hasn't eaten a thing all day.'

'Sure,' said Kidder, standing aside. 'I hope you feel better real soon. You look after him, Diana.'

Over dinner they talked in generalities, much to Denison's relief, and he was able to hold his own without much effort. There was not a single thing to trouble him until the coffee was served and that startling thought about the possible relationship between Diana and Meyrick came into his head. He looked at her speculatively and wondered what to do. For all he knew, Meyrick was an old ram.

He held the smile on his face and stirred his coffee mechanically. A waiter came to the table. 'Mrs Hansen?'

Diana looked up. 'Yes?'

'A telephone call.'

'Thank you.' She looked at Denison apologetically. 'I told someone I'd be here. Do you mind?'

'Not at all.' She stood up and left the restaurant, going into the lobby. He watched her until she was out of sight and then stopped stirring his coffee and put the spoon in the saucer with a clink. Thoughtfully he looked at the handbag on the other side of the table.

Mrs Hansen! He could bear to know more about that. He stretched out his hand slowly and picked up the handbag, which was curiously heavy. Holding it on his lap, below the level of the table, he snapped open the catch and bent his head to look inside.

When Diana came back the bag was back in its place. She sat down, picked it up, and took out a packet of cigarettes. 'Still not smoking, Harry?'

He shook his head. 'They still taste foul.'

Soon thereafter he signed the bill and they left, parting in the lobby, he to go to bed and she to go to wherever she lived. He had decided against making a pass at Mrs Diana Hansen because it was most unlikely that Dr Harold Feltham Meyrick would be having an affair with a woman who carried a gun – even if it was only a small gun.

CHAPTER TEN

The next day was boring. He obeyed instructions and stayed in the hotel waiting to hear from McCready. He breakfasted in his room and ordered English newspapers. Nothing had changed – the news was as bad as ever.

At mid-morning he left the room to allow the maid to clean up, and went down to the lobby where he saw the Kidders at the porter's desk. He hung back, taking an inordinate interest in a showcase full of Norwegian silver, while Kidder discussed in a loud voice the possibilities of different bus tours. Finally they left the hotel and he came out of cover.

He discovered that the bookshop on the corner of the street had a convenient entrance inside the hotel, so he bought a stack of English paperbacks and took them to his room. He read for the rest of the day, gutting the books, his mind in low gear. He had a curious reluctance to think about his present predicament and, once, when he put a book aside and tried to think coherently, his mind skittered about and he felt the unreasoning panic come over him. When he picked up the book again his head was aching.

At ten that night no contact had been made and he thought of ringing the Embassy and asking for McCready but the strange disinclination to thought had spread to action and he was irresolute. He looked at the telephone for a while, and then slowly undressed and went to bed.

He was almost asleep when there was a tap at his door. He sat up and listened and it came again, a discreet double knock. He switched on the light and put on Meyrick's bath robe, then went to the door. It was McCready, who came in quickly and closed the door behind him. 'Ready for the doctor?' he asked.

Denison frowned. 'At this time of night?'

'Why not?' asked McCready lightly.

Denison sighed. It was just one more mystery to add to the others. He reached for his underwear and took off the bath robe. McCready picked up the pyjamas which were lying neatly folded on top of the suitcase. 'You don't wear these?'

'Meyrick did.' Denison sat on the edge of the bed to put on his socks. 'I don't.'

'Oh!' McCready thoughtfully tugged at his ear.

When Denison picked up his jacket he turned to McCready. 'There's something you ought to know, I suppose. Diana Hansen carries ...'

'Who?' asked McCready.

'The redhead I took to dinner – her name is Diana Hansen. She carries a gun.'

McCready went still. 'She does? How do you know?'

'I looked in her handbag.'

'Enterprising of you. I'll tell Carey – he'll be interested.' McCready took Denison by the arm. 'Let's go.'

McCready's car was in the garage and when he drove out into the street he turned left which Denison knew was away from the Embassy. 'Where are we going?'

'Not far,' said McCready. 'Five minutes. Possess your soul in patience.'

Within two minutes Denison was lost. The car twisted and turned in the strange streets until his sense of direction deserted him. Whether McCready was deliberately confusing him he did not know, but he thought it likely. Another possibility was that McCready was intent on shaking off any possible followers.

After a few minutes the car pulled up outside a large building which could have been a block of flats. They went inside and into a lift which took them to the fifth floor. McCready unlocked a door and motioned Denison inside. He found himself in a hall with doors on each side. McCready opened one of them, and said, 'This is Mr Iredale. He'll fix up your side for you.'

Iredale was a sallow, middle-aged man, balding and with deep grooves cut from the base of his nose to the corners of his mouth. He said pleasantly, 'Come in, Mr Denison; let me have a look at you.'

Denison heard the door close behind him and turned to find that McCready had already gone. He whirled around to confront Iredale. 'I thought I was being taken to a doctor.'

'I am a doctor,' said Iredale. 'I'm also a surgeon. We surgeons have a strange inverted snobbery – we're called "mister" and not "doctor". I've never known why. Take off your coat, Mr Denison, and let me see the damage.'

Denison hesitated and slowly took off his jacket and then his shirt.

'If you'll lie on the couch?' suggested Iredale, and opened a black bag which could only have been the property of a doctor. Somewhat reassured, Denison lay down.

Iredale snipped away the bandages with a small pair of scissors and examined the slash. 'Nasty,' he said. 'But clean. It will need a local anaesthetic. Are you allergic to anaesthetic, Mr Denison?'

'I don't know – I don't think so.'

'You'll just feel three small pricks – no more.' Iredale took out a hypodermic syringe and filled it from a small phial. 'Lie still.'

Denison felt the pricks, and Iredale said, 'While we're waiting for that to take effect you can sit up.' He took an ophthalmoscope from his bag. 'I'd just like to look at your eyes.' He flashed a light into Denison's right eye. 'Had any alcohol lately?'

'No.'

Iredale switched to the left eye upon which he spent more time. 'That seems to be all right,' he said.

'I was stabbed in the side, not hit on the head,' said Denison. 'I don't have concussion.'

Iredale put away the ophthalmoscope. 'So you have a little medical knowledge.' He put his hands to Denison's face and palpated the flesh under the chin. 'You know what they say about a little knowledge.' He stood up and looked down at the top of Denison's head, and then his fingers explored the hairline. 'Don't knock the experts, Mr Denison – they know what they're doing.'

'What sort of a doctor are you?' asked Denison suspiciously.

Iredale ignored that. 'Ever had scalp trouble? Dandruff, for instance?'

'No.'

'I see. Right.' He touched Denison's side. 'Feel anything?'

'It's numb but I can feel pressure.'

'Good,' said Iredale. 'I'm going to stitch the wound closed. You won't feel anything – but if you do then shout like hell.' He put on rubber gloves which he took out of a sealed plastic bag and then took some fine thread out of another small packet. 'I'd turn your head away,' he advised. 'Lie down.'

He worked on Denison's side for about fifteen minutes and Denison felt nothing but the pressure of his fingers. At last he said, 'All right, Mr Denison; I've finished.'

Denison sat up and looked at his side. The wound was neatly closed and held by a row of minute stitches. 'I've always been good at needlework,' said Iredale conversationally. 'When the stitches are out there'll be but a hairline. In a year you won't be able to see it.'

Denison said, 'This isn't a doctor's surgery. Who are you?'

Iredale packed his bag rapidly and stood up. 'There'll be another doctor to see you in a moment.' He walked to the door and closed it behind him.

There was something about the way the door closed that vaguely alarmed Denison. He stood up and walked to the door and found it locked. Frowning, he turned away and looked about the room. There was the settee on which he had been lying, a table, two armchairs and a bookcase against the wall. He went over to the bookcase to inspect it and tripped over a wire which threatened to topple a telephone from a small table. He rescued the telephone and then stood looking down at it.

Iredale walked along the corridor and into a room at the end. Carey glanced up at him expectantly, breaking off his conversation with

McCready. Harding, the psychiatrist, sat in an armchair, his long legs outstretched and his fingertips pressed together. There was also another man whom Iredale did not know. Carey saw Iredale looking at him and said, 'Ian Armstrong of my staff. Well?' He could not suppress his eagerness.

Iredale put down his case. 'He's not Meyrick.' He paused. 'Not unless Meyrick has had plastic surgery recently.'

Carey blew out his breath in a long gasp. 'Are you sure?'

'Of course I'm sure,' said Iredale, a little testily.

'That's it, then.' Carey looked across at Harding. 'It's your turn, Dr Harding. Try to get out of him as much as you can.'

Harding nodded and uncoiled himself from the chair. He walked out of the room without speaking. As the door closed Carey said, 'You understand that, to the best of our knowledge, this alteration was made in the space of a week – not more.' He took a thin, cardboard file from the table. 'We've just received a lengthy cable from London about Denison and a photo came over the wire.' He took the photograph and handed it to Iredale. 'That's Denison as he was quite recently. It hardly seems possible.'

Iredale studied the photograph. 'Very interesting,' he commented.

'Could this thing be done in a week?' Carey persisted.

Iredale put down the photograph. 'As far as I could ascertain there was only one lesion,' he said precisely. 'That was at the outside corner of the left eyelid. A very small cut which was possibly held together by one stitch while it healed. It would certainly heal in a week although there might have been a residual soreness. I detected a minute inflammation.'

McCready said in disbelief, 'You mean that was the only cut that was made?'

'Yes,' said Iredale. 'The purpose was to draw down the left eyelid. Have you got that photograph of Meyrick?'

'Here,' said Carey.

Iredale put down his forefinger. 'There – you see? The eyelid was drawn down due to the skin contraction caused by this scar.' He paused and said sniffily, 'A bit of a butcher's job, if you ask me. That should never have happened.'

'It was a war wound when Meyrick was a boy,' said Carey. He tapped the photograph of Meyrick. 'But how the devil did they reproduce this scar on Denison without cutting?'

'That was very cleverly done,' said Iredale with sudden enthusiasm. 'As expert a job of tattooing as I've ever seen, as also was the birthmark on the right jaw.' He leaned back in his chair. 'In my field, of course, I come across a lot of tattooing but I specialize in removal rather than application.' He leaned forward again and traced a line on the photograph. 'The hairline was adjusted by depilation; nothing as crude as mere shaving and leaving the hair to grow out. I'm afraid Mr Denison has lost his hair permanently.'

'That's all very well,' said McCready, coming forward. He leaned over the table, comparing the two photographs. 'But just look at these two men. Denison is thin in the face, and he'd look thinner without the beard. Meyrick is fat-jowled. And look at the differences in the noses.'

'That was done by liquid silicone injection,' said Iredale. 'Some of my more light-minded colleagues aid film stars in their mammary development by the same means.' His tone was distasteful. 'I palpated his cheeks and felt it. It was quite unmistakable.'

'I'll be damned!' said Carey.

'You say that Denison lost a week of objective time?' asked Iredale.

'He said he'd lost a week out of his life – if that's what you mean.'

'Then I can hazard a guess as to how it was done,' said Iredale. 'He was drugged, of course, and kept unconscious for the whole week. I noticed a dressing on his left arm. I didn't investigate it, but that was where the intravenous drip feed was inserted to keep him alive.'

He paused, and Carey said in a fascinated voice, 'Go on!'

'The cut would be made at the corner of the eye, giving it a full week to heal. Any competent surgeon could do that in five minutes. Then I suppose they'd do the tattooing. Normally there'd be a residual soreness from that, but it would certainly clear up in a week. Everything else could be done at leisure.'

He picked up the two photographs. 'You see, the underlying bone structure of these two men, as far as the heads go, is remarkably similar. I rather think that if you had a photograph of Meyrick taken fifteen to twenty years ago he would look not unlike Denison or, rather, as Denison used to look. I take it that Meyrick has been used to expensive living?'

'He's rich enough,' said Carey.

'It shows on his face,' said Iredale, and tossed down the photographs. 'Denison, however, looks a shade undernourished.'

'Interesting you should say that,' said Carey, opening the folder. 'From what we have here it seems that Denison, if not an alcoholic, was on the verge. He'd just lost his job – fired for incompetence on June 24.'

Iredale nodded. 'Symptomatic. Alcoholics reject food; they get their calories from the booze.' He stood up. 'That's all I can do tonight, gentlemen. I should like to see Denison tomorrow with a view to restoring him to his former appearance, which won't be easy – that silicone polymer will be the devil to get out. Is there any more?'

'Nothing, Mr Iredale,' said Carey.

'Then if you'll excuse me, I'll go to bed. It's been a long day.'

'You know where your room is,' said Carey, and Iredale nodded and left the room.

Carey and McCready looked at each other in silence for some time, and then Carey stirred and said over his shoulder, 'What did you make of all that, Ian?'

'I'm damned if I know,' said Armstrong.

Carey grunted. 'I'm damned, too. I've been involved in some bizarre episodes in this game, but this takes the prize for looniness. Now we'll have to see what Harding comes up with, and I suspect he's going to be a long time. I think somebody had better make coffee. It's going to be a long night.'

Carey was right because more than two hours elapsed before Harding returned. His face was troubled, and he said abruptly, 'I don't think Denison should be left alone.'

'Ian!' said Carey.

Armstrong got up, and Harding said, 'If he wants to talk let him. Join in but steer clear of specifics. Stick to generalities. Understand?'

Armstrong nodded and went out. Harding sat down and Carey studied him. Finally Carey said, 'You look as though you could do with a drink, Doctor. Whisky?'

Harding nodded. 'Thanks.' He rubbed his forehead. 'Denison is in a bad way.'

Carey poured two ounces of whisky into a glass. 'How?'

'He's been tampered with,' said Harding flatly.

Carey handed him the glass. 'His mind?'

Harding sank half the whisky and choked a little. He held out the glass. 'I'll have water in the other half. Yes. Someone has been bloody ruthless about it. He has a week missing, and whatever was done to him was done in that week.'

Carey frowned. 'Iredale suggested he'd been unconscious all that week.'

'It's not incompatible,' said Harding. 'He was probably kept in a mentally depressed state by drugs during the whole week.'

'Are you talking about brain-washing?' asked McCready sceptically.

'In a manner of speaking.' Harding accepted his refilled glass. 'Whoever did this to Denison had a problem. The ideal would have been to get Denison into such a condition that he thought he *was* Meyrick – but that couldn't be done.' Harding paused for consideration. 'At least, not in a week.'

'You mean the possibility of such a thing is there?' asked Carey incredulously.

'Oh, yes,' said Harding calmly. 'It could be done. But this crowd didn't have the time for that, so they had to go about it another way. As I see it, their problem was to put Denison in the hotel as Meyrick and to make sure he didn't fly off the handle. They didn't want him to take the next plane to London, for instance. So they *treated* him.' From Harding's mouth the emphasis was an obscenity.

'How?' said Carey.

'Do you know anything about hypnosis?'

McCready snorted and Harding, staring at him with suddenly flinty eyes, said coldly, 'No, it is *not* witchcraft, Mr McCready. Denison was kept in a drug-induced hypnogogic state for a long time, and in that period his psyche was deliberately broken down.' He made a suddenly disarming gesture. 'I suspect Denison was already neurotically inclined and no doubt there were many ready-made tools to hand – irrational fears, half-healed traumas and so on – to aid in the process.'

'What do you mean by neurotically inclined?' asked Carey.

'It's hard to say, but I suspect that he was already a disturbed man before this was done to him.'

'Off his head?' intejected McCready.

Harding gave him a look of dislike. 'No more than yourself, Mr McCready,' he said tartly. 'But I think something had happened which threw him off balance.'

'Something did happen,' said Carey. 'He lost his job.' He took a thin sheaf of papers from the file. 'I didn't have time to discuss this with you before, but this is what we have on Denison. There'll be more coming but this is what we've got now.'

Harding studied the typed sheets, reading slowly and carefully. He said, 'I wish I'd seen this before I went in to Denison; it would have saved a lot of trouble.'

'He was a film director for a small specialist outfit making documentary and advertising films,' said Carey. 'Apparently he went off the rails and cost the firm a packet of money. They thought his drinking had got out of hand, so they fired him.'

Harding shook his head. 'That wasn't what threw him off balance. The drinking must have been a symptom, not a cause.' He turned back a page. 'I see that his wife died three years ago. She must have been quite young. Have you any idea how she died?'

'Not yet,' said Carey. 'But I can find out.'

'It would be advisable. I wonder if it was about that time he started to drink heavily.'

'That isn't the present point at issue,' said Carey.

Harding's voice took on an edge. 'It is for me,' he said curtly. 'I have to treat the man.'

Carey's voice was soothing. 'I know, Doctor; and you shall have all the relevant information as soon as we get it ourselves. But my present interest is in what was done to Denison and how it was done.'

Harding was placated. 'Very well. Denison was literally dismantled. All he retained was a name and a location – and the location wasn't very exact. Giles Denison of Hampstead. They could, of course, have induced complete amnesia, but that wouldn't do because Denison had to substitute for Meyrick and he would need enough active personality to carry out the role. Why Denison had to act as Meyrick I don't know.'

'I have ideas on that,' said Carey. 'Go on, Doctor.'

'At the same time Denison must not retain too much personality, certainly not enough for him to reject the persona that had been thrust upon him. He had to be kept in a sort of limbo. There were some very strong blocks inserted into his mind to the effect that he should not question his origins. In addition, to confuse the issue, he has been given selective false memories. For instance, he distinctly remembers playing a game of golf, but at the same time he knows that he has never played a game of golf in his life. So he is a very confused man and this leads to a paralysis of the will, enough to make him stay in one place – a hotel in Oslo – while he tries to sort things out.'

McCready stirred restlessly. 'Is all this possible?'

'Quite possible. If I draw an imaginary square on the floor of this room I could hypnotize you into avoiding it by a posthypnotic suggestion. You could spend the rest of your life coming in and out of this room but you would never walk on that imaginary square. More to the point, you would not be aware of the irrationality of your behaviour.'

McCready looked sceptical, and Harding said, 'I'm willing to give you a demonstration at any time.'

'No!' said McCready hurriedly. 'I believe you.'

Carey smiled grimly. 'Carry on, Doctor.'

'The mind is a self-stabilizing organism,' said Harding. 'If it wasn't we'd all go crazy. And to inquire is basic. When Denison did try to delve into his past life he encountered the blocks and was so shocked at the impossibility of what he found in his own mind that he took refuge in a fugue.' He saw the incomprehension on Carey's face, and said simply, 'He fell asleep. A typical hysterical symptom. He did it twice when he was talking to me. I let him sleep for a quarter of an hour each time, and when he woke up he'd forgotten the reason for it – wiped it out of his mind. It's a self-protective mechanism against insanity, and I rather think it's happened to him before.'

'I don't think I've got this straight,' said Carey. 'You're saying that Denison is half out of his mind and likely to fall asleep – or unconscious – at any time. How do you square that with the fact that he pulled the wool over one of my people's eyes very successfully, and that he encountered a very tricky situation which might have been the death of him and coped with it very well?'

'Oh, he's quite competent,' said Harding. 'It's only when he tries to question his own past that he faces the impossible and goes into a fugue. Judging by what you told me of the manner in which he was wounded I'd say that he's more competent than I would have expected under the circumstances.'

'He's bloody competent,' said McCready suddenly, and Carey turned to look at him. 'I haven't told you this, but he's tagged Mrs Hansen.'

'He's *what*?'

'He knows she carries a gun – he told me so. He said he thought I ought to know.'

Harding wore an I-told-you-so expression and Carey's face was a study in bafflement. 'Another thing,' said McCready. 'Alcoholic or not, he's on the wagon now. Mrs Hansen said he tried a whisky last night and he gave the impression that he'd swallowed prussic acid.'

'Interesting,' said Harding. 'The man's mind has been stirred like porridge. It would be remarkable if it has cured his alcoholism. However, I'm afraid the cure is much worse than the complaint. He'll have to be hospitalized, of course. I can make the arrangements for that.'

Carey stood up. 'Thank you, Dr Harding.'

Harding also arose. 'I'd like to see him again tomorrow. What's going to happen to him now?'

'I'll take good care of him,' said Carey smoothly.

'You'd better,' warned Harding. 'If he doesn't get skilled attention he's quite likely to go insane.' He yawned. 'Well, I'm off to bed.'

He left the room and Carey sat down again. He picked up the two photographs and brooded over them. McCready said, 'That's it, then; the whole thing's a bust. No Meyrick – no operation.'

Carey did not say anything, and McCready asked, 'What are you thinking?'

Carey said slowly, 'I'm thinking that, while we may not have Meyrick, we've got a bloody good substitute.'

McCready's jaw dropped. 'You mean you want to hang on to him? You heard what Harding just said – the man's likely to go crazy. It's not what I'd call ethical.'

'Don't talk to me about ethics,' said Carey harshly. 'I have a job to do.' He threw down the photographs. 'Iredale wants to give Denison his face back, and Harding wants to restore his past. If we let Harding at him tomorrow with his tricky bloody hypnotism then Denison is going to pick up his marbles and go home.'

He frowned and came to a decision. 'Take him back to the hotel,' he said abruptly.

'For Christ's sake!' said McCready. 'Do you know what you're doing?'

'I know,' said Carey. 'But just work this one out while you're taking Denison back. When the attempt was being made on Denison's life at the Spiralen who was being attacked – Denison or Meyrick?'

McCready opened his mouth slowly while his mind spun. Carey said, 'Denison must be watched The guard on his room stays and I want somebody outside keeping an eye on his window. And I want that whole bloody hotel sewn up tight. Now get cracking.'

McCready dropped Denison off in the garage of the hotel. 'I won't come up,' he said. 'But I'll see you tomorrow.' He looked at his watch.

'Which is today. God, it's nearly five o'clock in the morning. You get to bed.'

They had both been silent during the short drive. Now Denison said, 'What was all that about? I understood the first doctor, but the second was a psychiatrist, wasn't he?'

McCready said, 'Carey will be seeing you tomorrow. He'll explain everything.' He paused, biting his lip. 'I promise you.'

'All right,' said Denison. 'I'm too tired to argue now. But Carey had better come up with something good.' He nodded to McCready and walked towards the stairs. He did not look back, but if he had and if he had been able to interpret the look in McCready's eyes he might have recognized compassion.

Denison opened the door leading into the hotel lobby and saw suitcases stacked into a pile. There was a peal of laughter from the group of early arrivals, a crowd of young people who adorned the lobby like butterflies. He walked towards the porter's desk and stood waiting while the overworked night porter did his best to deal with the rush.

At last, Denison caught his eye, and said, 'Three-sixty, please.'

'Yes, Mr Meyrick.' The porter unhooked the key.

Denison did not see the girl who stared at him in surprise, but heard the cool voice behind him saying, 'Daddy!' He turned leisurely and was suddenly and horrifyingly aware that the young woman was addressing him.

CHAPTER ELEVEN

It was greatly to Denison's credit that he did not panic. His first impulse was to step back and deny he was Meyrick – that it was a question of mistaken identity. Hard on that decision came the realization that it would not do; the night porter knew his name and was within earshot, and, in any case, a disclaimer in the hotel lobby was sure to create a fuss. He cancelled the impulse.

She was kissing him and he felt his own lips hard and unresponsive. Perhaps it was his lack of reaction that caused her to step back, the smile fading from her face. She said, 'I was hoping to find you here, but I hardly expected to run into you in the same hotel – and at five in the morning. What are you doing up so early – or so late?'

She was young – not much more than twenty – and had the clear eyes and clear skin of youth. Her eyes were grey and her mouth wide and generous, perhaps too wide for perfect beauty. To the untutored male eye she wore no make-up but perhaps that was a tribute to skill.

He swallowed. 'I was visiting a friend; the talk tended to go on a bit.'

'Oh.' She thrust her hands deep into the pockets of her motoring coat and turned her head to look at the harassed porter. 'It's going to take hours before I get my room. Can I freshen up in yours? I must look a sight.'

His mouth was dry and, for a moment, he could not speak. She looked at him curiously. 'You *are* staying here?' Then she laughed. 'Of course you are; you have the key in your hand.'

'I just have to make a telephone call,' he said, and stepped away slightly, disengaging himself.

'Why not from the room?'

'It's just as easy from down here.' He walked away to the public telephones, fumbling in his pocket for coins.

The public telephones were not in booths but were surrounded by large transparent plastic hoods which theoretically would keep conversations private. He was aware that the girl had followed him and was standing close by. He took out his wallet, extracted a slip of paper, and dialled the number. The ringing sound buzzed in his ear six times, and then a voice said, 'Yes?'

He kept his voice low. 'I want Carey.'

'You'll have to speak up. I can't hear you.'

He raised his voice a little. 'I want to talk to Carey.'

Doubtfully: 'I don't think that's possible. He's in bed.'

'I don't care if he's in his coffin. Get him up. This is Denison.'

There was a sharp intake of breath. 'Right!'

In a remarkably short time Carey came on the line. 'Denison?'

'It's trouble. Meyrick's ...'

Carey cut in with a voice like gravel. 'How did you know to ring this number?'

'For God's sake! That can wait.'

'How did you know?' insisted Carey.

'There was a telephone in the room where I saw the doctors,' said Denison. 'I took the number off that.'

'Oh!' said Carey. Then with grudging respect, 'Harding said you were competent; now I believe him. All right; what's your problem?'

'Meyrick's daughter has just pitched up at the hotel.'

The telephone blasted in his ear. '*What!*'

'What the hell am I to do?' said Denison desperately. 'I don't even know her bloody name.'

'Jesus H. Christ!' said Carey. 'Wait a minute.' There was a confused murmur and then Carey said, 'Her name is Lyn – L-Y-N.'

'Do you know anything else about her?'

'How the devil would I?' demanded Carey. 'Not off the top of my head.'

'Damn you!' said Denison violently. 'I have to talk to this girl. I must know something about her. She's my *daughter*.'

'Is she there now?'

Denison looked sideways through the plastic hood. 'She's standing within ten feet of me. I'm in the hotel lobby and I don't know how soundproof this canopy is. She wants to come to my room.'

'I'll do what I can,' said Carey. 'Hold on.'

'Make it quick.' Out of the corner of his eye he saw the girl walking towards him. He put his head around the edge of the hood, and said, 'I won't be a minute, Lyn. Is there anything you want to take up to the room?'

'Oh, yes; my little travelling bag. I'll go and get it.'

He watched her walk across the lobby with a bouncing stride, and felt the sweat break out on his forehead. Carey came back on the line. 'Margaret Lyn Meyrick – but she prefers Lyn; Meyrick's daughter by his first wife.'

Denison digested that, and said quickly, 'Is her mother still alive?'

'Yes – divorced and remarried.'

'Name?'

'Patricia Joan Metford – her husband is John Howard Metford; he's something in the City.'

'What about Meyrick's present wife?'

'There isn't one. Also divorced three years ago. Her name was Janet Meyrick, née Austin.'

'About the girl – what does she do? Her work? Her hobbies?'

'I don't know,' said Carey. 'All this stuff is from Meyrick's dossier. We didn't delve into the daughter.'

'You'd better get something fast,' said Denison. 'Look, Carey; I don't know why I'm doing this for you. My impulse right now is to blow the whole thing.'

'Don't do that,' said Carey quickly. 'I'll get as much information on the Meyrick girl as I can and I'll let you have it as soon as possible.'

'How?'

'I'll send it in a sealed envelope by special messenger; she doesn't have to know what's on the sheet of paper you're reading. And if things get too tough I'll find a way of separating her from you. But, Denison – don't blow your cover, whatever you do.'

There was a pleading quality in Carey's voice and Carey, in Denison's brief experience of him, was not a man who was used to pleading. Denison thought it a good opportunity to turn the screw. 'I've been given the fast run around by you ever since this … this indecent thing was done to me. Now I want an explanation – a full explanation – and it had better be good.' He was aware that his voice had risen and that he was in danger of becoming hysterical.

'You'll get your explanation today,' promised Carey. 'Now do your best to handle that girl.'

'I don't know if I can. It's one thing fooling a stranger and another to try it on a member of Meyrick's family.'

'We may be lucky,' said Carey. 'I don't think they were too close. I think she was brought up by her mother.'

Denison turned to face the lobby. 'I'll have to go now – the girl's coming.' He put down the telephone and heard a faint, squawking noise just before the connection was broken. It sounded as though Carey had said, 'Good luck!'

He walked away from the telephone as she approached. 'All finished.'

She fell into step with him. 'You looked as if you were having an argument.'

'Did I?'

'I know you're an argumentative type, but I wondered who you'd found to argue with at five o'clock in the morning in the middle of Oslo.'

They stopped in front of the lifts and Denison pressed the button. 'Where have you just come from?'

'Bergen. I hired a car and drove over. Most of yesterday and all night.' She sighed. 'I feel a bit pooped.'

He kept his voice neutral. 'Travelling alone?'

'Yes.' She smiled, and said, 'Wondering about a boyfriend?'

He nodded towards the thinning group in the lobby. 'I just thought you were with that lot.' The lift arrived and they stepped inside. 'No wonder you're tired if you did all that driving. What it is to be young.'

'Right now I feel as old as Methuselah,' she said glumly. 'It's the hunger that does it. I'll feel better after breakfast, I dare say.'

He risked a probe. 'How old are you, Lyn? I tend to lose track.'

'Yes, you do, don't you? You even forgot my twenty-first – or did you forget?' There was an unexpected bitterness in her voice. 'Any father who could do that …' She stopped and bit her lip. 'I'm sorry, Daddy. It's my birthday next week.'

'That's all right.' There was an undercurrent of antagonism Denison did not understand. He hesitated, and said, 'Anyway, you're old enough to stop calling me Daddy. What's wrong with Harry?'

She looked at him in surprise and then impulsively squeezed his hand.

They had arrived at the room door and he unlocked it. 'Bedroom straight ahead – bathroom to the left.'

She walked ahead of him into the bedroom and put down the travelling bag. 'The bathroom for me,' she said. 'I want to wash off some of the grime.' She opened the bag, picked out a couple of small articles, and disappeared into the bathroom.

He heard the sound of water as she turned on a tap and then he picked up the telephone. 'This is room three-sixty. If there are any messages for Meyrick – or anything at all – I want to know immediately.' He put down the telephone and looked contemplatively at the travelling bag.

The bathroom noises continued so he crossed the room quickly and looked into the bag. It was more neatly packed than he had expected which made it easier to search. He saw the blue cover of a British passport and took it out and turned the pages. It was Lyn Meyrick's birthday on July 21, and she would be twenty-two. Her occupation was given as teacher.

He put the passport back and took out a book of traveller's cheques. As he flicked through them he whistled softly; the Meyrick family did not believe in stinting themselves. There was a wallet fitted with acetate envelopes which contained credit cards and photographs. He had no time to examine these in detail because he thought she might come out of the bathroom at any moment.

He thrust back the wallet and zipped open a small interior pocket in the bag. It contained the key for a rented car and a bunch of smaller keys. As he zipped it closed he heard all sound cease in the bathroom and, when she emerged, he was standing by the armchair taking off his jacket.

'That's much better,' she said. She had taken off the motoring coat and, in lime green sweater and stretch pants, she looked very trim. 'When is the earliest I can order breakfast?'

He checked his watch. 'Not much before half past six, I think. Perhaps the night porter can rustle up sandwiches and coffee.'

She frowned and sat on the bed. 'No, I'll wait and have a proper breakfast.' Blinking her eyes, she said, 'I still feel as though I'm driving.'

'You shouldn't push so hard.'

'That isn't what you told me the last time we met.'

Denison did not know what to make of that, so he said neutrally, 'No.' The silence lengthened. 'How's your mother?' he asked.

'She's all right,' said Lyn indifferently. 'But, my God, he's such a bore.'

'In what way?'

'Well, he just sits in an office and makes money. Oh, I know you're rich, but you made money by making *things*. He just makes money.'

Denison presumed that 'he' was John Howard Metford who was 'something in the City'. 'Metford isn't such a bad chap,' he said.

'He's a bore,' she said definitely. 'And it isn't what you said about him last time.'

Denison decided against making gratuitous judgements. 'How did you know I was here?' he asked.

'I got it out of Andrews,' she said. 'When he told me you were in Scandinavia I knew you'd be here or in Helsinki.' She seemed suddenly nervous. 'Now I'm not sure I should have come.'

Denison realized he was standing over her. He sat in the armchair and, perhaps in response, she stretched out on the bed. 'Why not?' he asked.

'You can't be serious when you ask that.' Her voice was bitter. 'I still remember the flaming row we had two years ago – and when you didn't remember my twenty-first birthday I knew *you* hadn't forgotten. But, of course, you didn't forget my birthday – you never forget anything.'

He was getting into deep water. 'Two years is a long time,' he said platitudinously. He would have to learn how to speak like a politician – saying a lot and meaning nothing.

'You've changed,' she said. 'You're … you're milder.'

That would never do. 'I can still be acid when I want to be.' He smiled. 'Perhaps I'm just becoming older and, maybe, wiser.'

'You always were wise,' said Lyn. 'If only you weren't so bloody right *all* the time. Anyway, I wanted to tell you something to your face. I was disappointed when I found you weren't in England, so I rushed over here.' She hesitated. 'Give me a cigarette.'

'I've stopped smoking.'

She stared at him. 'You *have* changed.'

'Temporarily,' he said, and stretched out his hand to open a drawer in the dressing-table. He took out the gold cigarette case and the lighter and offered her a cigarette. 'I've had a bad head cold.'

She took a cigarette and he lit it. 'That never stopped you before.' She drew on the cigarette nervously and blew a plume of smoke. 'I suppose you're surprised I'm not smoking a joint.'

Denison suspected that he was encountering something of which hitherto he had only heard – the generation gap. He said, 'Stop talking nonsense, Lyn. What's on your mind?'

'Direct and to the point as usual. All right – I've taken my degree.'

She looked at him expectantly and he was aware that she had dropped a bombshell. How he was supposed to react to it he did not know, but the damned thing had better be defused carefully. However, taking a degree was usually a matter for congratulation, so he said, 'That's good news, Lyn.'

She regarded him warily. 'You mean it?'

'It's the best news I've heard for a long time.'

She seemed relieved. 'Mother thought it was silly. She said that with all the money I'm going to have why should I worry about working – especially with a lot of snotty-nosed East End kids. You know what she's like. And the Bore didn't care one way or another.' For a moment she sounded pathetic. 'Do you really mean it?'

'Of course I do.' He found he was really glad for her and that put sincerity into his voice.

'Oh, Daddy; I'm so glad!' She scrambled off the bed and went to her bag. 'Look what it says in here. I had to get a new passport, anyway.' She opened the passport and displayed it. 'Occupation – teacher!' she said proudly.

He looked up. 'Was it a good degree?'

She made a wry face. 'Middling-good.' There was no smile on her face now. 'I suppose you think a Meyrick should have passed with honours.'

Mentally he damned Meyrick who, apparently, set a superhuman standard. This girl was set on a hair trigger and his slightest word could cause an explosion in which somebody would get hurt – probably Lyn. 'I'm very glad you've got your degree,' he said evenly. 'Where are you going to teach?'

The tension eased from her and she lay on the bed again. 'First I need experience,' she said seriously. 'General experience. Then I want to specialize. After that, if I'm going to have a lot of money I might as well put it to use.'

'How?'

'I'll have to know more about what I'm doing before I can tell you that.'

Denison wondered how this youthful idealism would stand up to the battering of the world. Still, a lot could be done with enthusiasm and money. He smiled, and said, 'You seem to have settled on a lifetime plan. Is there room in the programme for marriage and a family?'

'Of course; but he'll have to be the right man – he'll have to want what I want.' She shrugged. 'So far no one like that has come my way. The men at university could be divided into two classes; the stodges who are happy with the present system, and the idealists who aren't. The stodges are already working out their retirement pensions before they get a job, and the idealists are so damned naive and impractical. Neither of them suit me.'

'Someone will come along who will,' predicted Denison.

'How can you be so sure?'

He laughed. 'How do you suppose the population explosion came about? Men and women usually get together somehow. It's in the nature of the animal.'

She put out her cigarette and lay back and closed her eyes. 'I'm prepared to wait.'

'My guess is that you won't have to wait long.' She did not respond and he regarded her intently. She had fallen asleep as readily as a puppy might, which was not surprising considering she had been up all night. So had he, but sleep was the last thing he could afford.

He put on his jacket and took the keys from the zippered compartment of her bag. In the lobby he saw two suitcases standing before the desk and, after checking to make sure they were Lyn's, he said to the porter, 'I'd like these taken to my daughter's room. What's the number?'

'Did she have a reservation, Mr Meyrick?'

'It's possible.'

The porter checked and took down a key. 'Room four-thirty. I'll take the bags up.'

In Lyn's room Denison tipped the porter and put the two cases on the bed as soon as the door closed. He took out the keys and unlocked them and searched them quickly, trying not to disturb the contents too much. There was little that was of value to him directly, but there were one or two items which cast a light on Lyn Meyrick. There was a photograph of himself – or, rather, of Harry Meyrick – in a leather case. The opposing frame was empty. In a corner of one suitcase was a small Teddy-bear, tattered with much childish loving and presumably retained as a mascot. In the other suitcase he found two textbooks, one on the theory and practice of teaching, the other on child psychology; both heavyweights, the pages sprinkled with diagrams and graphs.

He closed and locked the suitcases and put them on the rack, then went down to his own room. As the lift door opened on to the third floor he saw Armstrong just stepping out of the other lift. Armstrong held out an envelope. 'Mr Carey told me to give you this.'

Denison ripped open the envelope and scanned the sparse typescript on the single sheet. The only thing it told him that he had not learned already was that Lyn Meyrick's sport was gymnastics. 'Carey will have to do better than this,' he said curtly.

'We're doing the best we can,' said Armstrong. 'We'll get more later in the day when people have woken up in England.'

'Keep it coming,' said Denison. 'And don't forget to remind Carey that I'm still waiting for an explanation.'

'I'll tell him,' said Armstrong.

'Another thing,' said Denison. 'She said she'd find me either here in Oslo or in Helsinki in Finland. That baffled me until I realized I don't know a bloody thing about Meyrick. Carey mentioned a dossier on Meyrick – I want to see it.'

'I don't think that will be possible,' said Armstrong hesitantly. 'You're not cleared for security.'

Denison speared him with a cold eye. 'You bloody fool!' he said quietly. 'Right now *I* am your security – and don't forget to tell Carey that, too.' He walked past Armstrong and up the corridor to his room.

CHAPTER TWELVE

Carey walked past the Oslo City Hall in the warm mid-afternoon sunshine and inspected the statuary with a sardonic eye. Each figure represented a different trade and the whole, no doubt, was supposed to represent the Dignity of Labour. He concluded that the Oslo City Fathers must have been socialist at one time.

He sat on a bench and looked out over the harbour and Oslofjord. A ship slid quietly by – the ferry bound for Copenhagen – and there was a constant coming and going of smaller, local ferries bound for Bygdøy, Ingierstrand and other places on the fjord. Camera-hung tourists strolled by and a tour bus stopped, disgorging more of them.

McCready walked up and sat on the bench. Carey did not look at him but said dreamily, 'Once my job was easy – just simple eyeball stuff. That was back in the days when Joshua sent his spies into the land of Caanan. Then the bloody scientists got busy and ballsed the whole thing up.'

McCready said nothing; he had encountered Carey in this mood before and knew there was nothing to do but wait until Carey got it off his chest.

'Do you realize the state we've got ourselves into now?' asked Carey rhetorically. 'I think you're George McCready, but I could be wrong. What's more, *you* could think you're George McCready and, if Harding is to be believed, still be wrong. How the hell am I supposed to cope with a situation like that?'

He disregarded McCready's opening mouth. 'The bloody boffins are lousing up the whole damned world,' he said violently, and pointed towards the line of statuary. 'Look at that crowd of working stiffs.

There's not a trade represented there that isn't obsolete or obsolescent. Pretty soon they'll put up a statue of me; there'll be a plaque saying "Intelligence agent, Mark II" and my job'll be farmed out to a hot-shot computer. Where's Denison?'

'Asleep in the hotel.'

'And the girl?'

'Also asleep – in her own room.'

'If he's had five minutes' sleep that's five minutes more than I've had. Let's go and wake the poor bastard up. Mrs Hansen will join us at the hotel.'

He stood up, and McCready said, 'How much are you going to tell him?'

'As much as I have to and no more,' said Carey shortly. 'Which may be more than I want to tell him. He's already putting the screws on me through young Ian. He wants to see Meyrick's dossier.'

'You can't expect him to carry out an impersonation without knowing something of Meyrick,' said McCready reasonably.

'Why did that damned girl have to turn up?' grumbled Carey. 'As though we don't have enough trouble. I had a row with Harding this morning.'

'I'm not surprised.'

'George – I have no option. With Meyrick gone I have to use Denison. I'll play fair; I'll tell him the truth – maybe not all of it, but what I tell him will be true – and let him make up his own mind. And if he wants out that's my hard luck.'

McCready noticed the reservation and shook his head. The truth, in Carey's hands, could take on a chameleon-like quality. Denison did not stand a chance.

Carey said, 'Something Iredale told me gave me the shudders. This silicone stuff that was rammed into Denison's face is a polymer; it's injected in liquid form and then it hardens in the tissues to the consistency of fat – and it's permanent. If Denison wants to get his own face back it will be a major surgical operation – they'll have to take his face apart to scrape the stuff out.'

McCready grimaced. 'I take it that's a part of the truth you're not going to tell him.'

'That – and a few other titbits from Harding.' Carey stopped. 'Well, here's the hotel. Let's get it over with.'

Denison woke from a deep sleep to hear hammering on his door. He got up groggily, put on the bath robe, and opened the door. Carey said, 'Sorry to waken you, but it's about time we had a talk.'

Denison blinked at him. 'Come in.' He turned and went into the bathroom, and Carey, McCready and Mrs Hansen walked through into the bedroom. When Denison reappeared he was wiping his face with a towel. He stared at Diana Hansen. 'I might have known.'

'You two know each other,' said Carey. 'Mrs Hansen was keeping tabs on Meyrick.' He drew back the curtain, letting sunlight spill into the room, and tossed an envelope on to the dressing-table. 'Some more stuff on the girl. We have quite a few people in England running about in circles on your behalf.'

'Not mine,' corrected Denison. 'Yours!' He put down the towel. 'Any moment from now she's going to start playing "Do you remember when?" No information you can give me will help in that sort of guessing game.'

'You'll just have to develop a bad memory,' said McCready.

'I need to know more about Meyrick,' insisted Denison.

'And I'm here to tell you.' Carey pulled the armchair forward. 'Sit down and get comfortable. This is going to take a while.' He sat in the other chair and pulled out a stubby pipe which he started to fill. McCready and Diana Hansen sat on the spare bed.

Carey struck a match and puffed at his pipe. 'Before we start on Meyrick you ought to know that we discovered how, and when, the switch was made. We figured how we'd do a thing like that ourselves and then checked on it. You were brought in on a stretcher on June 8 and put in room three-sixty-three, just across the corridor. Meyrick was probably knocked out by a Mickey Finn in his nightly Ovaltine or something like that, and the switch was made in the wee, small hours.'

'Meyrick was taken out next morning before you woke up,' said McCready. 'He was put into an ambulance, the hotel management co-operating, and driven to Pier Two at Vippetangen where he was put aboard a ship sailing to Copenhagen. Another ambulance was waiting there which took him God knows where.'

Carey said, 'If you'd contacted the Embassy as soon as it happened we'd have been able to work all that out so damned fast that *we* could have been waiting at Copenhagen.'

'For God's sake!' said Denison. 'Would you have believed me any the quicker? It took you long enough to check anyway with your doctor and your tame psychiatrist.'

'He's right,' said McCready.

'Do you think that's why it was done this way? To buy time?'

'Could be, said McCready. 'It worked, didn't it?'

'Oh, it worked all right. What puzzles me is what happened at the Spiralen the next day.' Carey turned to Denison. 'Have you got the doll and the note?'

Denison opened a drawer and handed them to Carey. He unfolded the single deckle-edged sheet and read the note aloud. ' "Your Drammen Dolly awaits you at Spiraltoppen. Early morning, June 10." ' He lifted the paper and sniffed delicately. 'Scented, too. I thought that went out in the 1920s.'

Diana Hansen said, 'This is the first I've heard of a note. I know about the doll, but not the note.'

'It's what took Denison to the Spiralen,' said McCready.

'Could I see it?' said Diana, and Carey passed it to her. She read it and said pensively, 'It could have been ...'

'What is it, Mrs Hansen?' said Carey sharply.

'Well, when Meyrick and I went to Drammen last week we lunched at the Spiraltoppen Restaurant.' She looked a little embarrassed. 'I had to go to the lavatory and I was away rather a long time. I had stomach trouble – some kind of diarrhoea.'

McCready grinned. 'Even Intelligence agents are human,' he said kindly.

'When I got back Meyrick was talking to a woman and they seemed to be getting on well together. When I came up she went away.'

'That all?' asked Carey.

'That's all.'

He regarded her thoughtfully. 'I think there's something you're not telling us, Mrs, Hansen.'

'Well, it's something about Meyrick. I was with him quite a lot during the last few weeks and he gave me the impression of being something of a womanizer – perhaps even a sexual athlete.'

A chuckle escaped from McCready. 'Did he proposition you?'

'He had as many arms as an octopus,' she said. 'I thought I wasn't going to last out this operation without being raped. I think he'd go for anything on two legs that wore skirts, with the possible exception of Scotsmen – and I wouldn't be too sure of that.'

'Well, well,' said Carey. 'How little we know of our fellow men.'

Denison said, 'He was divorced twice.'

'So you think this note was to set up an assignation.'

'Yes,' said Diana.

'But Meyrick wouldn't have fallen for that, no matter how horny he was,' said Carey. 'He was too intelligent a man. When you and he went to Drammen last week he checked with me according to instructions. Since you were going with him I gave him the okay.'

'Did Meyrick know Diana was working for you?' asked Denison.

Carey shook his head. 'No – we like to play loose. But Meyrick didn't find the note.' He pointed his pipe stem at Denison. 'You did – and you went to the Spiralen. Tell me, did the men who attacked you give the impression that they wanted to capture or to kill you?'

'I didn't stop to ask them,' said Denison acidly.

'Um,' said Carey, and lapsed into thought, his pipe working overtime. After a while he stirred, and said, 'All right, Mrs Hansen; I think that's all.'

She nodded briefly and left the room, and Carey glanced at McCready. 'I suppose we must tell him about Meyrick.'

McCready grinned. 'I don't see how you can get out of it.'

'I have to know,' said Denison, 'if I'm going to carry on with this impersonation.'

'I trust Mrs Hansen and she doesn't know,' said Carey. 'Not the whole story. I work on the "need to know" principle.' He sighed. 'I suppose you need to know, so here goes. The first thing to know about Meyrick is that he's a Finn.'

'With a name like that?'

'Oddly enough, it's his own name. In 1609 the English sent a diplomat to the court of Michael, the first Romanov Czar, to negotiate a trade treaty and to open up the fur trade. The courtiers of James I had to get their bloody ermine somewhere. The name of the diplomat was John Merick or Meyrick – and he was highly philoprogenitive. He left by-blows all over the Baltic and Harry Meyrick is the end result of that.'

'It seems that Harry takes after his ancestor,' commented McCready.

Carey ignored him. 'Of course, Meyrick's name was a bit different in Finnish, but when he went to England he reverted to the family name. But that's by the way.' He laid down his pipe. 'More to the point, Meyrick is a Karelian Finn; to be pedantic, if he'd stayed at home in the town where he was born he'd now be a Russian. How good is your modern history?'

'Average I suppose,' said Denison.

'And that means bloody awful,' observed Carey. 'All right; in 1939 Russia attacked Finland and the Finns held them off in what was known as the Winter War. In 1941 Germany attacked Russia and the Finns thought it a good opportunity to have another go at the Russkies, which was a pity because that put them on the losing side. Still, it's difficult to see what else they could have done.

'At the end of this war, which the Finns know as the Continuation War, there was a peace treaty and the frontier was withdrawn. The old frontier was too close to Leningrad, which had the Russians edgy. An artilleryman could stand in Finland and lob shells right into the middle of Leningrad, so the Russians took over the whole of the Karelian Isthmus, together with a few other bits and pieces. This put

Meyrick's home town, Enso, on the Russian side, and the Russians renamed it Svetogorsk.'

Carey sucked on his pipe which had gone out. It gurgled unpleasantly. 'Am I making myself clear?'

'You're clear enough,' said Denison. 'But I want more than a history lesson.'

'We're getting there,' said Carey. 'Meyrick was seventeen at the end of the war. Finland was in a hell of a mess; all the Karelian Finns cleared out of the isthmus because they didn't want to live under the Russians and this put the pressure on the rest of Finland because there was nowhere for them to go. The Finns had to work so bloody hard producing the reparations the Russians demanded that there was no money or men or time left over to build housing. So they turned to the Swedes and asked calmly if they'd take 100,000 immigrants.' Carey snapped his fingers. 'Just like that – and the Swedes agreed.'

Denison said, 'Noble of them.'

Carey nodded. 'So young Meyrick went to Sweden. He didn't stay long because he came here, to Oslo, where he lived until he was twenty-four. Then he went to England. He was quite alone all this time – his family had been killed during the war – but as soon as he arrived in England he married his first wife. She had what he needed, which was money.'

'Who doesn't need money?' asked McCready cynically.

'We'll get on faster if you stop asking silly questions,' said Carey. 'The second thing you have to know about Meyrick is that he's a bright boy. He has a flair for invention, particularly in electronics, and he has something else which the run-of-the-mill inventor doesn't have – the ability to turn his inventions into money. The first Mrs Meyrick had a few thousand quid which was all he needed to get started. When they got divorced he'd turned her into a millionairess and he'd made as much for himself. And he went on making it.'

Carey struck a match and applied it to his pipe. 'By this time he was a big boy as well as a bright boy. He owned a couple of factories and was deep in defence contracts. There's a lot of his electronics in the Anglo-French Jaguar fighter as well as in Concorde. He also did some bits and pieces for the Chieftain main battle tank. He's now at the stage where he heads special committees on technical matters concerning defence, and the Prime Minister has pulled him into a Think Tank. He's a hell of a big boy but the man-in-the-street knows nothing about him. Got the picture?'

'I think so,' said Denison. 'But it doesn't help me a damn.'

Carey blew a plume of smoke into the air. 'I think Meyrick inherited his brains from his father, so let's take a look at the old boy.'

Denison sighed. 'Must we?'

'It's relevant,' said Carey flatly. 'Hannu Merikken was a physicist and, by all accounts, a good one. The way the story runs is that if he hadn't been killed during the war he'd have been in line for the Nobel Prize. The war put a stop to his immediate researches and he went to work for the Finnish government in Viipuri, which was then the second biggest city in Finland. But it's in Karelia and it's now a Russian city and the Russians call it Vyborg.' He looked at Denison's closed eyes, and said sharply, 'I trust I'm not boring you.'

'Go on,' said Denison. 'I'm just trying to sort out all these names.'

'Viipuri was pretty well smashed up during the war, including the laboratory Merikken was working in. So he got the hell out of there and went home to Enso which is about thirty miles north of Viipuri. He knew by this time that no one was going to stop the Russians and he wanted to see to the safety of his papers. He'd done a lot of work before the war which hadn't been published and he didn't want to lose it.'

'So what did he do?' asked Denison. He was becoming interested.

'He put all the papers into a metal trunk, sealed it, and buried it in the garden of his house. Young Harri Merikken – that's our Harry Meyrick – helped him. The next day Hannu Merikken, his wife and his younger son, were killed by the same bomb, and if Harri had been in the house at the same time he'd have been killed, too.'

'And the papers are important?' said Denison.

'They are,' said Carey soberly. 'Last year Meyrick was in Sweden and he bumped into a woman who had given him a temporary home when he'd been evacuated from Finland. She said she'd been rummaging about in the attic or whatever and had come across a box he'd left behind. She gave it to him. He opened it in his hotel that night and looked through it. Mostly he was amused by the things he found – the remnants of the enthusiasms of a seventeen-year-old. There were the schematics of a ham radio he'd designed – he was interested in electronics even then – some other drawings of a radio-controlled model aircraft, and things like that. But in the pages of an old radio magazine he found a paper in his father's handwriting, and that suddenly made the papers buried in Merikken's garden very important indeed.'

'What are they about?' asked Denison.

Carey ignored the question. 'At first, Meyrick didn't realize what he'd got hold of and he talked about it to a couple of scientists in Sweden. Then the penny dropped and he bolted back to England and began to talk to the right people – we're lucky he was big enough to know who to talk to. The people he talked to got interested and, as an end result of a lot of quiet confabulation I was brought in.'

'The idea being to go and dig up the garden?'

'That's right. The only snag is that the garden is in Russia.' Carey knocked out his pipe in the ashtray. 'I have a couple of men scouting the Russian border right now. The idea was that as soon as they report Meyrick and I would pop across and dig up the papers.'

McCready snapped his fingers. 'As easy as walking down Piccadilly.'

'But Meyrick was snatched,' said Carey. 'And you were substituted.'

'Yes,' said Denison heavily. 'Why me?'

'I don't think we need to go too deeply into that,' said Carey delicately. He did not want Denison to ruminate about his past life and go off into a fugue. 'I think it could have been anybody who looked enough like Meyrick to need the least possible surgery.'

There was a whole list of other qualifications – someone who would not be missed too easily, someone who had the right psychological make-up, someone very easily accessible. It had been a job which had been carefully set up in England and back in London there was a team of ten men sifting through the minutiae of Denison's life in the hope of coming up with a clue to his kidnapping. It was a pity that Denison could not be directly questioned but Harding was dead against it, and Carey had a need for Denison – he did not want an insane man on his hands.

'Which brings us to the next step,' said Carey. 'Someone – call them Crowd X – has pinched Meyrick, but they're not going to broadcast the fact. They don't know if we've tumbled to the substitution or not – and we're not going to tell them.' He looked steadily at Denison. 'Which is why we need your co-operation, Mr Denison.'

'In what way?' asked Denison cautiously.

'We want you to carry on being Meyrick, and we want you to go to Finland.'

Denison's jaw dropped. 'But that's impossible,' he said. 'I'd never get away with it. I can't speak Finnish.'

'You've got away with it up to now,' pointed out Carey. 'You fooled Mrs Hansen and you're doing very well with Meyrick's daughter. It's quite true what Harding said – you're very competent.'

'But the language! Meyrick speaks Finnish.'

'He speaks Finnish, Swedish, Norwegian and English fluently and idiomatically,' said Carey easily. 'His French passes but his Italian and Spanish aren't too hot.'

'Then how the hell can I get away with it?' demanded Denison. 'All I have is English and schoolboy French.'

'Take it easy. Let me tell you a story.' Carey began to fill his pipe again. 'At the end of the First World War quite a number of the British troops married French wives and stayed in France. A lot of them were given jobs by the War Graves Commission – looking after the war cemeteries. Twenty years after, there came another war and another British Expeditionary Force. The new young soldiers found that the old soldiers had completely lost their English – their mother tongue – and could speak only French.'

He struck a match. 'And that's what's going to happen to Meyrick. He hasn't been back to Finland since he was seventeen; I don't think it's unreasonable to suppose he'd lose the language.'

'But why do you want me? I can't lead you to the papers – only Meyrick can do that.'

Carey said, 'When this happened my first impulse was to abandon the operation, but then I started to think about it. Firstly, we don't know that Meyrick was snatched because of this operation – it might have been for a different reason. In that case the papers are reasonably safe. Secondly, it occurred to me that you could be a good distracting influence – we could use you to confuse the opposition as much as they've confused us. If you go to Finland as Meyrick they won't know what the hell to think. In the ensuing brouhaha we might get a chance at the papers. What do you think?'

'I think you're crazy,' said Denison.

Carey shrugged. 'Mine is a crazy profession – I've seen crazier ploys come off. Look at Major Martin – the man who never was.'

'He didn't have to stand up to questioning,' said Denison. 'The whole thing is bloody ridiculous.'

'You'd be paid, of course,' said Carey casually. 'Well paid, as a matter of fact. You'd also get a compensatory grant for the injuries that have been done to you, and Mr Iredale is ready and willing to bring you back to normality.'

'Dr Harding, too?'

'Dr Harding, too,' confirmed Carey. He wondered to what extent Denison knew his mental processes to be abnormal.

'Suppose I turn you down,' said Denison. 'Do I still get the services of Iredale and Harding?'

McCready tensed, wondering what Carey would say. Carey placidly blew a smoke ring. 'Of course.'

'So it's not a matter of blackmail,' said Denison.

The unshockable Carey arranged his features in an expression of shock. 'There is no question of blackmail,' he said stiffly.

'Why are Merikken's papers so important? What's in them?'

'I can't tell you that, Mr Denison,' said Carey deliberately.

'Can't or won't?'

Carey shrugged. 'All right, then – won't.'

'Then I'm turning you down,' said Denison.

Carey put down his pipe. 'This is a question of state security, Denison; and we work on the principle of "need to know." Mrs Hansen doesn't need to know. Ian Armstrong doesn't need to know. You don't need to know.'

'I've been kidnapped and stabbed,' said Denison. 'My face has been altered and my mind has been jiggered with.' He raised his hand. 'Oh, I know that – Harding got that much across – and I'm scared to the marrow about thinking of who I once was. Now you're asking me to go on with this charade, to go to Finland and put myself in danger again.' His voice was shaking. 'And when I ask why you have the gall to tell me I don't need to know.'

'I'm sorry,' said Carey.

'I don't care how sorry you are. You can book me on a flight to London.'

'Now who is using blackmail?' said Carey ironically.

'It's a reasonable request,' said McCready.

'I know it is, damn it!' Carey looked at Denison with cold eyes. 'If you breathe a word of what I'm going to tell you you'll be behind bars for the rest of your life. I'll see to that personally. Understand?'

Denison nodded. 'I've still got to know,' he said stubbornly.

Carey forced the words through reluctant lips. He said slowly, 'It seems that in 1937 or 1938 Hannu Merikken discovered a way of reflecting X-rays.'

Denison looked at him blankly. 'Is that all?'

'That's all,' said Carey curtly. He stood up and stretched.

'It isn't enough,' said Denison. 'What's so bloody important about that?'

'You've been told what you want to know. Be satisfied.'

'It isn't enough. I must know the significance.'

Carey sighed. 'All right, George; tell him.'

'I felt like that at first,' said McCready. 'Like you, I didn't see what all the fuss was about. Merikken was doing a bit of pure research when he came across this effect before the war and in those days there wasn't much use for it. All the uses of X-rays depended upon their penetrative power and who'd want to reflect them. So Merikken filed it away as curious but useless and he didn't publish a paper on it.'

He grinned. 'The joke is that now every defence laboratory in the world is working on how to reflect X-rays, but no one has figured out a way to do it.'

'What happened to make it important?' asked Denison.

'The laser happened,' said Carey in a voice of iron.

'Do you know how a laser works?' When Denison shook his head, McCready said, 'Let's have a look at the very first laser as it was invented in 1960. It was a rod of synthetic ruby about four inches long and less than half an inch in diameter. One end was silvered to form a reflective surface, and the other end was half-silvered. Coiled around the rod was a spiral gas discharge lamp something like the flash used in photography. Got that?'

'All clear so far.'

'There's a lot more power in these electronic flashes than people imagine,' said McCready. 'For instance, an ordinary flash, as used by a professional photographer, develops about 4,000 horse power in the brief fraction of a second when the condensers discharge. The flash used in the early lasers was more powerful than that – let's call it – 20,000 horse power. When the flash is used the light enters the ruby rod and something peculiar happens; the light goes up and down the rod, reflected from the silvered ends, and all the light photons are brought in step with each other. The boffins call that coherent light, unlike ordinary light where all the photons are out of step.

'Now, because the photons are in step the light pressure builds up. If you can imagine a crowd of men trying to batter down a door, they're more likely to succeed if they charge at once than if they try singly. The photons are all charging at once and they burst out of the half-silvered end of the rod as a pulse of light – and that light pulse has nearly all the 20,000 horse power of energy that was put into the rod.'

McCready grinned. 'The boffins had great fun with that. They discovered that it was possible to drill a hole through a razor blade at a range of six feet. At one time it was suggested that the power of a laser should be measured in Gillettes.'

'Stick to the point,' said Carey irritably.

'The military possibilities were easily seen,' said McCready. 'You could use a laser as a range-finder, for instance. Fire it at a target and measure the light bouncing back and you could tell the range to an inch. There were other uses – but there was one dispiriting fact. The laser used light and light can be stopped quite easily. It doesn't take much cloud to stop a beam of light, no matter how powerful it is.'

'But X-rays are different,' said Denison thoughtfully.

'Right! It's theoretically possible to make an X-ray laser, but for one snag. X-rays penetrate and don't reflect. No one has found a way of doing it except Merikken who did it before the war – and the working of a laser depends entirely upon multiple reflection.'

Denison rubbed his chin, feeling the flabbiness. Already he was becoming used to it. 'What would be the use of a gadget like that?'

'Take a missile coming in at umpteen thousand miles an hour and loaded with an atomic warhead. You've got to knock it down so you use another missile like the American Sprint. But you don't shoot your missile directly at the enemy missile – you aim it at where the enemy will be when your missile gets up there. That takes time to work out and a hell of a lot of computing power. With an X-ray laser you aim directly at the enemy missile because it operates with the speed of light – 186,000 miles a second – and you'd drill a hole right through it.'

'Balls,' said Carey. 'You'd cut the damned thing in two.'

'My God!' said Denison. 'That's a death ray.' He frowned. 'Could it be made powerful enough?'

'Lasers have come a long way since the first one,' said McCready soberly. 'They don't use the flash any more on the big ones – they pour in the power with a rocket engine. Already they're up to millions of horse power – but it's still ordinary light. With X-rays you could knock a satellite out of orbit from the ground.'

'Now do you understand the significance?' asked Carey. When Denison nodded, he said, 'So what are you going to do about it?'

There was a long silence while Denison thought. Carey stood up and went to the window where he looked across to the *Studenterlunden*, his fingers drumming on the window sill. McCready lay back on the bed with his hands behind his head, and inspected the ceiling closely.

Denison stirred and unclasped his fingers. He straightened in his chair and stretched his arms, then he sighed deeply. 'My name is Harry Meyrick,' he said.

CHAPTER THIRTEEN

Three days later Denison, descending for breakfast, bought a newspaper at the kiosk in the lobby and scanned it over coffee. Diana Hansen joined him, and said, 'What's new?'

He shrugged. 'The world is still going to hell in a handcart. Listen to this. Item one. Two more skyjackings, one successful and one not. In the *unsuccessful* one – God save the mark – two passengers were killed. Item two – pollution. A tanker collision in the Baltic and a fifteen mile oil slick is drifting on to Gotland; the Swedes are understandably acid. Item three. There are strikes in Britain, France and Italy, with consequent riots in London, Paris and Milan. Item four ...'

He raised his head – '... do you want me to go on?'

She sipped her coffee. 'You sound a bit acid yourself.'

'Just how would you feel in my circumstances?' he asked a little grimly.

Diana shrugged. 'Where's Lyn?'

'The young sleep late.'

'I have a feeling she's sharpening her claws, getting ready to scratch my eyes out,' said Diana meditatively. 'She's made one or two odd remarks lately.' She stretched over and patted Denison's hand. 'She thinks her daddy is getting into bad company.'

'How right the child is.'

'Child!' Diana raised her eyebrows. 'She's only eight years younger than I am. She's no child – she's a healthy young woman with all her wits about her – so watch your step.'

Denison put his head on one side. 'Of course!' he said, somewhat surprised. Privately he thought that Diana was drawing the longbow a bit. He put her age at thirty-two which probably meant she was thirty-four; that would give her twelve years on Lyn, not much less than the fourteen years he had himself.

'Carey wants to see you,' said Diana. 'If you leave the hotel, turn left and walk about three hundred yards, you'll come to a place where they're building a memorial or something. Be around there at ten o'clock.'

'All right,' said Denison.

'And here's your darling daughter.' Diana raised her voice. 'Good morning, Lyn.'

Denison turned and smiled appreciatively at Lyn's *chic* appearance. It's the money that makes the difference, he thought; the grand ideas of the rulers of the fashion world are apt to look tatty when filtered through the salary of a junior London typist. 'Did you have a good night?'

'Fine' said Lyn lightly, and sat down. 'I didn't expect to see you at breakfast, Mrs Hansen.' She glanced sideways at Denison. 'Did you sleep in the hotel last night?'

'No, darling,' said Diana sweetly. 'I brought a message for your father.'

Lyn poured coffee. 'What are we doing today?'

'I have a business appointment this morning,' said Denison. 'Why don't you two go shopping?'

A shadow briefly crossed Lyn's face, but she said, 'All right.' Diana's answering smile was sickly in its sweetness.

Denison found Carey with his rump buttressed by a coping stone and his back to the Royal Palace. He looked up at Denison's approach and said brusquely, 'We're ready to move. Are you fit?'

'As fit as I'll ever be.'

Carey nodded. 'How are you getting on with the girl?'

'I'm tired of being Daddy,' said Denison bitterly. 'I'm only getting through by the skin of my teeth. She asks the damnedest questions.'

'What's she like?'

'A nice kid in danger of being spoiled rotten – but for one thing.'

'What's that?'

'Her parents were divorced and it's messed up her life. I'm beginning to realize what an unmitigated bastard Harry Meyrick is.' He paused. 'Or was.' He looked at Carey. 'Any news?'

Carey flapped his hand in negation. 'Tell me more.'

'Well, the mother is a rich bitch who ignores the girl. I don't think Lyn would care if she dropped dead tomorrow. But Lyn has always had a respect for her father; she doesn't like him but she respects him. She looks up to him like a ... like a sort of God.'

Denison rubbed his chin and said meditatively, 'I suppose people respect God, but do they really *like* him? Anyway, every time she tries to get near Meyrick he slaps her down hard. That's no way to bring up a daughter and it's been breaking her up.'

'I never did like his arrogance myself,' said Carey. 'It's the one thing that would have given you away in the end. You're not bloody-minded enough to be Meyrick.'

'Thank God for that,' said Denison.

'But you get on with her all right? As Meyrick?'

Denison nodded. 'So far – but no future guarantees.'

'I've been thinking about her,' said Carey. 'Suppose we took her to Finland – what would the opposition think?'

'For God's sake!' said Denison disgustedly.

'Think about it, man,' Carey urged. 'They'd check on her, and when they find out who she is they'd be bloody flummoxed. They might think that if you're good enough to deceive Meyrick's daughter you're good enough to deceive me.'

Denison was acid. 'That's not far short of the mark. I had to *tell* you who I was.'

'You can do it,' said Carey. 'It adds a bit of confusion, and there's nothing like confusion for creating opportunity. Right now we need all the luck we can create for ourselves. Will you ask her if she'll go with you to Helsinki tomorrow?'

Denison was troubled. 'It's all right for me.' he said. 'I'm going into this with my eyes open – but she's being conned. Will you guarantee her safety?'

'Of course I will. She'll be as safe as though she were in England.'

It was a long time before Denison made his decision. 'All right,' he said resignedly. 'I'll ask her.'

Carey slapped him lightly on the arm. 'Which brings us back to Meyrick's character. As you said – he's a right bastard. Bear that in mind when you're handling her.'

'You want her in Finland,' said Denison. 'I don't. If I really act like her father she's going to run and hide like she always has. Do you want that?'

'I can't say I do,' said Carey. 'But lean too far the other way and she'll know you're not Meyrick.'

Denison thought of the many ways in which he had hurt Lyn by his apparent forgetfulness. As in the case of her mascot, for instance; he had idly picked it up and asked what it was. 'But you *know*,' said Lyn in astonishment. He had incautiously shaken his head, and she burst out, 'But you *named* him.' There was a hurt look in her eyes. 'You called him Thread-Bear.'

He laughed sourly. 'Don't worry; I'm hurting her enough just by being myself.'

'It's settled then,' said Carey. 'You have an appointment at Helsinki University tomorrow afternoon with Professor Pentti Kääriänen. Your secretary arranged it.'

'Who the devil is he?'

'He was one of Hannu Merikken's assistants before the war. You are to introduce yourself as Merikken's son and pump him about what Merikken was doing in his laboratory from 1937 to 1939. I want to find out if there's been any other leakage about his X-ray researches.' He paused. 'Take the girl with you; it adds to your cover.'

'All right.' Denison gave Carey a level look. 'And her name is Lyn. She's not a bloody puppet; she's a human being.'

Carey's answering stare was equally unblinking. 'That's what I'm afraid of,' he said.

Carey watched Denison walk away and waited until he was joined by McCready. He sighed. 'Sometimes I have moments of quiet desperation.'

McCready suppressed a smile. 'What is it this time?'

'See those buildings over there?'

McCready looked across the road. 'That scrubby lot?'

'That's Victoria Terrace – there's a police station in there now. The authorities wanted to pull it down but the conservationists objected and won their case on architectural grounds.'

'I don't see the point.'

'Well, you see, it was Gestapo Headquarters during the war and it still smells to a lot of Norwegians.' He paused. 'I had a session in there once, with a man called Dieter Brun. Not a nice chap. He was killed towards the end of the war. Someone ran him down with a car.'

McCready was quiet because Carey rarely spoke of his past service. 'I've been running around Scandinavia for nearly forty years – Spitzbergen to the Danish-German border, Bergen to the Russo-Finnish border. I'll be sixty next month,' said Carey. 'And the bloody world hasn't changed, after all.' There was a note of quiet melancholy in his voice.

Next morning they all flew to Finland.

CHAPTER FOURTEEN

Lyn Meyrick was worried about her father, which was a new and unwanted experience. Her previous worries in that direction had always been for herself in relation to her father. To worry for her father was something new which gave her an odd feeling in the pit of her stomach.

She had been delighted when he suggested that she accompany him to Finland; a delight compounded by the fact that for the first time he was treating her like a grown-up person. He now asked her opinion and deferred to her wishes in a way he had never done before. Diffidently she had fallen in with his wish that she call him by his given name and she was becoming accustomed to it.

However, the delight had been qualified by the presence of Diana Hansen who somehow destroyed that adult feeling and made her feel young and gawky like a schoolgirl. The relationship between Diana and her father puzzled her. At first she had thought they were lovers and had been neither surprised nor shocked. Well, not *too* shocked. Her father was a man and not all that old, and her mother had not been reticent about the reasons for the divorce. And, yet, she had not thought that Diana Hansen would have been the type to appeal to her father and the relationship seemed oddly cold and almost businesslike.

And there were other things about him that were strange. He would become abstract and remote. This was nothing new because he had always had that ability to switch off in the middle of a conversation which made her feel as though he had dropped a barrier to cut her off. What was new was that he would snap out of these abstracted moments and smile at her in a way he never had before, which made her heart turn over. And he seemed deliberately to put himself out to please her.

And he was losing his memory, too. Not about anything big or important, but about minor things like … like Thread-Bear, for instance. How could a man forget a pun which had caused so much excitement in a little girl? If there was anything about her father that had annoyed her in the past it was his memory for detail – he usually remembered too much for her comfort. It was all very odd.

Anyway, she was glad he had invited her to go the University to meet the man with the unpronounceable name. He had been hesitant about it, and she said, 'Why are you going?'

'It's just that I want to find out something about my father.'

'But that's my grandfather,' she said. 'Of course I'm coming.'

It seemed strange to have a grandfather called Hannu Merikken. She sat before the mirror and contemplated herself, making sure that all was in order. I'm not bad-looking, she thought, as she regarded the straight black eyebrows and the grey eyes. Mouth too big, of course. I'm no raving beauty, but I'll do.

She snatched up her bag and went to the door on the way to meet her father. Then she stopped in mid-pace and thought, *What am I thinking of? It's my father … not … not …* She shook the thought from her and opened the door.

Professor Kääriänen was a jolly, chubby-faced man of about sixty, not at all the dry professorial stick Lyn had imagined. He rose from his desk to greet Denison, and shot out a spate of Finnish. Denison held up his hand in protest: 'I'm sorry; I have no Finnish.'

Kääriänen raised his eyebrows and said in English, 'Remarkable!'

Denison shrugged. 'Is it? I left when I was seventeen. I suppose I spoke Finnish for fifteen years – and I haven't spoken it for nearly thirty.' He smiled. 'You might say my Finnish language muscle has atrophied.'

Kääriänen nodded understandingly. 'Yes, yes; my own German was once quite fluent – but now?' He spread his hands. 'So you are Hannu Merikken's son.'

'Allow me to introduce my daughter, Lyn.'

Kääriänen came forward, his hands outstretched. 'And his granddaughter – a great honour. But sit down, please. Would you like coffee?'

'Thank you; that would be very nice.'

Kääriänen went to the door, spoke to the girl in the other office, and then came back. 'Your father was a great man, Dr … er … Meyrick.'

Denison nodded. 'That is my name now. I reverted to the old family name.'

The professor laughed. 'Ah, yes; I well remember Hannu telling me the story. He made it sound so romantic. And what are you doing here in Finland, Dr Meyrick?'

'I don't really know,' said Denison cautiously. 'Perhaps it's a need to get back to my origins. A delayed homesickness, if you like.'

'I understand,' said Kääriänen. 'And you want to know something about your father – that's why you've come to me?'

'I understand you worked with him – before the war.'

'I did, much to my own profit. Your father was not only a great research worker – he was also a great teacher. But I was not the only one. There were four of us, as I remember. You should remember that.'

'I was very young before the war,' said Denison defensively. 'Not even into my teens.'

'And you don't remember me,' said Kääriänen, his eyes twinkling. His hand patted his plump belly. 'I'm not surprised; I've changed quite a lot. But I remember you. You were a young rascal – you upset one of my experiments.'

Denison smiled. 'If guilty I plead sorrow.'

'Yes,' said Kääriänen reminiscently. 'There were four of us with your father in those days. We made a good team.' He frowned. 'You know; I think I am the only one left.' He ticked them off on his fingers. 'Olavi

Koivisto joined the army and was killed. Liisa Linnankivi – she was also killed in the bombing of Viipuri; that was just before your father died, of course. Kaj Salojärvi survived the war; he died three years ago – cancer, poor fellow. Yes, there is only me left of the old team.'

'Did you all work together on the same projects?'

'Sometimes yes, sometimes no.' Kääriänen leaned forward. 'Sometimes we worked on our own projects with Hannu giving advice. As a scientist yourself, Dr Meyrick, you will understand the work of the laboratory.'

Denison nodded. 'What was the main trend of my father's thought in those days before the war?'

Kääriänen spread his hands. 'What else but the atom? We were *all* thinking about the atom. Those were the great pioneering days, you know; it was very exciting.' He paused, and added drily, 'Not long after that, of course, it became too exciting, but by that time no one in Finland had time to think about the atom.'

He clasped his hands across his belly. 'I well remember the time Hannu showed me a paper written by Meitner and Frisch interpreting Hahn's experiments. The paper showed clearly that a chain reaction could take place and that the generation of atomic energy was clearly possible. We were all excited – you cannot imagine the excitement – and all our work was put aside to concentrate on this new thing.' He shrugged heavily. 'But that was 1939 – the year of the Winter War. No time for frivolities like atoms.' His tone was sardonic.

'What was my father working on when this happened?'

'Ah – here is the coffee,' said Kääriänen. He fussed about with the coffee, and offered small cakes to Lyn. 'And what do you do, young lady? Are you a scientist like your father and your grandfather?'

'I'm afraid not,' said Lyn politely. 'I'm a teacher.'

'We must have the teachers, too,' said Kääriänen. 'What was that you asked, Doctor?'

'I was wondering what my father was working on at the time he read the paper on atomic fission.'

'Ah, yes,' the professor said vaguely, and waved his hand a little helplessly. 'It was a long time ago, you know; so much has happened since – it is difficult to remember.' He picked up a cake and was about to bite into it when he said, 'I remember – it was something to do with some aspects of the properties of X-rays.'

'Did you work on that project?'

'No – that would be Liisa – or was it Olavi?'

'So you don't know the nature of the work he was doing?'

'No.' Kääriänen's face broke into a smile, and he shook with laughter. 'But, knowing your father, I can tell you it had no practical application. He was very proud of being a pure research physicist. We were all like that in those days; proud of being uncontaminated by the world.' He shook his head sadly. 'A pity we're not like that now.'

The next hour and a half was spent in reminiscences from Kääriänen interspersed with Denison's desperate ploys to fend off his inquiries into Meyrick's work. After allowing what he thought was a decent time he excused himself and he and Lyn took their leave of the professor with assurances that they would keep in professional contact.

They came out into Senate Square and made their way back to the hotel along Aleksanterinkatu, Helsinki's equivalent of Bond Street. Lyn was thoughtful and quiet, and Denison said, 'A penny for your thoughts.'

'I was just thinking,' she said. 'It seemed at one time as though you were pumping Professor Kääriänen.'

Did it, by God! thought Denison. *You're too bloody smart by half.* Aloud he said, 'I just wanted to know about my father, the work he did and so on.'

'You didn't give much back,' said Lyn tartly. 'Every time *he* asked a question you evaded it.'

'I had to,' said Denison. 'Most of my work is in defence. I can't babble about that in a foreign country.'

'Of course,' said Lyn colourlessly.

They were outside a jeweller's shop and Denison pointed. 'What do you think of that?'

She caught her breath. 'Oh, it's beautiful!'

It was a necklace – chunky, rough-hewn gold of an intricate and yet natural shape. He felt reckless and took her arm. 'Come on,' he said. 'Inside.'

The necklace cost him £215 of Meyrick's money which he paid by credit card. Apart from the fact that he thought that Meyrick ought to pay more attention to his daughter he thought it would take her mind off other things.

'Your birthday present,' he said.

Lyn was breathless with excitement. 'Oh, thank you, Da … Harry.' Impulsively she kissed him. 'But I have nothing to wear with it.'

'Then you'll have to buy something, won't you? Let's go back to the hotel.'

'Yes, let's.' She slipped her fingers into his. 'I have a surprise for you, too – at the hotel.'

'Oh? What is it?'

'Well, I thought that now you're back in Finland you ought to become reacquainted with the sauna.'

He laughed, and said cheerfully, 'I've never been to a sauna in my life.'

She stopped dead on the pavement and stared at him. 'But you must have. When you were a boy.'

'Oh, yes; I went then.' He cursed himself for the slip. Carey had given him books to read about Finland; language was one thing but there was a minimum any Finn would know, expatriate or not. The sauna definitely fitted into that category. 'I tend to regard my years in Finland as another life.' It was lame but it would have to do.

'It's about time you were reintroduced to the sauna,' she said firmly. 'I go often in London – it's great fun. I've booked for us both in the hotel sauna for six o'clock.'

'Great!' he said hollowly.

CHAPTER FIFTEEN

In the hotel he escaped to his room and rang the number he had been given. When Carey answered he gave a report on his interview with Kääriänen, and Carey said, 'So it all comes to this: Merikken *was* working on X-rays at the time but no one can remember exactly what he was doing. Those who would know are dead. That's encouraging.'

'Yes,' said Denison.

'You don't sound pleased,' said Carey.

'It's not that. I have something else on my mind.'

'Out with it.'

'Lyn has booked me in for the sauna this evening.'

'So?'

'She's booked us both in.'

'So?' There was a pause before Carey chuckled. 'My boy; I can see you have a wrong impression or an evil mind. This is not Hamburg nor is it the lower reaches of Soho; you're in Helsinki and the Finns are a decent people. I think you'll find there is one sauna for gentlemen and another for ladies.'

'Oh!' said Denison weakly. 'It's just that I don't know much about it. One gets the wrong impression.'

'Didn't you read the books I gave you?'

'I must have missed that one.'

'In any case, there's nothing wrong with a father joining his daughter in the sauna,' said Carey judicially. 'It may be done in your own home but not, I think, in an international hotel.' He paused. 'You'd better read up on it. Meyrick wouldn't have forgotten the sauna – no Finn would.'

'I'll do that.'

'Have fun,' said Carey, and rang off.

Denison put down the telephone and rummaged in his suitcase where he found a slim book on the sauna written for the benefit of English-speaking visitors to Finland. On studying it he was relieved to find that the sauna appeared to be little more than a Turkish bath in essence – with differences.

He turned back the pages and read the introduction. There was, apparently, one sauna for every six Finns which, he reflected, was probably a greater incidence than bathrooms in Britain. A clean people, the Finns – *mens sana in corpore sauna*. Stones were heated by birch logs or, in modern times, by electric elements. Humidity was introduced by *löyly* – tossing water on the stones. The booklet managed to convey an air of mystic ritual about what was essentially a prosaic activity, and Denison came to the conclusion that the sauna was the Finnish equivalent of the Japanese tea ceremony.

At quarter to six Lyn rang him. 'Are you ready?'

'Yes, of course.'

'I'll meet you afterwards in the swimming pool. Have you got your trunks?'

Denison mentally ran down a checklist of Meyrick's clothing. 'Yes.'

'At half past six, then.' She rang off.

He went up to the top floor of the hotel, found the sauna for men, and went into the change room where he took his time, taking his cue from the others who were there. He stripped and went into the ante-chamber to the sauna where he showered and then took a square of towelling from a pile and went into the sauna itself.

It was hot.

Out of the corner of his eye he saw a man lay his towel on a slatted, wooden bench and sit on it, so he followed suit. The wood beneath his feet was almost unbearably hot and sweat was already beginning to start from his skin. A man left the sauna and another took a bucket of water and sluiced it along the wood on which his feet were resting. Tendrils of steam arose but his feet were cooler.

Another man left the sauna and Denison turned and found a thermometer on the wall by his head. It registered 15 degrees. Not too bad, he thought; I can stand that. Then he looked again and saw that the thermometer was calibrated in degrees Celsius. Christ Almighty! Water *boils* at 100°C.

He blinked the sweat out of his eyes and turned his head to find that there was just himself and another man left – a broad-shouldered, deep-chested man, shaggy with hair. The man picked up a wooden dipper and filled it with water from a bucket. He paused with it in his hand, and said interrogatively, '*Löyly*?'

Denison answered with one of the few Finnish words he had picked up. '*Kiitos*.'

The man tossed the dipperful of water on to the square tub of hot stones in the corner. A blast of heat hit Denison like a physical blow and he gasped involuntarily. The man shot a sudden spate of Finnish at him, and Denison shook his head. 'I'm sorry; I have no Finnish.'

'Ah; first time in Finland?'

'Yes,' said Denison, and added, 'Since I was a boy.'

The man nodded. A sheen of sweat covered his hairy torso. He grinned. 'First time in sauna?'

Sweat dripped from Denison's nose. 'For a long time – many years.'

The man nodded and rose. He picked up the dipper again and, turning away from Denison, he filled it from the bucket. Denison gritted his teeth. Anything a bloody Finn can stand, I can; he thought.

With a casual flick of the wrist the man tossed the water on to the hot stones, then quickly went out of the sauna, slamming the door behind him. Again the wave of heat hit Denison, rising to an almost intolerable level so that he gasped and spluttered. A bloody practical joker – baiting a beginner!

He felt his head swim and tried to stand up but found that his legs had gone rubbery beneath him. He rolled off the top bench and tried to crawl to the door and felt the hot wood burning his hands. Darkness closed in on him and the last thing he saw was his own hand groping for the door handle before he collapsed and passed out.

He did not see the door open, nor did he feel himself being lifted up and carried out.

CHAPTER SIXTEEN

He awoke to darkness.

For a long time he just lay there, unable to think because of the throbbing pain in his head. Then his head cleared a little and he stirred and knew he was lying on a bed. When he moved he heard a metallic clinking noise. He moved again and became aware that he was naked, and a recollection of the sauna came back.

His first thought was that he had collapsed of heat prostration and had been taken to his own room, but when he lifted his hand that theory disintegrated quickly. There was a tug on both wrists and he felt cold metal, and when he twisted his hands around he heard that chinking sound again and felt the handcuffs.

He lay quiet for a while before he levered himself up on one elbow to stare into the blackness, then he swung his legs over the side of the bed and sat up. Tentatively he moved his feet apart; at least they were not manacled and he could walk. But walk where? He held his arms out before him and moved them sideways, first to the left and then to the right, until he encountered an object. It was flat with square edges and he concluded it was a bedside table. Exploring the top brought no joy; there was nothing on it.

Although his headache had eased he felt as weak as a kitten and he sat for a few moments to conserve his strength. Whether his weakness was a natural result of the heat of the sauna was debatable. He reasoned that if the sauna did that to everyone then it would not be so popular in Finland. Apart from that, he had no idea of how long he had been unconscious. He felt his skin and found it cool and with no moisture.

After a while he stood up with his arms out in front of him and began to shuffle forward. He had gone only a few feet when he stubbed his toe on something and the pain was agonizing. 'Damn!' he said viciously, and stepped back until he felt the bed behind his legs. He sat down and nursed his foot.

A sound came from the other side of the room and he saw a patch of greyness, quickly obscured and vanishing. A light suddenly stabbed at him and he blinked and screwed up his eyes against the sudden glare. A voice said in accented English, 'So Dr Meyrick is awake – and up, too.'

Denison brought up his hands before his eyes. The voice said sharply, 'Don't move, Meyrick. Stay on the bed.' Then, more coolly, 'Do you know what this is?'

The lamp dipped a little so that he could see the vague outline of a man in back-reflected light. He saw the glint of metal in an out-thrust hand. 'Well?' said the voice impatiently. 'What is it, Meyrick?'

Denison's voice was hoarse. 'A pistol.' He cleared his throat. 'I'd like to know what the hell this is all about.'

The voice was amused. 'No doubt you would.' As Denison tried to sort out the accent the light played over him. 'I see you've hurt your side, Dr Meyrick. How did that happen?'

'A pack of maniacs attacked me in Norway. They seem to have the same breed in Finland, too.'

'Poor Dr Meyrick,' mocked the voice. 'You seem to be continually in trouble. Did you report it to the police?'

'Of course I did. What else would you expect me to do? And to the British Embassy in Oslo.' He remembered what Carey had said about Meyrick's bloody-mindedness, and added irascibly, 'Bloody incompetents – the lot of them.'

'Who did you see at the Embassy?'

'A man called McCready picked me up at the police station and took me to the Embassy. Look, I've had enough of this. I'm answering no more questions. None at all.'

The pistol moved languidly. 'Yes, you will. Did you meet Carey?'

'No.'

'You're a liar.'

'If you think you know the answers, why ask me the questions? I don't know anyone called Carey.'

A sigh came out of the darkness. 'Meyrick, I think you ought to know that we have your daughter.'

Denison tensed, but sat quietly. After a moment he said, 'Prove it.'

'Nothing easier.' The pistol withdrew slowly. 'Tape recorders are made conveniently small these days, are they not?' There was a click and a slight hissing noise in the darkness beyond the flashlight, then a man spoke:

'Now tell me; what's your father doing here in Finland?'

'He's on holiday.'

That was Lyn's clear voice. Denison recognized it in spite of the slight distortion which was far less than that of a telephone.

'Did he tell you that?'

'Who else would tell me?' She sounded amused.

'But he went to see Professor Kääriänen this afternoon. That sounds more like business than pleasure.'

'He wanted to find out something about his father – my grandfather.'

'What did he want to find out?'

There was a raw silence, then the man said, *'Come now, Miss Meyrick; nothing will happen, either to you or to your father, if you answer my questions, I assure you that you will be released unharmed.'*

A switch snapped and the voices stopped. From the darkness: 'You see, Dr Meyrick! Of course, I cannot guarantee the truthfulness of my friend regarding his last statement.' The pistol reappeared, glinting in the light. 'Now, to return to Mr Carey – what did he have to say?'

'He hauled me over the coals for being in a road accident,' said Denison.

The voice sharpened. 'You can do better than that. Now, having put you and Carey together, I want to know just what you're doing here in Finland. I want it truthfully, and I want it quickly. And you'd better start thinking seriously of your daughter's health.' The gun jerked. 'Talk!'

Denison was never more conscious of the disadvantages of being naked; it took the pith out of a man. 'All right,' he said. 'We're here to see the Finnish government.'

'What about?'

'A defence project.'

'Who in the government?'

'Not really the government,' said Denison inventively. 'Someone in the army – in military intelligence.'

'The name?' When Denison was silent the gun jerked impatiently. 'The name, Meyrick.'

Denison was hastily trying to slap together a name that sounded even remotely Finnish. 'Saarinen.'

'He's an architect.'

'Not this one – this one's a colonel,' said Denison, hoping it was a rank in the Finnish army. He was listening intently but heard no sound other than an occasional rustle of clothing from the other side of the bright light.

'What's the project?'

'Electronic espionage – equipment for monitoring Russian broadcasts, especially on military wavelengths.'

There was a long silence. 'I suppose you know that this is already done.'

'Not the way I do it,' said Denison.

'All right; how do you do it? And let's not have me extract answers like pulling teeth or that girl of yours might have some of her teeth pulled.'

'I invented an automatic decoder,' said Denison. A barrier broke in his mind and a wave of panic and terror swept over him. He felt sweat trickle down his chest and then deliberately pushed the panic back where it had come from – but he retained the words that had come with it.

'It's a stochastic process,' he said, not even knowing what the word meant. 'A development of the Monte Carlo method. The Russian output is repeatedly sampled and put through a series of transformations at random. Each transformation is compared with a store held in a computer memory – if a match is made a tree branching takes place leading to a further set of transformations. There are a lot of dead ends and it needs a big, fast computer – very powerful.'

The sweat poured off him. He had not understood a word of what he had said.

'I got most of that,' said the voice, and Denison thought he detected a touch of awe. 'You invented this thing?'

'I developed the circuits and helped with the programming,' said Denison sullenly.

'There's one thing I don't understand – and this I really have to know. Why give it to the Finns?'

'We didn't,' said Denison. 'They gave it to us. They developed the basics. They didn't have the resources to follow up, so they gave it to us.'

'Professor Kääriänen?'

'Look,' said Denison. 'Let me hear that tape again.'

'Why?'

'I'm not saying another bloody word until I hear it,' said Denison stubbornly.

A pause. 'All right; here's a re-run.'

The gun vanished and there was a click.

'Now tell me; what's your father doing here in Finland?'

'He's on holiday.'

Denison strained his ears as he listened to the conversation and evaluated the voices. He raised his hands and slowly parted them so that the link of the handcuffs tightened.

'He wanted to find out something about his father – my grandather.'

'What did he want to find out? A pause. *'Come now, Miss Meyrick; nothing will happen, either to you or to your father, if you ans …'*

Denison lunged, moving fast. He had moved his legs under the bed, so that when he moved he was on the balls of his feet and utilizing the maximum thrust of his thighs. His hands were as wide apart as he could spread them and he rammed them forward as though to grab the man by the ears. The link between the handcuffs caught the man right across the larynx.

Both tape recorder and flashlight dropped to the floor; the flashlight rolled, sending grotesque shadows about the room, and the recorder babbled. Denison kept up his pressure on the man's throat and was aware of cloth as he pressed his hands to his opponent's face. In the shifting light he saw the glint of metal as the man raised the pistol from his pocket and he twisted his hand frantically and managed to grab the wrist as it came up.

With his left hand holding firmly on to his opponent's right wrist he thrust firmly so that the steel link cut into the man's throat. The gun was thus held close to the man's right ear, and when it went off with a blinding flare and a deafening explosion the man reeled away and dropped it.

Denison dived for it and came up again quickly. The door banged closed and the recorder chattered insanely. He made for the door and opened it, to find himself in a narrow corridor with another door at the end. As he ran for it heard Diana Hansen say, from behind him, *'Lyn, if you take this attitude it will be the worse for you.'*

He heard the words but they made little sense and he had no time to evaluate them. He burst through the door and found himself in the brightly lit hotel corridor. There was no one to be seen, so he ran to the corner where the corridor turned and came to the lifts, and skidded to a halt in front of an astonished couple in evening dress. One lift was going down.

He made for the stairs, hearing a startled scream from behind him, and ran down two flights of stairs, causing quite a commotion as he emerged into the lobby yelling for the police and wearing nothing but a pair of handcuffs and an automatic pistol.

CHAPTER SEVENTEEN

'Incredible!' said Carey. His voice was dead as though he, himself, did not believe what he was saying, and the single word made no echo in the quiet room.

'That's what happened,' said Denison simply.

McCready stirred. 'It would seem that more than water was thrown on to the hot stones in the sauna.'

'Yes,' said Carey. 'I have heard that some Finns, in an experimental mood, have used koskenkorva as *löyly*.'

'What's that?' asked Denison.

'A sort of Finnish vodka.' Carey put down his dead pipe. 'I dare say some smart chemist could come up with a vaporizing knock-out mixture. I accept that.' He frowned and shook his head. 'Could you repeat what you told this fellow about your bloody decoder?'

'It's engraved on my memory,' said Denison bitterly. 'I said, "It's a stochastic process – a development of the Monte Carlo method. The Russian output is repeatedly sampled and put through a series of transformations at random. Each transformation is compared with a store held in a computer memory – if a match is made a tree branching takes place leading to a further set of transformations. There are a lot of dead ends and it needs a big, fast computer – very powerful." '

'It would,' said Carey drily.

'I don't even know what stochastic means,' said Denison helplessly.

Carey took a smoker's compendium from his pocket and began to clean his pipe, making a dry scraping sound. 'I know what it means. A stochastic process has an element of probability in it. The Monte

Carlo method was first devised as a means of predicting the rate of diffusion of uranium hexafluoride through a porous barrier – it's been put to other uses since.'

'But I don't know anything about that,' expostulated Denison.

'Apparently you do,' said Carey. 'If you thought you were talking gobbledegook you were wrong. It would make sense to a mathematician or a computer man. And you were right about something else; you'd need a bloody powerful computer to handle it – the transformations would run into millions for even a short message. In fact, I don't think there is that kind of a computer, unless the programming method is equally powerful.'

Denison developed the shakes. 'Was I a mathematician? Did I work on computers?' he whispered.

'No,' said Carey levelly. 'What did you think you were doing when you reeled off all that stuff?'

'I was spinning a yarn – I couldn't tell him why we were really here.'

McCready leaned forward. 'What did you feel like when you were spouting like that?'

'I was scared to death,' confessed Denison.

'Of the man?'

There was violence in Denison's headshake. 'Not of the man – of myself. What was in *me*.' His hands began to quiver again.

Carey caught McCready's eye and shook his head slightly; that line of questioning was too dangerous for Denison. He said, 'We'll leave that for a moment and move on. You say this chap accepted you as Meyrick?'

'He didn't question it.'

'What made you go for him? That was a brave thing to do when he had a gun.'

'He wasn't holding the gun,' said Denison. 'He was holding the recorder. I suddenly tumbled to it that the recording was a fake. The threatening bit at the end had a different quality – a dead sound. All the other stuff was just ordinary conversation and could have happened quite naturally. It followed that this chap couldn't have Lyn, and that left me free to act.'

'Quite logical,' said Carey. 'And quite right.' There was a bemused look on his face as he muttered to himself, '*Competent!*'

McCready said, 'Lyn was in the hotel lounge yesterday afternoon and a chap sat at the table and began to pump her. Either the flower pot or the ashtray was bugged and the conversation recorded. Diana Hansen was around and caught on to what was happening and butted in, spoiling the game. Of course, she didn't know about the bug at the time.'

A look of comprehension came over Denison's face. 'I heard Diana's voice on the tape. She was threatening Lyn, too.'

McCready grinned. 'When this character was foiled he went away, and Diana and Lyn had a row. The bug was still there so that, too, was picked up on the tape. It seems that your daughter is trying to protect her father against the wiles of a wicked woman of the world.'

'Oh, no!' moaned Denison.

'You'll have to come the heavy father,' McCready advised.

'Does Lyn know what happened?'

Carey grunted and glanced at his watch. 'Six in the morning – she'll still be asleep. When you went missing I had Mrs Hansen tell her that the two of you were going on the town and you'd be late back. I didn't want her alarmed.'

'She's certain to find out,' said McCready. 'This is too good a story to suppress – the eminent Dr Meyrick capering in the lobby of the city's best hotel as naked as the day he was born and waving a gun. Impossible to keep out of the papers.'

'Why in hell did you do it?' demanded Carey. 'You were bawling for the police, too.'

'I thought I could catch the chap,' said Denison. 'When I didn't I thought of what Meyrick would have done – the real Meyrick. If an innocent man is threatened with a gun the first thing he does is to yell for the coppers. An innocent Meyrick would be bloody outraged – so I blew my top in the hotel lobby.'

'Still logical,' muttered Carey. He raised his voice. 'All right; the man in the sauna. Description?'

'He was hairy – he had a pelt like a bear.'

'I don't care if he was as hairy as Esau,' said Carey caustically. 'We can't go stripping the clothes off suspects to find how hairy they are. His face, man!'

'Brown eyes,' said Denison tiredly. 'Square face – a bit battered. Nose on one side. Dimple in chin.'

'That's the bloke who was quizzing Lyn Meyrick,' said McCready.

'The other man – the one with the gun.'

'I never saw him,' said Denison. 'The room was darkened and when I got my hands on him I found he was wearing some kind of a mask. But I ...' He stopped on a doubtful note.

'Carry on,' said Carey encouragingly.

'He spoke English but with an accent.'

'What sort of accent?'

'I don't know,' said Denison desperately. 'Call it a generalized middle-European accent. The thing is that I think I've heard the voice before.'

At that, Carey proceeded to put Denison through the wringer. Fifteen minutes later Denison yelled, 'I tell you I don't know.' He put his head in his hands. 'I'm tired.'

Carey stood up. 'All right; you can go to bed. We'll let you sleep, but I can't answer for the local cops – they'll want to see you again. Got your story ready?'

'Just the truth.'

'I'd leave out that bit about the decoder you invented,' advised Carey. 'It's a bit too much.' He jerked his head at McCready. 'Come on, George.'

They left Denison to his bed. In the lift Carey passed his hand over his face. 'I didn't think this job would call for so many sleepless nights.'

'Let's find some coffee,' proposed McCready. 'There's sure to be an early morning place open by now.'

They left the hotel in silence and walked along Mannerheimintie. The street was quiet with only the occasional taxi and the odd cyclist on his way to an early start at work. Carey said suddenly, 'Denison worries me.'

'You mean that stuff he came out with?'

'What the hell else?' The corners of Carey's mouth turned down. 'And more – but principally that. A man like Meyrick might design just such a contraption – but where did Denison get it from?'

'I've been thinking about it,' said McCready. His voice was careful. 'Have you considered the possibility of a double shuffle?'

Carey broke stride. 'Speak plainly.'

'Well, here we have a man whom we think is Denison. His past is blocked out and every time he tries to probe it he breaks into a muck sweat. You saw that.'

'Well?'

'But supposing he really is Meyrick – also with the past blocked out – who only thinks he's Denison. Harding said it was possible. Then anything brought out of the past in an emergency would be pure Meyrick.'

Carey groaned. 'What a bloody roundabout to be on.' He shook his head decisively. 'That won't wear. Iredale said he wasn't Meyrick.'

'No, he didn't,' said McCready softly. 'I can quote his exact words. Iredale said, "He's *not* Meyrick – not unless Meyrick has had plastic surgery recently." '

Carey thought that out. 'Stop trying to confuse me. That would mean that the man we had in the hotel in Oslo for three weeks was *not* Meyrick – that the ringer was the other way round.'

He stopped dead on the pavement. 'Look, George; let's get one thing quite clear.' He stabbed a finger back at the hotel. 'That man there is *not* Meyrick. I *know* Meyrick – he fights with his tongue and uses sarcasm as a weapon, but if you put him in a real fight he'd collapse. Denison is a quiet spoken, civil man who, in an emergency, seems to have the instincts of a born killer. He's the antithesis of Meyrick. Ram that into your mind and hold on to it fast.'

McCready shrugged. 'It leaves a lot to be explained.'

'It will be explained. I want Giles Denison sorted out once and for all back in London. I want his life sifted day by day and minute by minute, if necessary, to find out how he knows that mathematical jargon. And I want Harding brought here *tout de suite*.'

'He'll like that,' said McCready sardonically. 'I'll pass the word on.'

They walked for another hundred yards and McCready said, 'Denison is quite a boy. Who else would think of handcuffs as a weapon?' He chuckled. 'I think he's neither Meyrick nor Denison – I think he's Clark Kent.'

Carey's jaw dropped. 'And who the blazes is that?'

'Superman,' said McCready blandly.

CHAPTER EIGHTEEN

Denison slept, was interviewed by the police, and slept again. He got up at four, bathed and dressed, and went downstairs. Crossing the lobby he saw the receptionist stare at him, then turn and say something to the porter with a smile. Dr H. F. Meyrick was evidently the hotel celebrity.

He looked into the lounge, saw no one he knew, and then investigated the bar where he found Diana Hansen sitting at a table and reading a paperback. She looked up as he stood over her. 'I was wondering when you'd show.'

'I had to get some sleep. Yesterday was a bit wearing.' He sat down and picked up the ashtray to inspect its underside.

Diana laughed. 'No bugs – I checked.'

He put it down. 'Where's Lyn?'

'Out.' At his raised eyebrows she elaborated slightly. 'Sightseeing.'

A waiter came up. '*Mitä otatte*?'

'*Olut E, oikaa hyvä*,' said Denison. He looked at Diana. 'And you?'

'Nothing for me,' she said. 'Your Finnish is improving.'

'Only enough to order the necessities of life. Has Carey come to any conclusions about yesterday?'

'Carey isn't here,' she said. 'I'm to tell you to sit tight until he comes back.'

'Where is he?'

'He's gone to Sweden.'

'Sweden!' His eyes were blank. 'Why has he gone there?'

'He didn't tell me.' She stood up and picked up her book. 'Now that I've passed on the word I'll get about my business.' Her lips quirked. 'Don't take any wooden saunas.'

'Never again,' he said fervently. He bit his lip. 'But they might take another crack at me.'

'Not to worry,' she said. 'You're under Ian Armstrong's eye, and he's well named. He's sitting at the bar now. Don't acknowledge him – and don't move so fast he can't keep up with you.'

She went away as the waiter came up with his beer. He drank it moodily and ordered another bottle. Over at the bar Armstrong was making a single beer stretch a long way. Why Sweden? What could possibly have happened there to drag Carey away? No answer came.

He was half-way through the second bottle when Lyn entered the bar. She sat at his table and looked at his beer. 'You look dissipated.'

He grinned at her. 'I feel dissipated. I was up late.'

'So I'm told,' she said unsmilingly. 'I heard a strange story this morning – about you.'

He regarded her warily and decided to riposte. 'And I've heard something pretty odd about you. Why did you quarrel with Diana?'

Pink spots came into her cheeks. 'So she told you.'

'She didn't say anything about it,' said Denison truthfully.

Lyn flared up. 'Then who did if she didn't? We were alone.' She tugged viciously at the strap of her bag and looked down at the table. 'It doesn't feel nice to be ashamed of one's own father. I never really believed everything Mother said about you, but now I can see she was telling the truth.'

'Calm down,' he said. 'Have a drink. What will you have? A Coca-Cola?'

Her chin came up. 'A dry Martini.'

He signalled to the waiter, suppressing a smile, and gave the order. When the waiter had gone, she said, 'It was disgusting of you.'

'What's so disgusting about Diana Hansen?'

'You know what I mean. I've heard the jet set gets up to some queer things but, my God, I didn't expect it of you. Not my own father.' Her eyes were unnaturally bright.

'No, I don't know what you mean. What am I supposed to have done?' he asked plaintively.

A hurt look came into her eyes. 'I know you went out with that woman last night because she told me so. And I know how you came back. too. You must have been disgustingly drunk to do that. Did *she* have any clothes on? No wonder they had to send for the police.'

'Oh, my God!' said Denison, appalled. 'Lyn, it wasn't like that.'

'Then why is everyone talking about it? I heard it at breakfast this morning. There were some Americans at the next table – you ought to have heard them. It was dirty!' She broke into tears.

Denison hastily looked about the bar and then put his hand on Lyn's. 'It wasn't like that; I'll tell you.'

So he told her, leaving out everything important which would only complicate the issue. He was interrupted once by the waiter bringing the Martini, and then he bore in again to finish his story.

She dabbed at her eyes with a small handkerchief and sniffed. 'A likely tale!'

'If you don't believe me, would you believe the police?' he said exasperatedly. 'They've been on my neck all morning.'

'Then why did Diana tell me you were going out with her?'

'It was the best thing she could have done,' said Denison. 'She didn't want you worried. And about your quarrel – I heard a bit of it on the tape.' He explained about that, and said, 'The police have the tape now.'

Lyn was horrified. 'You mean everyone is listening to that quarrel?'

'Everyone except me,' said Denison drily. 'Have your Martini.'

Something else occurred to her. 'But you might have been hurt – he might have *killed* you!'

'But he didn't – and all's well.'

'Who could it have been?'

'I suppose I'm a fairly important man in some respects,' said Denison tiredly. 'I told you yesterday that I don't babble about my work. Someone wanted information and took direct action.'

She straightened her shoulders and looked at him with shining eyes. 'And didn't get it.'

He brutally chopped the props from under the hero worship. 'As for Diana Hansen, there's nothing in it – not the way you think. But even if there were it's got nothing to do with you. You're behaving more like an affronted wife than a daughter.'

The glow died. Lyn hunched her shoulders a little and looked down at the Martini glass. Suddenly she picked it up and drained the contents at a swallow. It took her breath away and she choked a little before putting down the empty glass. Denison grinned. 'Does that make you feel better?'

'I'm sorry,' she said miserably.

'That's all right,' he said. 'No harm done. Let's go for a walk.' He signalled to the waiter and paid the bill and, as he got up from the table, he glanced over at the bar and saw Armstrong doing the same. It was comforting to have a bodyguard.

They left the bar and went into the lobby. As they approached the entrance a porter came in loaded with baggage, and a burly figure followed. 'Hey, Lucy; look who's here,' boomed a voice. 'It's Harry Meyrick.'

'Oh hell!' said Denison, but there was no escape.

'Who is it?' asked Lyn.

'I'll introduce you,' said Denison grimly.

'Hi, Harry!' shouted Kidder, advancing across the lobby with outstretched hand. 'It's great to see you, it sure is.'

'Hallo, Jack,' said Denison without enthusiasm, and allowed his hand to be pulped.

'It's a small world,' said Kidder predictably. 'I was only saying that to Lucy the other day when we bumped into the Williamsons in Stockholm. You remember the Williamsons?'

'Of course,' said Denison.

'I guess we're all on the same Scandinavian round, eh? I wouldn't be surprised if the Williamsons don't turn up here, too. Wouldn't it be great if they did?'

'Great!' said Denison.

Lucy Kidder popped out from behind her husband. 'Why, Harry; how nice to see you. Did Jack tell you we saw the Williamsons in Stockholm?'

'Yes, he did.'

'It's a small world,' said Lucy Kidder.

'It sure is,' said Jack. 'If the Williamsons get here – and that nice friend of yours, Diana Hansen – we could get down to some poker. That gal is a mean player.'

Lyn said, 'Diana Hansen? Why, she's here.'

Surprise and pleasure beamed from Kidder's face. 'Now, isn't that just great? Maybe I'll be able to win some of my dough back, Lucy.'

'Lose it, more likely,' she said tartly. 'Jack really believes he can play poker.'

'Now then, Momma,' he said good-humouredly. 'Don't knock the old man.' He looked down at Lyn. 'And who's the little lady?'

'Excuse me,' said Denison. 'Jack Kidder – my daughter, Lyn – Lucy Kidder.'

They shook hands and Kidder said, 'You didn't tell me you had a daughter, Harry. You certainly didn't tell me you had a beautiful daughter. Where you been hiding her?'

'Lyn's been at University,' said Denison. 'She's now on vacation.'

Lucy said, 'I don't want to break things up, Jack, but I guess we gotta register. The desk clerk's waiting.'

'Sure,' said Kidder. 'I'll be seeing you around, Harry. Tell Diana to break out that deck of cards – we'll be playing poker.'

'I'll do that,' said Denison and, taking Lyn by the arm, he steered her out of the hotel. Under his breath he said, 'Over my dead body.'

'Who was that?' asked Lyn.

'The biggest bore from the North American continent,' said Denison. 'With his long-suffering wife.'

CHAPTER NINETEEN

Carey and McCready were being violently seasick. They clung to the rail of the small boat as it pitched in the summer gale which had blown up from the south and whistled up the narrow channel between the Swedish mainland and the island of Öland. There was but one significant difference between them – while Carey thought he was dying McCready *knew* he was dying.

They both felt better when they set foot ashore at Borgholm. There a car awaited them, and a police officer who introduced himself with a jerky bow as 'Hoglund, Olof.'

'I'm Carey and this is McCready.' The wind blew off the sea and riffled his short grey hair. 'Shall we get on with it?'

'Certainly. This way.' As Hoglund ushered them to the car he said, 'Your Mr Thornton arrived an hour ago.'

Carey stopped dead in his tracks. 'Has he, indeed?' He glanced sideways at McCready, and muttered, 'What the hell does he want?'

'He won't tell us,' prophesied McCready.

They were silent as they drove through the streets of Borgholm. It was not the time yet for talk; that would come later after they had seen what they had come to see. Carey's mind was busy with speculations arising from the presence of Thornton, and even if he wanted to discuss it with McCready he could not do so in the presence of Hoglund.

The car pulled up in front of a two-storey building and they went inside, Hoglund leading the way. He took them into a back room where there was a trestle table set up. On the table was a long shape covered with a white cloth. Behind the table stood a short man with a neat vandyke beard, who wore a white coat. Hoglund introduced him as Dr Carlson. 'You already know Mr Thornton.'

Thornton was a tall, dark man of cadaverous features, smooth unlined skin and indecipherable expression. He was a young-looking sixty or an aged forty – it was hard to determine which and Thornton was not going to tell anybody. It was not his habit to tell anyone anything that did not concern him and he was chary of doing even that. He could have been Carey's boss but he was not; Carey was proud and pleased to be in another department.

He lifted yellowed, dyspeptic eyes as Carey and McCready entered the room. Carey nodded to him curtly, and turned to Carlson. 'Good afternoon, Doctor,' he said in a weary voice. He was very tired. 'May I see it?'

Carlson nodded without speaking and drew back the cloth. Carey looked down with an expressionless face and motioned for the cloth to be drawn back farther. 'This is how he was found?'

'The body has been cleaned externally,' said Carlson. 'It was covered with oil. And the manacles have been removed of course.'

Carey nodded. 'Of course. There was no clothing?'

'The man was naked.'

McCready looked at Carey and raised his eyebrows. 'The same as ...'

Carey was unaccountably clumsy. He turned and trod heavily on McCready's foot. 'Sorry, George.' He turned to Carlson. 'What was the cause of death, Doctor?'

Carlson frowned. 'That will have to await the autopsy,' he said cautiously. 'At the moment it is a question of whether he was drowned or poisoned.'

Thornton stepped forward. 'Did you say poisoned?' Carey analysed the tone of voice. In spite of Thornton's habitual flatness of expression he thought he detected a note of genuine surprise.

'I'll show you,' said Carlson. He opened the jaws of the corpse and took a long spatula and thrust it down the throat. McCready winced and turned away. Carlson withdrew the spatula and held it out. 'A scraping from the inside of the throat.'

Carey inspected the blackened end of the spatula. 'Oil?'

When Carlson nodded Thornton said, 'I don't think it really matters if he drowned in oil or if it poisoned him.' His attitude was relaxed.

'I agree,' said Hoglund. 'Do you make the identification, Mr Carey?'

Carey hesitated. 'At this moment – no.' He nodded at Thornton. 'What about you?'

'I've never seen the man before in my life,' said Thornton.

A grim expression settled on Carey's face. 'The body will have to be ... preserved. Do you have facilities?'

'Not on Öland,' said Carlson.

'We can take it to the mainland as soon as Dr Carlson has completed the autopsy,' said Hoglund.

'No,' said Carey forcibly. 'I need a positive identification before the body is touched. That means the body must go to England or someone must come to Sweden. In any case, I want one of our own pathologists to assist at the autopsy.'

'This comes within our jurisdiction,' said Hoglund sharply.

Carey rubbed his eyes tiredly; the inside of his eyelids seemed to be covered in sand. This would have to be handled carefully considering the Swedish tradition of neutrality. He said slowly, 'As far as we are concerned this has now become a matter of State. I am going to push the question upstairs, and I suggest you also consult your superiors. Let our masters argue the question of jurisdiction, my friend; it will be safer for both of us.' As Hoglund considered the suggestion Carey added, 'In any case, the incident took place in international waters.'

'Perhaps that would be best,' said Hoglund. His manner was stiff. 'I will do as you suggest. Would you like to see the manacles?' When Carey nodded he strode to a shelf and took down a pair of handcuffs.

Carey examined them. 'British,' he commented. He handed them to Thornton. 'Wouldn't you think so?'

Thornton shrugged. 'It means little.' He turned to Hoglund. 'Is it established he did not come from the tanker?'

'The crew of the tanker are all accounted for,' said Hoglund. 'One man was killed but the body was recovered.' Carlson was replacing the sheet over the body as Hoglund gestured at it. 'This man probably came from the other boat. The captain of the tanker says it must have been running without lights.'

'He would say that,' said Carey cynically. 'He could be right, though. It has not been identified yet?'

'Not yet. No boat has been reported missing; no insurance claim has been made. We are making inquiries, naturally.' Hoglund frowned. 'Apart from the body there is the matter of the oil. It will cost a lot to clean the coasts of Gotland and someone must pay.'

'That's something I don't understand,' said McCready. 'If the oil is drifting on to Gotland how is it that the body turned up here on Öland? They are a long way apart.'

'The body was taken from the sea south of Gotland,' said Hoglund. 'But the ship was coming here.'

Carey cleared his throat. 'What have you got to go on in your inquiries?'

'Not a great deal. The captain of the tanker was not on the bridge at the time, and the boat sank within minutes. The captain estimated it as something between three hundred and four hundred tons. He derives this figure from the damage done to the bows of the tanker and its speed at the time of impact.'

'A small coaster,' said Carey thoughtfully. 'Or a biggish fisherman.'

Hoglund shrugged. 'We will soon find out.'

I wouldn't hold your breath, my friend, thought Carey. He turned to Carlson. 'There is no reflection on your ability as a pathologist, Dr Carlson. I hope you understand that. Will you begin preparations for the preservation of the body?'

Carlson looked warily at Hoglund, who nodded. 'I understand. I will do as you ask.'

'Then there's nothing more we can do here,' said Carey. 'Unless Mr Thornton has anything further to add.'

'Nothing,' said Thornton. 'I'll leave the details of the identification to you.'

They left the room. At the entrance of the building Carey paused to button up his coat, and turned to Thornton. 'Your arrival was unexpected. What brought you here?'

'I happened to be at the Embassy in Stockholm,' said Thornton easily. 'About another matter, of course. They're a bit short-handed so when this thing blew up I volunteered to come here and look after the British interest.'

Carey turned up his collar. 'How did you know there was a British interest?' he asked blandly.

Thornton was equally bland. 'The handcuffs, of course.' He nodded back towards the room they had come from. 'Who was he?'

'We'll know that when he's been identified.'

Thornton smiled. 'Your department has a vested interest in mysteries, I know – but you shouldn't let it become an obsession.' He pointed. 'Hoglund is waiting for you at the car.'

'Aren't you coming?'

'I came by helicopter,' said Thornton. 'Sorry I can't offer you a lift back, but I don't know where you came from, do I?' His smile was malicious.

Carey grunted and walked towards the car. Again there was silence in the car because Hoglund was there but, as they drew up to the quay side, Carey said abruptly, 'Was the British Embassy informed of the country of origin of those handcuffs?'

Hoglund furrowed his brow. 'I don't think so. Not by me.'

'I see. Thank you.'

The wind had moderated and the passage back to the mainland of Sweden was easier. Carey and McCready stayed on deck where it was possible to talk with some privacy. 'I didn't expect to see Thornton,' said McCready. 'What's he up to?'

'I don't know, said Carey broodingly. 'He tried to spin me a yarn. Can you imagine a Whitehall mandarin like Thornton volunteering for an errand boy's job which any Embassy whippersnapper could do? The mind boggles.' He thumped the rail with his fist. 'Damn these interdepartmental rivalries! We're all supposed to be on the same side, but I spend more time guarding my back against people like Thornton than I do on my job.'

'Do you suppose he knows about the switch on Meyrick?'

'I don't know. According to what he said back there he doesn't even know Meyrick.' Carey looked down at the grey sea. 'Somebody's luck ran out.'

'Meyrick's certainly did.'

'I was thinking of the people who snatched him. They got him to Copenhagen and put him on a boat to take him … where? And the boat was run down by a tanker travelling westwards.'

'So it was probably going east,' said McCready. 'Suggestive – to say the least.'

'Let's not jump to any fast conclusions,' said Carey irritably.

'I agree,' said McCready. 'Especially let's not jump to the conclusion that this oil-poisoned stiff is Meyrick. We've been had before.'

Carey gave him a withering look, and said abruptly, 'I want Iredale present at the autopsy to check for any signs of plastic surgery. I want the fingerprints of the corpse taken and a check made at Meyrick's home for matching prints. For legal identification I suggest one of Meyrick's ex-wives.'

'What's wrong with his daughter?'

'I'm trying to work that one out,' said Carey with a sigh. 'If I can do it before we get to the plane then maybe I can get some sleep on the flight back to Helsinki.' He did not sound too sanguine.

CHAPTER TWENTY

Carey sat in the Café Hildén on Aleksanterinkatu and sank a beer while waiting for Harding. After twelve hours' sleep he felt refreshed and no longer as depressed as he had been. He knew his depression had been caused by tiredness. All the same, rested and clear-headed though he was, the coming decision was not going to be easy to make.

He saw Harding come around the corner so he held up his hand. When Harding came over, he asked, 'You've seen Denison?' On Harding's nod, he said, 'Have a beer.'

Harding sat down. 'That'll be welcome. I didn't think it got as hot as this in the frozen north.'

Carey went to the counter and returned with two more beers. 'What's the verdict?'

Harding had his head on one side, apparently watching the foam rise in his glass. 'Oddly enough, he's improved since I last saw him. He's better integrated. What are his drinking habits like now?'

Carey tapped the side of his glass. 'He just has the odd beer.'

'In an odd sort of way this experience might have been therapeutic for him.' Harding smiled wryly. 'Although I wouldn't recommend it as a well-judged treatment. Now that we know more of his past history I'm better equipped to assess his present state.' He took a notebook from his pocket. 'Denison was something of a car enthusiast and ran a Lotus Elan. Three years ago he was driving with his wife, there was an accident for which he was partly – and only partly – to blame, and his wife was killed. They had been married eighteen months. She was pregnant at the time.'

'That's bad,' said Carey.

'He took *all* the blame on himself,' said Harding. 'And one thing led to another. He began to drink heavily and was on the verge of alcoholism when he lost his job for incompetence.'

'That baffles me,' said Carey. 'Because, he's bloody competent at what he's doing now.' He grinned. 'I'm thinking of offering him a permanent job.'

Harding sampled his beer. 'He can't remember his wife in any meaningful way because of what's been done to him. He remembers her and he remembers her death but it's as though it happened to someone else. Of course, that's just as it should be after three years. In a normal person the sharpness of grief is blunted by the passage of time and, in that respect, Denison is now normal.'

'I'm glad to hear it,' said Carey.

Harding gave him a sharp look. He mistrusted Carey's reasons for being glad. He said, 'Consequently he has lost his irrational guilt feelings and has no need to anaesthetize himself with booze. Hence the return to competency. I rather think that, with a little expert treatment, he can be made into a much better man than he was immediately prior to his kidnapping.'

'How long would that take?'

'Three to six months – that's just a guess.'

Carey shook his head. 'Too long; I want him now. Is he fit to carry on?'

Harding pondered for a moment. 'You know, I think he's actually enjoying himself right now. He likes the cut and thrust of this business – the opportunity to exercise his wits seems to be good for him.'

'So he's fit,' said Carey in satisfaction.

'I didn't say that,' said Harding testily. 'I'm not thinking of your damned operation – I'm thinking of Denison.' He thought for a while. 'The present pressures don't seem to worry him. I'd say the only danger is if his past is revealed to him in a traumatic manner.'

'That won't happen,' said Carey definitely. 'Not where I'm sending him.'

'All right,' said Harding. 'Then he's as fit as a man in his position can be – which isn't saying a hell of a lot.'

'Which brings me to another problem,' said Carey. 'Meyrick is dead.' He inspected that statement, found it wanting, and amended it. 'Probably dead. We have a body but once bitten, twice shy.'

'I see your difficulty,' said Harding with a half smile.

'I can't tell the girl her father's dead – not with Denison around. She'd blow up like a volcano and bang goes his cover as Meyrick – and I need him as Meyrick. The point is – do I tell Denison?'

'I wouldn't,' said Harding. 'Handling Lyn Meyrick is tricky enough for him as it is. If he knows her father is dead it might put him into a moral dilemma, assuming he's a moral man which I think he is.' He sighed. 'God knows we're not.'

'We represent the higher morality,' said Carey sardonically. 'The greatest good for the greatest number. I've always been a Benthamite at heart; it's the only way to keep my job bearable.' He drained his glass. 'That's it, then. Where is Denison now?'

'Sightseeing,' said Harding. 'He took his daughter to see the Sibelius Memorial.'

CHAPTER TWENTY-ONE

'It looks like an organ,' said Lyn judiciously. 'If it had a keyboard you could play it. A bit funny, that, come to think of it. Sibelius was an orchestra man, wasn't he?'

'I think so,' said Denison. He consulted his guide book. 'It weighs twenty-eight tons and was made by a woman. I suppose you could call it an early example of Women's Lib – the hand that rocks the cradle can also wield the welding torch. Let's sit and watch the passing parade.'

They sat on a bench and watched a tour group debark from a bus; transatlantic accents twanged the air. Denison saw Armstrong stroll along the path below the monument, then he lifted his eyes to look at the sea. The white sails of yachts dotted the deep blue which echoed the lighter blue of the cloudless sky. He wondered when Carey was going to make his move.

Lyn sighed comfortably. 'Isn't this beautiful? I didn't think Finland would be like this – it's more like the Mediterranean, like Ibiza. Remember when we went there?'

'Mmm,' said Denison neutrally.

Lyn laughed. 'That funny little hotel where there was no hot water and you couldn't have a hot bath. I've never heard you complain so angrily. What was the name of the owner – that little fat man?'

'I don't remember,' said Denison. That was safe enough; a man was not expected to remember every casual encounter.

'And then the seafood was bad and they took you off to hospital and pumped out your stomach.'

'I always had a delicate stomach,' said Denison. He pointed out to sea. 'I think they're racing out there.' He wanted to divert her mind to the present.

'Yes, they are,' she said. 'That reminds me – I suppose *Hesperia* is still laid up if you've not been sailing her this summer. The reason I ask is that if you're not going to sail her I'd like to. I sort of half promised Janice and Kitty – friends of mine – that we'd sail together.'

Denison was silent, not knowing what to say.

Lyn said, 'Don't be a spoilsport. Billy Brooks will put her in the water and I can rig her myself.'

'All right,' he said. 'But don't get into trouble. English waters aren't as calm as the Baltic. When are you intending going back?'

'I haven't made up my mind yet. I have to write to the girls and make plans, then I'll drop a line to Billy at the yard. You were going to get a new suit of sails two years ago – did you?'

'Yes.' He stood up quickly. 'Let's press on – it's quite late and I have to see someone at the hotel.'

'All very mysterious,' she said. 'What's the sudden appointment?' She grinned at him. 'It sounds rather like Wilde's excuse – "I must decline your invitation owing to a subsequent engagement." '

Had he been as transparent as that? He forced a smile, and said, 'It's just that I promised to have a drink before dinner with the Kidders, that's all.'

'Oh,' she said lightly. 'Then let's go. We mustn't keep the Kidders waiting.'

As they walked away Denison saw Armstrong rise from his bench and follow them. *What's the use of a bodyguard*? he thought. *The enemy is by my side and stabs with a sharp tongue*. More and more he was conscious of the injustice of the fraud he was perpetrating on Lyn Meyrick and he determined to see Carey and ask him to find a way of separation.

They got back to the hotel, and Lyn said, 'Do you mind if I come to your room?' She looked about the hotel lobby. 'There's something I want to talk to you about.'

'What?'

She pointed to the hotel entrance. 'Him, for one thing.' Denison looked around and saw Armstrong just coming in. 'He's been following us for the last two days.'

'He's supposed to,' said Denison. 'You might call him a bodyguard. If I go into the sauna again – which God forbid – he'll be in there with me.'

She said quietly, 'I think you'd better tell me what it's all about. There's a lot you're keeping from me. In your room?'

'All right,' he said resignedly. Then went up in the lift with three other people and Denison used the time to sort out what he was going to tell her – no lies but withholding most of the truth. He decided that a lot could be hidden behind the Official Secrets Act.

He unlocked the door and followed her in. 'What do you want to know, Lyn?'

'There's a big secret, isn't there?' She sat on the bed.

'Which I can't tell,' he answered. 'It's part of my work. Somebody had a go at me the other day so the Embassy sent that young fellow – he's called Armstrong, incidentally – to look after me. That's all.'

'No more?'

'Nothing you're entitled to know, Lyn. I'm sorry.' He spread his hands. 'I'm bound by the Official Secrets Act.'

Her face was drawn. 'I'm sorry, too, because it isn't enough.'

'My God, I *can't* tell you anything more. If I tattle about what I'm doing they'll assume I'm a bad security risk.' He laughed shortly. 'I'd never be allowed into my own factories – and that's the best that could happen. At the worst I could go to prison.' He sat on the bed next to her. 'It isn't that I don't trust you, Lyn; it's that if you knew what I know you'd be vulnerable. I don't want to put you in danger.'

She was silent for a while. Her face was troubled and her fingers plucked at the coverlet. She moistened her lips. 'I've been worried.'

'I know you have, but there's nothing to worry about. It's over, and Armstrong will see that it doesn't happen again.'

'It's not that I've been worrying about.'

'What, then?'

'Me,' she said. 'And you – principally you. There's something wrong somewhere.'

Denison felt his stomach churn. He said, 'There's nothing wrong with me. It's your imagination.'

It was as though she had not heard him. 'Nothing big – the big things were all right. It's the little things. Thread-Bear, for instance; how could you have forgotten Thread-Bear? And then there are the Kidders.'

'What about the Kidders?'

'Two years ago you'd have cut a man like that down to size in five words.' She looked at him steadily. 'You've changed. You've changed too much.'

'For the better, I hope,' said Denison, fighting a valiant rearguard action.

'I'd say so.' There was a slight waver in her voice. 'You're not nearly as hard to get on with.'

'I'm sorry if I gave you a bad time in the past,' said Denison soberly. 'As I said before: perhaps as I grow older I grow wiser.'

'It confused me,' she said. 'And I'm no different from anyone else; I don't like being confused. And I had a crazy idea – it was so crazy I thought I must be losing my mind.'

Denison opened his mouth but she covered it with her hand. 'No, don't speak. Let me sort it out myself. I don't want to be confused again.'

She took her hand away, and Denison said quietly, 'Go on, Lyn.'

'I found myself having strange thoughts about you.' She swallowed. 'The kind of thoughts a girl shouldn't have about her own father, and I felt ashamed. You were so *different*, you see; not like my father at all – and the change was too much. I tried to see how you'd changed and the only conclusion I could come to was that suddenly you'd become human.'

'Thanks,' said Denison.

'There's a bit of my old daddy come back,' she said vehemently. 'Oh, you could use irony and sarcasm like knife blades.'

'No irony intended,' said Denison sincerely.

'Then I saw the other things like Thread-Bear and the Kidders and the fact that you've stopped smoking. Look at your hands now – no nicotine at all. Then I got this wild idea.'

Denison stood up. 'Lyn, I think we'd better stop this now,' he said coldly. 'You're becoming hysterical.'

'No, we won't stop,' she shouted, and stood to face him. 'You knew all the works of Sibelius backwards and sideways, and why wouldn't you? You're a Finn! But this morning you only *thought* his work was for the orchestra. And I don't know about you – we've been parted for many years – but I've never been to Ibiza in my life and, to the best of my knowledge, you've never been to hospital with food poisoning.'

Denison was appalled. 'Lyn!'

She was merciless. 'There is no yacht called *Hesperia*. You always said that sailing is the most inefficient means of locomotion known to man, and everyone knows that efficiency is your god. And Billy Brooks doesn't exist – I invented him. And you said you'd bought a suit of sails for a non-existent yacht.'

Her face was white and her eyes brimmed with tears and Denison knew she was deathly frightened. 'You *can't* be my father,' she whispered. 'You're *not* my father. *Who are you*?'

CHAPTER TWENTY-TWO

'Where the hell is Denison?' said Carey irritably.

McCready was soothing. 'He'll be along. He's not very late.'

Carey was on edge. 'He could have been jumped again.'

'It's you that's jumpy. Armstrong's looking after him.'

Carey said nothing. He bent his head to re-read the lengthy cable. Presently he said, 'Well, that's cleared up. It was a hell of a problem while it lasted.'

'What was?' asked Harding interestedly.

'When Denison was lifted from the sauna he came out with a string of mathematical stuff to confuse the opposition. He didn't know what it meant himself but it was the jargon Meyrick might have used.' He tossed the cable on to the table. 'We couldn't see how Denison could possibly have known it.'

Harding said, 'It must have come out of his past somewhere.'

'Precisely,' said Carey. 'But he didn't have that kind of past.'

'Of course not.' Harding wrinkled his brow. 'He was a film director.'

'Of a special kind,' said McCready. 'He made documentaries. We found he'd done a series of educational films on mathematics for the public relations department of one of the big computer firms. I suppose a film director must have a working knowledge of his subject although, judging by some of the movies I've seen, you wouldn't think so. Anyway, somebody talked to the computer people and we find that not only did he have a ready grasp but a keen interest. The films were largely in cartoon style and the subject was probability theory. He knew the jargon, all right.'

'But it gave me a shudder at the time,' said Carey. 'Mrs Hansen, ring the hotel and find what's keeping Denison.'

Diana Hansen got up and crossed the room. She was about to pick up the telephone when it rang shrilly. She put it to her ear, then beckoned to Carey. 'For you – it's Armstrong.'

Carey took the telephone. 'Ian, what's the hold-up?'

'I was in my room,' said Armstrong. 'I had my door open so I could see the door of Denison's room. About twenty minutes ago Miss Meyrick busted out of there fast so I went into the corridor to find what was happening. She grabbed me and said Denison had had some kind of attack. I went into the room and found him on the floor, out cold. He came round about five minutes ago.'

'Is he all right now?'

'He says he is.'

'Then you'd better bring him along here,' said Carey. 'I'll have Harding have a look at him.'

There was a pause. 'Miss Meyrick says she's coming, too.'

'Nothing doing,' said Carey. 'Ditch her.'

'I don't think you understand,' said Armstrong. 'When she spoke to me in the corridor she said *Denison* had had an attack – not Meyrick.'

Carey's eyebrows crawled up his forehead. 'She *knows*?'

'Apparently so.'

'Bring her along and don't take your eyes off the pair of them. And be discreet.' He put down the telephone. 'The girl has caught on – and your patient is coming home to roost, Harding. He's had another of his thingummy attacks.'

'A fugue,' said Harding. 'It must have been the Meyrick girl.'

'She called him Denison,' said Carey flatly.

They waited for twenty minutes in silence. Carey produced his pipe and filled it, and then smoked jerkily. Harding stretched out his long legs and contemplated the tips of his shoes with an all-consuming interest. His forehead was creased into a frown. Diana Hansen smoked cigarettes one after the other, stubbing each out half-way down its length. McCready paced back and forward, wearing a groove in the carpet.

There was a tap at the door and everyone jerked to attention. McCready opened it, letting in Lyn and Denison, with Armstrong close behind. Carey stared at Denison. 'Harding would like a word with you in the other room. Do you mind?'

'No,' said Denison quietly, and followed Harding.

When the door closed behind them Carey stood up and said to Lyn, 'Miss Meyrick, my name is Carey and I'm from the British Embassy here. This is Mr McCready. Mrs Hansen you already know, and you've already met Mr Armstrong.'

Lyn Meyrick's face was pale but two pink spots deepened in her cheeks when she saw Diana Hansen. Then she flung out her arm at the door through which Denison had gone. 'Who is that man? And where is my father?'

'Please sit down,' said Carey, and nodded to McCready who brought up a chair.

'I don't understand,' said Lyn. 'He said his name was Denison and he told me an unbelievable story …'

'… which happens to be true,' said Carey. 'I wish it wasn't so.'

Lyn's voice rose. 'Then what's happened to my father?'

Carey wagged his eyebrows at Diana Hansen who stood up and went close to Lyn. He said, 'Miss Meyrick, I'm sorry to tell you this …'

'He's dead, isn't he?'

Carey nodded. 'We believe it to be an accident. His body was recovered from the Baltic three days ago. There had been a collision between an oil tanker and another ship.'

'Then what this man, Denison, said is correct?'

'What did he tell you?'

They listened as Lyn spoke and finally Carey nodded. 'He seems to have given you all that's relevant.' He noted that Denison had not told her of the contents of Merikken's papers; he had just said they were important. 'I'm sorry about your father.'

'Yes,' she said coldly. 'I suppose you are.'

Carey thought that she found no difficulty in holding back her grief but that might be understandable in the circumstances. He said deliberately, 'Miss Meyrick; after Denison had told you his story did you try to probe into his past?'

'Why, yes; I wanted to know who he was – who he is.'

'You must never do that again,' said Carey solemnly. 'It could be most dangerous for him.'

She flared up. 'If only a quarter of what he told me is true, what you're doing to that man is despicable. He ought to have psychiatric treatment.'

'He's getting that now,' said Carey. 'Dr Harding is a psychiatrist. How did Denison give himself away?' She told him and he nodded. 'We couldn't hope to get away with it for ever,' he said philosophically. 'But I did hope for another day. I was going to separate you tomorrow.'

'My God!' she said. 'Who the hell do you think you are? We're not chess pieces.'

'Denison is a volunteer,' said Carey. 'It's his own choice.'

'Some choice!' she said cuttingly.

The door behind Carey opened. He swung around in his chair and saw Harding alone. 'Ian, go and sit with Denison.'

'It won't be necessary,' said Harding. 'He'll be out in a minute. I've just given him something to think about.'

'How is he?'

'He'll be all right.'

'Does he remember spilling the beans to Miss Meyrick?'

'Oh, yes,' said Harding. 'It's just that he can't remember what Miss Meyrick was asking him just before he passed out.' He looked at Lyn with interest. 'What was it?'

'I wanted to know who he was,' Lyn said.

He shook his head. 'Don't try that again. I think I'll have to have a talk with you, young lady.'

'Don't bother,' said Carey grimly. 'She's going back to England.'

Lyn inspected Harding with a cold eye. 'Are you a doctor?'

Harding paused as he lit a cigarette. 'Among other things.'

'I think you must have been confused when you took the oath,' she said. 'You took the hypocritic oath instead of the Hippocratic oath.' Harding coloured but before he could answer she had rounded on

Carey. 'As for going to England, I most certainly am. A lot of people will be very interested in what I have to tell them.'

'Oh, I wouldn't try that,' said Carey quietly.

'Try to stop me,' she challenged.

Carey leaned back in his chair and glanced at McCready. 'It looks as though we'll have to keep her here, George. Arrange the necessary – booking her out of the hotel and so on.'

'And then what?' she asked. 'You can't keep me here for ever. I'll be back in England some time and I'll make sure the story gets around about what's been happening to this man. It will make interesting reading.'

McCready smiled. 'The papers won't print it. There's a thing called a "D" notice.'

She looked at him contemptuously. 'Do you think twenty universities full of students will take any account of your stupid "D" notices?' she asked in scorn.

'My God!' said McCready. 'She's right. You know what students are like.'

'So what are you going to do?' she asked interestedly. 'Kill me?'

'They're going to do nothing,' said Denison from behind Carey. He closed the door behind him. 'Or they'll have to get themselves another boy.'

Carey did not turn round. He merely said, 'Draw up a chair, Denison. We have a problem to solve.'

Denison sat next to Carey. 'Coercion won't solve it.'

'So I'm finding out,' said Carey caustically. 'So maybe we'll try persuasion. What exactly is it you want, Miss Meyrick?'

She was suddenly nervous. 'I want you to stop whatever it is you're doing to … to him.' Her hand trembled as she pointed at Denison.

'We're not doing anything to him. He's a volunteer – and he'll confirm it.'

She flared. 'How can he be a volunteer when he doesn't know who he is? Any court of law would toss out that argument.'

'Careful,' said Harding suddenly, watching Denison.

'He needs help,' she pleaded.

'He's getting it,' said Carey, and indicated Harding.

'You already know what I think of that.'

'Tell me something,' said Carey. 'Why are you so agitated about Denison? He is, after all, a stranger.'

She looked down at the table. 'Not any more,' she said in a low voice. She raised her head and regarded Carey with clear eyes. 'And aren't we supposed to care for strangers? Have you never heard of the parable of the Good Samaritan, Mr Carey?'

Carey sighed, and said dispiritedly, 'See what you can do, Giles.'

Denison opened his mouth and then closed it again. It was the first time Carey had addressed him by his Christian name, as he normally did with Armstrong and McCready. Was he now accepted as a member of the team, or was it just that the cunning old devil had decided to use psychology?

He looked across the table at the girl. 'I know what I'm doing, Lyn – and this operation is very important.'

'How can you know what you're doing?' she demanded. 'You're not competent to judge.'

'That's just what he is,' interjected Carey. 'Sorry, Giles; carry on.'

'That's not the point,' said Denison. 'It wasn't of my own free will that I was pitched into the middle of all this, but now that I'm in it I agree with Carey. If the operation is to be a success then I must continue to be Meyrick – to be your father. And that I'm going to do, regardless of what you think. I appreciate your concern, but this is too important for considerations like that.'

She was silent, biting her lip. She said, 'All right, Har … Giles. But on one condition.'

'What's that?'

'That I come with you – as Lyn Meyrick with her father.' There was a dead silence around the table, 'Well, isn't that what you wanted – for the masquerade to go on? You've used me unknowingly – now you can use me knowingly.'

Carey said softly, 'It might be dangerous.'

'So is having a father like Harry Meyrick,' she said bitterly. 'But that's my condition – take it or leave it.'

'Taken,' said Carey promptly.

'No!' said Denison simultaneously.

They stopped and looked at each other. 'She's stubborn,' said Carey. 'And she's got us by the short hairs. It's the answer.'

'Are you sure?' asked Denison. He might have been replying to Carey but he looked at Lyn.

'I'm sure,' she said.

'Well, that's it,' said Carey briskly. 'Now we can get on with the planning. Thank you, Dr Harding; I don't think we'll need you on this. I'll keep in touch with you.'

Harding stood up and nodded. He was walking to the door when Lyn said, 'No!' Her voice was sharp.

Harding stopped. 'No *what*?' said Carey exasperatedly.

'Dr Harding stays with Giles,' she said. 'The three of us stay together.'

'For Christ's sake!' said Carey, and a suppressed snort came from McCready.

Harding had a white smile. 'My dear Miss Meyrick; I'm hardly … I'm no … no …'

'No gunman, like the rest of them probably are? Well, let me tell you something. You won't be worth a damn as a psychiatrist unless you stay with your patient.'

Harding flushed again. Carey said, 'Impossible!'

'What's so impossible about it?' Lyn looked at Harding speculatively. 'But I'm willing to leave it to the doctor – and his conscience, if he has one. What about it, Dr Harding?'

Harding rubbed his lean jaw. 'Insofar as it will help Denison I'm willing to stay. But I warn you – I'm no man of action.'

'That's it, then,' said Lyn, parodying Carey.

Carey looked at her helplessly, and McCready said, 'It might not be a bad idea if the doctor is willing, as he seems to be.'

Carey gave up. 'Sit down, Harding,' he said ungraciously.

As he picked up his briefcase Denison murmured, 'You did say by the short hairs, didn't you?'

Carey ignored him and opened the briefcase. 'I have reason to believe that quite a lot of people are interested in the movements of Dr Meyrick. We're going to give them some movements to watch.'

He spread out a large map of Finland. 'George will fly to Ivalo, in Northern Lapland –' his finger stabbed down – 'here. That's as far north as you can fly in Finland. There'll be a car waiting and he'll drive still farther north to this place up by the Norwegian border – *Kevon Tutkimusasema* – that's a station for the exploration of the Kevo Nature Preserve, the jumping off place, as you might call it.'

He looked up at McCready. 'Your job is to cover the party from the outside. You'll inspect Kevo Camp, make sure it's clean – and I don't mean in the hygienic sense – and you'll keep an eye on the party all the time it's up there. But you won't acknowledge it – you'll be a stranger. Understand?'

'Got it,' said McCready.

'Denison and Mrs Hansen – and now, of course, Miss Meyrick and Dr Harding will travel by car from Helsinki. You will leave early tomorrow and it will take you two days to get to the camp at Kevo. George will already be there but you *don't* recognize him. He's your trump card should you get into trouble.' Carey's finger moved slightly south. 'You will then explore the Kevo Nature Park. It's rough country and you'll need packs and tents.' He wagged a finger at McCready. 'We'll need extra gear; see to it, George.'

'What's the point of all this?' asked Denison.

Carey straightened. 'From my reading of Meyrick's dossier and from what I know of his character he never did take an interest in natural history. Is that correct, Miss Meyrick?'

'He was a pure technologist,' she said. 'If he ever thought of natural history – which I doubt – it would be with contempt.'

'As I thought,' said Carey. 'So if Meyrick becomes interested now it will be out of character. The people who are watching him – as I am certain they are – will be mystified and will suspect an ulterior motive, which I will be careful to provide.' He tapped Denison's arm. 'You'll take some simple instruments – a theodolite and so on – and you'll act out a charade as though you're looking for something. Got the idea?'

'A red herring,' said Denison.

'Right. You'll spend three days at Kevo and then you'll move south to another Nature Park at Sompio. There you will put on the same act until you're recalled.'

'How will that be done?' asked McCready.

'There's a little village called Vuotso just outside. I'll send you a telegram to *poste restante* – "Come home, all is forgiven." It would be useful to have webbed feet at Sompio – it's very marshy.'

'Then there'll be wildfowl,' said Harding with sudden enthusiasm.

'Very likely,' said Carey uninterestedly.

'Let me get this straight,' said Denison. 'Meyrick is supposed to be looking for something – let's say buried – in a Nature Park, but he doesn't know which one. And all he has to go on are landmarks, hence the theodolite for measuring angles.'

'Just like in a treasure hunt,' said Lyn.

'Precisely,' said Carey. 'But the treasure doesn't exist – at least, not up there. I've even got a map for you. It's as phoney as hell but very impressive.'

Denison said, 'And what will you be doing while we're wandering all over the Arctic?'

Carey grinned. 'Young Ian and I will nip into Svetogorsk to dig up the loot while, hopefully, all eyes are on you.' He turned to Mrs Hansen. 'You're very quiet.'

She shrugged. 'What's there to say?'

'You'll be bodyguarding this lot from the inside. I had hoped you'd have but one person to worry about but, as you see, there are now three. Can you manage?'

'If they'll do as they're told.'

'They'd better,' said Carey. 'I'll give you something a bit bigger than the popgun you so incautiously let Denison see.' He looked about. 'Can anyone else here shoot?'

'I'm not bad with a shotgun,' said Harding.

'I doubt if a shotgun in a Nature Preserve would be appreciated,' said Carey ironically. 'But at least you'll know one end of a gun from the other. I'll let you have a pistol. What about you, Giles?'

Denison shrugged. 'I suppose I can pull the trigger and make the thing go bang.'

'That might be all that's needed.' Carey looked at Lyn, appeared to be about to say something, and changed his mind.

'Are you expecting shooting?' asked Harding. He looked worried.

'Let me put it this way,' said Carey. 'I don't know if there'll be shooting or not, but if there is, I hope you'll be on the receiving end and not me, because that's the object of this bloody exercise.' He put the map back into his briefcase. 'That's all. Early start tomorrow. George, I'd like a word with you before you go.'

The group at the table broke up. Denison went across to Lyn. 'Harding told me about your father. I'm sorry.'

'No need,' she said. 'I ought to feel sorry, too, but I can't.' She looked up at him. 'Carey said you are a stranger, but it's my father who was the stranger. I hadn't seen him for two years and when I thought I'd found him again, and he was different and nicer, I hadn't found him at all. So then I lost him again and it made no difference, after all. Don't you see what I mean?'

Denison followed this incoherent speech, and said, 'I think so.' He took her by the shoulders. 'I don't think you should come on this jaunt, Lyn.'

Her chin came up. 'I'm coming.'

He sighed. 'I hope you know what you've got yourself into.'

Carey filled his pipe. 'What do you think, George?'

'The girl's a bit of a handful.'

'Yes. Look after them as best you can.'

McCready leaned forward. 'It's you I'm worried about. I've been thinking about Meyrick. If the people who snatched him were the Russkies, and if he talked, you're in dead trouble. You're likely to find a reception committee awaiting you in Svetogorsk.'

Carey nodded. 'It's a calculated risk. There were no signs of physical coercion on Meyrick's body – burn marks or anything like that – and I doubt if he'd talk voluntarily. I don't think they had time to make him talk; they were too busy smuggling him around the Baltic. In any case, we don't know who snatched him.'

He struck a match. 'It's my back I'm worried about right now. I had a talk to Lyng last night on the Embassy scrambler. I told him that Thornton was nosing about. He said he'd do something about it.'

'What?'

Carey shrugged. 'They don't use guns in Whitehall but I believe they have weapons that are equally effective. It's no concern of yours, George; you won't have to worry about the Whitehall War until you get up to my level.'

'I'm not so worried about Whitehall as I am about Svetogorsk,' said McCready. 'I think it ought to be swapped around. Armstrong can go north and I'll come with you across the border.'

'He doesn't have the experience for what might happen up there. He's yet to be blooded, but he'll be all right with an old dog like me.'

'He'd be all right with me,' said McCready. 'He and I could cross the border and you could go up north.'

'Sorry,' said Carey regretfully. 'But I'm pushing sixty and I don't have the puff for that wilderness lark. And I don't have the reflexes for the fast action you might get. The plan stands, George.' His voice took on a meditative note. 'This is likely to be my last field operation. I'd like it to be a good one.'

CHAPTER TWENTY-THREE

The car slowed as it came to the corner. Harding, who was driving, said, 'This might be the turn-off. Check it on the map, will you?'

Denison, in the back of the car, lifted the map from his knee. 'That's it; we've just passed Kaamanen. The Kevo Camp is eighty kilometres up this side road and there's damn-all else.' He checked his watch. 'We ought to arrive before eleven.'

Harding turned on to the side road and the car lurched and bumped. After a few minutes he said, 'Make that midnight. We're not going to move fast on this road.'

Diana laughed. 'The Finns are the only people who could coin a word like *kelirikko*. It's a word Humpty-Dumpty would be proud of.'

Harding notched down a gear. 'What does it mean?'

'It means, "the bad state of the roads after the spring thaw".'

'Much in little,' said Harding. 'There's one thing I'm glad of.'

'What's that?'

'This midnight sun. I'd hate to drive along here in the dark.'

Denison glanced at Lyn who sat by his side. She was apparently asleep. It had been two days of hard driving, very tiring, and he was looking forward to his bed. He wound the window down to clear the dust from the outside surface, then looked at the countryside covered with scrub birch. Something suddenly caught him in the pit of the stomach. *What the hell am I doing here? Hundreds of miles north of the Arctic Circle in the Finnish wilderness?* It seemed preposterously improbable.

They had left Helsinki very early the previous morning and headed north out of the heavily populated southern coastal rim. Then they had left the rich farmlands very quickly and entered a region of forests and lakes, of towering pine and spruce, of white-trunked, green-leaved birch and the ever-present blue waters.

They took it in turns driving in two-hour shifts and made good time, sleeping that night in Oulu. After Oulu the land changed. There were fewer lakes and the trees were not as tall. A birch that in the south towered a hundred feet now had hardly the strength to grow to twenty, and the lakes gave way to marshes. As they passed through Ivalo, where there was the northernmost airstrip, they encountered their first Lapps, garish in red and blue, but there were really very few people of any kind in this country. Denison, under the prodding of Carey, had done his homework on Finland and he knew that in this most remote area of the country, Inari Commune, there were fewer than 8,000 people in a province the size of Yorkshire.

And there would be fewer still around Kevo.

Diana stretched, and said, 'Stop at the top of the next rise, Doctor; I'll spell you.'

'I'm all right,' said Harding.

'Stop anyway.'

He drove up the hill and was about to pull up when Diana said, 'Just a few yards more – over the crest.' Harding obligingly let the car roll and then braked to a halt. 'That's fine,' she said, taking binoculars from a case. 'I won't be a minute.'

Denison watched her leave the car and then opened his own door. He followed her back along the road and then into a growth of stunted birches. When he caught up with her she was looking back the way they had come through the glasses. 'Anything in sight?'

'No,' she said curtly.

'You've done this every hour,' he said. 'And you've still seen nothing. Nobody's following us.'

'They might be ahead,' she said without taking the glasses from her eyes.

'How would anyone know where we were going?'

'There are ways and means.' She lowered the glasses and looked at him. 'You don't know much about this business.'

'No, I don't,' Denison said reflectively. 'What's a nice girl like you doing in it? You're American, aren't you?'

She slung the binocular strap over her shoulder. 'Canadian. And it's just a job.'

'Just a civil servant,' he said ironically. 'Like any nine-to-five typist in Whitehall.' He remembered the occupation given in Meyrick's passport. 'Or like Dr Meyrick.'

She faced him. 'Let's get one thing straight. From now on you do not refer to Meyrick in the third person – not even in private.' She tapped him on the chest with her forefinger. 'You are Harry Meyrick.'

'You've made your point, teacher.'

'I hope so.' She looked around. 'This seems a quiet spot. How long is it since you've seen anyone?'

He frowned. 'About an hour. Why?'

'I want to find out how much you lot know about guns. Target practice time.' As they went back to the car, she said, 'Go easy on Lyn Meyrick. She's a very confused girl.'

'I know,' said Denison. 'She has every reason to be confused.'

Diana looked at him sideways. 'Yes,' she agreed. 'You could call it confusion – of a sort. It's not easy to fall in love with a man who looks like the father you hate, but she's managed it.'

Denison stopped dead. 'Don't be idiotic.'

'Me!' She laughed. 'You do a bit of thinking and then figure who's the idiot around here.'

Harding pulled the car off the road and into the trees. Diana loaded a pistol from a packet of cartridges and set an empty beer can on a fallen tree trunk. 'All right; let's see who can do this.' Almost casually she lifted her arm and fired. The beer can jumped and spun away.

They took it in turns to fire three shots each. Denison missed every time, Harding hit the can once and Lyn, much to her own surprise, hit it twice. Diana said to Denison caustically, 'You were right; you can make the gun go bang.'

To Lyn she said, 'Not bad – but what would you be like shooting at a man instead of a beer can?'

'I ... I don't know,' said Lyn nervously.

'What about you, Doctor?'

Harding hefted the gun in his hand. 'If I was being shot at I think I'd shoot back.'

'I suppose that's as much as I could expect,' said Diana resignedly. 'Let's go back to the car.'

She gave them each a pistol and watched them load. 'Don't forget to put on the safety catch. More important, don't forget to release it when you shoot. You'll put those in your bedrolls now. When we move off on foot tomorrow you'll need a more accessible place for them. Let's go.'

CHAPTER TWENTY-FOUR

Carey lit his pipe and said, 'Slow down.'

Armstrong eased his foot on the accelerator and hastily wound down his side window. He wished Carey would not smoke at all in the car or, at least, change his brand of horse manure.

'See that tower over there?' asked Carey. 'To the right.'

Armstrong looked past him. 'A water tower?' he hazarded.

Carey grunted in amusement. 'A Russian observation tower. That's Mother Russia.'

'We're *that* close to the frontier! It can't be more than a kilometre away.'

'That's right,' said Carey. 'You can turn round now; we'll go back to Imatra and book into the hotel.'

Armstrong came to a wide part of the road and slowed to a halt. As he turned the car, he said, 'Are there many of those towers around here?'

'All along the frontier. I suspect they're linked with electronic detection devices. The boys in those towers can record every footfall.' He looked at the spindly tower with a critical eye. 'The Russians have a suspicious nature – always trying to look over other people's walls. They're a funny crowd.'

Armstrong was silent, but his mind was busy with speculation. The trouble with Carey was that he was uncommunicative about his plans until the last moment, an idiosyncrasy apt to unnerve his subordinates. He wondered how they were going to cross the border.

He drove back into Imatra under Carey's direction and pulled up outside the entrance to the hotel. It was a big, rambling building constructed of stone with turrets and cupolas and towers. He thought it looked like a fairy tale castle as designed by Walt Disney had he been a more controlled artist. 'Some place!'

'The Valtionhotelli,' said Carey. 'Built at the turn of the century and genuine Art Noveau. Come on.'

The hotel foyer was elaborately luxurious in an old-fashioned style. The stonework of the entrance was carved with grotesque mythological beasts and was panelled in dark wood. They registered and entered a lift accompanied by a porter carrying the bags.

The porter unlocked a door and stood back deferentially. Carey strode in, followed by Armstrong. He led the way along a wood-panelled corridor into a very large circular bedroom. 'I'll take the bed on the left,' he said as he tipped the porter.

Armstrong looked about him. 'Not bad. Not bad at all.'

'Nothing but the best for us civil servants,' said Carey. 'Let's go upstairs and have a drink.'

'There's an upstairs?'

They climbed a broad winding staircase leading off the corridor. Carey said, 'This hotel was built back in 1902 when Finland was still a part of Russia. The Finns will give you arguments that it was ever a part of Russia, but facts are facts. Imatra was a playground for the St Petersburg aristocracy. The Czar stayed in the hotel – probably in this apartment.'

They emerged into another large circular room with windows all around. It was furnished with half a dozen easy-chairs and a long, low table of highly polished wood. A bear skin decorated the wall. Carey strode over to a built-in refrigerator while Armstrong looked through one of the windows. 'We must be at the top of the main tower.'

'That's right.' Carey pulled out a bottle. 'Skåne – that's Swedish; Linie – it's funny the Norwegians think that shipping their booze to Australia and back improves it. Koskenkorva – that's local. Stolichnaya – what the hell is that doing here? I call it damned unpatriotic. Ah, here's the beer.'

Armstrong turned and looked at the array of *snaps* bottles. 'Are we expected to be poured into Russia?'

Carey winked. 'The perquisites of the job. Besides, we might have to do a little entertaining.'

'Oh!' He held out field glasses he had found on a window ledge. 'Someone must have left these behind.'

Carey shook his head as he uncapped a beer bottle. 'Part of the room fittings. This apartment is where they bring the V.I.P.s to give them a little thrill.' He picked up a glass and joined Armstrong at the window. 'See those chimneys?'

Armstrong looked out of the window at the smoking factory chimneys. 'Yes?'

'That's Stalin's Finger,' said Carey. 'Svetogorsk!'

Armstrong put the binoculars to his eyes. The chimneys jumped closer and he could almost distinguish the separate bricks. 'My God!' he said. 'It's nearly part of Imatra.' He stared for a long time then slowly lowered the glasses. 'What did you say about Stalin?'

'Stalin's Finger – that's the local name. After the war the Russians wanted the frontier pushed back so there was the usual conference. Svetogorsk – or Enso, as it was then – is quite a nice little industrial town making paper. One of the Russians was drawing the revised frontier with a pen on the map but when he got to Enso he found that Stalin had put his finger in the way. He looked up at Stalin and Stalin smiled down on him, so he shrugged and drew the line around Stalin's finger. That put Enso in Russia.'

'The old bastard!' said Armstrong.

'Sit down and have a beer,' said Carey. 'I want to talk to you about procedure. I'll just nip down and get my briefcase.'

Armstrong took a beer from the refrigerator. When Carey came back he indicated the bear skin on the wall. 'Could that be a Russian bear with its hide nailed to the wall?'

'It could,' said Carey with a grim smile. 'That's part of what I want to talk to you about.' He put the briefcase on the table and sat down. 'As far as I'm concerned Svetogorsk is Svetogorsk – I'm a realist. But we'll be talking to some Finns and we'll refer to the town throughout as Enso. They're a mite sensitive about it.'

'I can understand that,' said Armstrong.

'You don't know the half of it,' said Carey flatly. 'This has been my stamping ground all the time I've been in the service, so listen to some words of wisdom from the old man. Back in 1835 a man called Lönrot gathered together a lot of folk tales and issued them in verse form – that was the Kalevela, the Finnish national epic. It was the first major literary work the Finns ever had of their own, and it formed the basis of the new Finnish culture.'

'Interesting,' said Armstrong. 'But what the hell?'

'Just listen,' said Carey sharply. 'The heartland of the Kalevela is Karelia – which is now in Russia. The village of Kalevela itself is now Russian.' He rubbed the side of his nose. 'There's no exact English parallel, but it's as though the French had occupied Cornwall and Nottinghamshire and taken over all the King Arthur and Robin Hood legends. Of course, it runs deeper than that here, and some Finns are bitter about it.'

'They think the Russians pinched their national heritage?'

'Something like that.' Carey drained his glass. 'Now to politics. After the war President Paasikivi adopted a foreign policy that was new to Finland, and the idea was to remain strictly neutral, rather like Sweden. In actual practice it's a neutrality in favour of Russia – at all costs no offence must be given to Big Brother in the east. This is known as the Paasikivi Line, and it's followed by the current President, Kekkonen. It's like walking a tightrope but it's difficult to see what else Finland can do. They already have the example of what happened to Estonia and the other Baltic States.'

He got himself another beer. 'We're going to meet some Finns tonight who don't agree with the Paasikivi Line. They're Right Wingers and, personally, I'd call them bloody reactionaries, but they're the boys who are going to get us into Enso. If Kekkonen knew what we were doing here, what little hair he has left would turn white. He's getting on with the Russians reasonably well and he wants it to stay that way. He doesn't want any incident on the frontier that could cause a diplomatic breach and give Moscow an excuse for making demands. Neither do we – so to the Finns we meet tonight we talk softly, and when we're in Enso we walk softly.'

He fixed Armstrong with a firm eye. 'And if we're caught over there we've done it on our own hook – no Finns were involved. That's bloody important, so keep it in mind.'

'I understand,' said Armstrong soberly.

'Of course, the whole idea is *not* to get caught.' Carey unzipped his briefcase. 'Here is a street plan of Enso, dated 1939.' He unfolded it and spread it on the table. His finger wandered over the surface and then went down. 'This is the house in which Hannu Merikken lived. He buried his box full of papers in the garden which is something under half an acre – but not much under.'

Armstrong bent his head over the plan. 'That's quite an area. How big is the box?'

'Meyrick described it as two feet by one-and-a-half by one.'

Armstrong did some mental arithmetic. 'If we dug a hole at random the chances against hitting it would be over eight hundred to one.'

'We can do better than that,' said Carey. 'The original idea was to have Meyrick point out the spot – he was present when the box was buried. But after all these years his memory had slipped a few cogs.' He dipped into the briefcase again. 'All he could come up with was this.'

Armstrong examined the large scale plan which was drawn meticulously in Indian ink. Carey said, 'There are four trees and the box is buried under one of them but he couldn't remember which one.'

'At least that's cutting it down to a maximum of four holes.'

'1944 is a long time ago,' said Carey. 'Three of the trees are no longer there. Look at these.' He produced some photographs. 'These were taken by our Finnish friends about three weeks ago.' As Armstrong looked at them, Carey said, 'I had hoped that taking Meyrick back would jog his memory, but we don't have Meyrick any more, so what we're left with is half an acre of ground and one tree.' He peered over Armstrong's shoulder and pointed. 'I think that's the one, but I'm not sure.'

'So we dig,' said Armstrong. 'It will have to be done under cover of darkness.'

Carey stared at him. 'What darkness? I know we're not in the Arctic Circle, but even so, there's precious little darkness at this time of year. The most we'll get is a deep twilight.'

'Do we have to jump in now?' asked Armstrong. 'Why not wait until later in the year?'

Carey sighed. 'Apart from the fact that these papers are of overwhelming importance, there's one very good reason why we have to go in now.' He tapped the street plan. 'When Merikken was living in this house it was in a good class suburb. But Enso has been expanding, the area has become run-down, and it's due for redevelopment. The bulldozers will be moving in before the autumn. We've got to get in first.'

'A pity Meyrick didn't make his great discovery a year earlier,' commented Armstrong. 'Anyone living in the house?'

'Yes; a Russian called Kunayev – he's a foreman in one of the paper mills. A wife and three children; one cat – no dogs.'

'So we just go along and start to dig holes all over his garden in broad daylight. He's going to like that!' Armstrong tossed down the photograph. 'It's impossible!'

Carey was unperturbed. 'Nothing is impossible, my lad. To begin with, the papers are in a tin trunk. That's a misnomer – a tin trunk is made of sheet steel and I have a natty metal detector, small but efficient.'

'Like a mine detector?'

'Something like that, but smaller. Small enough for us to take over the border without much risk. I had it specially made up. According to Meyrick's dicey memory there's not much more than two feet of earth on top of the box. I've tested this gadget with a similar box and even three feet under it gives a signal that blasts your eardrums.'

'So we get the signal and start to dig. What's Kunayev going to be doing while this is happening?'

Carey grinned. 'With a bit of luck he won't be there. The comrade will be toiling like a Stakhanovite in his bloody mill, reeling up the toilet paper, or whatever it is he does.'

'His wife will be there,' objected Armstrong. 'And his kids – and probably the next-door neighbours.'

'It won't matter. We'll take them all by the hand and lead them right up that bloody garden path.'

CHAPTER TWENTY-FIVE

The meeting with the Finns took place that night in a house on the outskirts of Imatra. 'There are three of them,' said Carey, as they drove towards the rendezvous. 'Lassi Virtanen and his son, Tarmo, and Heikki Huovinen.'

Armstrong giggled, perhaps more out of nervous tension than anything else. 'I never thought I'd meet the Son of Lassie.'

'If you have any more remarks like that left in your system bottle them up until this operation is over,' said Carey grittily. 'This particular crowd doesn't have a strong sense of humour. Old Virtanen was a fighter pilot during the war and he still reckons it's a bad thing the Germans lost. I still don't know which is topmost in him – the Nazi sympathizer or the Russian-hater – probably a fifty-fifty mixture of both. He's brought up his son in his own image. Huovinen is a shade more liberal, but still well to the right of Atilla the Hun. These are the tools we have to work with and I don't want them turning in my hand. Remember that.'

'I'll remember,' said Armstrong. He felt as thought Carey had suddenly thrown a bucket of ice water over him. 'What's the scheme?'

'The Finns are expert paper makers,' said Carey. 'And the Russians are quite willing to take advantage of their expertise. They're building a new paper mill in Enso; all the machinery is Finnish and the installation is done by Finns, most of whom live in Imatra. They go over the border every day.'

A great light broke on Armstrong. 'And we go with them. How convenient.'

Carey grunted. 'Don't shout too soon. It won't be as easy as all that.' He pointed. 'There's the house.'

Armstrong drew the car to a halt. 'Do these three go over to Enso?'

'That's it.'

Armstrong thought for a moment. 'If the Virtanens hate the Russians so much why do they help them build paper factories?'

'They belong to a half-baked secret society – very right wing, of course. They fondly believe they're spying and preparing for *Der Tag*.' Carey shrugged. 'It's my belief they're at the end of their rope and the government is going to hang them with it. One of the troubles with the Paasikivi Line is keeping to the middle ground between right and left. The government can't crack down too hard on the communists because of Russian pressure, but who the hell cares what happens to a lot of neo-Nazis? They're only left loose as a makeweight on the other end of the political see-saw, but if they get out of line they get the chop. So let's use them while we can.'

Lassi Virtanen was a hard-faced man in his middle-fifties who walked with a limp. His son, Tarmo, was about thirty and did not look much like his father; he was fresh-faced and his eyes sparkled with excitement. Armstrong measured him carefully and thought he would be too excitable to be relied on for anything important. Heikki Huovinen was dark with a blue chin. To look respectable he would have to shave twice a day but, to Armstrong's eye, he seemed not to have shaved for two days.

They sat around a table on which there was an array of dishes, the open sandwiches of Scandinavia. There were also a dozen bottles of beer and two bottles of a colourless spirit. They sampled the herring and then the elder Virtanen filled small glasses with the spirit, and raised his glass slightly. '*Kippis!*' His arm went up and he threw the contents of his glass down his throat.

Armstrong took his cue from Carey and did the same. The fierce spirit bit the back of his throat and burned in his belly. Carey put down his empty glass. 'Not bad,' he said. 'Not bad at all.' He spoke in Swedish for the benefit of Armstrong. Finding Finnish speakers for the Service was the very devil and it was fortunate that Swedish was the second language of Finland.

Tarmo Virtanen laughed. 'It's from the other side.'

'Their vodka is the only good thing about the Russians,' said Lassi Virtanen grudgingly. He refilled the glasses. 'Heikki is worried.'

'Oh!' Carey looked at Huovinen. 'What about?'

'It's not going to be easy,' said Huovinen.

'Of course it'll be easy,' said Lassi. 'Nothing to it.'

'It's all right for you,' said Huovinen. 'You won't be there. It's me who has to come up with all the explanations and excuses.' He turned to Carey. 'It can't be done for three days.'

'Why not?'

'You and your friend, here, are taking the place of the Virtanens – right? Well, the Virtanens have got work to do over there – I know, I'm their damned foreman. Tomorrow Lassi is working on the screening plates, but Tarmo hasn't much to do and he wouldn't be missed. The day after that Tarmo will be busy. The only time I can spare them both without too many questions being asked will be the day after, and even then I'll have to tell a hell of a lot of lies.'

Carey thought Huovinen was getting cold feet but not by any sign did he show it. He said, 'What about it, Lassi?'

'It's true enough – as far as it goes – but it doesn't have to be that way. Heikki, you could fix things so that no one works on the screens tomorrow. A little bit of sabotage?'

'Not with that Georgian bastard, Dzotenidze, breathing down my neck,' said Huovinen heatedly.

'Who's he?' asked Carey.

'The Chief Engineer for the Russians. He'll be Chief Engineer of the mill when it gets working, and he wants everything right. He watches me like a hawk.'

'No sabotage,' said Carey flatly. 'I want things to go right, too.'

Huovinen nodded vigorously. 'In three days,' he said. 'Then I can conveniently lose the Virtanens.'

Carey said, 'We'll come here in the evening the day after tomorrow. We'll spend the night here and we'll leave in the morning just as the

Virtanens would. Won't the rest of the crew be surprised at a couple of strangers joining in?'

'That's taken care of. They may be surprised, but they won't talk.' Huovinen drew himself up. 'They're Finns,' he said proudly. 'They're Karelians.'

'And you're a foreman.'

Huovinen smiled. 'That's got something to do with it, too.'

Carey regarded Lassi and Tarmo Virtanen. 'And you two will stay in the house that day and you won't go out. We don't want anyone asking questions about how in hell can you be in Imatra and Enso at the same time.'

Young Virtanen laughed and tapped the bottle of vodka. 'Leave us plenty of this and we won't go out.'

Carey frowned, and Lassi said, 'We'll stay in the house.'

'Very well. Did you get the clothing?'

'It's all here.'

Carey took two folded cards from his pocket. 'These are our passes – will you check them?'

Huovinen picked them up and studied them. He took out his own pass for comparison, then said, 'These are very good; very good, indeed. But they look new – they're too clean.'

'We'll dirty them,' said Carey.

Huovinen shrugged. 'It doesn't really matter. The frontier guards have got tired of looking at passes. You'll be all right.'

'I hope so,' said Carey drily.

Lassi Virtanen picked up his glass. 'That's settled. I don't know exactly what you're doing over there, Mr Englishman, but I know it will do *Ryssä* no good. *Kippis!*' He knocked back his vodka.

Carey and Armstrong both drank and immediately Virtanen replenished their glasses. Armstrong looked about the room and saw a photograph on the sideboard. He tipped his chair back to get a closer look and Lassi, following his gaze, laughed and got up. 'That's from the Continuation War,' he said. 'I had fire in my belly in those days.'

He passed the photograph over to Armstrong. It showed a much younger Lassi Virtanen standing next to a fighter aircraft decorated with the swastika insignia. 'My Messerschmitt,' said Virtanen proudly. 'I shot down six Russian bastards in that plane.'

'Did you?' said Armstrong politely.

'Those were the good days,' said Virtanen. 'But what an air force we had. Any aircraft that had been built anywhere in the world – we had it. American Brewsters and Curtis Hawks, British Blenheims and Gladiators, German Fokkers and Dorniers, Italian Fiats, French Moranc-Saulniers – even Russian Polikarpovs. The Germans captured some of those in the Ukraine and sent them to us. Unreliable bastards they were, too. What a crazy, mixed-up air force we had – but we still held the Russians off until the end.'

He slapped his leg. 'I got mine in '44 – shot down near Raisala and it took four of them to do it. That was behind the lines but I walked out with a bullet in my leg, dodging those damned Russian patrols. Good days those were. Drink up!'

It was late before Carey and Armstrong were able to leave because they had to listen to a monologue from Virtanen about his war experiences, interspersed with glasses of vodka. But at last they got away. Armstrong got behind the wheel of the car and looked eloquently at Carey. 'I know,' said Carey heavily. 'Drunken and unreliable. I'm not surprised they're getting nowhere.'

'That man lives in the past,' said Armstrong.

'There's a lot like him in England – men who've never really lived since the war. Never mind the Virtanens – they're staying here. It's Huovinen we have to rely on to get to the other side.'

'He was packing the stuff away as though he wanted to start a drought in vodka,' said Armstrong dispiritedly.

'I know – but they're all we've got.' Carey took out his pipe. 'I wonder how McCready and company are doing up north. They can't be doing worse than we are.'

CHAPTER TWENTY-SIX

'I'm tired,' said Harding. 'But I don't think I'll sleep.'

Denison inspected the narrow patch of ground for stones before he unrolled his sleeping bag. He flicked an offender aside and said, 'Why not?'

'I can't get used to broad daylight in the middle of the night.'

Denison grinned. 'Why don't you prescribe yourself a sleeping pill?'

'I might do that.' Harding picked a blade of grass and chewed it. 'How are you sleeping these days?'

'Not bad.'

'Dream much?'

'Not that I can remember. Why?'

Harding smiled. 'I'm your resident head-watcher appointed by that chit over there.' He nodded towards Lyn who was peering dubiously into a camp kettle.

Denison unrolled his sleeping bag and sat on it. 'What do you think of her?'

'Personally or professionally?'

'Maybe a bit of both.'

'She seems to be a well-balanced young woman.' There was amusement in Harding's voice. 'She certainly knew how to handle Carey – she caught him coming and going. And she jabbed me in a sore spot. She's very capable, I'd say.'

'She took her father's death pretty coolly.'

Harding threw away the blade of grass and lit a cigarette. 'She lived with her mother and stepfather and didn't have much to do with Meyrick apart from quarrelling. I'd say her attitude to her father's death was perfectly normal. She had other things to think about at the time.'

'Yes,' said Denison pensively.

'I don't think you need worry about Lyn Meyrick,' said Harding. 'She's used to making up her own mind – and the minds of others, come to that.'

Diana Hansen came down the hill looking trim and efficient in the neat shirt and the drab trousers which she wore tucked into the tops of field boots – a world removed from the cool sophisticate Denison had met in Oslo. She cast a look at Lyn and walked over to the two men. 'Time to do your bit with the theodolite, Giles.'

Denison scrambled to his feet. 'Are they still with us?'

'So I'm told,' said Diana. 'And there's another party. We're becoming popular. I'd go up on that ridge there – and stay in sight.'

'All right.' Denison took the theodolite out of its case, picked up the lightweight tripod, and walked up the hill in the direction Diana had indicated.

Harding smiled as he watched Denison's retreating figure. He thought that Lyn Meyrick would make up Denison's mind were she allowed to. From a psychiatric point of view it was most interesting – but he would have to have a word with the girl first. He got up and walked over to where Lyn was pumping the pressure stove.

Denison stopped on top of the ridge and set up the theodolite. He took the sheet of paper from his pocket, now much creased, and studied it before looking around at the view. This was the bit of fakery Carey had given him to make the deception look good. It had been written with a broadnibbed pen – 'No ballpoints in 1944,' Carey had said – and artificially aged. Across the top was scrawled the single word, *Iuonnonpuisto*, and below that was a rough sketch of three lines radiating from a single point with the angles carefully marked in degrees. At the end of each line was again a single word – *Järvi*, *Kukkula* and *Aukko* – going around clockwise. Lake, hill and gap.

'Not much to go on,' Carey had said. 'But it explains why you're wandering around nature preserves with a theodolite. If anyone wants to rob you of that bit of paper you can let him. Maybe we can start a trade in theodolites.'

Denison looked around. Below ran the thread of a small river, the Kevojoki, and in the distance was the blue water of a lake pent in a narrow valley. He bent his head and sighted the theodolite at the head of the lake. Every time he did this he had a curious sense of *déjà vu* as though he had been accustomed to doing this all his life. Had he been a surveyor?

He checked the reading on the bezel and sighted again on the hill across the valley and took another reading. He took a notebook from his pocket and worked out the angle between the lake and the hill, then he swept the horizon looking for a possible gap. All this nonsense had to look good because he knew he was under observation – Carey's red herring appeared to be swimming well.

It had been at lunchtime on the first day that Diana had said casually, 'We're being watched.'

'How do you know?' asked Denison. 'I've seen nobody.'

'McCready told me.'

McCready had not been in evidence at Kevo Camp and Denison had not seen him since Helsinki. 'Have you been talking to him? Where is he?'

Diana nodded across the lake. 'On the other side of the valley. He says that a party of three men is trailing us.'

Denison was sceptical. 'I suppose you have a walkie-talkie tucked away in your pack.'

She shook her head. 'Just this.' From the pocket of her anorak she took a small plate of stainless steel, three inches in diameter; it had a small hole in the middle. 'Heliograph,' she said. 'Simpler than radio and less detectable.'

He examined the double-sided mirror – that is what it amounted to – and said, 'How can you aim it?'

'I know where George McCready is now,' she said. 'He's just been signalling to me. If I want to answer I hold this up and sight on his position through the hole. Then I look at my own reflection and see a circle of light on my cheek where the sun comes through the hole. If I tilt the mirror so that the circle of light goes into the hole, then the mirror on the other side flashes light into George's eyes. From then on it's simply a matter of Morse code.'

Denison was about to experiment when she took the gadget from him. 'I told you we're being watched. I can get away with it by pretending to make up my face – you can't.'

'Has McCready any idea of who is watching us?'

She shrugged. 'He hasn't got near enough to find out. I think it's about time you started your act with the theodolite.'

So he had set up the theodolite and fiddled about checking angles, and had repeated the charade several times during the past two days.

Now he found what might, by a stretch of imagination, be called a gap and took the third reading. He calculated the angle, wrote it into his notebook, and put the notebook and the fake paper back into his pocket. He was dismantling the theodolite when Lyn came up the hill. 'Supper's ready.'

'Thanks,' he said. 'Hold this.' He gave her the theodolite. 'Did Diana say anything about another group following us?'

Lyn nodded. 'They're coming up from behind very fast, she says.'

'Where's the first group?'

'Gone on ahead.'

'We're like the meat in a sandwich,' Denison said gloomily. 'Unless it's all a product of Diana's imagination. I haven't seen anyone around – and I certainly haven't seen George McCready.'

'I saw him signalling this morning,' said Lyn. 'He was on the other side of the valley. I was standing next to Diana and saw the flash, too.'

Denison collapsed the tripod and they both set off down the hill. 'You and Harding have had your heads together lately. What do you find so interesting to talk about?'

She gave him a sideways glance. 'You,' she said quietly. 'I've been finding out about you; since I can't ask you I've been asking him.'

'Nothing bad, I hope.'

She smiled at him. 'Nothing bad.'
'That's a relief,' he said. 'What's for supper?'
'Bully beef stew.'
He sighed. 'I can't wait.'

CHAPTER TWENTY-SEVEN

McCready was desperately tired. He lay on a hillside in a grove of dwarf birch and watched the group of four men making their way up the valley on the other side of the river. He had had very little sleep in the last two days and his eyes were sore and gritty. He had long since come to the conclusion that it needed two men to do this job.

He lowered the binoculars and blinked, then rubbed his eyes before checking on the camp on the top of the bluff across the river. There was a new figure on the rock above the camp which looked like Denison. At three in the morning there was quite enough light to see; the sun had skimmed the horizon at midnight and was already high in the sky. It seemed that Diana had insisted that a watch be kept.

He shifted his elbows and checked on the higher reaches of the valley and his mouth tightened as he saw a movement. The three men of the first party were coming down, keeping close to the river. Earlier he had crossed the river to scout their camp and, although he had not got close enough to hear clearly what they had been talking about, he had heard enough to know they were not Finns. Their tones had Slavic cadences and he had seen that they were very lightly equipped with no tents or even sleeping bags.

He switched his attention to the group of four who were coming up the valley. The two groups could not see each other because of a bend in the river where the water swirled around the bluff. He judged that if both groups kept up the same pace they would meet under the bluff and just below Denison.

McCready frowned as he watched. If the first group was under-equipped the second was well-outfitted to the point of decadent luxury. He had watched them stop for a meal and had seen what seemed to be a collapsible barbecue. Two of the men carried coils of rope as though they might expect rock climbing. Maybe Finns, he had thought, but now he was not so certain; not even Finns made route marches at three a.m.

At the time he had first seen the second group he had been too far away to distinguish faces, but now the men were nearer and he had a better chance. As he waited patiently he pondered over the differences between the two parties and came to the conclusion that they were indeed quite separate. Two minutes later he was sure of it when he saw the face of the leading man of the four.

It was Jack Kidder, the big loud-mouthed American who had cropped up in Oslo and, later, in Helsinki.

Whatever the first group had been speaking it had been neither Finnish nor English. It was reasonable to assume that not only were the two parties quite distinct but also that neither knew of the existence of the other. Even more interesting, they were going to run into each other within twenty minutes.

McCready put down the binoculars and twisted around to open the pack which lay beside him. He took out what appeared to be the stock of a rifle and slapped open the butt plate which was hinged. From inside the hollow glassfibre stock he took out a barrel and a breech action and, within thirty seconds, he had assembled the rifle.

He patted the stock affectionately. This was the Armalite AR-7, originally designed as a survival rifle for the American Air Force. It weighed less than three pounds and was guaranteed to float in water whether knocked down or ready to fire, but what made it suitable for his purpose was the fact that, stripped down, it measured less than seventeen inches in length and so could be smuggled about unobtrusively in a back pack.

He inserted a magazine containing eight rounds of long rifle and put another clip in his pocket, then he crawled backwards out of the grove of trees and began to make his way down to the river along a ravine he had previously chosen for the eventuality. He came out to the river's edge opposite the bluff and right on the bend of the river, and took shelter behind boulders which a long-gone glacier had left in its passage.

From his position on the outside bend of the river he could see both groups although neither, as yet, was aware of the other. He looked at the bluff and could not see Denison who was farther back up the hill. Nothing like adding confusion, he thought, as he raised the rifle to firing position.

As both groups were about to round the bend he fired, not at Kidder but just in front of him, and the sand spurted at Kidder's feet. Kidder yelled and rolled sideways and, as if by magic, all four men disappeared.

McCready did not see that sudden transformation of the scene; he had already turned and slammed another shot at the leading man of the trio which ricocheted off a rock by his head. The man ducked instinctively and went to ground fast, but not so fast that McCready did not see the pistol that suddenly appeared in his hand.

McCready withdrew into his niche like a tortoise drawing its head into its shell and waited to see what would happen next.

Denison heard the shot from below and jerked to attention. Even before he took the second quick pace back to the camp he heard the flat report of the second shot which echoed from the hill behind him. Then there was no sound but the thudding of his boots on the rock.

He stooped to Diana's sleeping bag and found her already awake. 'Someone's shooting.'

'I heard. Wake the others.'

He roused Lyn and then went to Harding who, in spite of his pessimism, was fast asleep. 'Wassamatter?' he said drowsily, but came awake with a jerk as two more shots broke the early morning silence. 'What the hell?'

Diana was gesturing vigorously. 'Over the ridge,' she called. 'Away from the river.'

Harding hastily thrust his feet into his boots and cursed freely. Denison ran over to Diana who was helping Lyn. 'What about the gear?'

'Leave it. Leave everything except your gun. Get moving.'

He hauled Lyn to her feet and they ran for it, up the hill and over the top of the ridge, a matter of some three hundred yards. There they waited, breathless, until Diana and Harding caught up. Three more shots were fired in rapid succession, and Denison said, 'It sounds like a bloody battle.'

'We've got to get lost,' said Diana. 'There's cover over there.'

They ran for it.

On the other side of the river, at the water's edge, McCready watched and smiled. As he had figured, neither of the groups had time to find out where the shots had come from. They had taken cover immediately in the manner of professionals, and now they were dodging about on each side of the bluff in skirmish lines, ready for defence or attack. Kidder, on the left, caught a glimpse of a man on the right, and fired. He missed but, in firing, he exposed himself and someone took a shot at him. Another miss. Kidder pulled back and unslung his pack which was hampering him. As the others did the same McCready smiled. A typical battle situation was developing in miniature. Kidder, to improve mobility, was divesting himself of supplies, which might be a good idea considering he outnumbered the opposition – although he could not know that. But if he lost and was overrun and had to retreat then his supplies would be lost.

McCready patted his rifle again and withdrew, to worm himself up the ravine and back into his original position in the stand of stunted trees. On the way he heard three more shots fired. He picked up the glasses and studied the situation. Denison was gone from the rock and the camp was deserted, so it was likely that they had pulled back over the hill and gone to ground, which was the sensible thing to do.

He looked down at the river. The narrow strip of sand between the bluff and the water's edge was held at each end by two men, and both sides were engaged in a classic outflanking action. Kidder and another man were climbing the bluff on the left, obviously intending to come out on top. There they would have the advantage of height and dropping fire as well as greater numbers.

The only snag was that the opposition was doing the same with one man and he had got the idea first. McCready, enjoying his grandstand seat, watched their progress with interest and estimated that the deserted camp on top of the bluff would be the next battleground. If the single man on the right could get himself established on top of the bluff before Kidder and his friend arrived he would stand a good chance despite the two to one odds.

Meanwhile the holding action at the bottom of the bluff continued with a desultory exchange of shots more to indicate the presence of opposition than to press an attack. McCready stroked his rifle, and thought, *How to Start a War in One Easy Lesson.* He hoped no small nation got the idea – using atomic missiles instead of rifle bullets.

The man on the right made it to the top while Kidder and his man still had twenty yards to go. He came up slowly, looked at the deserted camp, and then ducked for cover behind a rock. Kidder came up to the top and also surveyed the camp from cover, then gestured to the other man to crawl farther along.

He shouted – a thin cry that came to McCready across the river – and they both broke into the open, running across the top of the bluff. The man in cover fired and Kidder's companion spun away and fell among the rocks. Kidder dropped into cover and simultaneously there was a renewed outburst of fire from the base of the bluff to which McCready transferred his attention.

There had been a casualty on the other side and from the way the man nursed his arm McCready judged it to be broken. He heard a confused and distant shouting; Kidder was worming his way among the rocks in the direction of his wounded friend, and suddenly the other man on the bluff broke away and retreated.

Within fifteen minutes both sides were retreating in opposite directions, Kidder's group going down-river, one man limping heavily with a bullet in his leg, and the others heading up-river. Honours were even in an inconclusive engagement, and McCready thought that neither party knew just exactly what had happened.

Diana Hansen waited an hour after the last shot before making a move, then she said, 'I'll go and see what's happening.'

'I'll come with you,' said Denison.

She hesitated. 'All right. I'll go to the left, you go to the right. We move alternately, one covering the other.' She looked back at the others. 'You two give us general cover. If anyone shoots at us you start banging away fast; it doesn't matter if you don't hit anything – just make a lot of noise.'

She went first and Denison watched her as she zigzagged forward up to the top of the ridge. Half-way up she stopped and waved him forward and he did his best to imitate what she had done. He flopped down when he was parallel with her and wondered how she had learned a trade like this.

She was on the move again and this time she got to the top of the ridge where she could look down on the camp. At her hand signal he also went forward and peered cautiously around a rock. The camp was deserted and nothing appeared to have been touched; he could even see a gleam from the open theodolite case where he had left it, forgetting to close the top.

She wriggled over to him. 'I'll go around to the left – you to the right – we'll come in on the camp from two sides. Don't be in too much of a hurry, and don't shoot at the first thing that moves – it might be me.'

He nodded. She was just going away when he took another look at the camp and saw a movement. He grabbed her ankle as he ducked back. 'Someone down there,' he whispered.

She turned. 'Where?'

'By the rock where we kept watch.'

After a while Diana said, 'I don't see anyone.'

'I saw it,' said Denison. 'A movement by that rock.'

Again they waited and watched until Diana said, 'Must have been your imagination.'

Denison sighed. 'I suppose so.' His hand suddenly tightened on hers. 'No – look! On the other side now.'

The figure of a man came over the edge of the bluff, paused a little wearily, and then walked slowly towards the camp. When he got there he stared about him and unslung his pack.

Diana clicked with her tongue. 'It's George McCready,' she said, and stood up.

McCready looked as though he was ready to drop on his feet. His clothing was soaked and his boots squelched when he walked. He saw them coming but made no move to advance. Instead he sat down and began to unlace his boots. 'That bloody river,' he said. 'That's the third time I've crossed it.'

'What was all the shooting?' demanded Diana.

McCready described what had happened. 'One crowd was American; I don't know who the others were. The language sounded vaguely Slav.'

'Russian?'

'Could be,' said McCready. 'I hope so. If they're chasing us up here there's a good chance they won't be on to Carey.' He wrung out his socks. 'When I'm sixty I'll be an arthritic cripple.'

'So you set them fighting each other,' said Denison. 'I don't know if that was a good idea. They might think it was us, and next time they'll come shooting.'

McCready nodded. 'Now's the time to lose them. The best way of doing that is to cross the river and go back on the other side. That will give us the three days that Carey wanted us here.'

'But we don't want to lose them,' objected Diana. 'That isn't the object.'

'I know,' said McCready. 'But I'd like to get back to the cars and away while they're licking their wounds. We can leave plenty of signs to indicate where we've gone. They'll beat around here for a while – if we're lucky they'll have another shooting match – and then they'll follow. It's still gaining time for Carey and it's less risk for us.'

Diana thought about it. 'All right.'

McCready cocked his head on one side and regarded Denison. 'The leader of the American mob was your old pal, Kidder.'

'Kidder!' said Denison incredulously.

'I thought he turned up a bit too opportunely in Helsinki,' said Diana. 'But the man sounded such a fool I discounted him.'

'If it's any consolation, so did I,' said McCready. 'But you know what it means – our cousins of the CIA are muscling in.' He took a pair of dry socks from a plastic bag. 'Unless he's a renegade or a double agent. I fancy the CIA myself.' He looked up at Denison who was deep in thought. 'What's the matter with you? You look as though you've just been sandbagged.'

'For God's sake!' said Denison. 'It was *Kidder!*' He shook his head in a bewildered manner. 'The man who questioned me after I was knocked out in the sauna. I thought I recognized the voice but I couldn't place it because the American accent had gone.'

'Are you sure?' Diana's voice was sharp.

'I'm certain. I didn't associate the man with Kidder because we'd left him behind in Oslo. He hadn't appeared in Helsinki at that time. Is it important?'

'Could be,' said McCready. 'There's one bunch who knows you're *not* Meyrick – the crowd who snatched you from Hampstead. But the man who questioned you assumed you were Meyrick. If it was Kidder then the CIA weren't responsible for the resculpting of that unlovely face of yours. All these bits of jigsaw come in handy.'

'Dr Harding and Lyn will be wondering what happened to us,' said Diana.

Denison turned. 'I'll bring them back.' He started to walk up to the top of the ridge but then veered over to the rock where he had kept watch. Something niggled at the back of his mind – he wondered how McCready could have got from one side of the camp to the other. The first movement he had seen from the top of the ridge had been by the rock, but McCready had come up the other side from the river.

Denison walked around the rock keeping his eyes on the ground. When McCready had come up his boots had been wet – waterfilled – and he had left a line of damp footprints over a smooth rock outcrop. Here there was also an outcrop but no footprints. He went to the other side of the rock and out of sight of Diana and McCready.

Something struck him on the back of the head and he felt a blinding pain and was driven to his knees. His vision swam and there was a roaring in his ears. The second thump on the head he did not feel but plunged headlong into darkness.

CHAPTER TWENTY-EIGHT

The bus rocked as it rolled along the narrow country road in the early morning. It was cold and Carey drew his coat closer about him. Armstrong, next to him, looked out of the window at the tall observation tower. It was drawing nearer.

The bus was full of Finns, most of whom were quiet at that early pre-work hour. Two seats ahead of Carey, on the aisle, sat Huovinen. He turned his head and looked back; his eyes were expressionless but Carey thought he could detect worry. Huovinen had been drinking again the previous night and Carey hoped his hangover did not get in the way of his efficiency.

Brakes squealed as the bus drew to a halt and Carey craned his neck to look through the forward windows. A soldier in Finnish uniform walked up and exchanged a few words with the driver, then he smiled and waved the bus on. It jerked into motion again.

Carey took out his pipe and filled it with steady hands. He nudged Armstrong, and said in Swedish, 'Why don't you have a cigarette? Have you stopped smoking?'

Armstrong looked at him in surprise, then shrugged. If Carey wanted him to smoke a cigarette, then he would smoke a cigarette. He felt in his pocket and took out a half-empty packet of Finnish cigarettes as the bus stopped again.

The bus driver leaned out of the cab and called to the advancing Russian soldier, '*Kolmekymmentäkuusi.*' The soldier nodded and climbed into the bus by way of the passenger door and surveyed the work party. He looked as though he was doing a head count.

Carey struck a match and lit his pipe, cupping his hands about the bowl and shrouding the lower part of his face. He seemed to be doing his best to make a smokescreen. Armstrong caught on fast and flicked on his cigarette lighter, guarding the flame with his hand as though the draught from up front was about to blow it out.

The Russian left the bus and waved it on and it lurched forward with a clash of gears and rolled past the frontier post. Armstrong averted his face from the window as the bus passed an officer, a square man with broad Slavic features. He felt a sudden tightening in his belly as he realized he was in Russia. He had been in Russia many times before, but not as an illegal entry – and that had been the subject of a discussion with Carey.

Armstrong had argued for going into Russia quite legitimately through Leningrad. 'Why do we have to be illegal about it?' he asked.

'Because we'd have to be illegal anyway,' said Carey. 'We couldn't get to Enso legally – the Russkies don't like foreigners wandering loose about their frontier areas. And they keep a watch on foreigners in Leningrad; if you're not back at the Europa Hotel they start looking for you. No, this is the best way. Over the border and back – short and sharp – without them even knowing we've been there.'

Black smoke streamed overhead from the factory chimneys as the bus trundled through Enso. It traversed the streets for some minutes and then went through a gateway and halted outside a very long, low building. The passengers gathered up their belongings and stood up. Carey looked at Huovinen who nodded, so he nudged Armstrong and they got up and joined the file behind Huovinen.

They went into the building through an uncompleted wall and emerged into an immense hall. At first Armstrong could not take in what he was seeing; not only was the sight unfamiliar but he had to follow Huovinen who veered abruptly to the right and out of the main stream. He led them around the end of a great machine and stopped where there was no one in sight. He was sweating slightly. 'I should be getting twice what you're paying me,' he said.

'Take it easy,' counselled Carey. 'What now?'

'I have to be around for the next hour,' said Huovinen. 'Laying out the work and a fifteen-minute conference with Dzotenidze. I have to put up with that every morning.' He coughed and spat on the floor. 'I can't lead you out before then.'

'So we wait an hour,' said Carey. 'Where?'

Huovinen pointed. 'In the machine – where else?'

Carey turned and looked at the half-constructed machine. Designed for continuous paper-making it was over three hundred yards long and about fifty feet wide. 'Get in the middle of there and take your coats off,' said Huovinen. 'I'll bring you some tools in about ten minutes. If anyone looks in at you be tightening bolts or something.'

Carey looked up at a crane from which a big steel roller hung. 'Just see that you don't drop that on my head,' he said. 'And don't be longer than an hour. Come on, Ivan.'

Armstrong followed Carey as he climbed inside the machine. When he looked back Huovinen had gone. They found a place where there was headroom and Carey took off his coat and looked around. 'In this snug situation a British working man would be playing cards,' he said. 'I don't know about the Finns.'

Armstrong bent and peered through a tangle of complexity. 'They're working,' he reported.

Carey grunted. 'Then let's look busy even if we're not.'

Presently a man walked by and stooped. There was a clatter of metal on concrete and footsteps hastened away. 'The tools,' said Carey. 'Get them.'

Armstrong crawled out and came back with a selection of spanners and a hammer. Carey inspected them and tried a spanner on the nearest bolt. 'What we do now,' he announced, 'is to take off this girder and then put it back – and we keep on doing that until it's time to go.' He applied the spanner to a nut and heaved, then paused with a thoughtful look on his face. 'Just pop your head up there and see what happens when we remove this bit of iron. I don't want the whole bloody machine to collapse.'

An hour and a half later they were walking through the streets of Enso. Armstrong still wore his overalls and carried a spade over his shoulder, but Carey had removed his and was now more nattily dressed. He wore, he assured Armstrong, the regulation rig of a local water distribution inspector. In his hand he carried, quite openly, the metal detection gadget. To Armstrong's approval it had a metal plate attached to it which announced in Russian that it was manufactured by Sovelectro Laboratories of Dnepropetrovsk.

As they walked they talked – discreetly and in Russian. Armstrong noted the old-fashioned atmosphere of the streets of Enso. It was, he thought, occasioned by the Russian style of dress and he could be in the nineteen-thirties. He always had that feeling when he was in Russia. 'I nearly had a heart attack when that bloody man wanted to know where Virtanen was,' he said.

It had been a tricky moment. The Chief Engineer, Dzotenidze, had stood by the machine quite close to them while he interrogated Huovinen as to the whereabouts of Lassi Virtanen. 'Those screens aren't right,' he said in Russian. 'Virtanen isn't doing his work properly.'

An interpreter transmitted this to Huovinen, who said, 'Virtanen hasn't been feeling too well lately. An old war wound. In fact, he's not here today – he's at home in bed.'

Dzotenidze had been scathing but there was nothing he could do about it. 'See that he's back on the job as soon as possible,' he said, and stalked away.

Armstrong said, 'I could have stretched out my hand and touched him.'

'Huovinen could have come up with a better story,' said Carey grimly. 'What happens if that engineer checks back and finds that the bus came in with a full crew? Still, there's nothing we can do about it.'

They walked on for five minutes in silence. Armstrong said, 'How much farther?'

'Not far – just around the corner.' Carey tapped him on the arm. 'Now, Ivan, my lad; you're a common working man, so let your betters do the talking. If you have to talk you're slow and half-witted and as thick as two planks as befits a man who wields an idiot stick.' He indicated the spade.

'The heroic worker, in fact.'

'Precisely. And I'm the technician controlling the magic of modern science and haughty to boot.' They turned the corner. 'There's the house.' Carey regarded it critically. 'It looks pretty run-down.'

'That's why it's being demolished.'

'Just so.' Carey surveyed the street. 'We'll start on the outside just for the sake of appearances – right here in the street.' He took a pair of earphones from his pocket and plugged the lead wire into a socket on the metal detector. 'Do I look technical enough?'

'Quite sweet,' said Armstrong.

Carey snorted and switched on the detector, then adjusted a control. Holding the detector close to the ground like a vacuum cleaner he walked along the pavement. Armstrong leaned on his spade and looked on with an expression of boredom. Carey went for about fifty yards and then came back slowly. There was a worried look on his face. 'I'm getting quite a few readings. This street must be littered with metal.'

'Maybe you've struck gold,' suggested Armstrong.

Carey glared at him. 'I'm not being funny,' he snarled. 'I hope to hell the garden of that house isn't the same.'

'You're arousing interest,' said Armstrong. 'The curtain just twitched.'

'I'll give it another run,' said Carey. He went through his act again and paused in front of the house, then took a notebook from his pocket and scribbled in it.

Armstrong lounged after him just as a small boy came out of the house. 'What's he doing?'

'Looking for a water pipe,' said Armstrong.

'What's that thing?'

'The thing that tells him when he's found a water pipe,' said Armstrong patiently. 'A new invention.' He looked down at the boy. 'Is your father at home?'

'No, he's at work.' The boy looked at Carey who was peering over the garden fence. 'What's he doing now?'

'I don't know,' said Armstrong. 'He's the expert, not me. Is your mother at home?'

'She's doing the wash. Do you want to see her?'

Carey straightened up. 'I think it runs through here,' he called.

'Yes,' said Armstrong. 'I think we do want to see her. Run inside and tell her, will you?' The boy dashed into the house and Armstrong went up to Carey. 'Kunayev is at work; Mrs K. is doing the wash.'

'Right; let's get to it.' Carey walked up to the front door of the house just as it opened. A rather thin and tired-looking woman stepped out. 'This is the ... er – ' Carey took out his notebook and checked the pages – 'the Kunayev household?'

'Yes, but my husband's not here.'

'Then you'll be Grazhdanke Kunayova?'

The woman was faintly alarmed. 'Yes?'

Carey beamed. 'Nothing to worry about, Grazhdanke Kunayova. This is merely a technicality concerning the forthcoming demolition of this area. You know about that?'

'Yes,' she said. 'I do.' The faint alarm turned to faint aggression. 'We're having to move just when I've redecorated the house.'

'I'm sorry about that,' said Carey. 'Well, under the ground there are a lot of pipes – gas, water, electricity and so on. My own concern is with the water pipes. When the demolition men come in there'll be bulldozers coming through here, and we don't want them breaking the water pipes or the whole area will turn into a quagmire.'

'Why don't you turn off the water before you start?' she asked practically.

Carey was embarrassed. 'That's not as easy as it sounds, Grazhdanke Kunayova,' he said, hunting for a plausible answer. 'As you know, this is one of the older areas of Svetogorsk, built by the Finns just after the First World War. A lot of the records were destroyed twenty-five years ago and we don't even know where some of the pipes are, or even if they connect into our present water system.' He leaned forward and said confidentially, 'It's even possible that some of our water still comes from over the border – from Imatra.'

'You mean we get it free from the Finns?'

'I'm not concerned with the economics of it,' said Carey stiffly. 'I just have to find the pipes.'

She looked over Carey's shoulder at Armstrong who was leaning on his spade. 'And you want to come into the garden,' she said. 'Is he going to dig holes all over our garden?'

'Not at all,' said Carey reassuringly. He lifted the detector. 'I have this – a new invention that can trace pipes without digging. It might be necessary to dig a small hole if we find a junction, but I don't think it will happen.'

'Very well,' she said unwillingly. 'But try not to step on the flower beds. I know we're being pushed out of the house this year but the flowers are at their best just now, and my husband does try to make a nice display.'

'We'll try not to disturb the flowers,' said Carey. 'We'll just go around to the back.'

He jerked his head at Armstrong and they walked around the house followed by the small boy. Armstrong said in a low voice, 'We've got to get rid of the audience.'

'No trouble; just be boring.' Carey stopped as he rounded the corner of the house and saw the garden shed at the bottom of the garden; it was large and stoutly constructed of birch logs. 'That's not on the plan,' he said. 'I hope what we're looking for isn't under there.'

Armstrong stuck his spade upright in the soil at the edge of a flower bed, and Carey unfolded a plan of the garden. 'That's the remaining tree there,' he said. 'One of the four Meyrick picked out. I'll have a go at that first.' He donned the earphones, switched on the detector, and made a slow run up to the tree. He spent some time exploring the area about the tree, much hampered by the small boy, then called, 'Nothing here.'

'Perhaps the pipe runs down the middle,' said Armstrong.

'It's possible. I really think I'll have to search the whole area.'

Which he proceeded to do. For the benefit of the small boy every so often he would call out a number and Armstrong would dutifully record it on the plan. After half an hour of this the boy became bored and went away. Carey winked at Armstrong and carried on, and it took him well over an hour to search the garden thoroughly.

He glanced at his watch and went back to Armstrong. 'We have two possibilities. A strong reading – very strong – on the edge of the lawn there, and a weaker reading in the middle of that flower bed. I suggest we have a go at the lawn first.'

Armstrong looked past him. 'Mrs K. is coming.'

The woman was just coming out of the house. As she approached she said, 'Have you found anything?'

'We may have found a junction,' said Carey, and pointed. 'Just there. We'll have to dig just a small hole, Grazhdanke Kunayova, you understand. And we'll be tidy and replace the turf.'

She looked down at the straggly lawn. 'I don't suppose it matters,' she said dispiritedly. 'My husband says the grass doesn't grow as well here as down south where we come from. Would you like something to eat?'

'We brought our own sandwiches,' said Carey gravely.

'I'll make you tea,' she said decisively, and went back to the house.

'Nice woman,' commented Carey. 'It's midday, when all good workers down tools for half an hour.'

They ate their sandwiches sitting on the lawn, and drank the glasses of lemon tea which the woman brought to them. She did not stay to make small talk, for which Carey was thankful. He bit into a sandwich and said meditatively, 'I suppose this is where Merikken and his family were killed – with the exception of young Harri.' He pointed to the house. 'That end looks newer than the rest.'

'Was there much bombing here?' asked Armstrong.

'My God; this place was in the front line for a time – the sky must have been full of bombers.'

Armstrong sipped the hot tea. 'How do we know the trunk is still here? Any keen gardener might have dug it up. What about Kunayev himself?'

'Let's not be depressing,' said Carey. 'It's time you started to dig. I'll give you a reading and then let you do the work, as befits my station in life.' He walked across the lawn, searched the area briefly with the detector, and stuck a pencil upright in the ground. 'That's it. Take out the turves neatly.'

So Armstrong began to dig. He laid the turves on one side and tried to put each spadeful of soil into as neat a heap as he could. Carey sat under the tree and watched him, drinking the last of his tea. Presently Armstrong called him over. 'How deep is this thing supposed to be?'

'About two feet.'

'I'm down two and a half and there's still nothing.'

'Carry on,' said Carey. 'Meyrick could have been in error.'

Armstrong carried on. After a while he said, 'I'm down another foot and still nothing.'

'Let's see what the gadget says.' Carey put on the earphones and lowered the detector into the hole. He switched on and hastily adjusted the gain. 'It's there,' he said. 'Must be a matter of inches. I've just had my ears pierced.'

'I'll go down a bit more,' said Armstrong. 'But it'll be difficult without enlarging the hole.' Again he drove the spade into the earth and hit something solid with a clunk. 'Got it!' He cleared as much as he could with the spade and then began to scrabble with his hands. After five minutes he looked up at Carey.

'You know what we've found?'

'What?'

Armstrong began to laugh. 'A water pipe.'

'Oh, for God's sake!' said Carey. 'Come out of that hole and let me see.' He replaced Armstrong in the hole and felt the rounded shape of the metal and the flange. He dug away more earth and exposed more metal, then he got out out of the hole.

Armstrong was still chuckling, and Carey said, 'Fill in that hole and go gently. It's an unexploded bomb.'

Armstrong's laughter died away thinly.

'250 kilograms, I'd say,' said Carey. 'The equivalent of our wartime 500-pounder.'

CHAPTER TWENTY-NINE

They were grouped around Denison who lay prone on the ground. 'Don't move him,' warned Harding. 'I don't know what he'll have apart from concussion.' Very carefully he explored Denison's skull. 'He's certainly been hit hard.'

Diana looked at McCready. 'Who by?' McCready merely shrugged.

Harding's long fingers were going over Denison's torso. 'Let's turn him over – very gently.' They turned Denison over on to his back and Harding lifted one eyelid. The eye was rolled right back in the head, and Lyn gave an involuntary cry.

'Excuse me, Doctor,' said Diana, and her hand went to Denison's shirt pocket. She got up off her knees and jerked her head at McCready. They walked back to the middle of the camp. 'The plan and the notebook are gone,' she said. 'He carried them in the button-down pocket of his shirt. The button has been torn off and the pocket ripped. The question is by whom?'

'It wasn't the Yanks,' said McCready. 'I saw them well off down-river. And it wasn't the other mob, either; I'll stake everything on that.'

'Then who?'

McCready shook his head irritably. 'By, God!' he said. 'There's someone around here cleverer than I am.'

'I'd better not comment on that,' said Diana tartly. 'You might get annoyed.'

'It doesn't really matter, of course,' said McCready. 'We were expecting it, anyway.'

'But we were expecting to use it to find out who the opposition is.' She tapped him on the chest. 'You know what this means. There are three separate groups after us.' She ticked them off on her fingers. 'The Americans; another crowd who is vaguely Slav – Russians, Poles, Bulgarians, Yugoslavs, take your pick – and now someone mysterious whom we haven't even seen.'

'It's what Carey was expecting, isn't it?'

'Yes, but it's worrying all the same. Let's see how Denison is.'

They went back to the rock where Lyn was saying worriedly, 'It is just concussion, isn't it?'

'I'm not too sure,' said Harding. 'Lyn, you'll find a black box in my pack about half-way down. Bring it, will you?'

Lyn ran off and McCready went down on his knees by Denison. 'What's wrong with him apart from a crack on the head?'

'His pulse is way down, and I'd like to take his blood pressure,' said Harding. 'But there's something else. Look at this.' He took Denison's arm by the wrist and lifted it up. When he let go the arm stayed there. He took the arm and bent it at the elbow, and again it stayed in the position into which he had put it.

McCready drew in his breath sharply. 'You can mould the man like modelling clay,' he said in wonder. 'What is it?'

'A form of catalepsy,' said Harding.

That did not mean much to McCready. 'Does it usually accompany concussion?'

'Not at all. It's the first time I've seen it induced by a knock on the head. This is most unusual.'

Lyn came back and held out the box to Harding. 'Is this what you wanted?'

He nodded briefly, took out an elastic bandage of a sphygmometer and bound it around Denison's arm. He pumped the rubber bulb, and said, 'His blood pressure is down, too.' He unwrapped the bandage. 'We'll carry him back and put him into a sleeping bag to keep him warm.'

'That means we don't move from here,' said McCready.

'We can't move him,' said Harding. 'Not until I can find out what's wrong with him and that, I'm afraid, is mixed up with what's been done to him.'

A bleak expression came over McCready's face. If they stayed at the camp they'd be sitting ducks for the next crowd of international yobbos.

Lyn said, 'Is he conscious or unconscious, Doctor?'

'Oh, he's unconscious,' said Harding. 'Blanked out completely.'

Harding was wrong.

Denison could hear every word but could not do a thing about it. When he tried to move he found that nothing happened, that he could not move a muscle. It was as though something had chopped all control from the brain. He had felt Harding moving his limbs and had tried to do something about it but he had no control whatever.

What he did have was a splitting headache.

He felt himself being lifted and carried and then put into a sleeping bag. After a few minutes he was lapped around in warmth. Someone had tucked the hood of the bag around his head so that sounds were muffled and he could not hear what was said very clearly. He wished they had not done that. He tried to speak, willing his tongue to move, but it lay flaccid in his mouth. He could not even move his vocal cords to make the slightest sound.

He heard a smatter of conversation. 'Still breathing … autonomic functions unimpaired … side … tongue out … choking …' That would be Harding.

Someone rolled him on to his side and he felt fingers inserted into his mouth and his tongue pulled forward.

After a little while he slept.

And dreamed.

In his dream he was standing on a hillside peering through the eyepiece of a theodolite. Gradually he became aware that the instrument was not a theodolite at all – it was a cine camera. He even knew the name of it – it was an Arriflex. And the small speck of blue lake in the distance became one of the blue eyes of a pretty girl.

He pulled back from the view finder of the camera and turned to Joe Staunton, the cameraman. 'Nice composition,' he said. 'We can shoot on that one.'

Great slabs of memory came slamming back into place with the clangour of iron doors.

'It's no good, Giles,' said Fortescue. 'It's becoming just that bit too much. You're costing us too much money. How the hell can you keep control when you're pissed half the time?' His contempt came over like a physical blow. 'Even when you're not drunk you're hung over.' Fortescue's voice boomed hollowly as though he was speaking in a cavern. 'You can't rely on the Old Pals Act any more. This is the end. You're out.'

Even in his dream Denison was aware of the wetness of tears on his cheeks.

He was driving a car, the familiar, long-since-smashed Lotus. Beth was beside him, her hair streaming in the wind.

'Faster!' she said. 'Faster!' His hand fell on the gear lever and he changed down to overtake a lorry, his foot going down on the accelerator.

The scooter shot, insect-like, from the side road right across his path. He swerved, and so did the lorry he was overtaking. Beth screamed and there was a rending, jangle of tearing metal and breaking glass and then nothing.

'Sorry about that,' said Staunton. 'This would have been a good one, but Fortescue won't have it. What will you do now?'

'Go home to Hampstead and get drunk,' said Denison.

Hampstead! An empty flat with no personality. Bare walls with little furniture and many empty whisky bottles.

And then ...!

In his dream Denison screamed.

He stirred when he woke up and opened his eyes to find Lyn looking at him. He moistened his lips, and said 'Beth?'

Her eyes widened and she turned her head. 'Mr Harding! Dr Harding – he's … he's awake.' There was a break in her voice. When she turned back to him he was trying to get up. 'No,' she said. 'Lie quietly.' She pushed him back.

'I'm all right,' he said weakly.

Harding appeared. 'All right, Lyn; let me see him.' He bent over Denison. 'How are you feeling?'

'Not too bad,' said Denison. 'Hell of a headache, though.' He put up his hand and tenderly felt the back of his head. 'What happened?'

'Somebody hit you.'

Denison fumbled with his other hand inside the sleeping bag, groping for his shirt pocket. 'They got the plan.'

'It doesn't matter,' said Lyn. 'Giles, it doesn't matter.'

'I know.' He levered himself up on one elbow and accepted the pills Harding gave him and washed them down with water. 'I think I gave you a shock, Doctor.'

'You were aware?' asked Harding in surprise.

'Yes. Another thing – I've got my memory back.'

'All of it?'

Denison frowned. 'How would I know? I'm not sure.'

'We won't go into that now,' said Harding quickly. 'How do you feel physically?'

'If you let me stand up I'll tell you.' He got out of the sleeping bag and stood up, supported on Harding's arm. He swayed for a moment and then shook himself free and took three steps. 'I seem all right,' he said. 'Except for the headache.'

'The pills ought to clear that up,' said Harding. 'But if I were you I wouldn't be too energetic.'

'You're not me,' said Denison flatly. 'What time is it? And where are the others?'

'It's just after midday,' said Lyn. 'And they're scouting to see if anyone else is around. I think the doctor is right; you ought to take it easy.'

Denison walked to the edge of the bluff, thinking of the perturbation in McCready's voice when he discovered that, because of the attack on himself, the party was pinned down. 'I ought to be able to cross the river,' he said. 'That might be enough.'

CHAPTER THIRTY

Armstrong was digging another hole. He had filled in the first one and left Carey to replace the turf. Carey did his best but still the lawn in that place was bumpy and uneven and, in the circumstances, he did not feel like stamping it down too hard. He looked towards Armstrong who appeared to be systematically wrecking a flower bed. 'Found anything?'

'Not yet.' Armstrong pushed again with the spade, and then stooped quickly. 'Wait! I think there's some –' before he finished the sentence Carey was by his side – 'thing here.'

'Let me see.' Carey put his hand down the hole and felt a flat surface. Flakes of something came away on his fingers and when he brought up his hand his fingertips were brown. 'Rust!' he said. 'This is it. Careful with that spade.'

He looked back at the house and thought it was fortunate that Mrs K. had gone shopping and taken her son with her. A bit of good for a lot of bad. Earlier in the afternoon she had been out in the garden hanging out the weekly wash to dry, and then she had come over and chatted interminably about the iniquities of the planning authorities, the ridiculous prices in the shops and other matters dear to the housewifely heart. A lot of time had been wasted.

He said, 'If the trunk is corroded we might be able to rip open the top and take out the papers without making the hole any bigger.'

'I forgot my tin opener,' said Armstrong. 'But this might do.' He put his hand to the side of his leg and from the long pocket of the overalls designed to take a foot rule he extracted a sheathed knife. 'Bought it in Helsinki; thought it might come in handy.'

Carey grunted as he saw the design. He took the knife from the sheath and examined the broad blade and the simple wooden handle. 'The Yanks think Jim Bowie invented these,' he said. 'Don't ever try to tackle a Finn with one; they're better at it than you. And probably the Russians, too, in these parts. It'll do quite nicely.'

He cleared earth from the top of the trunk until about a square foot of rusty metal was showing then he stabbed at it with the sharp point of the knife. The metal was rotten and the knife punched through with ridiculous ease. He enlarged the hole and bent up the metal into a tongue which he could hold in his fingers. He gripped it and pulled and there was a tearing sound.

Within five minutes he had made a hole in the trunk big enough to take his hand, and he groped inside and touched a hard square edge. His fingers curled around what felt like a book but when he tried to pull it out he found he was in the position of the monkey gripping the nut inside the bottle. The book was too big to come through the hole so he dropped it and concentrated on making the hole bigger.

At last he was able to get the book out. It was a school exercise book with hard covers and, when he flicked the pages, he saw mathematical symbols and lengthy equations in profusion. 'Jackpot!' he said exultantly.

The next thing out of the lucky dip was a roll of papers held by a rubber band. The rubber snapped at a touch but the papers, long rolled, held their curvature and he unrolled them with difficulty. The first pages were written in Finnish in a tight handwriting and the first mathematical equation came on the fourth page. From then on they were more frequent until the final pages were solid mathematics.

'How do we know what we're looking for?' asked Armstrong.

'We don't – we take the lot.' Carey dived into the hole again and groped about. Within ten minutes he had cleared the box which proved to be only half full but, even so, the books and papers made a big stack.

Carey took some folded paper bags from his pocket. 'Fill that hole; I'll take care of the loot.' He looked at his watch with worried eyes. 'We haven't much time.'

He filled three stout kraft-paper bags with documents and sealed them with sticky tape. Armstrong said, 'There's not enough earth to go back. It's filling the trunk.'

'I'll see to that,' said Carey. 'You nip along and fetch that wheelbarrow. You know where it's planted.'

'The empty house at the end of the street. I hope young Virtanen parked it in the right place.'

'You'll soon find out. Get going.' Carey began to fill in the hole and, as Armstrong had said, there was not enough earth, so he took more from other parts of the flower bed and took care not to pack it too tightly. It took him quite a while but when he had finished Armstrong had not yet returned.

He took the brown paper bags from where they had been lying among the long-stemmed flowers and hid them more securely in some shrubbery. His watch told him that time was running out; they had to get back to the paper mill and smuggle the papers aboard the bus. That had been arranged for but it would take time and there was little of that left.

Impatiently he went to the front gate and was relieved to see Armstrong trudging back with the wheelbarrow. 'What kept you?'

'The damn fool *hid* it,' said Armstrong savagely. 'What did you tell him to do?'

'To put it just inside the wall and out of sight.'

'He put the bloody thing in the cellar,' said Armstrong. 'I had to search the house to find it.'

'A misunderstanding – but we've got it. Come on.'

They put the documents into the wheelbarrow and covered the bags with dirty sacking. Armstrong put the spade and the detector on top and picked up the handles of the wheelbarrow. He was about to push off when he stopped. 'Someone's coming.'

Carey turned. A man was coming up the garden from the side of the house. His whole attitude was one of suspicion. 'What are you doing in my garden?'

Carey stepped forward. 'Grazhdaninu Kunayev?'

'Yes.'

Carey reeled out his story, then said, 'Your wife knows about it, of course. We've made very little disturbance.'

'You've been digging holes? Where?'

Carey pointed. 'There – on the lawn.' He refrained from drawing attention to the flower bed.

Kunayev walked over and prodded at the turf with his toe. 'You've been neat, I will say that.' He stamped hard with his foot, and Armstrong winced, thinking of the bomb below. 'Does this mean you'll be coming in earlier?'

Carey frowned. 'How do you mean?'

'With the bulldozers.'

'Not that I know of, comrade. That's not my department. I'm concerned only with water pipes.'

Kunayev looked at the house. 'I've liked living here; it's a good place. Now they want to pull it down and put up another damn factory. I ask you; is that right, comrade? Do you think it's right?'

Carey shrugged. 'Progress sometimes means sacrifice.'

'And I'm doing the sacrificing.' Kunayev snorted. 'I'm being transferred to the new housing development on the other side of town. A cheap, rotten, new house. Not like this house, comrade; those Finns knew how to build houses.'

'Meaning that Soviet workers don't?' asked Carey suavely.

'I didn't say that,' said Kunayev. He walked towards the wheelbarrow and picked up the detector. 'Is this your water diviner?'

Carey tightened his lips. 'Yes.'

'Like the mine detector I used during the war. I was at Stalingrad, comrade. Fourteen years old I was then.' He strolled towards the fence separating his garden from the one next door, still holding the detector. 'Boris Ivanevitch, are you there?'

'For Christ's sake!' whispered Armstrong. 'What do we do now?'

A woman called back. 'He's just going on duty.'

'Good afternoon, Irina Alexandrovna; ask him to come round here. I have something to show him.'

'Let's just leave,' urged Armstrong.

'We can't leave without that detector,' saId Carey through his teeth. 'It would look too suspicious.'

Kunayev came back from the fence. He had put on the earphones. 'Seems to work just like a mine detector, too. Not as big and heavy, of course; but they're clever with their electronics these days.'

'It works on a different principle,' said Carey. 'But we've finished here, Grazhdaninu Kunayev; we must go about our work.'

'No great hurry, comrade,' said Kunayev carelessly. He walked over to the patch of relaid turf. 'You say you found your water pipe here?'

'A pipe junction,' said Carey, gritting his teeth.

Kunayev flicked a switch and walked back and forth several times. 'It works,' he said. 'I could find that junction blind-fold – see if I can't.' He closed his eyes and walked back and forward again. 'Am I there?'

'Right on the spot,' said Armstrong.

Kunayev opened his eyes and looked past them. 'Ah, Boris Ivanevitch,' he said. 'You'll be interested in this.'

Carey turned around and felt a sinking feeling in his stomach. Boris Ivanevitch was a policeman.

CHAPTER THIRTY-ONE

'The chief study here at Sompio is the ecology of wetlands,' said Dr Matti Mannermaa. 'In northern Finland we have many marshes caused by the slow drying out of the shallow lakes. Sompio was chosen as a nature preserve because it not only has such a marsh but also has high ground of an altitude of over five hundred metres and a small part of Lake Loka. Thus we have a varied habitat for many creatures, especially birds.'

'Very interesting,' said McCready, hoping the interest showed in his face. He was bored to death.

'I am an ornithologist, of course,' said Dr Mannermaa. 'My work here is similar to that done at your English research station at Slimbridge.'

'I've been there,' said Harding with enthusiasm.

'So have I,' said Dr Mannermaa. 'I spent many months there investigating British methods. We have adopted the rocket-driven net for use here. We ring a lot of birds for the study of migratory patterns.'

McCready indicated the rack of shotguns on the wall of Mannermaa's office. 'I see you shoot them, too.'

'We must,' said Mannermaa. 'We have a continuing study in pesticide residues in body fat. We break a lot of eggs, too, Mr McCready – to study the thickness of the shells. Decreasing shell thickness is mainly a problem with the raptors, of course.' He laughed. 'I am not a sentimentalist about birds; I like roast duck just as much as anyone else.'

'I'm a wildfowler,' said Harding. 'We get good shooting in Norfolk.'

'I hope you don't take a shotgun into Sompio,' said Mannermaa. There was a twinkle in his eye, which belied the gravity of his voice. 'Well, now; let us look at the map and decide what is best for you to do.'

He stood up and went to a wall map. For a few minutes they discussed routes and possibilities. 'Here there is a hut,' said Mannermaa. 'On the edge of the marsh just below Nattaset – that's the mountain here. It's equipped with bunks and cooking facilities – rough living but better than tenting.'

'Most kind of you,' said McCready. 'Thank you very much.'

'A lot of our technical equipment is stored there. Please try not to disturb it.'

'We won't touch anything,' promised McCready. 'Thank you for everything, Dr Mannermaa.'

As they shook hands Mannermaa said, 'I hope your companions are successful in their shopping here. Vuotso is a small place and the range of choice may be restricted.'

'All we need are basic rations.'

'If you run out you'll find some tinned food in the hut,' said Mannermaa. 'You can pay for it when you get back.'

McCready and Harding left the office and emerged on to the main street of Vuotso. Harding said, 'Co-operative chap, isn't he? Those credentials Carey supplied must be really high-powered.'

'But we mustn't take a shotgun into Sompio,' said McCready. 'I wish we could take a machine-gun.'

'Do you think we'll be followed here?'

'It's a certainty – we left a trail like a bloody paper chase. Carey's plan is working and that's just fine for Carey, but I have a feeling that we're left holding the sticky end.' McCready sounded angry. 'It's all very well for him to set us up as targets but who likes being shot at? His plan that I should be an outside guard has already broken down. I have to sleep some time. It's too big a job for one man.'

'You'll be with us this time, then?'

McCready nodded. His brow was furrowed as he tried to cover all the angles. 'Another thing – how will Denison hold out?'

'He's got remarkable resilience,' said Harding. 'That crack on the head stirred things up and a lot of the blocks on his memory have been shaken loose. He's remembering more and more as time goes on, but he seems to have the ability to handle it.'

'What happens when he gets it all back? Does he crack up and go back on the bottle?' asked McCready sourly.

'I don't know. I tried him on whisky last night. He seems to have a positive aversion to it.'

McCready grunted. 'I hope he stays that way.'

In fact, Denison felt remarkably well. As they went on foot into the Sompio nature preserve he tried to analyse the reasons for his feeling of well-being and came to the conclusion that it was because of the absence of panic when he probed into his past. And then, of course, there was the immediate environment. He stopped and took a deep breath of the cool clean air and looked about him.

They were skirting the mountain called Nattaset and keeping to the high ground. Below there was a vista of the northern wilderness breathtaking in its beauty. Where there was firm ground the ever-present birches grew, but in between a multitude of islets there was a lacework intricacy of watercourses reflecting the blue of the sky, and in the distance an island-dotted lake shone like silver. Closer at hand white wreaths of last winter's snow lay all about.

Denison turned and saw McCready trailing about half a mile behind. He, too, appeared to have stopped and Denison thought he was doing a search with field glasses – and not just to look at the view. If beauty is in the eye of the beholder then, as far as McCready was concerned, this view would be bleak indeed. There were far too many places for a man – or even a regiment – to hide.

Denison hitched his pack to a more comfortable position and set off again, keeping up a fast pace, so as to catch up with the others. He drew abreast of Lyn, and said, 'It's lucky no one took a crack at us when we were leaving Kevo. I was so woozy I wouldn't have been much help.'

Lyn looked at him worriedly. 'How are you feeling now?'

'Fine,' he said lightly. 'I feel a lot better now I can remember things. This morning I remembered the name of the man in the flat above mine; Paterson – a nice chap.'

'And you remember being a film director?'

'Yes.' He laughed. 'Don't run away with the idea that I was one of your big-time movie moguls – my stuff wasn't shown in the West End. I make educational films mostly.' He frowned. 'Or, at least, I did. I was fired from my job.'

'Don't worry about that, Giles,' she said quietly.

'I'm not worrying; I have more important things on my mind at the moment. All the same,' he said, looking into his past, 'I don't seem to have been a nice character.'

There was violence in her voice. 'Forget it!' she said crossly.

He glanced at her face in profile. 'You worry about me, don't you?' There was a tinge of wonder in his voice; it had been a long time since anyone had worried about what happened to him. All Fortescue had worried about was whether the job would get done – he hadn't given a damn about Denison himself.

'What do you expect me to do? Cheer when you get slugged on the head?' She walked on a few more paces. 'You should never have agreed to this mad scheme.'

'Carey talked me into it – he's a very persuasive man. But you talked yourself into it. Nobody asked you to come. Now why did you do that?'

She offered him a wan smile. 'You know, you're rather like Hamlet; you let yourself be pushed around.'

He grinned. 'Ah, the fair Ophelia.'

'Don't class me with that damned ninny,' she snapped. 'I'm not going to go mad in white satin. But I still think that if Hamlet had had someone to give him advice, to put some backbone into him, things would have turned out differently. As it was, all he had was that wet, Horatio.'

He felt suddenly depressed. 'Are you offering to supply backbone?'

'All I'm saying is that you mustn't depend on this gang of Whitehall thugs. Don't believe everything Carey tells you. He's in business for himself, not you.' She seemed angry.

He was silent for a while. 'You could be right,' he said at last. 'I have no illusions about this job. I know I was thrown into it involuntarily but I carried on of my own will and with my eyes open. I know I'm being used and I don't particularly like it. At the time when Carey put the proposition I was mixed up, to say the least, and I dare say Carey took advantage. I don't blame him for it – I was all he had.'

'But you're becoming better,' said Lyn. 'You'll be getting ready to make your own decisions.'

'We'll see,' said Denison thoughtfully. 'We'll see.' He hitched the pack on his back. 'When do we get to this hut?'

They pressed on late that night because Diana wanted to reach the hut. 'No point in staying in the open when we can have a roof over our heads,' she said. Travelling late was no problem; the light never left the sky and they were able to move as fast at midnight as at midday and they saw the hut at two in the morning.

It was built of birch logs and was bigger than they had expected. It was in the form of a letter 'H', wings having been added as was necessary. The living quarters were in the crossbar of the 'H' and they were glad to divest themselves of the heavy packs. The two women began to prepare a meal and sent the men to get water.

Harding and Denison took buckets and went outside, and Harding stopped just outside the hut and looked across the marsh which seemed to consist of reeds and water for as far as the eye could see. 'Good wildfowling country,' he said appreciatively.

Denison slapped at his neck. 'Good mosquito country,' he grumbled.

'Don't worry; they're not malarial.'

'You mean I'm merely being eaten alive?' Denison slapped at himself again. 'Let's get the water.'

They went down to the water's edge and Harding inspected it critically. 'It looks all right; but we'd better boil it to make sure.' They filled the buckets and then Harding straightened. 'I wonder what that is.'

Denison followed the direction of his gaze and saw a low wooden hut on the water's edge about a hundred yards away. 'A sauna probably. The Finns like to have them on the edge of the water so they can jump right in. You won't catch me in there.'

'It doesn't look tall enough to be a sauna,' said Harding. 'The roof's too low. I think I'll take a look.'

'The girls will be screaming for water.'

'I won't be a minute.' Harding walked away following the shore line, and Denison shrugged. He picked up a full bucket and took it up to the main hut. Upon being told there was an insufficiency of water he went back for the other bucket. Harding called, 'Denison; look what I've found.'

Denison walked towards the little hut and thought Harding was probably right – the roof was so low that there would be barely sitting room in the hut, let alone standing room. He walked around it and found Harding squatting on his heels. 'What is it?'

'It's a gun punt,' said Harding. 'Haven't seen one for years.'

From this side Denison could see that the hut consisted of roof only and was merely a shelter over a flat boat which looked like an enlarged Eskimo kayak. 'So?'

Harding shook with laughter. 'Mannermaa told us not to bring a shotgun, and all the time he had this here. The old devil!'

Denison bent down beside Harding. 'I don't see what's funny.'

'You wouldn't. I bet the gun is up at the hut. I'll have to see if I can find it.' Harding pointed to the foredeck of the punt. 'Look there; that's where the breech ropes go.'

Denison looked at the two eyebolts – they told him nothing. 'You're not being very comprehensible.'

'I don't suppose I am. These things have gone out of fashion. There are a couple still in use on the east coast back at home, but I didn't expect to see one in Finland. You'll understand better when you see the gun, if I can find it.' Harding stood up. 'Let's go back.'

They went back to the hut, taking the second bucket of water. On the way they encountered McCready who was just coming in. He seemed tired and depressed. 'Not a sign of anyone,' he said. 'But that's not surprising.' He waved a hand at the marsh. 'How deep would you say that water is?'

'Not very deep,' said Harding. 'Not at the edges, anyway. Two or three feet, perhaps.'

McCready nodded. 'You could hide a bloody army in those reeds,' he said glumly. 'What's for supper?'

Denison smiled slightly. 'I'll lay you ten to one it's bully beef stew.'

'That's not very funny,' said McCready as he went into the hut.

After he had eaten McCready felt better. It had not been bully beef for once and, with his belly full, he felt sleepy. He glanced at the bunks in the corner of the room where Diana and Lyn were already asleep, huddled in their sleeping bags. 'Well, here we are – right in the middle of the bullseye,' he said. 'I suppose someone should keep watch.'

'You get some sleep,' said Denison. 'I'll toss with Harding as to who takes first watch.'

'Where is he?'

'Looking around for some kind of gun.'

McCready came alert. 'A gun?'

'Something to do with a boat he found. He's a wildfowler, you know. He didn't make much sense.'

'Oh, a sporting gun.' McCready lost interest. He stretched for the coffee pot, refilled his cup and then produced a flask. He laced the coffee with whisky and offered the flask to Denison. 'Want some?'

'No, thanks.'

'Lost the taste for it?'

'Seems so.'

McCready put away the flask and sipped his coffee. 'You can keep watch from the hut,' he said. 'Take a turn outside once every half-hour and keep an eye on the hillside. Not that it matters but it would be nice to have warning of anyone coming.'

'They'll come?'

'If not today then tomorrow. We give them what they want and maybe they'll go away. Maybe.' He shrugged. 'I'm not getting killed for the sake of a scrap of paper that doesn't mean a damned thing. Anyway, we've got her to think about.' He nodded towards the bunk where Lyn lay asleep.

'Nice of you to be so considerate,' said Denison.

'Don't be so bloody snippy,' said McCready without rancour. 'We didn't ask her to come – she forced it.' He stretched. 'I'm going to bed.'

Denison picked up the binoculars. 'I'll do a check outside.'

He went out of the hut and looked around, studying the hillside through the glasses, especially in the direction from which they had come. There was nothing to be seen. Next he turned his attention to the marsh. A long way out there were dots on an open stretch of water which, through the glasses, proved to be birds. They were unmoving and apparently asleep. Too big to be ducks they were, perhaps, geese. Harding might know. Not that it made any difference.

After a while he went back into the hut, moving quietly so as not to wake anybody. Harding had just come back; he beckoned to Denison and said in a low voice, 'I've found it – and look!' He opened the palm of his hand and revealed a dozen small copper cylinders rather like .22 cartridge cases without the bullets.

'What are they?'

'Detonators,' said Harding. 'I can't find any powder, though. Come and have a look at the gun.'

'All right,' said Denison. It was something to do until he had to go outside again.

He went with Harding into a room at the side of the hut which was used as a store. Rolled up netting hung neatly on pegs on the wall, and there were a lot of boxes which had been pulled away from the wall, presumably by Harding.

'I found it behind there,' said Harding. 'Not so much hidden as concealed from casual eyes. I knew it must be somewhere around because of the punt.'

Denison had not the faintest idea of what Harding was talking about but he obligingly stepped forward and looked behind the boxes. At first he did not realize what he was looking at; Harding had said something about a gun for a punt and that was what he expected to find – a shotgun to kill ducks. What he saw was something unexpected. True, it was a shotgun, as he realized as soon as his mind had shifted gear, but it was a shotgun of Brobdingnagian proportions.

'What the devil ...?'

Harding chuckled. 'I thought you'd be surprised.'

'Surprised isn't the word,' said Denison. 'Confounded is more like it. How long is this thing?'

'A bit over nine feet, taking in the stock. The barrel is about seven feet.'

Denison looked down at the monstrous object and bent to peer at the bore. He measured it with his thumb and found it to be over an inch and a half. He put his hand under the muzzle and lifted. 'It's damned heavy. How the hell can you shoot a thing like this? You couldn't get it to your shoulder.'

'You certainly couldn't,' agreed Harding. 'I estimate the weight as something over a hundred and twenty pounds. It'll fire about a pound and a half of shot.'

'Well, how *do* you shoot it?'

'It's a punt gun,' said Harding. 'It lies on the foredeck of that punt. You can see that the breech ropes are attached they run through the ring bolts on the punt and take up the recoil. The stock is merely for aiming it; if you put your shoulder to it when firing you'd end up with a broken shoulder.'

Denison scratched his jaw. 'An impressive piece of artillery. I've never heard of anything like this.'

'It was developed early in the nineteenth century,' said Harding. 'The idea is that you lie flat in the punt and propel yourself with paddles rather like ping-pong bats. It's quite easy because once all the weight is in the punt it has a freeboard of only about four inches. You stalk the birds on the water – going among the reeds – and you aim by pointing the whole punt. When you're in range you fire and, God willing, get yourself a dozen birds.'

'Not very sporting,' commented Denison.

'Oh, it isn't as easy as you'd think. Birds aren't as easy to stalk as all that; they have more chance of escaping than you have of killing them.'

'What kind of cartridge does it use?'

'It doesn't.' Harding grinned. 'Try going to a gunsmith some time and asking for quarter-bore cartridges – he'd think you'd gone mad. If you want cartridges you make up your own. You use ordinary black powder well rammed and with your shot on top with some wadding; you put a detonator on this nipple – I won't now because it makes quite a noise even without a charge in the barrel – and you pull the trigger. Down goes the hammer on the nipple, the detonator explodes, flame shoots down the hole in the centre of the nipple and ignites the main charge. Bang!'

'And the whole punt recoils a few feet.'

'You've got the idea,' said Harding. 'The detonator is a modern touch. The originals used flint and steel – very unreliable – but with detonators you shouldn't have one misfire in a hundred.'

'Interesting,' said Denison.

'But no use without powder.' Harding patted the heavy barrel. 'I'd have liked to try it out. Like Mannermaa, I'm not averse to roast duck.'

'Are you averse to sleep?' Denison checked his watch. 'I'm going to wake you in two hours for the second guard duty. You'd better get your head down.'

CHAPTER THIRTY-TWO

Denison woke up because someone was shaking him. He moaned in protest and opened his eyes to see Diana bending over him. 'Wake up – we've got a visitor.'

He sat up and rubbed his eyes. 'Who?'

'Come and see.'

McCready was at the window, binoculars to his eyes. As Denison joined him he said, 'It's one of the characters from Kevo – not the Yanks, the other crowd.'

Denison saw the man walking along the edge of the marsh towards the hut. He was about four hundred yards away. 'Alone?'

'I haven't seen anyone else,' said McCready. 'This boy has his nerve, I must say.'

'Perhaps he doesn't know we're here.'

'Then he's a damned fool,' said McCready. 'And they don't send fools on jobs like this. Diana, stand behind the door with your gun.'

The man tramped stolidly towards the hut. If it were not for his pack he would have looked like any holidaymaker on any beach. Within ten minutes he was within hailing distance and he put up his hands showing empty palms. Holding them up he came to a stop ten yards from the door and waited.

'He knows we're here,' said McCready. He took a pistol from his pack and worked the action to put a round into the breech. He went to the door and held the pistol behind his back. 'If he comes in you'll be behind him,' he said to Diana, and opened the door.

The man still had his hands raised as McCready said, 'What do you want?'

'I want to talk to Dr Harold Meyrick.' The man's English was good but heavily accented. Denison tried to identify the accent but made nothing of it.

'What if Dr Meyrick doesn't want to talk to you?'

'Why not let him make up his own mind?' asked the man.

'Whom shall I announce?' asked McCready suavely.

'Shall we say … Herr Schmidt?'

McCready had no trouble with the accent. 'I'd prefer Pan Schmidt – and even then I don't like it. Schmidt isn't a Czech name.'

The man shrugged. 'Many people in Czechoslovakia have German names.' When McCready did not respond he said, 'My arms are getting tired.'

'You put them up, you pull them down – but not just yet.' McCready made up his mind. 'All right, Mr Smith; step into my parlour.' He opened the door wide and stepped back. The man smiled as he came forward, his hands still high.

He walked into the hut and came to a dead stop four feet inside as McCready brought up the hand holding a gun. Diana closed the door behind him. 'Search him,' said McCready.

Schmidt half-turned and smiled as he saw the pistol in Diana's hand. 'So many guns,' he said. 'I am unarmed, of course.'

'There's no of course about it,' said McCready as Diana checked. When she had finished and found nothing McCready wagged the gun. 'Now take off your pack slowly.'

Schmidt eased the pack from his shoulders and lowered it to the floor. 'That's better,' he said, flexing his arms. 'You people use guns too easily. That's why I came with my hands up – I didn't want to be shot by accident. Why did you shoot at me at Kevo?'

'We didn't, said McCready. 'You ran into another crowd.'

'You expect me to believe that?'

'I don't give a damn if you believe it or not – but you started a war with the United States. I was watching it – three of you against four Yanks. One of your chaps had a broken arm and an American had a bullet in his leg. I had a ringside seat on the other side of the river.'

'So?' said Schmidt. 'The Americans also.' He smiled pleasantly at Denison and then turned back to McCready. 'What Dr Meyrick carries must be very important.'

'And what is it to you?'

'I've come to get it,' said Schmidt composedly.

'Just like that?'

'Just like that, Mr McCready.' He grinned. 'You see that I know your name. In fact, I know the names of everyone here. Mrs Hansen, Dr Harding, Dr Meyrick and, of course, Miss Meyrick. It wasn't hard.'

'No doubt it wasn't,' said McCready. 'But what makes you think that Dr Meyrick will give you anything?'

Schmidt looked Denison in the eye. 'I should think he values the safety of his daughter. It is unwise to go treasure hunting while in possession of a greater treasure, Dr Meyrick.'

Denison glanced at Lyn, then cleared his throat. 'But we have you, Mr Schmidt – if that's your name.'

Schmidt smiled and shook his head. 'I can see you're no tactician, doctor. You see, I am no treasure. I am sure Mr McCready is ahead of you in his thinking.'

'You've got the place surrounded, then?' said McCready.

'Of course. There are more than three of us this time.' Schmidt looked at his watch. 'The time is up in twenty-five no, twenty-four – minutes.'

From the window Harding said, 'He could be pulling a bluff. I've seen no one.'

'The answer to that is easy,' said Schmidt. 'Call my bluff. I'm prepared to wait – if I can sit down.' He took a very slow step sideways and hooked a chair forward with his foot, never taking his eyes off McCready's pistol.

McCready leaned against the table. 'All right,' he said. 'Tell me what Meyrick has that interests you Czechs so much.'

A pained look appeared on Schmidt's flace. 'Don't be stupid, McCready.' He jerked his thumb at Denison. 'He babbled about it in Stockholm. He discovered what was in his father's papers and where they were, and he talked about it to some Swedish friends. You ought to know scientists can't keep secrets. But then he realized exactly what he was talking about so he shut up and went back to England.'

He stopped. McCready's face was blank. 'Go on.'

'Why?' asked Schmidt. 'You know the answers. By then it was too late; the secret was out. Nothing travels faster than the news of a scientific breakthrough. Scientists like to believe in what they call the community of ideas, so the news got around Sweden, to Germany and to Czechoslovakia.'

'And to the United States,' commented McCready.

Schmidt hunched his shoulders. 'Everyone knows the reputation of old Merikken and everyone knows his history. The guess is that he puts his papers somewhere for safe keeping. The way you're behaving leads us to think he buried them – or had them buried – somewhere in northern Finland. So it's a treasure hunt, as I said, and you've got a map with a cross on it. That or the equivalent.' He straightened. 'I want it.'

McCready slanted his eyes towards Denison. 'You see what comes of talking too much.' They were going to give in – that was the plan – but they must not collapse too easily because that would lead to suspicion. 'Let's be democratic,' he said. 'We'll vote on it. Harding?'

'I think he's bluffing,' said Harding flatly. 'I don't think there is anyone out there. Tell him to go to hell.'

Schmidt smiled but said nothing. McCready looked at Denison. 'What about you, Meyrick? You know the importance of this more than anyone.'

'I'm not the only one to be considered,' said Denison. 'Let him have what he wants.'

'Very wise,' said Schmidt.

'Shut up,' said McCready unemotionally. 'Diana?'

'I'm against.'

McCready turned his head. His face was away from Schmidt and he winked at Lyn. 'What do you say?'

'I vote with my father.'

McCready turned back to Schmidt. 'It seems I have the casting vote – yours doesn't count.'

'It will.' Schmidt nodded towards the window. 'My votes are out there.'

'I think you're going to have to prove that,' said McCready. 'You might be bluffing and you might not, but I'm going to call you regardless.'

'This is more dangerous than a game of poker.'

McCready smiled. 'When you came in here you said you didn't want to be shot by accident, so my guess is that if you do have a loaded vote outside you won't use it too forcibly against this hut. You see, you're inside it, too.'

'It's your guess,' said Schmidt.

'And it's your life.' McCready raised his pistol. 'If one bullet comes into this hut you're dead. If I don't kill you Diana will. And there's always Harding in reserve.'

Schmidt looked around at Diana who had a gun trained on him. He glanced at Harding who had also produced a pistol. His hand went to the pocket of his anorak. 'Do you mind if I smoke?'

McCready said nothing. Schmidt shrugged and lit a cigarette. He blew a perfect smoke ring. There was a crackling silence in the hut that went on and on and on.

CHAPTER THIRTY-THREE

Armstrong's hands sweated as he gripped the handles of the wheelbarrow and trundled it along the pavement at a speed that was positively dangerous to the pedestrian population of Enso. Beside him Carey walked quickly to keep pace, every now and then breaking into a little trot. Armstrong came to a halt at a street corner, stopped by the traffic flow.

'Damn Boris Ivanevitch!' said Carey. 'God save us all from talkative coppers. I hope he gets hell for being late on duty.'

'Not far now,' said Armstrong. 'Only another block. You can see the paper mill from here.'

Carey craned his neck and suddenly groaned. 'And I can see that bloody bus – it's just leaving.'

'Is it coming this way? Perhaps we can flag it down.'

'No, damn it! It's going away from us.' Carey checked his watch. 'Dead on time. Huovinen is chicken-livered; he could have delayed it somehow.'

There came a gap in the traffic and Armstrong jolted the barrow over the kerb. 'What now?' he asked as they crossed the street.

'I don't know,' said Carey heavily. 'Let's find a place where we're not too conspicuous.'

'The mill is as good a place as any.'

'No; there'll be a watchman. Go around the next corner and we'll see what we can find.'

They were lucky. A trench was being dug along one side of the street. Carey said, 'Just the thing; we'll stop here.'

Armstrong stopped and lowered the barrow. 'Why here?'

Carey sighed and plucked at his jacket. 'Don't be dim. This uniform and those exposed pipes go together. We look natural.'

Armstrong glanced around. 'A good thing the gang's knocked off work for the day.'

'Yes,' said Carey. 'Jump in the hole and you'll look natural.' Armstrong dropped into the trench and Carey squatted on his heels. 'Got any bright ideas?'

'There's the empty house where I found the barrow. We could lie low in the cellar.'

'Until tomorrow?' Carey pondered and shook his head. 'The problem is the head count at the frontier post. They'll be two short and that might make it a bit unhealthy around here before long.'

Armstrong snapped his fingers. 'There's a railway goes from here to Imatra. Maybe we could get a ride.'

'Nothing doing. Railway police are notoriously efficient especially at frontiers. All it needs is a telephone call from that frontier post to say there are two Finns missing and they'll be doubly efficient.'

'There's a copper coming up just behind you,' said Armstrong.

Carey did not turn. 'Not Boris Ivanevitch, I hope.'

'No.'

'Then have a look at that pipe and tell me what you see.'

Armstrong ducked down into the trench. His voice floated up. 'It's not cracked.'

'It must be cracked somewhere,' said Carey loudly. He heard the crunch of boots on road gravel behind him. 'We'll have to do a smoke test.' He looked up and saw the policeman. 'Good evening, comrade.'

The policeman's face was expressionless. 'Working late?'

'I always have to work late when something goes wrong,' said Carey in a grumbling voice. 'If it isn't one thing it's another, and they always pick on me. Now it's a pipe that's sprung a leak which no one can find.'

The policeman looked into the trench. 'What's this for?'

'Drainage for the new paper mill over there.'

The policeman looked at Carey. His eyes were like stones. 'You won't drain a paper mill through a pipe that size.'

'Not the main drainage for the mill,' said Carey. 'This is what you might call the domestic drainage for the lavatories and the canteen and so on.' An idea suddenly came into his mind, the brilliance of which astounded him. 'Perhaps the leak is in the mill. I might have to go in and see if I can find it there.' He stood up. 'You never can tell what a bad leak will do underground – undermine walls, anything.' He frowned. 'There's some heavy machinery in there.'

'So they tell me,' said the policeman. 'Imported from Finland.'

'I don't know why we can't use our own Russian stuff,' said Carey disgustedly. 'But Russian or Finnish, it will collapse if the foundations are washed from under it. I'd better go and have a look.'

'You're keen on your job,' said the policeman.

'That's how I got to where I am,' said Carey. He jerked his thumb at Armstrong. 'Now, take that young chap; he'll never rise to be an inspector if he lives a hundred years. He never raises a finger unless someone tells him to.' He turned to the trench. 'Come on, useless; we're going into the mill. Bring your barrow with your spade – we might need them.'

He walked away as Armstrong climbed out of the trench and the policeman fell into step beside him. 'You're right,' said the policeman. 'Some of these young chaps *are* useless.'

'Do you have many like that in your lot?' asked Carey.

The policeman laughed. 'They wouldn't last long with us. No, it's the layabouts I come across in the course of duty who grate on my nerves. Youngsters of fifteen and sixteen with hair half-way down their backs and swilling vodka until they're rotten drunk. I don't know how they can afford it. I can't – not on my pay.'

Carey nodded. 'I'm having something of the same trouble with my own son. This generation is as soft as putty, but what can you do, comrade? What can you do?'

'Well, I'll tell you,' said the policeman. 'Just tell that son of yours to keep out of my way. I'm getting a bit heavyhanded these days.'

They stopped at the mill entrance. 'Perhaps you're right,' said Carey. 'Maybe that's what's needed.'

'It is,' said the policeman. He flicked a hand in farewell. 'I hope you find your leak, comrade.'

'Just a minute,' said Carey. 'I've just thought of something. The watchman might not let us in.'

The policeman grinned. 'I'll have a word with him; it'll be all right.'

He walked into the mill and Carey winked at Armstrong. 'Not bad chaps, these Russian coppers, when you get to know them – in spite of Boris Ivanevitch. Come on.'

'Thanks for the testimonial,' said Armstrong. 'It's just the thing I need to get a job around here. Why are we going in?'

'You park the barrow near that temporary office in the corner. Then you go away and keep the watchman busy while I do a spot of burglary.'

'You can't burgle in front of a copper.'

'He won't stay around,' said Carey. 'He has his beat to cover.'

'All right; you do your burglary – then what?'

Carey grinned. 'Then we get ourselves booted out of Russia.'

Half an hour later, when they were walking up to the frontier post, Carey said, 'It was the papers that bothered me. Leaving Russia is easy, but not with Merikken's papers. Then I started talking to the copper about the mill and it gave me the idea. I'd seen those blueprints in that office this morning.'

Armstrong trundled the wheelbarrow. 'I hope it works. There's the frontier post.'

'Remember you don't know any Russian,' said Carey. 'It would be uncharacteristic in a Finn of your class.'

'I don't know any Finnish either,' said Armstrong. 'And that's bloody uncharacteristic.'

'Then keep your mouth shut,' said Carey. 'If you have to talk at all use Swedish; but don't talk if you can help it. Leave the talking to me. And hope that none of these guards are studying engineering or mathematics.'

They bore down on the frontier post at a steady three miles an hour. Armstrong was still wearing working overalls but Carey had covered his uniform. He had stopped being a Russian and was now a

Finn. The guard regarded them with mild surprise as they approached. 'This is as far as you go,' he said in Russian, and accompanied the statement with a smile.

Carey answered in fast Finnish. 'Did the bus driver tell you we were coming? The fool left us behind. We've had to walk from the paper mill.'

The smile left the guard's face as he heard the Finnish. 'Where the devil have you come from?' he asked in Russian.

'I don't speak Russian,' said Carey. 'Don't you know Finnish?'

'Sergeant!' yelled the guard, passing the buck.

A sergeant came out of the guard house, leisurely fastening his belt. 'What's the matter?'

'These two Finns popped up. They came from back there.'

'Oh, they did, did they?' The sergeant stepped over and inspected them critically, his eyes dwelling for a time on the barrow. In exceedingly bad Finnish he asked, 'Where did you come from?'

'The paper mill,' said Carey, speaking slowly. 'The bus driver left us behind.' He indicated the barrow. 'We had to collect these papers to take to the boss in Imatra. It took us a while to find them and when we came out the bus had gone.'

'What are the papers?'

'Machine drawings and calculations. See for yourself.' Carey threw aside the sacking on top of the barrow and picked up the top document. He unfolded it to reveal a blueprint which he gave to the sergeant. 'That's one of the drawings.'

The sergeant studied the complexity of lines with uncomprehending eyes. 'Why take them back to Imatra?'

'For revision,' said Carey. 'It happens all the time. When you build a complicated machine it doesn't always fit together right, usually because some fool of a draughtsman has made a mistake. So the drawings have to be amended.'

The sergeant raised his head and eyed Carey and then looked at the blueprint again. 'How do I know this is what you say it is? I know nothing about paper machinery.'

'In the bottom righthand corner there's the name of our company and a description of the drawing. Can you read that much Finnish?'

The sergeant did not reply. He handed the blueprint back to Carey. 'Are they all like this?'

'Help yourself,' said Carey generously.

The sergeant bent and rooted about in the wheelbarrow. When he straightened he was holding a hardbound exercise book. He opened it and glanced at a solid block of mathematical equations. 'And this?'

'I wouldn't know until I saw it,' said Carey. 'It could be about the chemistry or it could be mechanical. Let me see.' He leaned over to look at the page the sergeant was examining. 'Ah, yes; those are the calculations for the roller speeds. This machine is very advanced – very technical. Do you know that the paper goes through at seventy kilometres an hour? You have to be very exact when you're working at those speeds.'

The sergeant flicked through the pages and then dropped the book into the barrow. 'What do you mean – chemical?'

Carey was enthusiastic. 'Papermaking is as much a chemical process as mechanical. There's the sulphite and the sulphate and the clay – all have to be worked out in exact formulae for the making of different kinds of paper. I'll show you what I mean.' He dug into the wheelbarrow and brought up a roll of papers. 'These are the calculations for that kind of thing. Look; these are the equations for making tissue paper of cosmetic quality – and here – the calculations for ordinary newsprint.'

The sergeant waved away the papers from under his nose.

'I'm sorry,' he said. 'I have no authority to let you pass. I will have to consult my captain.' He turned to go back into the guard house.

'*Perrrkele!*' swore Carey, giving the 'r' its full Finnish value. 'You know damned well by the head count that thirty-six came in and only thirty-four went out.'

The sergeant halted in mid-stride. Slowly he turned and looked at the guard who shrugged helplessly. 'Well?' he asked acidly.

The guard was out of luck. 'I haven't put it in the book yet.'

'How many went out tonight?'

'Thirty-four, plus the driver.'

'How many came in this morning?'

'I don't know. I wasn't on duty this morning.'

'You don't know!' The sergeant was apoplectic. 'Then what's the use of doing a head count?' He took a deep breath. 'Bring me the book,' he said arctically.

The guard bobbed his head and went into the guard house at the double. He emerged in less than fifteen seconds and handed the sergeant a small record book. The sergeant turned the pages and then gave the guard a look that ought to have frozen the blood in his veins. 'Thirty-six came in,' he said softly. 'And you didn't know.'

The luckless guard had the sense to keep his mouth shut. The sergeant checked his watch. 'When did the bus go through?'

'About three-quarters of an hour ago.'

'About!' the sergeant screamed. 'You're supposed to know to the second.' He slapped the page. 'You're supposed to record it in here.' He snapped his mouth shut into a straight line and the temperature fell. 'For *about* three-quarters of an hour two foreign nationals have been wandering on the wrong side of the frontier without anyone knowing about it. Am I supposed to tell that to the captain?' His voice was low.

The guard was silent. 'Well, speak up!' the sergeant yelled.

'I … I don't know,' said the guard miserably.

'You don't know,' repeated the sergeant in freezing tones. 'Well, do you know this? Do you know what would happen to me – ' he slapped himself on the chest – 'to me if I told him that? Within a week I'd be serving on the Chinese frontier – and so would you, you little turd, but that wouldn't make me any happier.'

Carey tried to look unconcerned; he was not supposed to know Russian. He saw the beginnings of a grin appear on Armstrong's face and kicked him on the ankle.

'Stand to attention!' roared the sergeant, and the guard snapped straight, his back like a ramrod. The sergeant went very close to him and peered at him from a range of six inches. 'I have no intention of serving on the Chinese frontier,' he said. 'But I will guarantee one thing. Within a week you'll be wishing you were on the Chinese frontier – and on the Chinese side of it.'

He withdrew. 'You'll stay there until I tell you to move,' he said quietly, and came over to Carey. 'What's your name?' he asked in Finnish.

'Mäenpää,' said Carey. 'Rauno Mäenpää. He's Simo Velling.'

'Your passes?'

Carey and Armstrong produced their passes and the sergeant scrutinized them. He handed them back. 'Report here when you come in tomorrow. Report to me and no one else.'

Carey nodded. 'We can go?'

'You can go,' said the sergeant tiredly. He swung around and yelled at the unfortunate guard, 'Well, what are you waiting for? The grass to grow between your toes? Raise that barrier.'

The guard was electrified into sudden action. He raised the barrier and Armstrong pushed the wheelbarrow to the other side. Carey was about to follow when he paused. He turned to the sergeant and said, 'Papermaking is very interesting, you know. When the factory is working you ought to go and see it. Very spectacular.'

'I might do that,' said the sergeant.

Carey nodded pleasantly and followed Armstrong. He took a deep breath as though it was a different kind of air.

CHAPTER THIRTY-FOUR

Schmidt consulted his watch. 'One minute.' He dropped a cigarette stub on the floor and put his foot on it.

'We'll wait,' said McCready. He nodded to Denison. 'Check the windows – see if there's anyone out there. You too, Harding.'

Denison went to the window. All was quiet and nothing moved except water ripples in the distance and the reeds which swayed stiffly in the light breeze. 'All quiet.'

'Here, too,' said Harding, who was at the back window. 'Not a thing stirring on the mountain.'

'I think you're trying to pull a fast one,' said McCready. 'It would be a hell of a joke if there was just one man out there.'

Schmidt shrugged. 'Wait for it.'

Denison saw a movement in the reed bed at the edge of the marsh. 'There's something – or someone out there. It's a man. He's …'

His words were cut off by staccato explosions. In front of the hut the ground danced and soil fountained under the impact of bullets. An upthrown stone hit the pane of glass in front of Denison and the glass fractured and starred. He ducked hastily.

The noise stopped, chopping off into a dead silence.

McCready let out his breath. 'Automatic weapons. At least three.'

'Five,' said Schmidt. 'Seven men – eight including me.' His hand dipped into his pocket and came out with the packet of cigarettes. 'I've just cast my vote.'

McCready casually laid down his pistol on the table. 'Power grows out of the barrel of a gun. Your guns are bigger.'

'I thought you'd see sense,' said Schmidt approvingly. 'Where's the map, or whatever it is?'

'Give it to him,' said McCready.

Denison took a folded sheet of paper from his pocket and held it out to Schmidt who examined it with interest. His interest turned to bafflement. 'Is this all?'

'That's all,' said Denison.

'This word – ' Schmidt stumblingly pronounced it – '*Iuonnonpuisto*. What does it mean?'

'A literal translation would be "nature park",' said McCready. 'The other three words mean lake, hill and gap. The numbers are co-ordinates in degrees of a circle. If you can find a lake, a hill and a gap in that exact relationship, all in a nature park, then you've solved the problem.' He smiled at Schmidt. 'I can't say I wish you better luck than we've had.'

'Not much to go on,' said Schmidt. 'And this is a photocopy.'

'Someone snatched the original at Kevo. Our friend there got a bump on the head. So it wasn't you, then?'

'Obviously it wasn't,' said Schmidt. 'The Americans?'

'I don't think so.'

'I do think so,' stated Schmidt. 'Because they aren't here. Perhaps they're back at Kevo measuring angles with a theodolite like he was doing.' He pointed at Denison.

'Maybe,' said McCready non-committally.

Schmidt stared at the paper. 'This is foolishness. Why didn't he give the name of the nature park?'

'Why should he?' asked McCready. 'He knew it. That just an *aide-mémoire* – just for the figures. You see, Merikken *knew* where the papers were and expected to dig them up himself – he didn't expect to be killed in an air raid. But since one bit of rough country looked very much like another he took the precaution of measuring those angles.' He offered Schmidt a derisory smile. 'Those papers will be a hell of a job to find – especially with interference.'

Schmidt had a sour expression on his face as he folded the paper and put it into his pocket. 'Where's your theodolite?'

'Over there in the corner.'

'You don't mind if I borrow it?' His voice was heavily ironic.

'Go ahead; we can get another.'

Schmidt stood up, went to the door and opened it. He shouted something in Czech and came back into the room. 'Put your guns on the table.'

McCready hesitated, then said, 'All right, everybody; put your guns with mine.'

'You're showing sense,' said Schmidt. 'Neither of us can afford a shooting incident especially if people are killed.' He laughed. 'If only I have the guns we'll both be safe.'

Diana reluctantly laid down her gun and Harding followed suit. When the door opened to admit another man there were five pistols laid out. The man was carrying an automatic rifle and when Schmidt saw that McCready was looking at it with wary interest he laughed, and said, 'We borrowed some of your NATO weapons. They're not bad.' He spoke to the man and pointed at the back packs, then he picked up the pistols, put three of them into his pockets and held the other two in his hands.

'You spoke of interference,' he said to McCready. 'You will not interfere. You are out of the game.'

The other man was dumping the contents of the packs on to the floor. He gave a startled exclamation as he came upon McCready's collapsible rifle. Schmidt smiled, and said, 'Always trying, Mr McCready – but that I expect. You will stay in this hut. If you attempt to leave it there is a grave danger of being shot dead.'

'How long for?'

Schmidt shrugged. 'For as long as I consider necessary.'

Diana spoke up. 'We'll need water.'

Schmidt regarded her speculatively, then nodded abruptly. 'I am not an inhumane man.' He pointed to Harding and Denison. 'You and you will bring water now. The rest will stay here.'

Denison picked up the two empty buckets, and Harding said, 'We'll need as much as possible. I'll take the bowls.'

The man with the automatic rifle slung it over his shoulder together with McCready's rifle. He picked up the theodolite and its tripod and left the hut followed by Denison and Harding, and Schmidt brought up the rear, a gun in each hand.

McCready watched them go down to the edge of the marsh, and cocked an eye at Diana. 'They seem to have bought it,' he said softly. 'For the next few weeks all the nature parks in Finland will be crawling with Czechs wielding theodolites. That ought to make the Finns properly suspicious.'

Denison walked down to the marsh acutely aware that the man behind him was holding a pair of pistols. He bent down and began to fill the buckets. Schmidt lobbed the pistols one at a time into the marsh, using an overarm throw like a cricketer. He spaced them well out and Denison knew they would be irrecoverable. He straightened his back and said, 'How will we know when it's safe to come out of the hut?'

There was a grim smile on Schmidt's face. 'You won't,' he said uncompromisingly. 'You'll have to take your chances.'

Denison stared at him and then looked down at Harding who shrugged helplessly. 'Let's go back to the hut,' he said.

Schmidt stood with his hands on his hips and kept his eyes on them all the way to the hut. The door closed behind them and he hitched his pack into a more comfortable position, spoke briefly to his companion, and set off along the edge of the marsh in the same direction from which he had come, keeping up the same stolid pace as when he had arrived.

CHAPTER THIRTY-FIVE

It seemed to Denison that of all the episodes he had gone through since being flung into this hodge-podge of adventures the time he spent in the hut at Sompio was characterized by a single quality – the quality of pure irritation. The five of them were pent up – 'cribbed, cabined and confined', as Harding ironically quoted – and there was nothing that any of them could do about it, especially after McCready tested the temperature of the water.

After two hours had gone by he said, 'I think we ought to do something about this. I'll just stick my toe in and see what it's like.'

'Be careful,' said Harding. 'I was wrong about Schmidt – he doesn't bluff.'

'He can't leave his men around here for ever,' said McCready. 'And we'd look damned foolish if there's no one out there.'

He opened the door and stepped outside and took one pace before a rifle cracked and a bullet knocked splinters from a log by the side of his head so that white wood showed. He came in very fast and slammed the door. 'It's a bit warm outside,' he said.

'How many do you think there are?' asked Harding.

'How the hell would I know?' demanded McCready irritably. He put his hand to his cheek and pulled out a wood splinter, then looked at the blood on his fingertips.

'I saw the man who fired,' said Denison from the window. 'He was just down there in the reeds.' He turned to McCready. 'I don't think he meant to kill. It was just a warning shot.'

'How do you make that out?' McCready displayed the blood on his hand. 'It was close.'

'He has an automatic rifle,' said Denison. 'If he wanted to kill you he'd have cut you down with a burst.'

McCready was on the receiving end for the first time of the hard competency which Carey had found so baffling in Denison. He nodded reluctantly. 'I suppose you're right.'

'As for how many there are, that's not easy to say,' said Denison. 'All it needs is one at the front and one at the back, but it depends on how long Schmidt wants to keep us here. If it's longer than twenty-four hours there'll be more than two because they'll have to sleep.'

'And we can't get away under cover of darkness because there isn't any,' said Harding.

'So we might as well relax,' said Denison with finality. He left the window and sat at the table.

'Well, I'm damned!' said McCready. 'You've got it all worked out, haven't you?'

Denison looked at him with a half-smile. 'Have you anything to add?'

'No,' said McCready disgustedly. He went over to Diana and talked to her in a low voice.

Harding joined Denison at the table. 'So we're stuck here.'

'But quite safe,' said Denison mildly. 'As long as we don't do anything bloody foolish, such as walking through that door.' He unfolded a map of the Sompio Nature Park and began to study it.

'How are you feeling?' asked Harding.

'Fine.' Denison looked up. 'Why?'

'As your personal head-shrinker I don't think you'll be needing me much longer. How's the memory?'

'It's coming back in bits and pieces. Sometimes I feel I'm putting together a jigsaw puzzle.'

'It's not that I want to probe into a delicate area,' said Harding. 'But do you remember your wife?'

'Beth?' Denison nodded. 'Yes, I remember her.'

'She's dead, you know,' said Harding in an even uninflected voice. 'Do you remember much about that?'

Denison pushed away the map and sighed. 'That bloody car crash – I remember it.'

'And how do you feel about it?'

'How the hell would you expect me to feel about it?' said Denison with suppressed violence. 'Sorrow, anger – but it was over three years ago and you can't feel angry for ever. I'll always miss Beth; she was a fine woman.'

'Sorrow and anger,' repeated Harding. 'Nothing wrong with that. Quite normal.' He marvelled again at the mysteries of the human mind. Denison had apparently rejected his previous feelings of guilt; the irrational component of his life had vanished. Harding wondered what would happen if he wrote up Denison's experiences and presented them in a paper for the journals – 'The Role of Multiple Psychic Trauma in the Suppression of Irrational Guilt'. He doubted if it would be accepted in a serious course of treatment.

Denison said, 'Don't resign yet, Doctor; I'd still like to retain your services.'

'Something else wrong?'

'Not with me. I'm worried about Lyn. Look at her.' He nodded towards Lyn who was lying on her back on a bunk, her hands clasped behind her head and staring at the ceiling. 'I've hardly been able to get a word out of her. She's avoiding me – wherever I am, she's not. It's becoming conspicuous.'

Harding took out a packet of cigarettes and examined the contents. 'I might have to ration these,' he said glumly. 'I've also been wondering about Lyn. She is a bit withdrawn – not surprisingly, of course, because she has a problem to solve.'

'Oh? What's her problem? Apart from the problems we all have here?'

Harding lit a cigarette. 'It's personal. She talked to me about it – hypothetically and in veiled terms. She'll get over it one way or another.' He drummed his fingers on the table. 'What do you think of her?'

'She's a fine person. A bit mixed up, but that's due to her upbringing. I suppose the problem has to do with her father.'

'In a manner of speaking,' said Harding. 'Tell me; what was the difference in age between your wife and yourself?'

'Ten years,' said Denison. He frowned. 'Why?'

'Nothing,' said Harding lightly. 'It's just that it could make things a lot easier – your having had a wife so much younger than yourself, I mean. You used to wear a beard, didn't you?'

'Yes,' said Denison. 'What the hell are you getting at?'

'I'd grow it again if I were you,' advised Harding. 'The face you're wearing tends to confuse her. It might be better to hide it behind a bush.'

Denison's jaw dropped. 'You mean … Diana said something … she can't … it's imposs …'

'You damned fool!' said Harding in a low voice. 'She's fallen for Denison but the face she sees is Meyrick's – her father's face. It's enough to tear any girl in half, so do something about it.' He pushed back his chair and stood up. 'Talk to her, but go easy.' He went to the other end of the room and joined McCready and Diana, leaving Denison staring at Lyn.

McCready organized watches. 'Not that anything is likely to happen,' he said. 'But I'd like advance notice if it does. Those not on watch can do what they like. My advice is sleep.' He lay on a bunk and followed his own advice.

Harding wandered off into the storerooms and Denison resumed his study of the map of Sompio. From time to time he heard scrapings and bangings as Harding moved boxes about. Diana was on watch at a window and she and Lyn conversed in low tones.

After a couple of hours Harding came back looking rumpled and dishevelled. In his hand he carried what Denison took to be a gallon paint can. 'I've found it.'

'Found what?'

Harding put the can on the table. 'The powder.' He prised the lid off the can. 'Look.'

Denison inspected the grainy black powder. 'So what?'

'So we can shoot the punt gun. I've found some shot, too.'

McCready's eyes flickered open and he sat up. 'What gun?'

'The punt gun I was telling you about. You didn't seem interested in it at the time.'

'That was when we had guns of our own,' said McCready. 'What is it? A shotgun?'

'You could call it that,' said Harding, and Denison smiled.

'I think I'd better look at it,' said McCready, and swung his legs over the side of the bunk. 'Where is it?'

'I'll show you.' Harding and McCready went out, and Denison folded the map and went to the window. He looked out at the unchanging scene and sighed.

'What's the matter?' asked Diana. 'Bored?'

'I was wondering if our friends are still around.'

'The only way to find out is to stick your head outside.'

'I know,' said Denison. 'One of us will have to do it sooner or later. I think I'll have a crack at it. It's three hours since McCready tried.'

'No,' said Lyn. The word seemed to be torn out of her involuntarily. 'No,' she said again. 'Leave that to the … the professionals.'

Diana smiled. 'Meaning me? I'm willing.'

'Let's not argue about it,' said Denison peaceably. 'We're all in this together. Anyway, it's a sure cure for boredom. Keep your eye on those reeds, Diana.'

'All right,' she said as he walked to the door. Lyn looked at him dumbly.

He swung open the door slowly and waited a full minute before going outside, and when he did so his hands were above his head. He waited, immobile, for another minute and, when nothing happened, he took another step forward. Diana shouted and simultaneously he saw a movement in the reeds on the edge of the marsh. The flat report of the rifle shot coincided with a clatter of stones six feet in front of him and there was a shrill *spaaang* as the bullet ricocheted over his head.

He waved both his hands, keeping them over his head, and cautiously backed into the hut. He was closing the door when McCready came back at a dead run. 'What happened?'

'Just testing the temperature,' said Denison. 'Somebody has to do it.'

'Don't do it when I'm not here.' McCready went to the window. 'So they're still there.'

Denison smiled at Lyn. 'Nothing to worry about,' he assured her. 'They're just keeping us in a pen.' She turned away and said nothing. Denison looked at McCready. 'What do you think of Harding's gun?'

'He doesn't think much of it,' said Harding.

'For God's sake!' said McCready. 'It's not a shotgun – it's a light artillery piece. Even if you could lift it – which you can't – you couldn't shoot it. The recoil would break your shoulder. It's bloody useless.'

'It's not meant for waving about,' said Harding. 'It's designed for use on the punt, like a 16-inch gun on a battleship. You don't find many of those on land because of the difficulty of absorbing the recoil – but you can put half a dozen on a ship because the recoil is absorbed by the water.'

'Just my point,' said McCready. 'It's as useless as a 16-inch gun would be if we had one. The powder is something else; maybe we can do something with that.'

'Like making hand grenades?' queried Denison sardonically. 'What do you want to do? Start a war?'

'We have to find a way of leaving here.'

'We'll leave when the Czechs let us,' said Denison. 'And nobody will get hurt. They've fallen for your fake treasure map, so what's the hurry now?' There was a cutting edge to his voice. 'Any fighting you do now will be for fighting's sake, and that's just plain stupid.'

'You're right, of course,' said McCready, but there was an undercurrent of exasperation in his voice. 'Your watch, Harding; then Denison and then me.'

'You don't mind if I mess about with the gun while I keep watch?' asked Harding. 'It's of personal interest,' he added apologetically. 'I *am* a wildfowler.'

'Just don't cause any sudden bangs,' said McCready. 'I don't think my heart could stand it. And no one goes outside that door except on my say-so.'

Denison stretched his arms. 'I think I'll try to sleep for a while. Wake me when it's my watch.' He lay on his side on the bunk and for a while regarded Harding who had struggled in with the punt gun. He had some paper and appeared to be making small paper bags.

Denison's eyelids drooped and presently he slept.

He was awakened by Harding shaking his shoulder. 'Wake up, Giles; your watch.'

Denison yawned. 'Anything happening?'

'Not a thing to be seen.'

Denison got up and went to the window. Harding said, 'I think I've figured out the gun. I've even made up some cartridges. I wish I could try it.' There was a wistful note in his voice.

Denison looked about the room. The others were asleep which was not surprising because it was midnight. 'You'd better rest. When we move we'll probably move quickly.'

Harding lay on his bunk and Denison inspected the view from the window. The sun shone in his eyes, just dipping over the horizon far over the marsh; that was the lowest it would set and from then on it would be rising. He shaded his eyes. The sun seemed to be slightly veiled as though there was a thickening in the air over the marsh, the slightest of hazes. Probably a forest fire somewhere, he thought, and turned to the table to find the results of Harding's handiwork.

Harding had made up six cartridges, crude cylindrical paper bags tied at the top with cotton thread. Denison picked one up and could feel the small shot through the paper. The cartridges were very heavy; he bounced one in his hand and thought its weight was not far short of two pounds. A pity Harding could not get his wish but, as McCready had pointed out, firing the gun was impossible.

He bent down and picked up the punt gun, straining his back and staggering under the weight. He cradled it in his arms and attempted to bring the butt to his shoulder. The muzzle swung erratically in a wild arc. It was impossible to aim and the recoil as two pounds of shot left the barrel would flatten the man who fired it. He shook his head and laid it down.

An hour later the view from the window was quite different. The sunshine had gone to be replaced by a diffuse light and the haze over the marsh had thickened into a light mist. He could still see the boathouse where the punt lay, and the reeds at the marsh edge, but farther out the light was gone from the water and beyond that was a pearly greyness.

He woke McCready. 'Come and look at this.' McCready looked at the mist thoughtfully, and Denison said, 'It's been thickening steadily. If it keeps to the same schedule visibility will be down to ten yards in another hour.'

'You think we ought to make a break?'

'I think we ought to get ready,' said Denison carefully. 'And I think we ought to find out if our friends are still there before the mist gets any thicker.'

'We meaning me,' said McCready sourly.

Denison grinned. 'It's your turn – unless you think Harding ought to have a go. Or Diana.'

'I suppose I volunteer – but let's wake up the others first.'

Ten minutes later it was established beyond doubt that the besiegers were still there. McCready slammed the door. 'That bastard doesn't like me; I felt the wind of that one.'

'I saw him,' said Denison. 'The range is a hundred yards not more. He could have killed you, but he didn't.'

'The mist has thickened,' said Diana. 'Even in the last ten minutes.'

'Let's get everything packed,' said McCready.

They started to repack their gear, all except Denison who went to the window to stare out over the marsh. Fifteen minutes later McCready joined him. 'Aren't you coming?'

'Visibility down to fifty yards,' said Denison. 'I wonder what would happen if someone went outside now.'

'If Johnny is still in those reeds he wouldn't see.'

'What makes you think he's still in the reeds? If he has any sense he'll have closed in. So will the others.'

'Others?'

'Logic says there are at least four – two to watch back and front, and two to sleep.'

'I'm not so sure of that,' said McCready. 'It's only theory.'

'Try climbing out of the back window,' said Denison drily. He rubbed his jaw. 'But you're right in a way; it doesn't make sense, does it? Not when Schmidt could have put two men right here in the hut with us. He'd have saved two men.'

McCready shook his head. 'He's too wise a bird to fall for that. When you have a rifle that'll kill at a quarter mile you don't guard at a range of three yards. Guards that close can be talked to and conned into making a false move. We can't talk to these jokers outside and they talk to us with bullets.'

He tapped on the glass. 'But Schmidt didn't reckon on this mist. It's thickening rapidly and when the visibility gets down to ten yards I think we'll take a chance.'

'Then you take it on your own,' said Denison flatly. 'If you think I'm going to go stumbling around out there when there are four men armed with automatic rifles, you're crazy. They might not want to kill us by design but they could sure as hell kill us by accident. I don't go – nor does Lyn. Nor does Harding, if I have any say.'

'A chance like this and you won't take it,' said McCready disgustedly.

'I'm not in the chance-taking business, and in this case it doesn't make sense. Tell me; suppose you leave this hut what would you do?'

'Head back to Vuotso,' said McCready. 'We couldn't miss it if we skirted the edge of the marsh,'

'No, you couldn't,' agreed Denison. 'And neither could the Czechs miss you. You'd be doing the obvious. Come over here.' He walked over to the table and spread out the map, using Harding's cartridges to hold down the corners. 'I'm not recommending leaving the hut at all – not the way things are now – but if it's necessary that's the way to go.'

McCready looked at the way Denison's finger pointed. 'Over the marsh! You're crazy.'

'What's so crazy about it? It's the unexpected direction. They wouldn't think of following us across there.'

'You're still out of your mind,' said McCready. 'I had a good look at that marsh from up on the mountain. You can't tell where the land begins and the water ends, and where there's water you don't know how deep it is. You'd stand a damned good chance of drowning, especially if you couldn't see ten yards ahead.'

'Not if you took the punt,' said Denison. 'The two girls and one man in the punt – two men alongside pushing. Where the water becomes deep they hang on and are towed while the people in the punt paddle.' He tapped the map. 'The marsh is two miles across; even in pitch darkness you could get through in under four hours. Once you're across you head west and you can't help but hit the main road north from Rovaniemi.' He bent over the map. 'You'd strike it somewhere between Vuotso and Tankapirtti, and the whole journey wouldn't take you more than seven or eight hours.'

'Well, I'll be damned!' said McCready. 'You've really been working all this out, haven't you?'

'Just in case of emergency,' said Denison. He straightened. 'The emergency hasn't happened yet. We're a bloody sight safer here than we would be out there. If there was a life and death reason for getting out of here I'd be in favour of it, but right now I don't see it.'

'You're a really cool logical bastard,' said McCready. 'I wonder what it takes to make you angry. Don't you feel even annoyed that we're being made fools of by those Czechs out there?'

'Not so annoyed as to relish stopping a bullet,' said Denison with a grin. 'Tell you what – you were so keen on the democratic process when you were stringing Schmidt along, so I'll settle for a vote.'

'Balls!' said McCready. 'It's either the right thing to do or it isn't. You don't make it right just by voting. I think you're right but I don't ...'

He was interrupted by a single shot from outside the hut and then there was a sustained rapid chatter of automatic fire. It stopped, and McCready and Denison stared at each other wordlessly. There was another report, a lighter sound than the rifle fire, and a window of the hut smashed in.

'Down!' yelled McCready, and flung himself flat. He lay on the floor of the hut and then twisted around until he could see Denison. 'I think your emergency has arrived.'

CHAPTER THIRTY-SIX

All was silent.

Denison lay on the floor and looked at McCready who said, 'I think that was a pistol shot; it sounded different. I hope it was.'

'For God's sake, why?'

McCready was grim. 'Just pray they don't start shooting at this hut with those bloody rifles. They're NATO issue and they pack a hell of a wallop. In Northern Ireland the army found they were shooting through houses – through one wall and out the other.'

Denison turned his head. 'Are you all right, Lyn?'

She was flat on the floor by her bunk. 'I ... I think so.' Her voice was tremulous.

'I'm not,' said Harding. 'I think I was hit. My arm is numb.'

Diana crossed the hut at a low run and flopped down beside Harding. 'Your face is bleeding.'

'I think that was the flying glass,' he said. 'It's my arm that's worrying me. Can you have a look at it?'

'Christ!' said McCready savagely. 'One lousy bullet and he has to get in the way. What do you think now, Denison? Still think it's not time to leave?'

'I haven't heard anything more.' Denison crawled over to the window and cautiously raised himself. 'The mist is much thicker. Can't see a damned thing.'

'Get down from there,' snapped McCready. Denison pulled down his head but stayed in a crouch below the window. 'How's Harding?'

Harding answered. 'The bone is broken,' he said. 'Can someone get my black box? It's in my pack.'

'I'll get it,' said Lyn.

McCready crawled over to Harding and inspected his arm. Diana had torn away the shirt sleeve to get at the wound, a small puncture. Harding's arm was a curious shape; it seemed to have developed an extra joint. 'It was a pistol shot,' said McCready. 'If you'd have been hit by one of those rifle bullets at that range you'd have no arm left.'

Again came the sound of automatic fire but from a greater distance. It sounded like a noisy sewing machine and was interspersed with other single shots. It stopped as quickly as it had begun.

'Sounds like a battle,' said McCready. 'What do you think, Denison?'

'I think it's time to leave,' said Denison. 'We've had one bullet in here – we might get more. You and I will go down to the punt; Diana and Lyn can help Harding along as soon as we've made sure it's safe. We leave the packs and travel light. Bring a compass, if you have one.'

'I've got one in my pocket.' McCready looked down at Harding and saw he had filled a syringe and was injecting himself in the arm. 'How are you, Doctor?'

'That will keep it quiet,' said Harding, taking out the needle. 'If someone can slap a bandage around it.'

'I can do better than that,' said Diana. 'I can make splints.'

'Good,' said Harding. 'I have a broken arm – not a broken leg. I can walk and I'll be ready to move in five minutes. Did you say something about going by punt?'

'Denison's idea.'

'Then why don't we take the gun?'

'Haul that bloody great …!' McCready stopped and glanced at Denison. 'What about it?'

Denison thought of two pounds of birdshot. 'Might give someone a fright.'

'Tie that tighter,' said Harding to Lyn. 'Then bring me those cartridges from the table.' He raised his head. 'If you are going scouting we'll have the gun loaded when you get back.'

'All right,' said McCready. 'Let's go.' All the frustration had dropped from him now that he had something to do. 'When we go out of the door we go flat on our bellies.'

He opened the door and wreaths of mist drifted into the hut. When he put his head around the corner of the door at floor level he found the visibility to be ten to fifteen yards, shifting in density as the mist drifted in from the marsh. He wriggled out and waited until Denison joined him, then put his mouth to Denison's ear and whispered, 'We separate but keep in sight of each other – ten yards should do it. We go one at a time in ten yard runs.'

At Denison's nod he went forward, then dropped to the ground ten yards ahead and, after a moment, waved Denison on. Denison angled away until he was parallel with McCready; he lay and stared into the mist but could see nothing. McCready went ahead again and dropped and then Denison followed, and so on until Denison put his hand wrist-deep in cold water. They were at the edge of the marsh.

He lay there, turning his head from side to side, trying to penetrate the pearly mist, his ears strained for the slightest sound. When he looked up he could see the tops of the stiff reeds, and all he could hear was a rustling as the lightest of airs brushed through them. From the marsh came the occasional call of a bird.

McCready edged up next to him. 'Where's the punt?'

'To the left – a hundred yards.'

They went slowly and separately, McCready leading because of his experience. At last he stopped and when Denison drew up with him he saw the loom of the boathouse through the mist. McCready put his lips next to Denison's ear. 'There could be someone in there. I'll take it from the other side. Give me exactly four minutes then close in from this side.' He wriggled away and was lost to sight.

Denison lay there watching the sweep second hand on his watch. Four minutes seemed a hell of a long time. At exactly two minutes there was a renewed burst of firing which made him start; it seemed to come from the direction of the hut but he could not be sure. He found he was sweating despite the cool clamminess of the mist.

At four minutes he went forward carefully and looked into the dimness under the roof of the boathouse. He saw no one until a movement on the other side made his stomach roll over until he realized it was McCready. 'All safe,' said McCready.

'We'd better take the punt out and run it up on to the beach,' said Denison in a low voice. He waded into the water, trying not to splash, and floated out the punt. Between them they ran it up on to the shingle which crunched loudly. 'For Christ's sake, be quiet!' whispered McCready. 'Did you hear that last lot of shooting?'

'I thought it came from behind me.'

'I thought it came from the marsh,' said McCready. 'You can't tell with mist, though. It distorts sounds. Let's go back and get the others.'

They made it back to the hut uneventfully. McCready closed the door and said, 'There doesn't seem to be anyone out there – not towards the marsh, anyway. That idea of yours might be a good one.'

'I wouldn't go in any other direction,' said Denison briefly. 'Ready to move, Lyn?'

Her face was pale but her chin came up in the resolute gesture he had come to know. 'I'm ready.'

'McCready and I will go first. You follow and help Harding if he needs it. We won't be going too fast if we're carrying the gun.'

'It's loaded – but quite safe,' said Harding. His face was drawn. 'It can't be fired until it's cocked and a detonator cap put on the nipple.'

'We'd better know what we're going to do,' said McCready. 'Are you sure this gun will shoot, Doctor? I don't want us to be lumbered with a load of old iron.'

'It'll shoot,' said Harding. 'I tested the powder and it burns well; and I tested a detonator while they were shooting out there.'

Denison did not know what sound a detonator would make but that might account for his impression that a shot had come from the direction of the hut. He said, 'I think we ought to play safe until we get well into the marsh. Harding ought to go in the punt from the beginning because of his wound – and you, too, George, in case there's shooting. The girls and I will tag on behind.'

McCready nodded, but Harding said, 'I want Denison in the punt with me.'

McCready stared at him. 'Why?'

'Put it down to crankiness or, maybe, loss of blood,' said Harding. 'But that's the way I want it. Believe me, I know what I'm doing.'

McCready looked blankly at Denison. 'What do you say?'

'All right with me. If that's what he wants, that's what he gets.'

'Good,' said Harding. 'Come over here.' He took Denison to where the gun lay. 'It's all ready for going on to the punt. There'll be no difficulty in fixing it – it just drops into place and I have the breech ropes all ready to reeve through the eye-bolts.' He paused. 'There are two important items to remember when you shoot one of these things.'

'Go on.'

'First; keep your head well back when you pull the trigger. There'll be a blowback from the touch-hole which could make a nasty burn on your face. Secondly; you'll be lying flat on your belly when you shoot, and you've got a limited amount of lateral aim by shifting the butt – there's enough play in the breech ropes to allow for that. But just before you pull the trigger raise your knees from the bottom of the punt. That's important.'

'Why?'

Harding shook his head. 'I don't think you realize yet what sort of gun this is. If your knees are in contact with the punt when the recoil comes you're likely to have a couple of shattered kneecaps. Watch it.'

'God Almighty!' said Denison. He looked at Harding curiously. 'Why did you pick me instead of McCready?'

'McCready knows too much about guns,' said Harding. 'He might fall into the error that he knows about this one. I want somebody who'll do exactly as I say without contaminating it with what he thinks.' He smiled wryly. 'I don't know whether we're going to fire this gun – under the circumstances I hope not – but, believe me – when you pull that trigger you'll probably be just as surprised as the man you're shooting at.'

'Let's hope it never happens,' said Denison. 'How's your arm?'

Harding looked down at the improvised sling. 'It'll be fine as long as the drug holds out. I'm leaving my kit but I have a syringe loaded with pain-killer in my pocket. Just one more thing. If we shoot in the marsh it's going to be difficult to reload the gun. It will have to be done in shallow water with McCready at the front of the punt with a ramrod. I'll have a word with him about that.'

He went to McCready and Denison bent to examine the gun. It was suddenly much more real, no longer looking like an old piece of iron piping but a weapon deadly of purpose. He straightened to find Lyn at his side. 'An extra sweater,' she said, holding it out. 'It's always cold on the water.'

'Thanks,' he said, and took it from her. 'It'll be even colder in it. You shouldn't have come, Lyn; this is no place for you. Will you promise me something?'

'That depends.'

'If we get into trouble out there – shooting perhaps, promise to duck out of it. Get down among the reeds and out of sight. Don't take any chances you don't have to.'

She nodded towards Harding. 'And what about him?'

'Leave him to the professionals. They'll look after him.'

'If it weren't for me he wouldn't be here,' she said sombrely. 'And you're a fine one to talk about not taking chances.'

He shrugged. 'All right – but there is something you can do for me. Find a ball of string. Harding might know where there is some.'

McCready came over. 'We're ready to move. Help me with the gun.' As they lifted it they heard several single shots. 'What the hell's going on out there?' said McCready. 'We're not being shot at – so who is?'

Denison took the strain at the butt end of the gun. 'Who cares? Let's take advantage.'

It was better this second time despite the hampering weight of the gun; they had a better sense of direction and knew where to go. Within five minutes they were lowering the gun on to the foredeck of the punt; it slotted neatly into place and Harding, hovering over it, wordlessly indicated how to fit the breech ropes.

Denison uncoiled the thirty-foot length of string that Lyn had found. He gave one end to McCready. 'Keep at the end of that,' he whispered. 'If you get into trouble tug and I'll stop. Two tugs and I'll back water.'

'Bloody good idea.'

Denison tapped Harding on the shoulder. 'Get in before we launch her.' Harding obeyed and Denison and McCready pushed the punt forward until it was afloat. Again there was the crunch of shingle and they waited with held breath to see if they had attracted attention. Denison climbed aboard over the stern and settled behind the gun. He gave the other end of the string to Harding. 'If you feel a tug let me know. Where are the paddles?'

'On the bottom boards next to the gun butt.'

He scrabbled and found them, short-handled and broadbladed. Before he put them into the water he stared ahead. He was lying prone with his eyes not more than a foot above the level of the water. Ahead of him, on the foredeck, stretched nine feet of gun. It looked less clumsy on the punt, more as if it belonged. The weapons system was complete.

'Wait!' whispered Harding. 'Take this needle and push it down the touch-hole.'

Denison stretched out his hand and drew back the hammer. It clicked into place at full cock and he jabbed the needle into the hole in the nipple and felt it pierce the paper cartridge. He waggled it about to enlarge the hole which would allow the flame to reach the powder, and then passed it back to Harding who gave him a detonator cap. Harding whispered, 'I'd keep that in your hand until you're ready to shoot. It's safer.'

He nodded and picked up the paddles and took a short, easy stroke as quietly as he could. The punt moved forward, more quickly than he had expected. Ripples ran backwards vee-shaped from the bow as the punt glided into the mist.

Denison had already determined to stay close to the banks of reeds. From the point of view of paddling the punt he would have been better in mid-channel but there he would be more exposed. Besides, he had the others to think of; they were wading and the water was more likely to be shallow by the reeds.

Harding whispered, 'McCready gave me his compass. What's the course?'

'North-west,' said Denison. 'If we have to make any course changes try to make them north rather than west.'

'Then steady as you go.'

It was an awkward position in which to paddle and he quickly developed aches, particularly at the back of his shoulders. And his breastbone ground against the bottom boards until he thought he was rubbing the skin off his chest. Whoever used the punt must have had a cushion there.

When he estimated they had travelled about two hundred yards he stopped and rested. From behind he could hear faint splashes and, when he looked back, he saw the faint figures of the other three. Beyond there was nothing but greyness. McCready came alongside, water up to his waist. 'What have you stopped for?'

'It's bloody hard work. Unnatural position. I'll be all right.'

From the land came a series of rapid shots, the stammer of an automatic rifle. McCready breathed, 'They're still at it. I'd like to know what …'

There was another shot, so shockingly close that McCready instinctively ducked and Denison flattened himself even closer to the bottom of the punt. There was a splashing noise to the left as though someone was running in shallow water; the sound receded and everything was quiet again.

McCready eased himself up. 'That was right here in the marsh. Let's move.'

Denison pushed off again quietly and the punt ghosted into the mist. He was aware that Harding had not said anything, so he turned his head. 'Are you okay?'

'Carry on,' said Harding. 'A bit more to the left.'

As they penetrated the marsh there were flaws in the mist – sudden thinnings and thickenings of the vapour apparently caused by a light air which stroked Denison's cheek with a delicate touch. Visibility would be no more than five yards and then, ten seconds later, the mist would swirl aside so that he could see, perhaps, forty yards. He did not like it; it was unpredictable and could not be relied on.

Behind, McCready plodded thigh-deep in the water. The footing was treacherous – mostly rotting vegetation but with the occasional ankle-twisting stone or, sometimes, an unexpected hole. He cast a glance over his shoulder and saw that Lyn, much shorter than he, had the water to her waist. He grinned at her and she smiled back at him weakly. Diana brought up the rear, turning her head constantly to look back.

They went on for fifteen minutes and then there was a choked cry from behind McCready. He looked back and saw that Lyn was neck-deep and already beginning to swim. Since he himself was in the water to his armpits this was not surprising so he gave two sharp tugs on the string. The punt ahead drifted back silently as Denison back-paddled gently, and came to a halt alongside McCready.

'You'll have to change course. We're getting out of our depth.'

Denison nodded and silently pointed the way he intended to go, keeping close to the reeds and heading towards what seemed to be a promontory about fifty yards away. As the mist closed in again to blot it out he commenced paddling again.

Once more the gentle, vagrant wind parted the mist and Denison, peering forward along the barrel of the gun, saw a movement and dug both paddles into the water as quietly as he could. The punt slowed to a halt. Again the mist closed in but he waited, hoping that McCready would have the sense not to come forward again to find out what was wrong.

When he felt the slight air pressure on his cheek increase he was ready for the diminution of the mist and the suddenly increased visibility. There was a man standing on the promontory which was just a shingle bank out-thrust into the channel. Another man was walking towards him, splashing through water, and they waved to each other.

Denison put forth his hand and slipped the detonator cap on the nipple below the hammer, and with his other hand wielded a paddle gently. The punt came around slowly and with it the gun barrel. As the primitive foresight drifted across the target he back-paddled one stroke to arrest the movement.

His finger was on the trigger but he was hesitant about firing. For all he knew these men were innocent Finns caught up in a fortuitous battle with those gun-happy, crazy Czechs. One of the men turned and there was a sharp cry and Denison knew the punt had been seen. The other man brought up his arm stiffly and he saw two brief flashes just as the mist began to close in again.

That did it – no innocent Finn would shoot on sight. He squeezed the trigger, only remembering at the last moment to pull back his head and jerk up his knees from the bottom boards.

There was a pause of a single heart beat and then the gun went off. Flame flared from the touch-hole under the hammer and dazzled him but not so much that he could not see the monstrous flame that bloomed from the muzzle of the gun. Orange and yellow with white at its heart, it shot out twelve feet ahead of the punt, blinding him, and was accompanied by a deep-throated *booom*. The punt shivered and jerked back violently in the water and the bottom boards leaped convulsively under him. Then it was gone and a cloud of black smoke lazily ascended and there was the acrid stink of burnt powder in the air.

Although deafened by the concussion he thought he heard a shriek from ahead. Retinal images danced before his eyes as he tried to penetrate the suddenly dense mist and he could see nothing. An automatic rifle hammered from behind and suddenly the water ahead fountained in spurts right across the channel as someone traversed in a blind burst. There was a whipping sound overhead and bits of reed dropped on to his face as he looked up.

The rifle fire stopped.

After a moment Harding said weakly, 'What about reloading?'

'How long?'

'Five minutes.'

'Christ, no!' Denison burst into activity. 'We've got to move and bloody fast.' He brought up his legs and sat on his haunches so as to give the paddles a better grip in the water. This was no time to hang around and dead silence was not as important as getting clear. He jabbed the paddles into the water and made the punt move. As he skirted the promontory he kept a careful watch, not wanting to run aground, and still less wanting to meet whoever had been there.

The violence of that single shot was scared into him. What, in God's name could it have been like at the receiving end? He looked sideways but there was only the drifting mist, and all he could hear was the quickened splashing of the others as they increased their pace to his speed.

He paddled until he was thoroughly weary, occasionally changing course as the channel wound among marshy islands or as Harding dictated from the compass. After half an hour at top speed he was exhausted and stopped with his shoulders bowed and paddles trailing in the water. His breath rasped in his throat and his chest felt sore.

Harding touched him on the shoulder. 'Rest,' he said. 'You've done enough.'

McCready came up, half wading and half swimming. 'Jesus!' he said. 'You set a pace.'

Denison grinned weakly. 'It was that last rifle burst. A bit too much for me. All I wanted to do was to get away.'

McCready held on to the side of the punt and surveyed the gun. 'When this thing went off I was sure the barrel had burst. I've never seen anything like it.'

'How far have we come?' asked Denison.

Harding used his good hand to fish in the bottom of the punt. He came up with the map, soggy and running with water, and gave it to Denison who unfolded it. He pointed over Denison's shoulder. 'I think we've just crossed that wide bit of water.'

'It was deep as well as wide,' said McCready. 'We had to swim.'

'That's much more than half-way,' said Denison. 'Dry land not far ahead.'

Diana and Lyn splashed up along the reeds in the shallower water. They were soaked and bedraggled. Denison pushed with a paddle and eased the punt towards them. 'You all right?' he asked quietly.

Diana nodded wearily and Lyn said, 'How much more of this?'

'Not far,' said Denison. 'You can travel the rest of the way in the punt.'

McCready nodded. 'I think we've got clear. I haven't heard any shooting for quite a while.'

Harding was still doing something at the bottom of the punt. 'I'm afraid we're in trouble,' he said. 'I thought this water was the accumulated drips from the paddles, but I think we have a leak. The punt is sinking.'

'Oh, hell!' said McCready.

'My fault,' said Harding unhappily. 'I think I overloaded the gun. The strain on the punt was too much.'

Denison blew out his breath. McCready could have been right; the barrel *could* have burst. He said, 'It seems you'll have to walk the rest of the way, Doctor. Do you think you can make it?'

'I'll be all right when I've given myself another injection.'

'We'll jam the boat into the reeds,' said McCready. 'And then get going. I think the mist is lifting and I want to be out of this swamp by then.'

CHAPTER THIRTY-SEVEN

Carey strolled through a stand of tall timber and looked towards the house. It was not the sort of house you'd expect to see in Britain because the architecture was all wrong, mainly in matters of detail, but he supposed that if it had been in England it would have been called a manor house – one of the lesser stately homes.

He stopped and lit his pipe, ruminating on history. In the days when Finland was a Grand Duchy and part of Imperial Russia the house would have been the residence of one of the minor nobility or, possibly, a bourgeois Swedish Finn of the merchant class. More recently it had belonged to a company in Helsinki who used it as a holiday home for top staff and as a venue for executive conferences. Now it was rented by British Intelligence for their own undisclosed purposes.

Certainly Carey, as he strolled in the grounds clad in Harris tweed and puffing contemplatively on his pipe, looked every inch – or centimetre – the squire or whatever was the Finnish equivalent. He struck another match and, shielding it with his hand, applied it to his recalcitrant pipe. If he was worried it did not show in his manner. With the back of his mind he worried about McCready and his party who had not yet shown up, but with the forefront he worried about what was happening back in London. Apparently his boss, Sir William Lyng, had been unable to do much about Thornton and the in-fighting in Whitehall was becoming severe.

He achieved satisfaction with the drawing of his pipe and glanced towards the house again to see Armstrong approaching. He waited until he was within easy conversational reach, then said, 'Is that boffin still fiddling with those equations?'

'He's finished.'

'About time. Has he found it?'

'No one tells me anything,' said Armstrong. 'But he wants to see you. Another thing – George McCready phoned in. He couldn't say much on the phone but I gather he has a tale to tell. He wants medical supplies for a bullet in the arm.'

'Who?'

'Dr Harding.'

Carey grunted. 'Any other casualties?'

'None that George mentioned.'

'Good! Let's go to see the boffin.'

Armstrong fell in step with him. 'And there's a man to see you – a chap called Thornton.'

Carey's pace faltered. 'He's here now?'

'I put him in the library.'

'Has he seen the boffin?'

'I don't think so.'

'He mustn't.' Carey looked sideways at Armstrong. 'Do you know anything about Thornton?'

'I've seen him around,' said Armstrong. 'But not to speak to. He's a bit above my level on the totem pole.'

'Yes,' said Carey. 'One of the Whitehall manipulators and as tricky as they come. These are my specific instructions regarding Thornton. You're to go back to the library and offer him tea – he'll like that. You're to keep him busy until I see him. I don't want him prowling around; he makes me nervous. Got that?'

'Yes,' said Armstrong. 'What's the trouble?'

'There's a bit of an argument about policy going on back home and Thornton is pushing a bit too hard. It's nothing that should concern you as long as you obey orders – my orders. If Thornton tries to order you around refer him to me.'

'All right,' said Armstrong.

'I'll tell you something about Thornton,' said Carey candidly. 'He's a bastrich – that's a word worthy of Lewis Carroll. It means a combination of a bastard and a son of a bitch. So you don't say a word about this operation in Thornton's presence. That's another order from me.'

'Not even if he asks me directly?'

'Refer him to me,' said Carey. 'And you won't get into trouble. I know he's high-powered and you are but an underling, but you are in a different department. If he tries anything on just tell him to go to hell in a polite way, and I'll back you up.' He smiled. 'And Lyng will back me so you have support all the way to the top.'

Armstrong looked relieved. 'That's clear enough.'

Carey nodded shortly. 'Good. You attend to Thornton. I'll see the boffin.'

The man whom Carey called the boffin was Sir Charles Hastings, F.R.S., a physicist not without eminence. Carey, whose opinion of scientists was low, treated him robustly and with a lack of deference which Sir Charles, who had a sense of humour, found refreshing. Carey now, on entering the room, said, 'What's the score?'

Sir Charles picked up a set of papers. 'The answer is unequivocal. This is the crucial document. In it Dr Merikken outlines the germ of an idea, and develops it in a most interesting way. As you may know, the concept of the grazing angle has been utilized in the X-ray telescopes we now use, but Merikken took the idea much farther – which is strange considering he worked so many years ago.'

Sir Charles paused, contemplating a vision of genius. 'Merikken not only worked out the theory but subjected it to tests in the laboratory – the only way, of course. Here is a list of his tests, the results of which are frankly astounding. In his first test he was able to obtain an X-ray reflectance of nearly 25 per cent of the incident illumination.'

'Hold on a minute,' said Carey. 'How does that compare with what we've been able to do up to now?'

Sir Charles laughed shortly. 'There's absolutely no comparison. Apart from anything else, this is going to revolutionize X-ray astronomy; it makes possible an X-ray lens of considerable resolution. But that was just the first of Merikken's tests; in his final test before he ended the series he'd done considerably better than that – and his apparatus was not up to modern standards.'

Carey felt his hands empty and took out his pipe. 'So if we put a team on to this, gave it a hell of a lot of money and a reasonable amount of time, we could improve on what Merikken did. Would you agree with that, Sir Charles?'

'Indeed I would. There's nothing in here that offends any of the laws of physics. It reduces itself to a matter of engineering – advanced engineering, mark you, but nothing more than that.' He spread his hands. 'The X-ray laser has now moved from the barely possible to the probable.'

Carey gestured with his pipe. 'Anything else of value in those papers?'

Sir Charles shook his head. 'Nothing at all. This, for instance,' – he picked up the hardbound exercise book – '... this is a series of calculations of nuclear cross-sections. Quite primitive and totally useless.' His voice was a trifle disparaging. 'All the rest is the same.'

'Thank you, Sir Charles.' Carey hesitated. 'I'd be obliged if you would stay in this room until I return. I don't think I'll be more than a few minutes.' He ignored Sir Charles' expression of polite surprise and left the room.

Outside the library he paused and squared his shoulders before opening the door. Thornton was lounging in a leather chair and Armstrong stood at the window. Armstrong looked harassed and was visibly relieved when he saw Carey. 'Good morning,' said Thornton. His voice was cheerful. 'I must say you have your staff well trained, Carey. Mr Armstrong is a positive oyster.'

'Morning,' said Carey curtly.

'I just popped in to find out how Sir Charles Hastings is doing. You must know we're all very keen to see the results of your labours.'

Carey sat down, wondering how Thornton knew about Sir Charles. More and more he was certain there was a leak in Lyng's office. He said blandly, 'You'll have to get that from Sir William Lyng.'

Thornton's cheerfulness diminished a shade. 'Well, I'm sure we can excuse Mr Armstrong while we have a discussion on that matter.' He turned to Armstrong. 'If you don't mind.'

Armstrong made as though to move to the door but stopped as Carey snapped, 'Stay where you are, Ian.'

Thornton frowned. 'As you know, there are certain er … details which Mr Armstrong is not entitled to know.'

'He stays,' said Carey flatly. 'I want a witness.'

'A witness!' Thornton's eyebrows rose.

'Come off it,' said Carey. 'When this operation is finished I make out a final report – including what I hear in this room. So does Armstrong – independently. Got the picture?'

'I can't agree to that,' said Thornton stiffly.

'Then you don't have to talk. What you don't say Armstrong can't hear.' Carey smiled pleasantly. 'What time is your plane back to London?'

'I must say you're not making things easy,' said Thornton querulously.

Carey was blunt. 'It's not my intention to make things easy. You've been getting underfoot all through this operation. I haven't liked that and neither has Lyng.'

All cheerfulness had deserted Thornton. 'I think you misunderstand your position, Carey,' he said. 'You're not yet so big that you can't be knocked over. When the Minister reads my report I think you'll be in for a shock.'

Carey shrugged. 'You make your report and I'll make mine. As for the Minister I wouldn't know. I don't rub shoulders with the Cabinet – I leave that to Lyng.'

Thornton stood up. 'After this is over Lyng may not be around. I wouldn't rely on him to protect you.'

'Lyng can fight his own battles,' said Carey. 'He's been very good at it so far. Ian, will you escort Mr Thornton to his car. I don't think he has anything more to say.'

'Just one small item,' said Thornton. 'There are, of course, people other than those in your department who have been involved. You had better make sure that Denison and the Meyrick girl are silenced. That's all I have to say.'

He stalked out, followed by Armstrong. Carey sighed and took out his matches to light his pipe but stared at it in disgust and put it down unlit. Presently he heard a car door slam and the sound of tyres on gravel. When Armstrong came back he said, 'He's gone?'

'Yes.'

'Then give me a cigarette, for God's sake!'

Armstrong looked surprised but produced a packet of cigarettes. As he held a match for Carey, he said, 'You were a bit rough on Thornton, weren't you?'

Carey puffed inexpertly, and coughed. 'It's the only way to handle a bastard like that. He's the biggest con man in Whitehall, but if you hit him over the head hard enough he gets the message.'

'I'm surprised he took it from you. Aren't you afraid he'll jerk the rug from under you? I thought he was a big boy in the corridors of power.'

'Corridors of power!' Carey looked as though he was about to spit. 'I wonder if C. P. Snow knew he was coining *the* cliché of the twentieth century. I'm not afraid of Thornton; he can't get at me directly. Anyway, I'm coming up to retirement and I'll spit in his eye any time I feel like it.'

He drew on the cigarette and expelled smoke without inhaling. 'It's nothing to do with you, Ian. You just soldier on and don't worry your head about policy.'

'I don't even know what it's all about,' said Armstrong with a smile.

'You're better off that way.' Carey stood up and stared out of the window. 'Did you notice anything odd about that conversation?'

Armstrong thought back. 'I can't say that I did.'

'I did. Thornton got so mad at me that he slipped.' Carey drew on the cigarette and blew a plume of smoke. 'How did he know about Denison? You tell me that, my son, and you'll win a big cigar.' He held out the cigarette and looked at it distastefully, then stubbed it out in an ashtray with unnecessary violence. He said curtly, 'Let me know when Denison and McCready arrive.'

CHAPTER THIRTY-EIGHT

Denison lay in the old-fashioned bath with steaming water up to his ears. He lay passively letting the hot water untie all the knots. His shoulders still ached abominably because of the paddling in the marsh of Sompio. He opened his eyes and stared at the elaborately moulded ceiling and then looked at the ceramic stove in the corner, a massive contraption big enough to heat a ballroom let alone a bathroom. He deduced from that that winters in Finland could be chilly.

When the water turned tepid he got out of the bath, dried himself and put on his – or Meyrick's – bath robe. He looked down at it and fingered the fabric. From what Carey had said in the few brief remarks he had offered his days of high living were over. That suited Denison. In the past few days there had been less chance of high living than of low dying.

He left the bathroom and walked along the panelled corridor towards the bedroom he had been given. It seemed that British Intelligence were not averse to a spot of high life; this country house reminded him of those old-fashioned detective plays in which the earl was found dead in the study and, in the last act, it was the butler what done it. Playwrights in those days seemed to think that everybody but butlers had butlers.

He was about to go into his room when the door opposite opened and he saw Lyn. 'Giles, do you have a moment?'

'Of course.' She held the door open in invitation and he went into her bedroom. 'How is Harding?'

'He's quite a man,' she said. 'He took out the bullet and set the arm himself. He said it wasn't as bad as taking out his own appendix, as some doctors have had to do. Diana and I helped to bandage him.'

'I don't think he'll encounter any more bullets,' said Denison. 'From what I gathered from Carey this job is just about over. He said something about us flying back to England tomorrow.'

'So it was successful – he got what he wanted?'

'Apparently so. There was a scientist here who checked the stuff. Diana and Ian Armstrong went back with him to England.'

She sat on the bed. 'So it's all over. What will you do now?'

'Go back into films, I suppose.' He rubbed his jaw and felt the unshaven stubble. 'Carey said he wanted to talk to me about that because it might not be too easy, not with someone else's face.' He waved his arm largely. 'All this Scandinavian stuff is supposed to be kept secret, so I can't very well go back to Fortescue as I am. He'd ask too many questions which I can't answer. The trouble is that the film world is small and if it isn't Fortescue asking awkward questions it will be someone else.'

'So what's the answer?'

'A man called Iredale, I suppose,' he said morosely. 'He's a plastic surgeon. I can't say I fancy the idea; I've always had a horror of hospitals.'

'Do it, Giles,' she said. 'Please do it. I can't …'

He waited for her to go on but she was silent, her head averted. He sat next to her and took her hand. 'I'm sorry, Lyn. I'd have given anything for this not to have happened. I didn't like the deception I played on you, and I told Carey so. I was about to insist that it be put to an end when you … you found out. I wish to hell we could have met under different circumstances.'

She still said nothing and he bit his lip. 'What will you do?'

'You know what I'll do. I've got a not very good degree so I'll teach – as I told my father.' Her voice was bitter.

'When will you start?'

'I don't know. There's a lot to be straightened out about Daddy's death. Carey said he'll pull strings and make it easy from the legal angle, but there'll still be a lot to do – his will and things like that. There's a lot of money involved – shares in his companies – and there's his house. He once told me that the house would be mine if he died. That was just like him, you know – he said "if" instead of "when".'

Arrogant bastard, thought Denison. He said, 'So you won't start teaching for a long time.'

'Those different circumstances,' said Lyn. 'Perhaps they could be arranged.'

'Would you like that?'

'Oh, yes; to start again.'

'To start again,' mused Denison. 'I suppose it's a wish we all have from time to time. Usually it's impossible.'

'Not for us,' she said. 'After you've had the operation you'll be convalescent for a while. Come to the house and stay with me for that time.' Her hand tightened on his. 'If I could see Giles Denison's face in my father's house perhaps we could start again.'

'A sort of exorcism. It might work.'

'We can try.' She brought her hand up to his face and touched the scar on his cheek. 'Who did this to you, Giles? And who kidnapped my father to let him drown in the sea?'

'I don't know,' said Denison. 'And I don't think Carey knows, either.'

In the room directly below McCready was giving his report to Carey. He had nearly finished. 'It was a right shambles,' he said. 'The Czechs were shooting up everything in sight.' He stopped and considered. 'Except us.'

'Who were the opposition?'

'I don't know. They were armed with pistols, nothing bigger. We only saw them once in the marsh when Denison tickled them up with that overgrown shotgun. Remarkable man, Denison.'

'I agree,' said Carey.

'He keeps his cool in an emergency and he's a good tactician. It was his idea that we cross the marsh. It was a good idea because we didn't run into the Czechs at all. When the punt sank he led us out.'

McCready grinned. 'He had us all lined up on a thirty-foot length of string. And his estimation of speed was accurate; we hit the main road just seven hours after leaving the hut.'

'Did you have any trouble in Vuotso?'

McCready shook his head. 'We nipped in quietly, got into the cars, and drove out. Not far from Rovaniemi we changed into decent clothing to make ourselves presentable for the flight south.' He grimaced. 'There's a Dr Mannermaa in Vuotso – a bird watcher. He's going to be a bit peeved about losing his punt and his gun.'

'I'll straighten that out,' said Carey. 'You said the Czechs were also at Kevo.'

'Czechs, Americans – and a crowd of Germans hovering on the outskirts. I didn't tell the others about them because they never really came into the game.'

'East Germans or West Germans?' asked Carey sharply.

'I don't know,' said McCready. 'They all speak the same lingo.'

'And then there was the chap who knocked Denison on the head and took the original map.'

'I never spotted him from start to finish,' said McCready. 'I think he was a singleton – working on his own.'

'Four groups,' said Carey thoughtfully. 'And we can't identify any Russians for certain.'

'Five,' said McCready. 'There's the gang that substituted Denison for Meyrick. They wouldn't have come chasing after us to Kevo and Sompio. They knew better.'

Carey grunted. 'I have my own ideas about who did the dirty on Denison and Meyrick – and I don't think the Russians came into it.'

'You said Thornton was here. What did he want?'

'I didn't find out,' said Carey. 'I wouldn't let him speak to me except in front of a witness and he turned chicken. He's too fly to be caught that way. But he knew about Sir Charles Hastings, and he knew about Denison.'

'Did he, by God? We'll have to seal that leak when we get back to London. What did Hastings say?'

'Oh, we've got the goods all right. He's taken photocopies back to London. Now we can prepare for the next stage of the operation. I hope nothing happens tonight because I'd like to get Denison and the girl out of it. They're leaving tomorrow on the ten o'clock flight from Helsinki.'

'Where are the original papers now?'

'In the safe in the library.'

'In that antique? I could open it with my grandmother's hat-pin.'

Carey smiled blandly. 'Does it matter – under the circumstances?'

'No, I don't suppose it does,' said McCready.

CHAPTER THIRTY-NINE

Denison went to bed early that night because he had a lot of sleep to catch up on and because he had to get up fairly early to catch the flight to London. He said good night to Lyn and then went into his bedroom where he undressed slowly. Before getting into bed he drew the curtains to darken the room. Even though he was now below the Arctic Circle there was still enough light in the sky to make falling asleep annoyingly difficult. It would get darker towards midnight but never more than a deep twilight.

He woke up because someone was prodding him, and came swimming up to the surface out of a deep sleep. 'Giles; wake up!'

'Mmmm. Who's that?'

The room was in darkness but someone looked over him. 'Lyn,' she whispered.

He elbowed himself up. 'What's the matter? Turn on the light.'

'No!' she said. 'There's something funny going on.'

Denison sat up and rubbed his eyes. 'What sort of funny?'

'I don't really know. There are some people in the house down in the library. Americans. You know the man you introduced me to – the man you said was a bore.'

'Kidder?'

'Yes. I think he's down there. I heard his voice.'

Kidder! The man who had interrogated him in the hotel in Helsinki after he had been kidnapped from the sauna. The man who had led the American party at Kevo. The overjovial and deadly boring Jack Kidder.

'Christ!' said Denison. 'Hand me my trousers – they're on a chair somewhere.' He heard a noise in the darkness and the trousers were thrust into his groping hand. 'What were you doing prowling in the middle of the night?'

'I couldn't sleep,' said Lyn. 'I was standing at my bedroom window when I saw these men in the grounds – there's still just enough light to see. They didn't seem to be up to any good – they were dodging about a bit. Then they all disappeared and I wondered what to do. I wanted to find Carey or McCready but I don't know where their rooms are. Anyway, I looked down the stairs and there was a light in the library, and when I got to the door I heard Kidder's voice.'

'What was he saying?'

'I don't know. It was just a rumble – but I recognized the voice. I didn't know what to do so I came and woke you.'

Denison thrust his bare feet into shoes. 'There's a sweater on the back of the chair.' Lyn found it and he put it on. 'I don't know where Carey's room is, either. I think I'll just nip downstairs.'

'Be careful,' said Lyn. 'I've heard enough shooting already.'

'I'll just listen,' he said. 'But you be ready to scream the place down.'

He opened the bedroom door gently and went into the dimness of the corridor. He trod carefully on his way to the stairs to avoid creaking boards, and tiptoed down, his hand running along the balustrade. The door to the library was closed but illumination leaked out from under the door. He paused by the door and listened and heard the deep sound of male voices.

He could make nothing of it until he bent and put his ear to the keyhole and then he immediately recognized the gravelly voice of Kidder. He could not distinguish the words but he recognized the voice. Another man spoke in lighter tones and Denison knew it was Carey.

He straightened up and wondered what to do. Lyn had spoken of men in the plural which would mean there were others about besides Kidder. He could cause a disturbance and arouse the house but if Kidder was holding up Carey at gunpoint that might not be good for

Carey. He thought he had better find out what was really going on before doing anything drastic. He turned and saw Lyn standing by the staircase and he put his finger to his lips. Then he took hold of the door knob and eased it around very gently.

The door opened a crack and the voices immediately became clearer. Carey was speaking. '… and you ran into trouble again at Sompio?'

'Jesus!' said Kidder. 'I thought we'd run into the Finnish army but it turned out they were goddamn Czechs – we wounded one and he was cussing fit to bust. Who the hell would expect to find Czechs in the middle of Finland? Especially carrying automatic rifles and some sort of crazy flame-thrower. That's why I'm bandaged up like this.'

Carey laughed. 'That was our crowd.'

Denison swung the door open half an inch and put his eye to the crack. He saw Carey standing by the safe in the corner but Kidder was not in sight. Carey said, 'It wasn't a flame-thrower – it was a bloody big shotgun operated by no less than the eminent Dr Meyrick.'

'Now, there's a slippery guy,' said Kidder.

'You shouldn't have snatched him from the hotel in Helsinki,' said Carey. 'I thought you trusted me.'

'I trust nobody,' said Kidder. 'I still wasn't sure you weren't going to cross me up. You were playing your cards close to your chest – I still didn't know where the papers were. Anyway, I got nothing out of Meyrick; he gave me a lot of bull which I nearly fell for, then he nearly busted my larynx. You breed athletic physicists in Britain, Carey.'

'He's a remarkable man,' Carey agreed.

Kidder's voice changed and took on a more incisive quality. 'I reckon that's enough of the light conversation. Where are Merikken's papers?'

'In the safe.' Carey's voice sharpened. 'And I wish you'd put that gun away.'

'It's just window dressing in case anyone snoops in,' said Kidder. 'It's for your protection. You wouldn't want it getting around that you're … shall we say … co-operating with us, would you? What's with you, Carey? When the word came that you were willing to do a deal no one would believe it. Not such an upright guy like the respected Mr Carey.'

Carey shrugged. 'I'm coming up to retirement and what have I got? All my life I've lived on a thin edge and my nerves are so tight I've got a flaming big ulcer. I've shot men and I've been shot at; during the war the Gestapo did things to me I don't care to remember. And all for what? When I retire I get a pension that'll do little more than keep me in tobacco and whisky.'

'Cast away like an old glove,' said Kidder mockingly.

'You can laugh,' said Carey with asperity. 'But wait until you're my age.'

'Okay, okay!' said Kidder soothingly. 'I believe you. You're an old guy and you deserve a break. I know your British Treasury is penny-pinching. You should have worked our side of the fence – do you know what the CIA appropriation is?'

'Now who is making light conversation?' said Carey acidly. 'But now that we're talking of money you'd better make sure that the sum agreed goes into that Swiss bank account.'

'You know us,' said Kidder. 'You know we'll play fair – if you do. Now how about opening that safe?'

Denison could not believe what he was hearing. All the mental and physical anguish he had suffered was going for nothing because Carey – Carey, of all people – was selling out. It would have been unbelievable had he not heard it from Carey's own lips. Selling out to the bloody Americans.

He considered the situation. From what he had heard there were only the two of them in the library. Carey was where he could be seen, over by the safe. Kidder faced him and had his back to the door – presumably. It was a good presumption because nobody conducts a lengthy conversation with his back to the person he is talking to. But Kidder had a gun and, window dressing or not, it could still shoot.

Denison looked around. Lyn was still standing in the same position but he could not ask for her help. He saw a large vase on the hall table, took one step, and scooped it up. When he got back to the door he saw that Carey had opened the safe and was taking out papers and stacking them on top.

Kidder was saying, '... I know we agreed to chase Meyrick and McCready just to make it look good but I didn't expect all those goddamn fireworks. Hell, I might have been killed.' He sounded aggrieved.

Carey stooped to pull out more papers. 'But you weren't.'

Denison eased open the door. Kidder was standing with his back to him, a pistol held negligently by his side, and Carey had his head half-way inside the safe. Denison took one quick pace and brought down the vase hard on Kidder's head. It smashed into fragments and Kidder, buckling at the knees, collapsed to the floor.

Carey was taken by surprise. He jerked his head and cracked it on top of the safe. That gave Denison time to pick up the pistol which had dropped from Kidder's hand. When Carey had recovered he found Denison pointing it at him.

Denison was breathing heavily. 'You lousy bastard! I didn't go through that little bit of hell just for you to make a monkey of me.'

Before Carey could say anything McCready skidded into the room at top speed. He saw the gun in Denison's hand and where it was pointing, and came to a sudden halt. 'Have you gone m ...'

'Shut up!' said Denison savagely. 'I suppose you're in it, too. I thought it strange that Carey should have got rid of Diana and Armstrong so fast. Just what's so bloody important in London that Diana should have been put on a plane without even time to change her clothes, Carey?'

Carey took a step forward. 'Give me that gun,' he said authoritatively.

'Stay where you are.'

From the doorway Lyn said, 'Giles, what is all this?'

'These bloody patriots are selling out,' said Denison. 'Just for money in a Swiss bank account.' He jerked the gun at Carey who had taken another pace. 'I told you to stay still.'

Carey ignored him. 'You young idiot!' he said. 'Give me that gun and we'll talk about it more calmly.' He went nearer to Denison.

Denison involuntarily took a step backwards. 'Carey, I'm warning you.' He held out the gun at arm's length. 'Come any closer and I'll shoot.'

'No, you won't,' said Carey with certainty, and took another step.

Denison's finger tightened on the trigger and Carey's arm shot out, the hand held palm outwards like a policeman giving a stop sign. He pressed his hand on the muzzle of the pistol as Denison squeezed the trigger.

There was no shot.

Denison found his arm being forced back under the steady pressure of Carey's hand against the muzzle of the gun. He pulled the trigger again and again but nothing happened. And then it was too late because Carey's other hand came around edge on and chopped savagely at his neck. His vision blurred and, at the last, he was aware of but two things; one was Carey's fist growing larger as it approached, and the other was Lyn's scream.

McCready's face was pale as he looked at the sprawled figure of Denison. He let out his breath in a long whistle. 'You're lucky he had the safety catch on.'

Carey picked up the pistol. 'He didn't,' he said shortly.

Lyn ran over to where Denison lay and bent over his face. She turned her head. 'You've hurt him, damn you!'

Carey's voice was mild. 'He tried to kill me.'

McCready said, 'You mean the safety catch *wasn't* on. Then how …'

Carey bounced the pistol in his hand. 'Kidder went shopping for this locally,' he said. 'On the principle of "patronize your local gunsmith", I suppose. It's a Husqvarna, Model 40 – Swedish army issue. A nice gun with but one fault – there's about a sixteenth of an inch play in the barrel. If the barrel is forced back, the trigger won't pull.' He pressed the muzzle with the palm of his left hand and pulled the trigger. Nothing happened. 'See!'

'I wouldn't want to stake my life on it,' said McCready fervently. 'Apart from that will it shoot normally?'

Carey cocked an eye at him. 'I suppose Kidder has friends outside. Let's invite them in.' He looked about. 'I never did like that style of vase, anyway.' He raised the gun and aimed it at a vase at the other end of the room, a companion to the one Denison had broken over Kidder's head. He fired and the vase exploded into pieces.

Carey held the gun by his side. 'That ought to bring them.'

They waited quietly in an odd tableau. Lyn was too busy trying to revive Denison to pay much attention to what was happening. She had started at the shot and then resolutely ignored Carey. Kidder lay unconscious. The bandages around his lower jaw had come adrift revealing what seemed to be bloody pockmarks from the birdshot he had received in the marsh of Sompio. Carey and McCready stood in the middle of the room, silent and attentive.

The drawn curtain in front of the french window billowed as though blown by a sudden breeze. A woman's voice said, 'Drop the gun, Mr Carey.'

Carey laid down the pistol on the table and stepped aside from it. The curtains parted and Mrs Kidder stepped into the room. She was still the same mousy, insignificant little woman but what was shockingly incongruous was the pistol she held in her hand. There were two large men behind her.

'What happened?' Her voice was different; it was uncharacteristically incisive.

Carey gestured towards Denison. 'Our friend butted in unexpectedly. He crowned your husband – if that's what he is.'

Mrs Kidder lowered the gun and muttered over her shoulder. One of the men crossed the room and bent over Kidder. 'And the papers?' she asked.

'On top of the safe,' said Carey. 'No problems.'

'No?' she asked. 'What about the girl?' The gun came up and pointed at Lyn's back.

'I said it and I meant it,' said Carey in a hard voice. 'No problems.'

She shrugged. 'You're carrying the can.'

The other man crossed to the safe and began shovelling papers into a canvas bag. Carey glanced at McCready and then his eyes slid away to Kidder who was just coming round. He muttered something, not loudly but loud enough for Carey to hear.

He was speaking in Russian.

The mumbling stopped suddenly as the man who was bending over Kidder picked him up. He carried him to the french window and, although Carey could not see properly, he had the strong impression that a big hand was clamped over Kidder's mouth.

The man at the safe finished filling the bag and went back to the window. Mrs Kidder said, 'If this is what we want you'll get your money as arranged.'

'Don't make any mistake about that,' said Carey. 'I'm saving up for my old age.'

She looked at him contemptuously and stepped back through the window without answering, and the man with the canvas bag followed her. Carey waited in silence for a moment and then walked over and closed the window and shot the bolts. He came back into the middle of the room and began to fill his pipe.

'You know that Kidder tried to con me into believing he was with the CIA. I always thought that American accent of his was too good to be true. It was idiomatic, all right, but he used too much idiom – no American speaks with a constant stream of American clichés.' He struck a match. 'It seems the Russians were with us after all.'

'Sometimes you get a bit too sneaky for me,' said McCready.

'And me,' said Lyn. 'Giles was right – you're a thorough going bastard.'

Carey puffed his pipe into life. 'George: our friend, Giles, has had a rough day. Let's put him to bed.'

CHAPTER FORTY

Denison walked across St James' Park enjoying the bland, late October sunshine. He crossed the road at the Guards Memorial and strolled across Horse Guards Parade and through the Palace arch into Whitehall itself, neatly avoiding a guardsman who clinked a sabre at him. At this time of the year the tourists were thin on the ground and there was not much of a crowd.

He crossed Whitehall and went into the big stone building opposite, wondering for the thousandth time who it was wanted to see him. It could only have to do with what had happened in Scandinavia. He gave his name to the porter and stroked his beard while the porter consulted the appointment book. Not a bad growth in the time, he thought somewhat vaingloriously.

The porter looked up. 'Yes, Mr Denison; Room 541. I'll get someone to take you up. Just sign this form, if you please, sir.'

Denison scribbled his signature and followed an acned youth along dusty corridors, into an ancient lift, and along more corridors. 'This is it,' said the youth, and opened a door. 'Mr Denison.'

Denison walked in and the door closed behind him. He looked at the desk but there was no one behind it and then he turned as he saw a movement by the window. 'I saw you crossing Whitehall,' said Carey. 'I only recognized you by your movements. God, how you've changed.'

Denison stood immobile. 'Is it you I've come to see?'

'No,' said Carey. 'I'm just here to do the preparatory bit. Don't just stand there. Come in and sit down. That's a comfortable chair.'

Denison walked forward and sat in the leather club chair. Carey leaned against the desk. 'I hope your stay in hospital wasn't too uncomfortable.'

'No,' said Denison shortly. It had been damned uncomfortable but he was not going to give Carey even that much.

'I know,' said Carey. 'You were annoyed and worried. Even more worried than annoyed. You're worried because I'm still with my department; you would like to lay a complaint, but you don't know who to complain to. You are frightened that the Official Secrets Act might get in the way and that you'll find yourself in trouble. At the same time you don't want me to get away with it – whatever it is you think I'm getting away with.' He took out his pipe. 'My guess is that you and Lyn Meyrick have been doing a lot of serious talking during the last fortnight. Am I correct?'

Carey could be a frightening man. It was as though he had been reading Denison's mind. 'We have been thinking something like that,' he said unwillingly.

'Quite understandable. Our problem is to stop you talking. Of course, if you did talk we could crucify you, but by then it would be too late. In some other countries it would be simple – we'd make sure that you never talked again, to anyone, at any time, about anything – but we don't do things that way here.' He frowned. 'At least, not if I can help it. So we have to convince you that talking would be *wrong*. That's why Sir William Lyng is coming here to convince you of that.'

Even Denison had heard of Lyng; he was somebody in the Department of Defence. 'He'll have his work cut out.'

Carey grinned and glanced at his watch. 'He's a bit late so you'd better read this. It's secret, but not all that much. It represents a line of thought that's in the air these days.' He took a folder from the desk and tossed it into Denison's lap. 'I'll be back in a few minutes.'

He left the office and Denison opened the folder. As he read a baffled look came over his face, and the more he read the more bewildered he became. He came to the end of the few pages in the folder and then started to read from the beginning again. It had begun to make a weird kind of sense.

Carey came back half an hour later; with him was a short, dapper man, almost birdlike in the quickness and precision of his movements. 'Giles Denison – Sir William Lyng.'

Denison got up as Lyng advanced. They shook hands and Lyng said chirpily, 'So you're Denison. We have a lot to thank you for, Mr Denison. Please sit down.' He went behind the desk and cocked his head at Carey. 'Has he ...?'

'Yes, he's read his homework,' said Carey.

Lyng sat down. 'Well, what do you think of what you've just read?'

'I don't really know,' said Denison, shaking his head.

Lyng looked at the ceiling. 'Well, what would you call it?'

'An essay on naval strategy, I suppose.'

Lyng smiled. 'Not an essay. It's an appreciation of naval strategy from quite a high level in the Department of Defence. It deals with naval policy should the Warsaw Pact and NATO come into conflict in a *conventional* war. What struck you about it? What was the main problem outlined?'

'How to tell the difference between one kind of submarine and another. How to differentiate between them so that you can sink one and not the other. The subs you'd want to sink would be those that attack shipping and other submarines.'

Lyng's voice was sharp. 'Assuming this country is at war with Russia, what conceivable reason can there be for not wanting to sink certain of their submarines?'

Denison lifted the folder. 'According to this we wouldn't want to sink their missile-carrying submarines – the Russian equivalent of the Polaris.'

'Why not?' snapped Lyng.

'Because if we sank too many of them while fighting a conventional war the Russians might find themselves losing their atomic edge. If that happened they might feel tempted to escalate into atomic warfare before they lost it all.'

Lyng looked pleased and glanced at Carey. 'He's learned the lesson well.'

'I told you he's a bright boy,' said Carey.

Denison stirred in the chair. He did not like being discussed as though he were absent.

Lyng said, 'A pretty problem, isn't it? If we don't sink their conventional submarines we stand a chance of losing the conventional war. If we sink too many of their missile-carriers the war might escalate to atomic catastrophe. How do you distinguish one submarine from another in the middle of a battle?' He snapped his fingers. 'Not our problem – that's for the scientists and the technologists – but do you accept the validity of the argument?'

'Well, yes,' said Denison. 'I see the point, but I don't see what it's got to do with what happened in Finland. I suppose that's why I'm here.'

'Yes, that's why you're here,' said Lyng. He pointed to the folder in Denison's hand. 'That is just an example of a type of thought. Do you have anything to say, Carey?'

Carey leaned forward. 'Ever since the atomic bomb was invented the human race has been walking a tightrope. Bertrand Russell once said, "You may reasonably expect a man to walk a tightrope safely for ten minutes; it would be unreasonable to do so without accident for two hundred years".' He hunched his shoulders. 'Well, we've walked that tightrope for thirty years. Now, I want you to imagine that tightrope walker; he carries a long balancing pole. What would happen if you suddenly dropped a heavy weight so that it hung on one end of the pole?'

'He'd probably fall off,' said Denison. He began to get a glimmer of what these two were getting at.

Lyng leaned his elbows on the desk. 'A man called Merikken invented something which had no application when he invented it. Now it turns out to be something capable of carving up missiles in mid-flight. Mr Denison, supposing Russia developed this weapon – and no one else. What do you think might happen?'

'That depends on the ratio of hawks to doves in the Russian government, but if they were sure they could stop an American strike they might just chance their arm at an atomic war.'

'Meyrick blabbed in Stockholm before he came to us,' said Carey. 'And the news got around fast. Our problem was that the papers were in Russia, and if the Russians got to them first they'd hold on tight. Well, the Russians *have* got the papers – but so have we, in photocopy.'

Denison was suspicious. 'But you sold them to the Americans.'

'Kidder was a Russian,' said Carey. 'I let it be known that I was willing to be bought, but the Russians knew I'd never sell myself to them. After all, I do have certain standards,' he said modestly. 'So they tried to pull a fast one. I didn't mind.'

'I don't quite understand,' said Denison.

'All right,' said Carey. 'The Russians have the secret and they'll know, when we tell them, that we have it, too, and that we'll pass it on to the Yanks. And we'll let the Yanks know the Russians have it. We drop the heavy weight on *both* ends of the balancing pole.'

Lyng spread his hands. 'Result – stalemate. The man remains balanced on the tightrope.'

'There were a lot of others involved but they were small fry,' said Carey. 'The Czechs and the West Germans.' He smiled. 'I have reason to believe that the man who bopped you on the head at Kevo was an Israeli. The Israelis would dearly like to have a defence against the SAM III missiles that the Syrians are playing around with. But, really, only America and Russia matter. And maybe China.' He glanced at Lyng.

'Later, perhaps.' Lyng stared at Denison. 'This country has just lost an Empire but many of its inhabitants, especially the older ones, still retain the old Imperial habits of thought. These modes of thought are not compatible with the atomic era but, unfortunately, they are still with us. If it became public knowledge that we have handed over to the Russians what the newspapers would undoubtedly describe as a super-weapon then I think that one of the minor consequences would be the fall of the government.'

Denison raised his eyebrows. 'Minor!'

Lyng smiled wintrily. 'The political complexion of the government of the day is of little interest. You must differentiate between the government and the state; governments may come and go but the state remains, and the real power is to be found in the apparatus of state, in the offices of Whitehall, in what Lord Snow has so aptly described as the corridors of power.'

Carey snorted. 'Any day I'm expecting a journalist to write that the winds of change are blowing through the corridors of power.'

'That could very well happen,' said Lyng. 'The control of power in the state is not monolithic; there are checks and balances, tensions and resistances. Many of the people I work with still hold on to the old ideas, especially in the War Office.' He looked sour for a moment. 'Some of the senior officers in the Navy, for instance, were destroyer commanders during World War II.'

His hand shot forward, his finger pointing to the folder in Denison's lap. 'Can you imagine the attitude of such men, steeped in the old ideas, when they are expected to issue orders to young officers to sink one type of enemy submarine and not another?' He shook his head. 'Old habits die hard. They're more likely to say, in the old tradition, "Full speed ahead, and damn the torpedoes." They fight to win, forgetting that no one will win a nuclear war. They forget balance, and balance is all, Mr Denison. They forget the man on the tightrope.'

He sighed. 'If the news of what has been done in Finland were to be disclosed not only would the present government fall, a minor matter, but there would be a drastic shift of power in the state. We, who strive to hold the balance, would lose to those who hold a narrower view of what is good for this country and, believe me, the country and the world would not be the safer for it. Do you understand what I am saying, Mr Denison?'

'Yes,' said Denison. He found that his voice was hoarse, and he coughed to clear it. He had not expected to be involved in matters of high policy.

Abruptly the tone of Lyng's voice changed from that of a judge reviewing a case to something more matter-of-fact. 'Miss Meyrick made a specific threat. She derided the efficacy of "D" notices and said that the students of twenty universities would not be bound by them.

I regret to say that this is probably quite true. As you know, our student population – or some sections of it – is not noted for its coolheadedness. Any move towards implementing her threat would be potentially disastrous.'

'Why don't you talk to her about it?' said Denison.

'We will – but we believe you have some influence with her. It would be a pity if Miss Meyrick's anger and compassion were to cause the disruption I have described.'

Denison was silent for a long time then he sighed, and said, 'I see your point. I'll talk to her.'

'When will you see her?' asked Carey.

'I'm meeting her at the Horse Guards at twelve o'clock.'

'That's in ten minutes. You talk to her, and I'll have a word with her later.' Carey stood up and held out his hand. 'Am I forgiven?'

'I wanted to kill you,' said Denison. 'I very nearly did.'

'No hard feelings,' said Carey. 'I seem to remember hitting *you* pretty hard.'

Denison got up and shook Carey's hand. 'No hard feelings.'

Lyng smiled and busied himself with the contents of a slim briefcase, trying to efface himself. Carey stood back and looked at Denison critically. 'I wouldn't have believed it, the change in you, I mean.'

Denison put his hand to his face. 'Iredale unstuck the eyelid – that was easy – and took away the scar. He had a go at the nose and that's still a bit tender. We decided to leave the rest – getting the silicone polymer out would amount to a flaying operation so we gave it a miss. But the beard covers up a lot.' He paused. 'Who did it, Carey?'

'I don't know,' said Carey. 'We never did find out.' He looked at Denison quizzically. 'Has Iredale's handiwork made much difference with Lyn?'

'Er … why, yes … I think …' Denison was unaccountably shy.

Carey smiled and took out a notebook. 'I'll need your address.' He looked up, 'At the moment it's Lippscott House, near Brackley, Buckinghamshire. Can I take it that will be your address until further notice?'

'Until further notice,' said Denison. 'Yes.'

'Invite me to the wedding,' said Carey. He put away his notebook and glanced through the window down into Whitehall. 'There's Lyn,' he said. 'Admiring the horses. I don't think there's any more, Giles. I'll keep in touch. If you ever need a job, come and see me. I mean it.'

'Never again,' said Denison. 'I've had enough.'

Lyng came forward. 'We all do what we think is best.' They shook hands. 'I'm glad to have met you, Mr Denison.'

When he had gone Lyng put his papers back into his briefcase and Carey stood at the window and lit his pipe. It took him some time to get it going to his satisfaction. Lyng waited patiently, and then said, 'Well?'

Carey looked down into Whitehall and saw Denison crossing the street. Lyn ran towards him and they kissed, then linked arms and walked past the mounted guards and under the arch. 'They're sensible people; there'll be no trouble.'

'Good!' said Lyng, and picked up the folder from where Denison had left it.

Carey swung around. 'But Thornton is a different matter.'

'I agree,' said Lyng. 'He's got the Minister's ear. We're going to have a rough ride with this one regardless of whether Denison keeps silent.'

Carey's voice was acid. 'I don't mind if Thornton plays the Whitehall warrior as long as the only weapon he shoots is a memorandum. But when it comes to a deliberate interference in operations then we have to draw a line.'

'Only a suspicion – no proof.'

'Meyrick's death was bad enough – although it was accidental. But what he did to Denison was abominable and unforgivable. And if he'd got hold of Merikken's papers his bloody secret laboratories would be working overtime.'

'Forget it,' said Lyng. 'No proof.'

Carey grinned. 'I told a lie just now – the only lie I've told to Denison since I've known him. I've got the proof, all right. I've got a direct link between Thornton and his crooked plastic surgeon – Iredale was able to put me on to that one – and it won't be long before

I find the sewer of a psychologist who diddled around with Denison's mind. I'm going to take great pleasure in peeling the skin off Thornton in strips.'

Lyng was alert. 'This is certain? Real proof?'

'Cast iron.'

'Then you won't touch Thornton,' said Lyng sharply. 'Let me have your proof and I'll deal with him. Don't you see what this means? We can neutralize Thornton – he's out of the game. If I can hold that over him I can keep him in line for ever.'

'But ...' Carey held himself in. 'And where does justice come in?' he asked heavily.

'Oh, justice,' said Lyng indifferently. 'That's something else again. No man can expect justice in this world; if he does then he's a fool.' He took Carey by the elbow and said gently, 'Come; let us enjoy the sunshine while we may.'

Desmond Bagley

The Freedom Trap

An agent of the British Government is sent on a new and deadly assignment – to snare The Scarperers (a notorious gang of criminals who organise gaol-breaking for long-term prisoners) and Slade, a notorious Russian double agent whom they have recently liberated. The trail leads him to Malta, where he comes face-to-face with these ruthless killers and must outwit them to save his own life.

Night of Error

The only discernable bond in the relationship of brothers Mark and Mike Trevelyan is their fascination with the sea and its secrets.

When Mike hears of his brother's death, during an expedition to a remote Pacific atoll, the circumstances are suspicious enough to force him to investigate and, when he is the victim of a series of violent attacks, his search for the truth becomes even more desperate. Mike has only two clues – a notebook in code and a lump of rock – enough to trigger off a hazardous expedition and a violent confrontation far from civilisation.

DESMOND BAGLEY

RUNNING BLIND

It all begins with a simple errand – a package to deliver. But for Alan Stewart, standing on a deserted road in Iceland with a murdered man at his feet, the mission looks far from simple.

Set amongst some of the most dramatic scenery in the world, Stewart and his girlfriend, Erin, are faced with treacherous natural obstacles and deadly threats, as they battle to carry out the mission. The contents of the package are a surprise for the reader as much as for Stewart in a finale of formidable energy.

'In this sort of literate, exciting, knowledgeable adventure, Mr Bagley is incomparable'

– *Sunday Times*

THE SNOW TIGER

A small mining community in New Zealand is devastated when 'the snow tiger' (an avalanche) rips apart their entire township in a matter of minutes, killing fifty-four people.

In the course of the ensuing enquiry, the antagonisms and fears of the community are laid bare, and a ruthless battle for control of a multi-million pound international mining group is exposed. The tension in the courtroom mounts as each survivor gives his graphic account of the terrifying sequence of events.

'The detail...is immaculately researched. The action...has the skill to grab your heart or your bowels'

– *Daily Mirror*

DESMOND BAGLEY

THE SPOILERS

When film tycoon, Sir Robert Hellier, loses his daughter to heroin, he declares war on the drug peddlers. London drug specialist, Nicholas Warren, is called in to organise an expedition to the Middle East, in an attempt to track down the big-time dope runners, inveigle themselves into their confidence and make them an offer they can't refuse. No expense is spared in the plans for their capture, but with a hundred million dollars' worth of heroin at stake, the 'spoilers' must use methods as ruthless as their prey.

WYATT'S HURRICANE

A US Naval aircraft on a routine weather patrol in the Caribbean encounters 'Mabel', a ferocious hurricane that should, nevertheless, pass harmlessly among the islands. But David Wyatt, civilian weather expert, has developed a sixth sense about hurricanes and is convinced that Mabel will change course and strike the island of San Fernandez and its capital, St Pierre. Scientific evidence is against him, the Commander of the US Base refuses to evacuate, and Wyatt's lone voice is finally overwhelmed when a rebellion against the tyrannical dictator who rules San Fernandez sweeps down on St Pierre. Wyatt is forced to pit himself against insuperable odds, aided only by a small and diverse group of English and American civilians – and by Hurricane Mabel herself.

Made in the USA
San Bernardino, CA
15 January 2014